The Sorcerer's
VENGEANCE

BROCK E.
DESKINS

"Pick up the pace, people!" Azerick shouted.

Azerick pulled out a scroll, read it on the fly, and released a searing bolt of lightning directly into the path of the pursuing worms. The electrical bolt blasted into the leading ranks of monsters closest to the surface. Those behind tore into the wounded, drawn by their thrashing and screeches of pain. Still more continued their dogged pursuit but suffered deep gashes from the shards of glass the lightning created when it struck the sand. The uninjured sandworms ripped into those that had the bad luck of being cut by the glass shards.

The creatures were right on Azerick's heels and struck with frightening speed. Strong hands grabbed him and pulled him up onto the rocks at the same time as he swung his staff at one of the lunging beasts. The sorcerer turned around and found himself standing between Maude and Malek, several feet up the side of the ridge surrounding the ancient fortress.

"We made it! I really was not sure we would. I half expected to get stuck out in the middle with no way back or forward!" Azerick exclaimed, breathing heavily and trying to catch his breath.

"You didn't think we would make it, but you tried it anyway?" Borik demanded. "What in the fiery plains of the abyss is wrong with you wizards? Are you all crazy?"

"A little bit, I suppose, to varying degrees."

"Let's go find the horses and make camp. I don't know about you all, but I'm exhausted, and I don't feel like traveling very far right now," Maude suggested.

"That sounds like a good idea," Azerick agreed. "Let's get a little ways away from here before we make camp."

There was no argument as they set off to find a good place to collapse and bleed off the exhaustion they were all feeling.

CHAPTER I

General Baneford stepped out of the blazing sun and into his command tent, eager to get out of the fiery orb's merciless glare. He and his men had been riding hard for several days, and he was exhausted. When he saw the black-robed wizard sitting in his chair once again, it failed to startle or even impress him. He had gotten used to the spellslinger's sudden appearances.

He did take note of several large trunks that he was unfamiliar with stacked along the back of his tent. The wizard smiled under his hood, vacated the chair, and chose one nearby. The general pulled at the straps of his armor, let it fall to the floor, and removed his sweat-soaked helm, the only part of his armor that was not of the fabled artifact.

"You failed to eliminate Jarvin's treasure hunters," the wizard said without preamble.

General Baneford sat down heavily in his chair and poured the wizard and himself a glass of wine. "I hadn't expected the elf to bring down half the blasted mountain on top of our heads, but we got their wizard. It should be a simple matter to get the rest of them with a similar trap."

"That will not be necessary. I have an agent already within their ranks who will not only kill them for us but also hand-deliver the remaining piece of your—my armor. Do you see the nice things I do for you? It is important that partners help each other when they can. I believe it builds trust, an essential element for any successful partnership."

General Baneford was relieved that the wizard was not upset at their partial victory, or complete failure, depending on one's point of view. It could have led to a rather ugly confrontation. He had lost many good men thanks to that blasted wizard, and he was in no mood for a lecture or reprimand.

His hands and fingernails still bore indications of the abuse they had suffered digging their way out of tons of fallen rubble. Besides, he had put up with enough mistreatment from Ulric, and he would be damned if he was going to take any more. He was his own man now and would be subservient to no one.

The general allowed himself a small smile as he pictured Ulric swinging from the king's gibbet in the middle of Rose Plaza. All it would take was one little letter from him telling Jarvin all about Ulric's attempted coup. Nevertheless, he had taken several oaths, and he would not betray them even now. Besides, he would likely swing right next to him.

General Baneford snapped out of his contemplations and fixed the wizard with a look. "Have you come to deliver the things promised in our bargain then?"

The wizard clapped his hands together. "Indeed I have, General, indeed I have."

Krendall strode over to the trunks and popped the lids open with a wave of his hand. General Baneford stood and leaned over the trunks, and gave the contents inside a disinterested look. He set his glass on a nearby shelf and pulled out a breastplate. The finish was exceptionally smooth; no blemishes caused by the smith's hammer warped or marred its brilliant surface in any way. Elaborate designs were etched into the steel, but the surface remained as smooth as glass, leaving no imperfections that would allow an arrow or weapon to gain purchase.

The general had seen more than one wealthy young nobleman die from a lance, spear, or arrow because he wore armor with more ornament than function. The tip of the weapon had bitten into the steel because of some stamped coat of arms, where it would have skipped off harmlessly had the armor been plain and smooth. This magnificent armor somehow managed to accomplish both.

He pulled out pieces at random from the different chests. All were of extraordinary craftsmanship, even if they had not been enchanted, but that was what he had been promised.

"How am I to know that these bear any kind of beneficial enchantments?" the general asked the wizard.

"I can cast a spell that would make any item with magical properties glow with a faint aura, but you would have to trust me in that as well. I do know a spell that would make a perfectly mundane item appear to have a magical enchantment upon it. Unless you have a spellcaster amongst your men, whom you trust implicitly, you will have to take me at my word that these arms and armor are precisely what we agreed upon."

"I will take your word for it." General Baneford did actually believe the mage, something that surprised him.

"Excellent. Your personal equipment is in that trunk there. How you distribute the others is, of course, up to you."

The wizard handed him a large facetted black gem. "My agent will contact you through this. All you need to do is take it in your hand and concentrate your thoughts upon it. You will hear his voice through the gem and vice versa. You will know when he is trying to contact you because the gem will become warm and emit a tingling sensation so long as it is within a few feet of you."

The general took the gem into his hand with trepidation. Magical swords and armor were one thing, strange speaking gems were another. As beneficial as this arrangement had been, not counting the losses of the last mission, he would be glad to terminate his relationship with this enigmatic man.

"Now, I think we have covered everything here. I hope to see you again in the next week so you can fulfill your part of our agreement and conclude our most mutually beneficial business transaction. Good day, General," the wizard said, then stepped through the magical gate that sprang up behind him.

Maude and her reformed company once more found themselves riding through the parched, scrubby wasteland with the obstinate and almost intelligently rude camel in tow. The wizard Azerick, had actually purchased him outright because he feared they may not be coming back through Sandusk and did not want the man who rented him out to suffer the loss. That small act of selflessness did more to settle any concerns over trusting the stranger with such an important mission than anything else.

Maude missed Tarth terribly. She missed his peculiarity even if he did botch some spells as often as not. He was possibly the best friend she ever had, probably because he was so different. She felt just a little less peculiar herself when he was around. He was the only person other than her mother allowed to call her by her full name. Somehow, it just sounded natural coming from the elf's mouth.

She knew Azerick was probably not going to stay on beyond delivering the helm to King Jarvin, if he even went that far. The wizard seemed completely indifferent to any form of reward that Maude mentioned, even hypothetically. She had asked him if he could have anything in the world, what it would be, and he simply told her that the one thing he wanted could never be granted by another. He doubted even the gods could give him what he truly desired.

His apparent lack of greed gave her some misgivings. If he did not want gold, nobility, or power, what was his motivation, and what made him change his mind about joining her group? The assassin had tried to kill him, but Azerick said he was not the first to try. She had gotten that much out of him. She asked what he did when he was not trekking through the desert, and he said he ran an orphanage in North Haven!

A thought occurred to her, and she could kick herself for not having caught it sooner. Not only had he been near the two artifacts when they met in Sandusk, he already knew the location of the helm! Was he trying to acquire it for himself? It would be near useless without the rest of the suit, and what would a wizard do with it?

Maude was certain that the men who had ambushed them were likely the same group that had killed the king's Special Guard and recovered at least two of the pieces from them. She even saw the large man wearing that unnaturally black armor in the temple, which had to have been Dundalor's armor.

If Azerick had been with those men, surely he would have made his presence known and stopped their retreat. She, Borik, and Malek had ridden hard straight back to Sandusk, and Azerick had shown up only a couple of hours after they returned. Then again, who knew how fast he could travel with his powers.

Damn it, Maude, you are going to think yourself into a state of paranoia if you keep this up! He changed his mind, that's all. He has so far shown himself to be honest and honorable, even if he is reserved in talking about himself. You need him. If he tries to betray us, you will catch him and take off his head, or he will use his magic to fry us all dead.

She decided that she would talk to Malek about it later. He had magical powers of his own that may help quell her doubts or validate her concerns. She knew Borik would be no help. He lost his objectivity long before he reached the bottom of his first cold mug of beer. Azerick was the long-lost brother for whom he would gladly trade his mother. It did not help that Borik talked him into stuffing six small kegs of near-frozen ale into his magic sack.

She was starting to think Borik might be developing a drinking problem. He nearly wet himself giggling so hard when Azerick stuck a wooden stick into a mug of beer and froze it solid for him. He followed Azerick around like a puppy, licking the frozen beer treat in his hand. She should be grateful. This was about ten times longer than Borik had ever gone without grousing about *something*. The dwarf even complained in his sleep for the gods' sake!

Azerick led the party south once more but in the opposite direction from the way Maude said she had traveled to find the boots. His wards did a good job of protecting him from the constant blowing dust and the heat of the day. Maude had tried to draw information from him a few times about his history and what had motivated him to go on this quest. So far, he thought he had done a decent job of talking without really saying anything.

He wore the persona of a quiet, secretive person as if it was his own skin, which really was not far from the truth. Azerick was not sure if his evasive nature had worked or put her more on her guard. She was big and strong for a woman but far from stupid. In the end, he decided it did not really matter so long as they did not become so suspicious of his motivations that they tried to stop him before he could carry out his plans.

She had told him why they were risking their lives to gain even one piece of the armor, and it made sense to him. However, if his plan worked as he hoped, his method would prove even more beneficial to the king and the kingdom at large, even though he would have to betray his new companions to pull it off. He was not too worried about Maude and the dwarf. Simple fighters were easy to defeat if you sprang the trap on them first and they did not have any protection against magic. Azerick had checked and none of them did. The cleric, on the other hand, could pose a problem.

He was one of the few priests whom a god had actually entrusted to wield a small portion of its power. A true cleric carrying the god's divine favor was even rarer than a wizard, and a close second to a sorcerer. He knew that many wizards turned their noses up at the divine power of clerics as being grossly inferior to their ability to pull power from the Source, but they were fools.

Wizards learned flashy spells that could kill a man even with the relatively minimal skills of a journeyman or apprentice, but a true Chosen priest, with a good affinity with his or her god, could call upon magic that could quickly ruin a man's, or even an army's, plans. They were not people to underestimate. As with the warriors though, Azerick should have the element of surprise, and that advantage should allow him to defeat the three without issue.

They had trouble finding the pass that would allow them to cross the Bloodstone Mountains into the Great Sand Desert beyond, but they discovered it early yesterday and made it through. It was the one time they found it necessary to travel during the blistering day. Even Maude had to appreciate the frozen beer treats that Azerick made them. Every time she glanced back at Borik, he would look up from the beer-based chunk of ice, smile like a little boy with a new puppy, and wave enthusiastically.

They spotted the unusual rock formation a night after crossing into the sandy desert thanks to the full moon illuminating the honey-colored sands. It took four more hours of ponderously slow travel before they reached the base of the hundred-foot-tall rock wall. They picketed the horses and the camel that made up for Borik's lack of complaining with continual bellowing gripes of his own.

The rock formation was not hard to climb. It was steep, but with so many protrusions and handholds, it was like climbing something between a ladder and a massive set of stairs. The view from the top of the formation was impressive. The desert was so flat, with the exception of large dunes, that even in the moonlight they could see for miles around. However, the truly amazing view was directly in front of them. The rock formation made a colossal ring little more than half a mile across and a hundred feet tall with almost no visible variance in height.

Inside the ring were the remains of an ancient lost citadel and several crumbling buildings. The smashed remains looked like the remnants of some god's meal sitting in the bottom of his soup bowl. Azerick could see how this would have made an incredibly defensible position, but he wondered what the ancient army had done for a cavalry. It would have been impossible to get them over the natural stone walls, and he could not imagine an army stationing itself out here without mounts.

The party climbed down the inside slope of the giant bowl. Their feet sank into the sand when they stepped off the rocky slope and onto the floor of the massive crater-like landscape. The soft sand beneath their feet gave them the perception of significant depth, which left them feeling a bit unnerved at the thought of sinking below the soft silica.

Despite their misgivings, the loose grains only swallowed them up to the tops of their boot heels. The party stomped toward the ruins lying in the heart of the enormous natural ring. The sand pulled at their boots with every step making their feet feel as though they had large rocks tied to them.

The group was thoroughly exhausted by the time they reached the ruins of the ancient citadel. They took a seat on what looked to be a fallen section of wall and dumped out the sand that had managed to worm its way into their boots as they slogged through the gritty, arid land.

"These ancients sure picked the darnedest places to build their castles and hide their empire-dominating artifacts," Maude said in a voice heavy with fatigue.

Azerick pointed his gaze at the rock wall. "Just imagine trying to charge the citadel under a hail of arrows even if you were able to surmount what would have been well-defended walls"

Malek shook his head, sending his sweat-laden blond curls dancing. "I still don't see why anyone would bother building a fortress in the middle of nowhere."

Azerick pointed to a low, mortared, circular stone wall about ten feet across. "It was the well. When it held water instead of sand, this was probably a major trading post. There were probably hundreds, even thousands, of tents pitched inside and outside of the stone ring. Whoever controlled this well held enormous power and influence in the region."

"Well, let's get this over with so we can get back to a place where the landscape doesn't shift every time the wind blows," Maude suggested, standing up.

It did not take long to search the few stone buildings whose walls had withstood the ravages of time. The citadel's tower had fallen long ago as well as the floors within the fortress itself. Having finished looking within the few standing walls, they began searching through the rubble. Azerick and Malek created light, and split up into two teams, peeking into the nooks and crannies and hollows created by the fallen walls and tumbled stones.

"I think I got something over here!" Borik shouted.

Azerick and Maude looked up from the fallen stones they were searching under and spotted Borik and Malek on their hands and knees wiping several inches of sand off something on the ground. Azerick saw that they had uncovered what appeared to be a large stone slab about eight feet by four feet trapped beneath a couple of large blocks of stone that had fallen atop it.

It took all four of them to shove the blocks off the stone slab. For once, the sand was actually a help instead of a hindrance. After they cleared the blocks and sand from the slab, Borik identified the stone as grey granite someone must have hauled hundreds of miles from where it had originated. The slab was set flush into the bedrock with such precision that Azerick doubted he could slip a piece of parchment between the seams.

Maude looked at the slab dubiously. "Anyone have any ideas on how to pry this thing up?"

"There's no way you're gonna pry that thing out with the tools we have available," Borik pointed out. He then lay atop the slab, pressed his ear to the solid surface, and gave it several sharp raps with the pommel of his dagger. "That thing weighs at least two tons, maybe more depending on how thick it is. I put it at about eight inches thick, give or take about an inch. The good news is that there is definitely a chamber or a passage beneath it."

Azerick studied the stone for a moment. If it had been natural stone and not carved, he could have used the same spell he had in the dragon's cave and disintegrated it. However, since it was worked stone, the natural energies had been changed, and that spell would no longer have an effect on it. Instead, he went to work on it with his sunder spell. It strongly resisted his tampering, but in the end, his persistence won out over the stone's stubbornness, and he managed to sink a couple of flaws into it.

Azerick borrowed Malek's shield, propped it against his legs, and had everyone else stand back. He summoned his staff to his hand and struck the slab with all his might. Several runes flared brightly the instant the arcanum ball struck the granite surface. A sharp crack, like a large tree snapping in strong winds, echoed across the sands as jagged pieces of stone flew up and clattered against Maude's steel armor and the shields protecting Azerick's body.

The majority of the stone slab broke into large chunks and toppled down the stone stairs that lay hidden beneath it. The rest had turned into a blast of tiny projectiles, and Azerick's arms bled in several places where the sharp stone shards had pierced his magical wards and ruined yet another of his shirts. Malek helped him wash the wounds out and used a minor healing spell to close the mostly superficial injuries.

"Nice trick with the stick, wizard. Can you pull a rabbit out of a hat too?" Borik asked sardonically.

"No, but I could probably pull an untold number of creatures out of that wild habitat of a beard hanging from your chin."

Borik looked offended at the slight against his beard and used his hand to try to pull out some of the tangles and smooth it down.

"It looks like we go down from here," Maude stated, looking down into the gloomy interior.

"Nice choice of words, Maude," Borik grumbled.

The party descended the stairs single file and soon reached the broken remains of the stone slab. A long, dark corridor waited for them at the bottom of the steps nearly thirty feet below the surface.

Small alcoves held statues of men in strange armor and billowing clothing similar to robes. Most held weapons, mainly large, curved swords, but others held open tomes and stared sagely down at those who walked between them. Larger alcoves created small rooms where old wooden desks, stools, and beds still stood, almost untouched by the ravages of time.

The passage continued for several hundred feet, at the end of which was a brass-bound set of double doors, each door standing ten feet tall and four feet wide. Ornate brass rings hung in the jaws of a brass lion's head at chest height near the split between the doors.

"Looks like maybe you get to play sapper again," Borik told Azerick as they stepped up to the closed doors.

Azerick pulled on one of the rings, and the door swung open, dislodging a small amount of dust, which floated down in a multitude of motes illuminated by his light.

"Darn, too bad," Borik grumbled.

A beam of light shone through an unseen opening at the far end of the large chamber, highlighting the statue of a warrior in a softly glowing aura. They saw more statues standing in silent guard along the walls as they walked toward the moonbeam and the figure it illuminated.

The statue was made of a pure white marble, unmarred by any other colors or patterns. On the warrior's proud head, standing in stark contrast to the white stone, was a helm of absolute black, its edges traced in gold. The white marble of the statue glittered under the moonbeam, but the helm seemed to absorb it, not letting any of it reflect off its liquid black surface.

"I think we found it," Malek said unnecessarily.

"So that is what we have been searching for," Maude stated in awe.

Borik elbowed Azerick in the hip. "Coming up is the part when the statues come to life and try to kill us, or ghosts appear to devour our souls."

"I guess we had better be ready then," Azerick said as he climbed onto the large marble plinth upon which the statue stood.

Borik pulled several wooden wedges from his pack and lodged them firmly beneath the open bronze door. "Because you know it's gonna slam shut and lock us in with a horde of baddies."

Azerick looked at the dwarf. "Good idea."

"This ain't my first dance at the ball."

Azerick reached up and lifted the helm from the sculpture's regal brow. As the sorcerer stepped down from the pedestal, a low thrum like a single giant heartbeat echoed through the floor, a deep vibration they all felt roll through them, setting their flesh and bones to tingling.

"Oh great, here we go," Borik growled. He unlimbered his axe and prepared for the inevitable fight for their lives.

Azerick dropped the helm into his magic bag and prepared to defend himself. The adventurers unconsciously formed themselves into a circle looking outward and waited for any signs of attack. After several minutes with no indication of any foes, everyone started to relax. The statues stood just as rigidly as statues were supposed to, no monsters came charging down the halls, and no ghosts or specters appeared.

"Well, how about that. It's about damn time we caught a break," Borik said brightly, hooking his axe back onto the harness on his back.

Azerick was not quite as optimistic as the dwarf. He had no idea what the ominous pulse heralded, but he sincerely doubted that whoever had created the effect would have gone to the trouble without good reason. Perhaps whatever guardians it was supposed to summon were long dead, or the trap that was supposed to have sprung had crumbled to dust ages ago. Maude led them back toward the surface and wisely remained alert as they traveled down through the long, gloomy corridor and back up the stairs.

"If we hurry, we can get out of here before the sun rises and tries to bake us like a loaf of bread," Maude said, stepping out onto the sand.

A tingle of warning shot through Azerick. Without pausing to think, he grabbed Maude by the collar of her breastplate and pulled her backward with all his strength, dropping her unceremoniously onto her backside by his feet.

"What in blazes—" Maude started to shout.

Two brown and sand-patterned snake-like creatures burst out of the sand right where the woman's feet had been a split second before. The creatures were as big around as a large man's thigh, but Azerick had no idea how long they were. Part of their length was hidden below the sand. Their mouths were enormous. Their jaws were hinged at least a foot back from the tip of their snouts and filled with long, sharp teeth.

"Holy cripes, that thing almost ate me!" Maude cried as she jumped back to her feet and drew her huge two-handed sword from her back.

The party stared out at the expanse of sand all around them and saw the flickering movement of the sandworms gliding just below the surface like a huge school of fish in a feeding frenzy.

Azerick picked up a fist-sized stone and threw it out into the sand as far as he could. The instant the rock thumped into the sand, numerous sandworms struck out at it, the fastest worm snatching it up in its jaws and pulling it below the surface. The sand all around them, for as far as they could see, writhed and undulated as untold numbers of the sandworms swarmed toward the thrown rock.

"Gods in paradise, they're everywhere," Malek said softly.

"Wizard, I hope you got a spell to fly us all over the ridge, or a flying carpet in that bag of yours," Borik said.

Azerick shook his head. "I have nothing that will span that distance. I have a gate spell that allows us to step across a wide expanse, but it reaches only three or four hundred yards at best. It is several times that distance to the ridge."

"Why aren't they trying to eat us right now?" Maude asked.

"The fortress was built on a bed of sandstone. The sand is only a few inches deep here. It looks like the sandworms cannot or will not come all the way out of the sand."

"So how do we get out of here?" Borik demanded.

"I think that is the purpose. The helm was not difficult to get to; it did not need to be since the thief was never going to leave here alive. That pulse we felt probably woke the creatures who act as natural guardians. It is quite ingenious and effective."

"Well, I'm so glad you're impressed with the method of our death, wizard. I would sure hate to think we were going to die in some boring fashion like old age in our own beds," Borik complained. "Got another ice beer?"

Azerick pulled out a skin of beer, cups, and small sticks he had collected for the task and froze everyone an ice beer. The sorcerer then sat down on a block of stone, nibbling at the frozen treat, and wracked his brain for a solution to their current problem.

Maude could tell that, despite appearances, the wizard was deep in thought, so she followed his example and sat down as well. She only hoped his ponderings were focused on getting them out of here. If it were Tarth, the gods only knew what would be going through his mind at a moment like this. Then again, even the gods were probably wary of treading in the elf's mind for fear of going mad themselves. Thinking of her lost friend brought a new wave of despondency, but she let it come, having no pressing need to shove it aside at the moment.

Azerick finished his ice beer and stood up. He took small steps forward, shoving the tip of his staff into the sand. Even that slight vibration set the nearest sandworms into motion a few yards away. He drew a long line with the staff where he felt the bedrock drop away. He then grabbed his staff by the end and rhythmically thumped the ground with the arcanum ball.

Almost immediately, several sandworms struck with the speed and aggression of barracuda. One of the creatures bit down on the end of the staff, swallowing the gleaming orb at the end like a fish on a lure. Azerick triggered one of the engraved runes on the staff, which briefly flared with a blue light, sending a powerful jolt of electricity through the arcanum sphere.

"Help me hold on to this!" Azerick shouted as the creature involuntarily clamped down and began thrashing about as the electricity coursed through its body.

Maude leapt up, grabbed the staff just above Azerick's hands, and heaved back so that she was not stepping across the line. The frantic writhing caught the interest of the other sandworms, which began attacking their wounded and flailing brethren. Borik and Malek darted forward and used their weapons to hack at the sandworms, which were intent on cannibalizing one of their own.

Maude and Azerick managed to land the beast largely intact. Azerick pulled his staff from the creature's mouth, glad to find that it had not damaged it in any way, hunkered down, and examined the carcass.

The creature's snout was cone-shaped, and long thorns or thick hairs covered its body. Azerick could find no sign of eyes or ears. Using the knife he had taken off the Rook, Azerick cut one of the thorns from the sandworm's hide. He set the small horn on a flat stone and pressed the sharp blade down upon it, cutting it in half. Azerick nodded thoughtfully when he found that the horn-like structure was hollow and filled with a fluid similar in consistency to lamp oil.

Azerick looked up at the others, who were watching him intently. "It senses us by our vibrations through these protrusions. I imagine they are incredibly sensitive. No matter how softly we tried to walk, they would feel exactly where we were and devour us, and at the rate they can travel, we could never outrun them."

"So what do we do? Sit here until we starve?" Borik asked sourly.

Malek shook his head. "That could take a very long time. Azerick has enough food in that bag of his to feed an army, and I have a prayer that will create water. We would die of old age before we starved."

"Or die of boredom," Borik quipped. "Does that prayer of yours make beer too?"

"Nope, just water."

"Rather throw myself to the sandworms," Borik muttered.

Azerick was not about to admit defeat just yet. There was a way out of this. He did not know a spell to get them across without touching the sand, but he could make a minor change to a spell he knew. It was not like creating an entirely new spell, such a thing would be impossible unless they were going to spend months sitting on this slab of rock, which they may end up doing if he did not figure something out.

He had spent a great deal of time thinking about what Duncan had said about sorcery and rune carving, that the only limits were a caster's imagination and ability to control the power they drew. Azerick had practiced altering some of the spells he had already mastered, with varying degrees of success. He simply needed to figure out which one might contain the solution to their dilemma.

"Could we make a bridge out of the stone blocks lying about?" Maude asked, looking at the toppled ruins.

"I don't think so, Maude," Borik answered. "Those stones weigh over a thousand pounds apiece. Without rollers and pulleys, it would be near impossible. Plus we would have to step onto the sand to place them unless we could roll them across the one just set down."

"I might be able to make a bridge," Azerick said.

"You got a hundred or so dwarven bridge builders in that bag too?" Borik asked sardonically.

"No, but I have a spell that will create a series of stone spikes to jut up from the ground."

"I hate to picture what would happen if one of us slipped off and landed on the tip," Borik interrupted. "Frozen beer on a stick is delicious. Dwarf on a stick, not so much."

"I think I can modify the spell to make cylindrical columns instead of tapering to an impaling point," Azerick continued. "If I have them jut straight up and tightly packed together, I should be able to create a walkway a few feet above the sand. Keep a weapon handy in case these worms try and strike at you though."

"Sounds better than the plan I came up with," Maude said.

"What plan was that?" Malek asked.

"Don't give Borik a drink for a few hours and then throw a wineskin out as far as we can. When he goes running after it, drawing away all the sandworms, we run in the other direction."

"Oh, hardy har, har. You're about as funny as you are feminine," Borik retorted.

"On second thought, save the wineskin and just throw the dwarf."

Azerick was unsure how far away he could cast his stone spike spell and how long he could make a single path. He re-examined the changes he would have to make to the spell and stood just behind the line he had drawn marking the end of the bedrock. He bent his focus to the Source and drew upon its seemingly limitless power. A hundred yards away, dozens of stone cylinders, each a foot across, sprouted out of the sand like a multitude of tree stumps four feet tall.

"Hate to tell you this, wizard, but that's a mighty long jump for someone whose legs are barely two feet long," Borik informed him.

"If I tried to make a solid path we would be lucky if I could span half the distance we need to go, and that is greatly exaggerating my ability."

Azerick cast another spell and opened a magical gate between them and the end of the raised stone path.

"Be careful when you step through; it causes some disorientation for a moment. Walk straight through, and do not step to either side."

Maude took a deep breath and crossed through the portal. She stepped out onto the narrow ledge and felt the ground swaying and spinning under her feet. The warrior forced herself not to try to compensate for the dizzying effects of the long step. She closed her eyes, took a deep breath, and carefully took a few tiny steps forward.

When she opened her eyes, she felt more stable and turned just in time to catch Malek as he stepped through and almost tumbled over the edge. Arms frantically windmilling, Malek breathed a sigh of relief when Maude grabbed the end of his war hammer and pulled him up straight.

Borik stared warily at the shimmering rip in the air before him, not at all trusting such a mode of travel. "Maybe you could all go back and make, I don't know, a flying boat or something and come back to pick me up. Just leave me the beer. I can eat one of them sandworms if I get hungry."

"It is perfectly safe, Borik. Maude and Malek are both on the other side and ready to catch you if you fall. I have used it several times. Trust me, it's safe."

"What if it closes before I get all the way through and half my leg stays here and the rest of me is way over there?"

Azerick reached into his bag and pulled out a wineskin. "Do you know what this is, Borik? This is the last of our beer," Azerick threw it through the portal where it slapped onto the narrow stone bridge.

"Hey, what'd ya go and do that for!" Borik darted forward, reaching for the skin.

"Welcome across," Malek said when the dwarf crossed onto the path and scooped up the thrown wineskin. "How is your balance?"

"Eh? Oh fine, I got a low center of gravity," Borik replied, then showed off by hopping from one foot to the other while draining the wineskin.

Azerick stepped through with little problem, being somewhat used to the aftereffects. The portal snapped shut as soon as Azerick crossed over, and they all walked in single file toward the far end of the path. Maude had to lead since there was no room for anyone to get past.

Azerick repeated both spells once more. A couple of the more aggressive sandworms tried to snap at the adventurers as they stood upon the bridge, but they were mostly out of striking range. Two of them got some deep wounds for their efforts thanks to Maude's sword and Borik's axe. Their cannibalistic brethren attacked and devoured the wounded creatures.

Before they were halfway to the safety of the rocks, Azerick could no longer cast his stone spike and dimensional gate spell and was forced to tap into the power stored in his staff. If he had not been wearing the ring that Xornan had given him to fight in the arena, he would never have been able to make it across even with his staff.

Azerick crossed through the gate and onto the path about five hundred yards from the low ridge of stone. "We have a problem. I don't think I can cast both a stone spike spell and a dimension gate, and neither will get us all the way to the rocks by itself."

"How short will we be?" Maude asked.

"My gate will get us the farthest, so a hundred yards, give or take."

"We'll never make it. Those things are on us almost the second we step through," Malek said.

"Our only hope is to draw them off and try to make a run for it before they turn around and can catch us."

"Can you draw them off?" Maude asked.

"I think so. I should be able to use the runes in the staff to create a racket and strike the ground with rather significant force. It should be sufficient to get their attention."

"I would like to once more draw everyone's attention to my short legs. Dwarves are many things, but fleet of foot is not one of them."

Maude smiled wryly at the dwarf. "Don't worry, Borik. Malek and I will make sure you keep up. Go ahead and cast your spells, Azerick."

Azerick pushed up his sleeves, faced the opposite direction from their route of travel, and triggered several runes on his staff. About three hundred yards away, the minuscule amount of moisture in the air froze solid, creating balls of ice the size of melons, which plummeted from the sky and slammed into the ground sending sprays of sand several feet into the air. By the suddenly shifting sands, the party could see that the sandworms were all racing toward the sound of the disturbance. Sharp cries of pain screeched from dozens, possibly scores, of mouths as the strikes pummeled the creatures.

Azerick turned toward the distant ridgeline and spent the last of his and the staff's power casting a gate spell. Maude, Malek, and Borik sprinted through the instant the gate snapped open, and Azerick followed closely behind. Having the hundred-foot-tall ridge appear three hundred yards closer in a fraction of a second was by far the most disorienting experience they had endured thus far. Even Borik staggered while his short legs pumped up and down as fast as he could make them go.

Maude and Malek each grabbed one of the dwarf's thick wrists and half carried him across the sand, suspended between them like a child holding the hands of its parents. Azerick glanced behind him just as the last of the ice strikes crashed down. The moment the frozen barrage ceased, the sandworms sped toward the fleeing humans with relentless abandon.

"Pick up the pace, people!" Azerick shouted.

Azerick pulled out a scroll, read it on the fly, and released a searing bolt of lightning directly into the path of the pursuing worms. The electrical bolt blasted into the leading ranks of monsters closest to the surface. Those behind tore into the wounded, drawn by their thrashing and screeches of pain. Still more continued their dogged pursuit but suffered deep gashes from the shards of glass the lightning created when it struck the sand. The uninjured sandworms ripped into those that had the bad luck of being cut by the glass shards.

The creatures were right on Azerick's heels and struck with frightening speed. Strong hands grabbed him and pulled him up onto the rocks at the same time as he swung his staff at one of the lunging beasts. The sorcerer turned around and found himself standing between Maude and Malek, several feet up the side of the ridge surrounding the ancient fortress.

"We made it! I really was not sure we would. I half expected to get stuck out in the middle with no way back or forward!" Azerick exclaimed, breathing heavily and trying to catch his breath.

"You didn't think we would make it, but you tried it anyway?" Borik demanded. "What in the fiery plains of the abyss is wrong with you wizards? Are you all crazy?"

"A little bit, I suppose, to varying degrees."

"Let's go find the horses and make camp. I don't know about you all, but I'm exhausted, and I don't feel like traveling very far right now," Maude suggested.

"That sounds like a good idea," Azerick agreed. "Let's get a little ways away from here before we make camp."

There was no argument as they set off to find a good place to collapse and bleed off the exhaustion they were all feeling.

CHAPTER 2

Zeb sailed north on the *Iron Shark* with his most experienced crew and the biggest, strongest men he could find in the city. It was late afternoon bordering on evening, which came rather early this time of the year and lasted for close to eighteen hours, when they finally dropped anchor just two hundred yards from shore. They would wait until morning before setting out in their separate directions for the hunt. The shoreline was lost from sight by the thickening fog that rolled in before the night was able to steal it away first.

"Captain Zeb," Balor called out, "you might want to take a look at this."

"What is it, lad?"

"Look out there, maybe a quarter mile inland." Balor pointed a finger out past the fog-blanketed shoreline.

Zeb squinted at the dark, murky landscape. His vision was not as good as it once was, and although the cold evening air pushed the fog down to a height of five or six feet, it was still difficult for him to make anything out beyond a slight contrast in the few shrubs and pathetic trees that managed to sprout up far enough to peek out over the miasma.

The mists parted just slightly and Zeb was barely able to make out what had attracted his first mate's attention. "Ah, I see it. You make it out to be a small fire?"

"Most likely. It flickers too much to be a lamp and is a bit large for a torch."

The mists closed back in and swallowed the only bit of color in the entire landscape. "Not much to see, is it? I'm impressed you spotted it in this soup."

"It was Derran who brought it to my attention; otherwise I doubt I would have seen it."

"That figures. What I wouldn't give to have that boy's eyes. I'd trade him ten years of my experience for them and ten years of his youth. Make that fifteen," Zeb said with a smile.

"Who would be this far north, the Thule maybe?" Balor asked, referencing the small, tan-skinned nomadic people who lived at least part of the year in the most northern extremes of the known land and beyond.

Zeb shook his head. "From what I know of them, which like most people is very little, they should be farther east and south chasing the caribou herds. The Eislanders should be somewhere to the south this time of year, but I only know a little more of those people than I do the Thule. I do know enough that between the two we had better hope it's a Thule party."

Balor nodded his agreement. The small Thule were a strange and reclusive people but friendly when they chose to approach the few Utgardr, or southern people, who managed to travel so far north. The Eislanders, on the other hand, were the exact opposite. Fair of skin and hair, they were a huge and aggressive people, rivaling Toron in size and strength. The only thing that distinguished them from the dark-haired barbarians farther to the south and east was a fair sophistication in ship and weapon manufacturing.

Eislanders originally hailed from a series of rocky and inhospitable islands to the far north, hundreds of miles west of Valeria. However, in the past hundred years or so, they had established a few large settlements four or five hundred miles to the south of where they were now, near the coastline.

They had made occasional raids to the south as far as North Haven in the past, but the city had grown too large and the southerners' ships too advanced for their pirating to be profitable. Most of their raids these days were limited to their barbarian neighbors and northern island nations closer to their ancestral homelands, at least the Eislanders who still plied the seas.

A few large groups had moved farther inland, which created tension between them and the scattered Akkadian barbarian tribes. The name Akkadian was a term used by the elves as a reference for all of the human barbarians of the Northern Great Forest since the Akkadians themselves had no name for their people other than that used for individual tribes.

The Akkadians could be dealt with fairly as long as you were invited into their territory. The few people who made the long and arduous journey far enough north to trade steel for raw gold or the occasional gems often had to camp for days just outside the nearest tribe's territory. There they waited until one of the tribal representatives came to examine their goods and decide if they were desirable enough to allow them farther into their territory where they established a temporary trade camp days from the nearest Akkadian village.

Zeb seriously doubted that any Akkadian band had ventured so far from their bountiful home ranges, but it was only slightly more unlikely than the Eislanders doing so. The only thing that Zeb could think of was that perhaps an Eislander or Akkadian had learned the value of the pristine white furs of the far northern animals and had struck out to bring such rare treasures home.

If that were the case, then there should be little cause for conflict. Neither party would claim this remote land as a personal hunting ground. Eislanders may choose to raid them if they thought they had the numbers and the spoils were worth the potential losses. Akkadians were not above using bows in either hunting or warfare, but Eislanders used missile weapons purely for hunting, disdaining their use in combat as a coward's weapon, which gave the sailors a slight advantage if it came to blows.

As the two sailors pondered the significance of the campfire, several pairs of blue eyes watched the ship's lanterns from the shoreline, the men's heavy white and grey furs rendering them nearly invisible to anyone more than a few feet away. Large, calloused hands twisted on the smooth wooden hafts of the battle-axes they carried.

"What do you make of the Utgardr ship, Magni?" one of the powerfully built Eislanders asked. "Do you think they are the ones responsible and followed us north to continue their evil black magic?"

"I do not know, Modi," Magni replied through his thick, blond, braided beard, "but if they have, we will find out soon enough. Then we will spill so much of their blood that the snows will melt and the rivers will run red. By Djev's radiant axe, I swear it!"

There were no further signs of human life for the rest of the night nor were there in the morning as the sailors loaded up their longboats with the gear each party would need for their hunting forays. Zeb and Toron's party required the most equipment despite being one of the smaller groups. One longboat was sufficient to ferry every man in the party to shore, but three more were required to haul their gear.

Balor led two longboats carrying two score of men who would go in search of seals, and perhaps a few small whales, out on the ice floes. The long spiraled tusks of the unicorn whale were especially desirable, and the meat, blubber, and oil were all prized on the southern markets as well.

Another group of men in two longboats dropped nets near the mouth of the river and spent much of their days fishing for salmon, ensuring that the ship did not run into any trouble, and providing a rescue force if either of the other groups did not return at their scheduled time.

Derran was also part of Zeb and Toron's crew, his sharp eyes invaluable when it came to spotting prey. They and the nine burly rowers set about unloading the longboats. They assembled the sleds before strapping their gear onto them to make for easier traveling and hauling the results of their hunting.

Two tents, each with a small iron stove and a sack of coal, provided their shelter and heat when wood was unavailable. Foodstuffs went on next, as well as spare clothing, rope, and traveling gear. Half the men carried heavy crossbows while the other half wielded lighter and less cumbersome light crossbows for smaller game such as foxes and hares, reserving the powerful arbalests for ice bears—or Eislanders if it came to a fight.

The last things they loaded were a pair of scorpios. Scorpios were nothing more than very heavy crossbows mounted on bases and were too large and too heavy for anyone to wield, with the possible exception of Toron, although even he would have found the things far too cumbersome. Each scorpio was manned by a team of three who were trained to set it up and have it ready to fire in less than a minute.

The scorpios were weapons for dire emergencies. The heavy crossbows and pikes could take down an ice bear, even the big ones that stood over twelve feet tall and could reach a weight near fifteen hundred pounds. However, even the powerful crossbows and large spears would do little to deter a dire ice bear.

Dire ice bears were essentially dire bears that had made their home in the far north, their fur growing in white to help conceal themselves from prey in the largely colorless landscape. These fearsome beasts often exceeded three thousand pounds and could shake off all but the most powerful weapons. The scorpios were the humans' only real defense against such creatures and not an impressive one at that.

With the men's crossbows at the ready and spears close at hand, Zeb ordered their professional hunter and Derran to lead them out, with most of the men pulling and pushing the sleds, which would only get heavier as their hunting became successful. Whoever had been out here last night was gone now and had left no trace of ever having been present. Zeb started to wonder if perhaps they had not seen a will o' the wisp. Maybe they were just all delusional.

"Whoever or whatever was out here seems to be gone now," Derran said, seemingly reading the captain's current thoughts.

"Yeah, but for how long, I wonder."

The hunting party followed the ice-inundated river, which was more ice than liquid water at the surface. In another month, possibly less, it would be frozen solid along with most of the bay. Winter set in this far north later than in the south. For some unknown reason, it seemed to lag behind by an entire season. Just as spring started in the south, winter set in up here with an unforgiving fierceness.

Derran, Zeb, and another man who was an experienced hunter and tracker walked a hundred yards ahead of Toron and the rest of the group who had the important but thankless job of hauling the sleds. By the time they made camp that evening, they boasted a brace of hares, two foxes, and four snow-white ptarmigans. They would eat the rabbits and birds that very night, the skins scraped and prepared, and the feathers bagged.

Zeb stepped out of the tent and approached Derran who was scouring the flat countryside with his eyes. "Any sign of our friends?"

"No, sir, but with this damnable fog that's no real surprise. There could be a hundred men surrounding us no more than fifty yards away, and unless one of them sneezed or broke wind, we'd never even know," the young sailor replied.

"I've ordered the men to build a berm around the camp before they turn in. A wall of snow is no great defense, but it's better'n nothing at all. Here they come now. Go on and give 'em a hand. It'll take your mind off it for a bit."

Derran gave his captain a nod, grabbed a shovel from one of the sleds, and lent his muscles to the task. Zeb stared out at the thick fog that had rolled in once more as they were making camp. He had seen a lot of fog in his time, it was a regular part of a sailor's life, but never had he been in mists this thick, cold, and *dry*. A fog like this should soak a man to his skin as quickly as a light rain, but this stuff acted more like scentless smoke than any kind of precipitation.

It was so thick now that a man could lose his way trying to return to camp from using the privy they had dug just a few yards from the tents. Zeb would have to order another privy dug, one inside the growing berm. It would not do to lose someone answering the call of nature. That was no way for a man to die. With a sigh of helplessness, Zeb grabbed a shovel and decided he would dig the privy hole himself while his men packed snow into a six-foot-tall ring surrounding their small camp.

Zeb walked up to Toron as the big minotaur stood just outside one of the tents and noted the huge, billowing puffs of steam erupting from his large bovine-like nostrils in apparent agitation. "What's up, Toron?

You look fit to charge off and sink your axe into somebody."

"We were being watched…closely," the minotaur replied without turning his head. "I got a scent of them when they got up and moved. I never did see them through this blasted fog."

"What do you make of 'em?"

"Eislanders. I am almost certain of it. At least two were spying on us, which means there are likely at least ten men in their party."

A look of concern flashed across Zeb's weathered features. "You have some knowledge of Eislanders then?"

The minotaur nodded his large head, his horns swinging back and forth. "Aye, our two peoples often ply the same waters and run across each other as we raid our way along the northern isles. Eislanders like to engage us to test their strength and battle prowess, as we are one of the few people they respect as warriors. To take a minotaur's horns in battle is one of their highest honors."

"Don't sound like very good neighbors to me."

"They are worthy adversaries," Toron answered, bestowing upon the Eislanders the highest praise a minotaur could give.

"What do you think they will do?"

Toron shook his head. "They will confront us, but I cannot say when, only that it will likely be soon. Eislanders have less patience than even my people do. Whether they will open with words or axes is anyone's guess. We are lucky not to be on their land, or the answer would almost certainly not be in our favor. As it stands, I would give us an even chance of supping with them or being buried by them within the next day or two."

The sailors-turned-hunters struck camp and loaded the sleds before the fog burned fully away. By the time they were prepared to depart, the mist had dissipated enough to travel, its obscuring properties all but gone. They found signs of the Eislanders not far from their camp, but they had deliberately scoured their prints away, probably by dragging heavy furs or canvas behind them. That by itself did nothing to prevent someone from following the track, but it effectively made it impossible to judge their numbers. To complicate their ability to track them, several drag marks diverged in different directions a hundred yards away, and Zeb had no desire to split up even if he were willing to follow the dangerous northerners, which he had no intention of doing.

Zeb's crew continued following the river as it veered sharply south. Evergreen trees began populating its banks, and animal life became more numerous. Despite the increase of life and color, it would still take at least two days of hard traveling to reach anything they could call a forest. The small trees that grew this far north were weak and twisted things, widely spread out or growing in small clusters of three and four.

Fox, ptarmigans, and snowshoe hare became more abundant, and as the morning moved on into afternoon, the number of furs and wrapped meat piled on the sleds became a legitimate load. It was perhaps two hours before dusk when Derran sprinted ahead and to the party's left, his snowshoes kicking up clumps of snow. The young sailor stopped a hundred feet or so away then waved furiously to the others.

Zeb and the leading party veered to their left to see what had attracted his attention. When Zeb and the other three men approached, Derran was squatting down next to a series of prints nearly as large as those left by his snowshoes. The biggest difference was the pointed marks extending from the front of the impressions, proof of the four to five-inch-long claws of the ice bear.

"What do ya make of those tracks, Farley?" Zeb asked their least competent sailor but undisputed master huntsman.

The burly, wiry-haired, black-bearded man spit a gob of tobacco juice and saliva onto the ground as he crouched next to the track, making the only dirty brown spot in the vast sheet of white for miles in any direction.

"Ice bear, but even you sea dogs could tell that. It's a big one, to be sure. He's ten, twelve feet standing on his hind legs and well over a thousand pounds, given the size and depth of the track. Hard to say how long ago he passed. These dry, freezing climes don't like to tell their secrets much. I once followed the tracks of a huge stag north of End's Run for three days. When I finally found it, it had been torn apart by wolves—more'n two days past."

The hunter touched the sharp edge of the print and watched the tiny bits of dry snow crumble into the deep impression. "I'm pretty sure this'n is fresh though, real fresh. Can't be more'n about an hour or two old."

Zeb considered his options for a moment. "Me, Farley, Toron, Derran, and Ruben will take a sled and one of the scorpios, just in case the bear's got a big brother with him, and follow the tracks. If we don't find it by the time the sun sets, we'll turn around and come back. The rest of you pitch the tents, build a palisade, and put some warm food on. We should be back shortly after dark with or without the bear hide. I don't need to remind you boys to keep a sharp lookout. We have company out here, and we don't know what their intentions are, so you all stay alert and keep your weapons close at hand. Keep those crossbows loaded and the strings dry."

The men unloaded one of the sleds and strapped down the bare essentials that Zeb and his hunting party needed for the hunt, plus a little extra in case they could not make it back to camp that night. It was meager provisioning, but it would allow them to survive a night in the frigid region.

The sailors erected the tents first, then began shoveling up piles of snow for the berm, packing it just inside the area they had dug up to make the wall, creating a trench around the outside. Two men went out and cut down dozens of the spindly pines, sharpened the ends, and stuck them into the wall of packed snow around the camp. It was minimal defense against a determined enemy, but it was far better than nothing at all.

Toron pulled while Ruben pushed the sled along, Farley kept his eyes pointed at the ground, and Derran scanned the land between them and the horizon. Zeb kept pace in the middle, the cold angering the rheumatism that had started to trouble him the last couple of years. He was thinking that if this was not his last hunting trip to the far north it was very near to it.

It was not the best command decision for him to insist on leading the hunting party. It was a task far better-suited to the younger and stronger men, but he loved the hunt and was loath to give it up. It was also the most dangerous part of their journey, not counting the ship-crushing ice packs and high seas, and he was not the type of captain to send others where he would not dare to go himself. Maybe next year he would put Balor in charge of the hunting party and keep himself to the ship. The ship was a captain's rightful place after all.

Derran dropped two hares and the fox that was hunting one of the rabbits. His keen eye and masterful use of the crossbow brought them down without a missed shot, but they had yet to spot the bear. Even Farley was having trouble determining if they were getting any closer to their quarry, and the snow's refusal to help the hunter in any way was making him surlier than usual.

"Damn all this snow! If it were snowing now I could tell you if we were getting closer, if there were some wind I could tell you, if the damn thing would even so much as take a crap it would give me something to go off, to at least make a guess! For all I know, these tracks were made before the elves packed up and moved out of Valeria," the hunter complained, taking a swig of powerful spirits from a small flask he wore around his neck and tucked under his shirt.

"I think I see something," Derran whispered, even though such stealth was rather pointless after Farley's rant.

"What do you see, lad?" asked Zeb, glad to break the churlish master hunter out of his tantrum.

"Movement atop the hill near the horizon."

Zeb squinted in the direction Derran pointed, but he could make out nothing other than the expanse of white. The terrain was gently rolling with low hills, little more than broad mounds, and low-lying regions that resembled the undulating swells of the open sea. Even though the hillock was near the horizon, the ground sloped upward and was not such a great distance away. In a land where standing atop even a tiny hill would allow a man to see for miles in every direction in the flatter areas, this was far from a bad thing.

"I'll take your word for it. You think it's our bear?"

"I'm almost certain of it. It was big and four-legged. I didn't see it until it turned its side to us. I would swear the thing was looking right at us, watching us as if it knew we were following it."

Farley spit a large brown glob onto the snow. "That's a load of crap, boy. It's just an animal. Maybe it saw us, but it'll be more concerned with us stealing its prey than us hunting it. It don't matter none if it saw us anyhow. He knows he's a big boy, and there ain't nothin' out here gonna challenge him 'cept another bear, and he knows that humans ain't prey. Only important thing now is gettin' to him before he runs off. "

Derran fell in behind the hunter even though he was not so sure the man was right in his assertions of the bear's motives or its idea of its and the humans' place on the food chain.

They reached the mound where Derran had seen the bear. "Damn thing is circling back the way it came. Probably inspecting the borders of its territory," Farley growled while examining the yellow snow made by the bear to mark its range.

The tracks went down the back side of the knoll and continued around and behind another substantial white mound where they disappeared from sight. The men had stayed closer together since they started following the tracks, not concerned with scaring off smaller animals with the larger party and sled. The impressions veered south but seemed to be keeping to the lower side of the hills, a typical tactic for bears to use when hunting so as not to frighten off any potential prey by skylining themselves against the horizon.

The bear charged without warning and seemed to appear from nowhere. One second there was no sound or signs of life other than the humans and their own breathing, the next the top of a mound seemed to explode, and a bellowing roar split the air as the huge bear charged the sled from just a few yards away. Toron and the humans all spun at the sudden burst of movement and angry roar. Most creatures would have frozen in shock at such a fierce and unexpected attack and been destroyed by the awesome animal. These were all experienced men who had faced more than one kind of danger in their lives, and that experience was the critical difference between predator and prey.

Experience won out over youthful reflexes as Farley let fly the broad-headed quarrel from his heavy crossbow, striking the bear in its huge white side just behind the shoulder. It was an amazing shot, or just extremely lucky, given the animal's incredible speed and the way it bounded through the thick snow in its effort to reach the men near the sled.

Derran's shot struck just a foot behind and slightly lower than the hunter's had. It was still a good shot but nowhere near lethal for a creature this big and so outraged at the intrusion of the soft-skinned humans who dared to hunt a hunter.

Zeb let his own quarrel fly, but it sailed harmlessly past, just over the ice bear's back. The old captain dropped the crossbow with a curse and ran for the sled not more than fifteen yards behind him. Farley and Derran were also slogging toward the sled, knowing that they had nowhere near enough time to crank the windlass on the heavy crossbow before the bear ripped Toron and Ruben to shreds. It took less than a second for the three men to realize that they would not reach the sled and the spears it carried until after the bear had gotten to their comrades.

Toron had been pulling the sled by a ten-foot length of rope attached to its front end when the massive white creature burst over the top of the rise to their left. Knowing he had no time to grab one of the pikes from the sled, get in front of the bear, and set himself before it was on top of Ruben, he swung his trusty battle-axe off his broad back and charged at the ice bear's flank with a mighty roar only slightly less impressive than the bear's. The minotaur and the bear's charge intersected at a point less than ten feet from where Ruben was fumbling at one of the pikes lying atop the sledge.

The gleaming head of the double-bladed axe hissed as it cut through the air and raised a spray of bright red blood, made even more pronounced by the infinite whiteness of the bear's hide and the surrounding countryside, as Toron's axe cut deeply into the creature's muscled chest and shoulder.

Despite the grievous wound and the powerful intensity of Toron's strike, the mighty ice bear managed to swing a paw bigger than a man's head at the creature that was interfering with its kill. The huge mitt with its five dagger-like claws raked Toron across his shoulder, gouging deep furrows through the thick jacket and his tough hide without the bear breaking its stride toward the human who was desperately trying to bring his weapon to the ready.

Less than a couple of yards and two seconds separated Ruben and the charging ice bear. He turned toward the massive animal in time to see the big minotaur cut deeply into the bear's chest before the massive animal spun him to the ground with a powerful swipe that likely would have killed or at least crippled a human.

Death flashed before his eyes in the form of a huge mouth that opened far enough to swallow his head and part of his shoulders whole. Ruben had barely got the butt of the pike set onto the flat, wooden square of his snowshoe when all fifteen hundred pounds of the bear slammed into him and bore him to the ground. Fire erupted across his chest as the lethal claws tore through his thick fur coat and several layers of sturdy clothing, slicing through his flesh and muscle as if it were paper.

Blood sprayed his face as the bear roared its defiance and snapped at his head, its fangs protruding from black gums a full two inches. The only thing that saved his skull from being crushed like an eggshell and his brain pierced by the ivory daggers was that the awesome weight of the bear had shoved his entire torso two or three feet under the loose snow. Despite his gruesome wound, fear and the instinct for survival made him lash out, shoving the big head to the side, gouging at its eyes with his thumbs, and using his strong arms to keep the bear's fangs from getting a grip on his head or throat.

The fetid stench of carrion on the ice bear's breath was enough to choke him, but the oarsman hardly noticed, so involved was he in keeping himself alive long enough for one of his mates to kill the creature. He just prayed it would be within the next two to three seconds, figuring that was about how long he had before the bear tired of the game and tore his head from his shoulders like a child popping the head off an immature dandelion.

Ruben could see nothing beyond the flashing ivory fangs and huge gaping maw of the ice bear, but he heard Toron's roar of rage even over the behemoth's growls of fury.

With a roar of challenge and defiance, Toron sprinted the several steps to the sled, pushed himself high into the air as he leapt from its railing, and brought his axe crashing down with a mighty two-handed blow, cutting through the back of the ice bear's neck, severing its spinal cord, and nearly decapitating it.

The animal fell silent and crashed down on top of Ruben, the snow bank supporting enough of its dead weight to keep from crushing what little life Ruben had left in him.

Toron tossed his axe to the side as Zeb and the others ran up to him and began trying to roll the ponderous beast off their fallen comrade, but the animal was wedged into the crevice it had created when it had shoved Ruben beneath the snow and would not budge. Toron began tearing at the snow beside the dead bear with his large hands as Zeb shouted to the others to grab shovels to dig the oarsman out from beneath it.

In less than a minute, their furious digging uncovered Ruben's grinning face. "I always wanted me a nice fur coat, but I'd rather the original owner took it off first."

"Just hold on, Ruben. We almost got you out. Are you injured?" Zeb asked.

A flash of pain crossed Ruben's face. "Oh yeah, he got me real good. Don't know if he got to any of my innards, but he raked my chest real deep and bit the hell outta my arms. My skull probably looks akin to scrimshaw carving too."

They finally cleared enough snow away beside the wounded sailor to pull him out from beneath the ice bear's dead weight and examine his wounds more closely. Several deep lacerations on his skull bled profusely, and deep puncture wounds riddled his forearms, but the most serious were the ragged slashes across his chest.

They lifted him up onto the sled. When Zeb stripped off the man's tattered jacket and shirts, he winced at the severity of Ruben's wounds. He could see his lungs inflate between a couple of ribs that had been parted by the bear's powerful claws. At least three of them were fractured. The ends of one no longer aligned with one splintered end protruding above the other. Fortunately, the captain did not detect any frothing or signs that the lungs had been punctured.

Being of no further use, Toron and Farley went to dress and skin the massive bear that had lured them into a cunning trap and nearly killed one of them, and could have possibly killed them all, if they had not reacted with the quick-thinking and level-headedness of professional men. The two men were able to roll the partially excavated bear onto its side where Farley sliced the bear from groin to throat with a well-practiced hand. The offal dropped out, carried by its own weight into the shallow depression Toron had dug just beneath and beside the enormous creature.

They easily removed the head, Toron having done most of the work already with his axe, then began jerking and slicing away the tissues that kept the skin stubbornly attached to the animal. Optimally, they would have hung the bear upside down from a tree or rigged up a large tripod with a hoist and let gravity do some of the work for them, but all the trees within several miles were considerably smaller than the bear, and they had not brought timbers to erect a trivet.

In the meantime, Zeb and Derran cleaned and dressed Ruben's wounds as best they could. Zeb blessed Azerick under his breath for insisting that each ship carry a supply of healing draughts that he cooked up from time to time, and he used one on his wounded man after setting the broken rib back in place and wrapping his chest with strips of clean cloth. The potion closed most of the wounds, but it would be some time before Ruben would be back on his feet and hunting with them again. His hunting season was most assuredly over, but Zeb would find him some light camp duties to attend to. Men like Ruben needed to be kept employed to keep their spirits up.

The men kept glancing at the rapidly setting sun as they each tended to their business. Derran began helping Toron and Farley cut huge slabs of meat from the bear as Zeb made Ruben as comfortable on the sled as he could. Ruben was doing his part by complaining that he did not need such attentions, that he could probably walk. The bear had shredded his arms after all, not his legs. Both men knew his protests were groundless, but bravado in the face of horrible injury was simply an accepted part of being a rough and tough sailor.

Bear meat, particularly ice bears that lacked the more omnivorous plant diet of their southern cousins, tended to be a bit gamey and far from the most sought-after food in the kingdom. It was perfectly edible, particularly in well-seasoned stews, and a majestic animal like the mighty ice bear deserved to be utilized to its fullest and not wasted. Even the strong sinew that attached muscle to bone would be used for crossbow strings and suchlike.

"Gentlemen, I hate to rush you, but that sun is not going to wait for us or any other mortal men," Zeb said as he eyed the glowing orange disc nearly touching the horizon.

The crew was unable to clean the carcass as well as they would have liked, but the arctic scavengers would ensure that not even the bones would go to waste. Even so, they had the sled loaded with several hundred pounds of meat, not counting Ruben whom they covered with the huge bearskin, folded several times to keep it from dragging in the snow.

With the exception of Ruben and Farley, who as a hunter was adept at finding his way in the wilderness, they were all experienced sailors and knew how to navigate by the stars. This skill was put to use shortly after the sun disappeared while they were barely halfway back to the camp, but the fog rolled in and made that skill useless. Their only chance of reaching the camp now lay in navigating a straight line, hoping they could stay on course while blinded by the thick vapors, and get close enough to be heard.

The men back at the camp eyed the increasing thickness of the fog with growing concern. A fire burned in one of the small iron stoves, its top removed to allow the flames to leap out and provide a weak beacon for the absent hunting party.

"Bah, it's no use. I lose sight of that fire no more than a hundred feet out. They'll burn themselves on the side before they see the blasted thing," Matt complained.

"They planned for the event of not being able to make it back, Matt. I wouldn't worry too much," Rick replied.

"Then why do you look like someone just pinched your last copper?"

"It ain't the cold I'm worried about."

"The Eislanders," Matt said, both of the same mind.

"We ain't seen 'em, they ain't tried nothin', but I know they're there watching us, just waiting to slit our throats in our sleep," Rick said as a shiver ran down his spine.

"So what are they waitin' for? We're five shorter than we were last night. Why not attack us now if it were numbers they was worried about? They know we ain't got that big minotaur with us. That's like being short three men just by itself." Matt scratched his chin with a mittened hand. "Maybe they followed the cap'n. Maybe that's why they ain't made it back yet."

"I doubt it. Eislanders may be big brutes, but they ain't stupid, especially when it comes to fightin'. They'd take on us eight and know it's gonna be an easier fight than takin' on the cap'n with Toron by his side. I got as much pride in my strength and fightin' skill as any man alive, but I wouldn't provoke that big bull-headed beast for all the gold in the kingdom."

"Aye, I'll be glad to have him back too. Hey, I got an idea. Get a couple men to set up one of the scorpios, in fact, set 'em both up."

"Whatcha got in mind, Matt?"

"You'll see."

The men set up the scorpios; one atop a high mound for defense, the other on the side of another mound pointed up at a sharp angle in the direction Zeb and the others had traveled.

"All right," Matt said to the assembled sailors. "We take this strip of cloth and tie it to the end of the picket. We wrap another around the tip, roll it in animal fat, and set her aflame. Set it in the scorpio, and…voila!" Matt cried, triggering the big mounted crossbow.

The flaming brand streaked high across the low-lying fog more than a hundred feet in the air and over three hundred yards distant into the night.

"We launch one every fifteen minutes until we run out of stakes. That should last us until a bit after midnight. If Zeb and them don't catch sight of one by then, they won't be comin' back tonight."

"Pretty clever for a landlubbing desert rat," Rick ribbed his friend.

"Hey, the desert eats them that ain't clever enough to avoid its traps or move away. I was smart enough to do both."

Matt continued firing his improvised flares into the sky while Rick rhythmically banged the back of his cutlass against the side of the iron stove. Matt was halfway through his brands when a shout overrode Rick's thrumming on the stove side.

"Knock off that racket before you wake the dead." Zeb's gravelly voice broke through the stillness of the night and the oppressive fog.

Rick nearly dropped his cutlass as he leapt to his feet. No one had been sleeping, only partly due to Rick's banging, and they crossed to where their captain's voice had cut through the fog. Even as close as Zeb and the rest of the group were, it was difficult to determine the direction. The thick fog caused the sound to bounce around inside it, causing nearly as much trouble hearing as it did seeing.

"Zeb, thank the gods you made it back!" Matt shouted as Zeb and Derran appeared out of the mists.

"You can thank 'em if ya want. I'll give my thanks to you lads for launching them brands into the air and over this blasted fog. You boys knock a hole in the wall. We got a man down, and he don't need to be tossed over the top like a sack of feed."

Several men grabbed their shovels and hastened to obey the captain's orders. "What happened? Who's hurt?"

"Ruben got tackled by the granddaddy of all ice bears. He got his pike set just in time, but the weight of the beast split the base on his snowshoe and drove him and the spear butt a couple of feet into the snow. Even with two heavy quarrels in his side and a spear through his chest, that bear was determined to get at least one of us, and Ruben was the one unfortunate enough to be picked. Toron took a nasty swipe that woulda likely as not torn my top half from my bottom half before he leapt up and nearly took the beast's head off."

"How's Ruben doing?" Rick asked before they all heard Ruben's protests that he was fine to walk on his own.

"We were gettin' mighty worried that you all wouldn't make it back tonight," Matt said.

Zeb clapped Matt on the shoulder. "We likely wouldn't have if you boys hadn't been firing off them flares and bangin' on that stove. We weren't much more than a couple of degrees off from my dead reckoning, but even that took us a couple hundred yards to the south of the camp, and we would have walked right on by it. The fog got so thick for a while we couldn't even follow our own tracks back. I was about to order the tent pitched when Derran saw the first flash over the fog. We thought it was a shooting star at first until the next one went by near the same spot."

"I wasn't sure if it would work with all this fog. I'm glad to see it did. I know you all would have been all right for a night out there on your own, but it's still good to all be together. This place just don't seem right to me," Matt said with a small shudder.

"I know exactly what ya mean, lad. Now did ya keep some stew on the fire like I asked?" Zeb said with a grin.

Zeb's crew finished off the last of the pot of stew. They put Ruben in one of the tents and insisted he eat on his pallet then get some rest. He nearly punched Rick when the fellow oarsman tried to feed him, teasing him about needing to have the meat chunks chewed for him first.

They filled the opening in the palisade with packed snow and established a guard roster for the rest of the night. They slept tightly packed, not bothering to unload the second tent from the sled, which carried the big bear hide and meat. It was not until after midnight, and all but the two men on watch had gone to sleep, that the attack came.

There was no warning, no call to battle, or shouted challenge. The huge Eislanders simply walked out of the mists right in front of a man named Carter, grabbed his head in their calloused hands, and twisted with such strength that his head was nearly torn off his shoulders. Then all hell broke loose.

CHAPTER 3

It took them nearly an hour to circle around to where they had left the horses tethered. Despite everyone's fatigue, Azerick convinced the rest of the group that it would be prudent to get out of the area before establishing their camp. They rode for two hours before deciding they had gone far enough to avoid being seen by anyone searching for the ruins. The party set up in a small depression that would hide them from view unless someone walked right on top of them.

When it came time for Azerick to pull his watch shift, he made a comfortable seat in the sand, leaned against his saddle, and pulled the black gem from his pocket. He gripped the stone tightly in his palm, bent his concentration upon it, and tried to make contact with General Baneford.

It took a solid minute before Azerick felt the first touch of the general's sending and another minute before the man was able to focus his thoughts enough for his words to come through intelligibly.

"Uh, hello?" the general's clumsy sending came.

"You are General Baneford?"

"Yes. Gods this is eerie. I'm Baneford."

"I have recovered the helm. Where shall I meet you?"

"Have you eliminated the others?"

"Not yet. I thought you might have use for them as captives. Besides, this is a rough land, and I may still need them to help me reach you. You can capture them or kill them at your leisure then. I should have little problem neutralizing them once we meet."

"Adventurers are generally in business for personal gain. If I can sway their allegiance, I may have a use for them. If not, I certainly owe them for the death of so many of my men."

General Baneford described where he and his men were waiting and even managed to provide a rough mental picture of the area. He was not far, perhaps two days to the northwest in the abandoned ruins of some ancient outpost. These harsh lands were dotted with them. As wells dried up and the desert sands changed the geography, whole towns packed up and moved to more hospitable areas, leaving nothing behind but the desiccated remains of their stone and brick buildings.

Azerick woke the others as the sun was setting. After a quick meal of dry trail bread and cheese, he took the lead, setting a quick pace toward the northwest. He deflected inquiries about the helm by telling Maude and the others that it was best that it remain inside his magical bag because it would prevent any magical scrying, and an artifact as powerful as the helm would be like a brilliant beacon on a clear night for anyone attempting to divine its location.

"If we head straight west, we should cross the trade road that runs south to Langdon's Crossing. It will make for easier traveling," Maude suggested.

Azerick shook his head. "We do not know where the men who are looking for the helm are, and we run the risk of crossing their path if we ride the roads. There are also reports of at least two large bands of marauders looting towns inside the kingdom. Langdon's Crossing was one of the first towns hit. It would be a bitter pill to swallow to have finally gotten one of the pieces you have worked so hard to find, just to get robbed by a bunch of highwaymen on your way to present it to the king."

Maude could not argue with the mage's reasoning, but she could not fully banish the nagging feeling of unease in the shadowy recesses of her mind.

As the party rode through their second night of travel, it seemed to Maude that Azerick was even more aloof than usual, answering any questions with the briefest of answers but otherwise remaining silent.

The dark silhouette of stone ruins protruded out of a low, rocky hilltop on the distant horizon, breaking up the clear, starry night sky.

Just before they reached the first sand-scoured, tumbledown blocks of former buildings, Azerick reined in Horse and dismounted.

"This looks like a good place to rest up. It will be nice to have some shelter from the wind for a while," Azerick told the group.

The others followed Azerick's lead, swinging out of their saddles and proceeding to walk deeper into the ruins. They found a small roofless building with three walls still standing, which by using a length of rope to cordon off the open end, made a good stable for the horses.

"With luck, there will be another structure somewhat intact that will provide us with some decent shelter," Azerick told them as he walked further into the ruins.

A creaking sound to the right drew Maude's attention. A few yards away, an iron crow's cage swung from a pole. Maude thought that it contained a pile of clothing and bones until she saw a long-fingered, delicate hand slip through the bars. Maude crept closer and gasped as the cage gently rotated in the breeze and she saw the gaunt face of the prisoner inside.

"Tarth!" Maude shouted, then ran at the cage. "Oh, Tarth, what happened to you? Are you all right?" Maude grabbed the hand that was thrust through the bars.

"Oh, Maudeline, it is awful!" Tarth wailed. "I have not had a bath in days, my robes are torn and soiled, and my fingers have the most awful cuticles…cuticles, Maudeline! I think my arm may be broken too, but I have been unable to focus on such an inconsequential thing."

Several men chose that moment to separate themselves from the shadows of the ruins ahead and to each side of them. Maude, Borik, and Malek drew their weapons and prepared to defend themselves.

Azerick spun and dropped a ward of silence on the cleric and followed it with a binding spell, paralyzing all three adventurers before they even had the chance to understand what was happening. Rage burned through Maude when she realized Azerick's betrayal.

Gritting her teeth, she forced her muscles to move and broke free of the invisible chains that seemed to freeze her in place. With a savage snarl, she ran at Azerick, sword held high. A rune flared brightly on Azerick's staff and threw Maude painfully onto her back. Before she regained her feet, stone pillars surrounded her in a makeshift cage.

"You traitorous bastard!" Maude shouted, pounding on the stone rods with her gauntleted fists.

Azerick reached into his bag and pulled out the gleaming black helm, its edges outlined in gold, as a large man wearing the armor that obviously went with the helm approached. Azerick casually tossed the helm to General Baneford when he came forward, his face split in a wide grin.

"You have done most excellently, changeling," the general congratulated him. "I'll admit that I know very little of your kind, but I had thought that you could only mimic your victim's appearance, not their abilities. I see from the way you handled these fools that I was mistaken."

"Actually, General, you are quite correct in your understanding. A doppelganger would not be able to steal a spellcaster's ability to wield magic."

General Baneford furrowed his brow, taking a second to comprehend exactly what this creature meant.

This is the wizard, not the changeling!

Before he could even shout an order to his men, runes flared brightly on the staff in the sorcerer's hand. Stone spikes and towering walls of flames encircled the small area in which they stood, separating the general from his men.

"Now, General, you will tell me who has you collecting these artifacts, and who hired the assassin that tried to kill me; a man known as the Rook."

General Baneford shook his head and chuckled without a hint of mirth. "You stupid young fool. You have no way to force me to answer any of your questions," he said, donning the helm.

General Baneford felt a powerful surge suffuse his body. He felt stronger, faster, and invincible. He began to second-guess his bargain with the black wizard. With this armor, he could keep the gifts that the wizard had given him as well as Dundalor's armor, and no man could ever take it away. No man, no army could stop him! With a concerted effort, he suppressed his sudden power-hungry greed. He made a deal and gave his word, and he never went back on his word, unless the one he had given it to betrayed him. So far, the wizard had dealt fairly.

"You just gave up the only chance you had of overpowering me," General Baneford said, his voice sounding hollow from within the confines of the helm.

He drew the magnificent sword the wizard had given him along with the other arms and armor and stalked toward the sorcerer.

"You are a powerful young man. Join me, and I promise you a place in my command; otherwise I will have to cut you and these other fools down where you all stand."

"No chance, General. Tell me who the wizard is, or you will not live to enjoy that armor or any other."

The fearsome-looking general laughed again as he continued stalking toward the young mage.

"Bad choice, General."

The hard stone opened beneath General Baneford's feet. His hands went up and out in an attempt to arrest his fall, but the smooth sides of the shaft gave him no purchase. He struck the bottom perhaps twelve feet down. General Baneford looked up and saw the grim face of the young sorcerer peering down at him.

"Now that I have your undivided attention, General, tell me who hired the assassin and who sent you after this armor."

"You cannot maintain that fire forever, and when it goes out my men will cut you down!"

Even now, they could all hear the angry shouts from the men on the other side of the flaming barrier.

Azerick shook his head. "You are at my mercy, General. I can kill you before those flames disappear and be long gone. Now tell me what I want to know."

"You cannot harm me, not while I wear this armor! I am invulnerable to your magic and your weapons!"

"General Baneford, do you consider yourself a good student of history?" Azerick asked in a conversational tone.

"What nonsense are you spewing now?"

"I myself am quite fond of history. So much can be learned from our forefathers. In fact, it can almost be said that one well versed enough in history can foretell the future. Do you recall anyone throughout history by the name of King Bertrand or Emperor Bertrand?" Azerick quizzed the angry general.

"No, and why in the world would I care?"

Azerick smiled down at the trapped general. "Lord Bertrand managed to steal Dundalor's armor from King Archibald through a rather audacious plot to overthrow his rule and replace the Ollander bloodline with his own. Now, if he were truly invincible, as the armor purports the wearer to be, why was he never king?"

If Azerick could have seen through the glossy black helm, he would have seen the general's face pale as he quietly replied. "He failed. He had the armor but he still failed."

"That's right, General, he failed. Do you know how he failed?"

Azerick saw the general shake his head.

"Lord Bertrand and his men were lined up on the south bank of the Crook River at Ballinger's Bridge. King Archibald arrayed his own troops on the north bank of the river before Bertrand could get his men across uncontested. Archibald knew he could not defeat Bertrand and his soldiers, and Bertrand knew that he could not get his men across the bridge without suffering horrendous losses. His intent was to march his forces to a wide, natural ford several leagues downstream, but that would take days of marching, and Archibald's troops could reach it just as fast as he could, and he would still be forced to fight at a disadvantage though not nearly as great a one as crossing the bridge would cause. Are you still following me, General?" Azerick asked his captive audience. "The most important part is coming up."

"Yeah, I'm listening to your drivel!" Baneford yelled up at the arrogant, young spellcaster.

General Baneford had never shown fear in the face of an enemy, and he would certainly not do so in front of this whelp, but something in the young wizard's voice and demeanor greatly unnerved him. Coupled with the fact that he was stuck in a hole and unable to do anything about it, it was beyond maddening.

"Archibald knew he could punish Bertrand's troops at the ford, but he could not defeat them. So, against all common sense, King Archibald strode out onto the center of the bridge and challenged Bertrand to single combat with undisputed rule of the realm as the prize. Lord Bertrand laughed all the way to the center of the bridge where he gladly accepted Archibald's foolish challenge. Most people were quite aware of the armor's power. Its history was still fresh in most people's minds.

"In an even more bizarre move, Archibald stripped off all of his armor except for his breastplate and gauntlets, loudly proclaiming that Bertrand was a pathetic usurper who relied on magical armor to see him to victory because he was too weak and too stupid to achieve it by his own strength and wits.

"Bertrand was furious and attacked Archibald before he was even set to begin the battle. Archibald narrowly deflected the cowardly attack and set himself to receive Bertrand in a test of arms. Lord Bertrand, thoroughly incensed, thought to use the greater strength his armor provided him to overwhelm the king's skill. He also had no fear of being struck, because he knew that Archibald's blade could never harm him.

"Bertrand's tactic would have worked just as it had several times before in his many battles, but Archibald was canny and was just as aware of Bertrand's advantages. It was several minutes into the fight, both men were near the rail of the bridge, their sword hilts locked together as Bertrand's magical strength slowly shoved Archibald to his knees. With a sudden surge of strength, Archibald shoved with all his might and sent them both over the rail and into the muddy waters of the river below."

General Baneford continued to look up and listen to the young sorcerer's recitation, seemingly compelled to hang on his every word, then swallowed nervously as he looked upon the young man's smile, the very smile he imagined that King Archibald wore just before he threw them both into the frigid river.

"I think you see where this is going, General. Archibald shed his breastplate and gauntlets and swam to the distant shore. Bertrand was not seen again until Archibald's men managed to dredge his corpse out of the river several days later. The king knew that the armor was too dangerous to leave intact, so he had his most trusted wizards scatter the pieces throughout the realm. Now, tell me, General, how long can you hold your breath?" Azerick asked, his smile sliding from his face, replaced with a cold look of unchallengeable purpose.

Azerick raised his staff, and a dwarven rune for stone and water flared. The solid granite at General Baneford's feet lost all cohesion and flowed over the tops of his boots.

"What do you want from me!" he shouted, feeling more vulnerable and helpless than he ever had in his life.

"I told you what I want, General. It is a very simple request."

General Baneford sighed. He hated to tell this wizard, or demon, or whatever the hell he was, anything, but he had never actually pledged any sort of loyalty to the Black Tower wizard as he had Ulric. He had fulfilled the spirit of their bargain to the best of his ability.

"I don't know who sent the assassin, but I do know the Rook is affiliated with the Black Tower wizards who are the same ones that asked me to get them the armor."

Black Tower wizards. A great deal was starting to make sense to him now. The Black Tower wizards were an order of mages bent on reclaiming the power they once wielded in the realm. Even the king treaded lightly where the black wizards were concerned. The slow but inevitable attrition of wizards who were able to attain truly powerful levels of magic eventually allowed the good people of Valeria to cast them out of the kingdom. They rebuilt their great black tower in a city a few days' ride southeast of Langdon's Crossing in Sumara.

The Rook was affiliated with the Black Tower who had his father attempt to smuggle a piece of the armor into the kingdom. He got caught, and the Tower sent the Rook to silence him. But why did the Rook come after him? He had nothing to do with the armor or the politics behind its acquisition.

The attack on Miranda was no mere hold-up. Could it have been a kidnapping, and was it linked to all of this? The bandits had failed because of him. It was possible someone had sent the Rook in retaliation. Whatever the reason, it appeared that someone in the Black Tower would have answers.

"Tell me about Darius Giles and his murder."

"I don't know anyone by that name."

"He was a prisoner in Southport. He had one of the pieces that I assume you recovered somehow," Azerick explained. "Someone killed him in his cell. I am surmising it was the work of the Rook as well."

"I don't know anything about that. I haven't stepped foot in Southport in nearly eight years. I was told to recover the gauntlets from some king's men around that time, and that was a hundred miles from

Southport. Now, get me out of this blasted hole, or leave so my men may retrieve me, we had a deal!"

"I am well aware of our deal, General. I am a man of my word, are you?" Azerick asked.

General Baneford shed his ebony and gold helm. "I am a man of my word, wizard."

"I will free you, but you must order your men to stand down and leave us all in peace. You will take your soldiers wherever you please, but you will not trouble Valeria and her people any longer."

"I will do as you say. Now, get me out of here."

"First, you must remove the armor—all of it," Azerick told the general.

With a huff and a curse, Baneford tore at the priceless artifact and shed it like an old skin. He was soon standing on top of the jumbled mass of armor in his sweat-stained padded doublet, glaring up at the audacious young man who had him at his mercy. Azerick lowered the end of his staff into the hole and struggled to pull the larger man up and out.

Once the general was clear, Azerick raised his staff then pointed it down at the bottom of the pit. The armor clanged loudly as it fell another twenty feet when the ground below it disappeared. Azerick repeated the spell, and the armor fell another twenty feet. Twice more Azerick caused the pit to deepen until the armor was nearly a hundred feet below the surface. His efforts were tiring him, but he was not finished yet.

As General Baneford looked on in a sort of fascination, a dozen runes flared brightly on the sorcerer's staff. Runes of stone and fire blazed so brightly that it made the light from the wall of flames appear no more than a candle next to a forest fire. As the general's eyes blinked away the glowing dwarven runes swimming in his overwhelmed vision, he saw an orange glow radiating up from the bottom of the deep pit, and it was growing nearer.

It reminded him of a piece of steel heated white hot, ready to be forged by a blacksmith. As the glow reached the surface, General Baneford finally recognized it for what it was: magma, the molten rock he had heard sailors and scholars describe that shot from mountains and fissures on some faraway islands near the southern tip of Lazuul.

Azerick was bathed in sweat, and it was not from the heat of the lava, which was slowly bubbling up to the surface like some glowing, boiling brew from a witch's cauldron.

Once the nearly white-hot magma reached the surface, Azerick stopped its rise and allowed it to simmer. He did not know if the molten stone would destroy the armor, but anyone seeking to retrieve it was going to have a very difficult time digging it out. When he could sustain the magma no more, he released the flow of power he was pouring into the stone from both his staff and himself. As the molten rock began solidifying, Azerick cast a few spells below the surface of the rock. The wards would make the stone all around highly resistant to mundane pickaxes and hammers as well as magical detection and destruction.

"Tell your men to put away their weapons, and I will lower the flames," Azerick told the general, leaning heavily upon his staff.

General Baneford strode as close as he could to the wall of flames and shouted to his men on the other side. "Captains, can you hear me?"

"Aye, sir, we hear you. Have you slain the wizard?" one of his men shouted back.

General Baneford thought a moment before answering. "We have reached an accord. Sheath your weapons. There will be no further battles here today."

The moment Azerick dropped the flames, Baneford's men began threading their way through the stone spikes and converged upon their commander.

"Sir, what happened?"

"I was defeated, men. I was defeated fairly by a craftier foe and my own hubris. Remember the lesson this night, gentlemen. No matter how powerful you think you are, no matter how unassailable you believe your position may be, a clever man can defeat you. And if you let your pride rule your actions, you have just given him the key to do it."

General Baneford stepped past his men and approached Azerick, who walked over to Maude, touched the stone bars that trapped her, and turned them to dust. Borik and Malek moved quickly but warily to Maude's side when Azerick released the spell on them.

"Maude, I hope you will accept my apology for deceiving you. I had to convince the general and his men that I was somebody else with entirely different motives, and I felt the best way to do that was subterfuge against all involved," said Azerick, his voice heavy with fatigue.

Maude glared then sheathed her sword. "I despise deception, but in this case I suppose the ends justify the means. Fortunately, I am in a joyous mood since we found the companion we all thought lost."

Maude turned away and lowered the crow's cage holding the disheveled elf. Malek shattered the lock with his hammer, not wasting time asking anyone to use the key someone most certainly possessed. Maude reached in and pulled Tarth out of the cage and laid him gently onto the ground. Tarth reached toward Maude with a trembling hand and croaked something she could not make out.

"Borik, get him some water, quickly!" Maude commanded.

The dwarf ran forward with a full skin and shoved it into the elf's hand. Tarth focused his gaze on the life-giving water skin, shook his head, and contemptuously tossed it aside.

"I don't understand what you want, Tarth," Maude said, then lowered her head toward the elf's parched lips.

"H-hairbrush!" Tarth rasped.

General Baneford walked over to the visibly exhausted young sorcerer. "My offer still stands. I could really use a man like you."

"I have other responsibilities and some tasks I need to take care of. Sorry I had to destroy your armor, but I could not allow it to fall into anyone's hands. Too many good people have already died because of its existence."

"I'd wager it would be more accurate to say you have some people to take to task." Baneford chuckled. "To be honest with you, I'm not sorry to see it go. I have also seen too many good men's lives thrown away for something that would just make people miserable, although it does put me in a bind with those Black Tower wizards. They already paid me to recover it and hand it over to them, and I'm not sure I could talk my men into returning what we were given."

Azerick smiled wanly at the general. "I would not worry too much about the Black Tower wizards for long, General. Keep your men on the move, and they will have a difficult time finding you. They are going to have far bigger problems to deal with before long."

"Coming from any other man that would sound like overconfident boasting." General Baneford extended his hand. "Good hunting, and good luck."

Azerick gripped the general's proffered hand. "Good luck to you as well, General. You seem to be a decent man. I do not know how you got caught up in this sordid business, but I hope you find what you are looking for."

"What I'm looking for is some peace and freedom for me and my men, but that will likely only come after a great deal of fighting."

"That is one of the few things worth fighting for, General. It is the very reason I am here now and doing what I must do," Azerick replied, then turned away and made his way toward Maude and the others.

Maude was brushing the elf's hair while she made him drink some water. Azerick received some cold looks, but none were overtly hostile.

"Maudeline, really, I can do it myself. I am fine," Azerick heard Tarth protest.

"Hold still and drink more water. I can do it," Maude ordered in a tone most would think harsh but was full of affection.

"Maudeline, I love you dearly, but I have seen your hair, and I will crawl back into that crow's cage before I let my hair look like yours."

"How is he?" Azerick asked.

"Bird-brained and useless like always," Borik grumbled to disguise the small amount of pleasure in his voice. "Say, can you teach him that beer freezing trick?"

"Sorry, Borik, I would have no way of knowing how to teach it to a wizard."

Borik's faced turned red. "Why the heck not? You're both wizards! I thought your kind traded spells all the time?"

"Because he is not a wizard, you hairy-faced little cretin; he is a sorcerer," Tarth informed the dwarf.

"What are we supposed to do now, Azerick?" Malek asked. "You destroyed the armor or at least put it out of reach."

"Tell Jarvin that you have taken the armor out of enemy hands and secured it in a way that it is unlikely anyone will ever be able to use it again. If I were he, I would call that an unexpected but acceptable conclusion to his problems."

"I suppose it is. So where will you go now? I presume you are not traveling back with us to Brelland."

"No, my business is not yet finished."

"Despite your ruse, I think you have good intentions. I wish you luck in your journeys," Malek said, voicing a sentiment the others grudgingly shared.

"For good or ill, my intentions are my own."

Azerick forced himself to walk back to where Horse was picketed and led him out of the makeshift stable before mounting and riding toward Langdon's Crossing. He knew he would not be riding far. He felt as drained as his staff. After an hour or so, he directed Horse into a shallow basin, removed his saddle, and fell asleep with his head and shoulders resting on its padded seat.

CHAPTER 4

"Joshua!" Shakrill shouted for her apprentice. "Joshua! You have until the count of three to get your lazy, useless hide in here! One!—"

"Yes, mistress, I'm here!" a young, sandy-haired man in his late teens declared breathlessly as he burst into his mistress's chambers.

"Set up my scrying bowl, you lazy little wart. I don't know why I put up with your ineptitude."

If Joshua took offense at his mistress's verbal abuse, he dared not show it. He was used to it by now; she had never used a kind voice when she addressed him or any of the other apprentices or novices of the Black Tower. Of course, its commonness did not make the hateful words sting any less.

Joshua averted his gaze, not even daring to look her in the eye. "Yes, mistress."

Joshua went about following his mistress's command with efficient practice. He retrieved a stone bowl from where it sat upon a bookshelf amongst other assorted magical accessories. The bowl was carved from a dark grey, almost black, stone with red swirling patterns and was about six inches deep, as big around as a dinner plate, and had four small nubs for legs, like a tiny cauldron. He set it on the dark wooden table where his mistress preferred to work. Joshua then returned to the bookshelf, retrieved a blown glass bottle of pure elemental water, and began pouring it into the bowl.

"What are you doing, you imbecile?" Shakrill shouted. "I need the dragon's blood, you incompetent little twit!"

Shakrill would have been considered beautiful by most standards, with her long black hair, pale blue eyes, and alabaster skin, if it were not for the perpetual scowl that never left her face. She gave off such an aura of malice that any man who made the mistake of trying to consort with her would wither under her fierce glare and waspish tongue. She was the most feared, if not the most powerful, wizard in the Black Tower.

Joshua poured the precious liquid back into the bottle, careful not to spill a drop lest his mistress whip him, not that she needed such a reason, as he was well aware. He took a clean rag and thoroughly dried the bowl before filling the bottom inch of the vessel with the thick, black liquid.

"It is ready for you, mistress."

Shakrill looked up from the tome she was reading and stalked over to where Joshua was awaiting her approval before leaving. Without warning, she grabbed her apprentice firmly by the wrist and slashed his hand with a razor-sharp knife she materialized from inside her black robes. Joshua knew better than to so much as flinch away from the unexpected assault and remained perfectly still while Shakrill held his hand above the bowl, adding his blood to the preserved black liquid already in the small basin.

Joshua staunched his wound with the rag he had used to dry the scrying bowl as soon as his mistress released her grasp. She would beat him if he bled on her floor as she had on occasion after she had been the one who caused him to bleed in the first place.

"I assume you were doing something useful before you came to me?" Shakrill asked as she stared into the seemingly bottomless bowl.

"Yes, mistress."

"Then get back to it! What are you, a porter waiting around for a gratuity? Be gone!" Shakrill screeched at his fleeing back.

Shakrill sat and bent over the bowl, a sinister smile adorning her cold but perfect face. "Klaraxis," the dark wizard called softly.

The viscous black blood rippled in the bowl, and a face from one's worst nightmares glared up from the depths of the shallow vessel. The face was jet black, and long fangs and sharp teeth spiked from its upper and lower jaws. The reflection showed the base of blood-red horns jutting forward out of the creature's head just above its pronounced brow before disappearing from view. Its wide nose looked like it once belonged to some great ape from the jungles of Lazuul.

"What do you want, Shakrill?" the demon lord asked impatiently, glaring at the wizard with its malevolent scarlet eyes, which shone like brilliant rubies.

"We are nearly ready for your transcendence, my prince. You should be able to sense the essence of your soon-to-be host."

"Ah yes, he will be acceptable, Shakrill. You have done well."

"It is my pleasure to serve you, my prince. Joshua is useless as an apprentice, but he is young and strong and will serve well as the vessel to your essence."

"How much longer until you can perform the ritual?" Klaraxis asked.

"In precisely seven days, the planets will be in the most beneficial alignment we can expect for at least the next several years."

"Very well, Shakrill. I see no reason for you to disturb me until then," the demon cautioned the wizard, then faded from her view.

Klaraxis leaned back contentedly on his throne made from the bones of some of the more powerful creatures to have displeased him. The bones of the lesser creatures he had slain over the millennia formed the sixty-foot-tall wall that encircled his palace of black soul stone. It was only seven more days until he could travel from his domain on the fifth circle of the abyss to the realm of mortals. The demon prince was not known for his patience, but he had waited almost a thousand years to return to the realm of mortals, and he could wait another seven days.

"Skunk! Get in here!" Klaraxis shouted into the empty air.

A small winged demog materialized before the demon lord's throne with a puff of sulfurous smoke and a flash of fire, and hovered near his master.

"Yes, oh great and terrible lord of all, what can the dutiful *Skulk* do for you?" the little demog demon groveled.

Without warning, Klaraxis shot out a red-taloned hand, grabbed the smaller demon by the throat, and pulled him close to his fanged mouth.

"Did you just correct me, *Skunk?*"

Skulk tried to swallow, but the iron grip of the demon lord would not allow even that small measure of movement. "No, my most exalted and all-powerful master who could never be mistaken. Your most loyal and humble Skunk would never dare presume so much."

Klaraxis contemptuously tossed the demon through the air where he flitted back to hover several yards from the irritable demon lord. "Bring me a sacrifice, make it two. I feel like celebrating."

"At once, my majestic and universally feared master of all he surveys," the demog replied, then fluttered away down the black halls of the palace.

"*Skunk do this, Skunk do that,*" Skulk mocked in a whisper as he did his master's bidding. "*You're a worthless little slime, Skunk. I wouldn't use your bones to build my privy, Skunk.* Big bagalesh's ass thinks he can abuse Skulk just because he can. Big bagalesh's ass would be lost without Skulk. He can get his own stupid sacrifices next time if Skulk is so worthless."

"Skunk, move it!" Klaraxis's voice rang out from down the hall loud enough for Skulk to feel it.

"Yes, great omnipotent one!" Skulk shouted and raced away in terror.

Shakrill leaned back in her chair with a wintery smile, a perfect imitation of the demon lord. Joshua was almost worthless in her eyes, which made him one of the best apprentices she had ever had, and she had gone through quite a few in her time. He would be hard to replace, but the power Klaraxis would bring her and the Black Tower in exchange for freeing him would be worth far more than the inconvenience.

Ballizarr and the other wizards of the Black Tower told her she was foolish to enter such a pact, that the demon prince could not be trusted. Of course he could not be trusted. He was a demon, a lord of demons at that, which is why she did not leave their compact to trust. She had discovered the demon's soul name, and with it, she could control and command him to do her bidding. Klaraxis was unaware of this fact, but she would enlighten him once he arrived.

With the demon completely under her control, she would not only restore the Black Tower to its former glory, but replace that old wretch Ballizarr as head of the order as well. Her smile grew even wider and more malevolent as she pictured the current master of the Tower kneeling before her and kissing her feet. In seven days, she would command the Black Tower and all those who resided within its dark halls. Then she would rule the realm, no, the world!"

The sand dragon flew swiftly back to her cave, a fat goat gripped tightly in her long talons. She hated to hunt the beasts that belonged to the humans, but she had had no luck finding wild game, and her baby was hungry. Her foraging had taken her far from her normal hunting range as well. She knew those hated wyverns roosted along the cliffs to the north, and she made certain to avoid their territory. She thought of her young one waiting hungrily back at their cave and pumped her wings for more speed. As a sand dragon, she was far more at home burrowing under the soft sands than she was flying, but the tasty goats and camels that were her usual prey did not burrow, and they were rarely found near her home.

Only a slight disturbance in the air gave her any warning before a sharp pain lanced across her brassy scales on her right side. She banked hard to the left in an attempt to avoid the wyverns' attack. They had flown out of the sun, executing a rather clever ambush for the otherwise stupid creatures. Humans and other two-legged peoples called them two-legged dragons, but that was an insult to dragons. No true dragon would claim the vicious and stupid creatures as even a distant relative.

She barely had time to register the shadows of the other wyverns as they dove at her. She dropped the goat, knowing she was going to have to fight her way past these disgusting beasts. She was not as swift a flyer as many of the other types of dragons and knew she could not outfly them.

Another pain flared across her broad back when a second wyvern raked her with its sharp claws, cutting through her glittering scales, tearing a triple row of deep furrows in her flesh, and drawing dark blood. She banked again, and a third wyvern flew past, barely missing her vulnerable wing.

The sand dragon roared in fury and dove at the back of the wyvern that had fatally misjudged his attack. Her almost disproportionately long, hard claws tore into the softer scales of the wyvern. Her serpentine neck snaked forward and clasped the thin neck of the wyvern just behind its narrow, wedge-shaped head. One powerful bite from her strong jaws crushed the bone and cartilage just beneath the hide and muscle.

The paralyzed and dying wyvern plummeted like a stone and struck the ground a few seconds later, spraying a large geyser of sand into the air. A sixth sense warned her of another impending attack. She dipped her left wing and twisted her stout body, flipping over in midair. The sudden loss of lift sent her plummeting toward the ground but also served to drop her below the clutches of the attacking wyvern. She released a searing blast of fire up at the creature, incinerating its dry, leathery wings, and scorching its face and chest.

She could hear the beast screeching in pain as it fell to its death as she righted herself before she struck the sand next to it. Just as she snapped her wings out to regain lift, another set of claws tore into her back, and an even sharper pain wracked her body when the wyvern's vicious stinger knifed between her shoulder blades. The crippling poison burned as it coursed through her bloodstream.

She dipped sharply left and right, dislodging her attacker and diving for the ground before the effects of the paralyzing poison took full effect. She already felt her muscles responding sluggishly as she raced for the safety of the drifting sands. If she could just reach the ground, she could burrow below the sand and rest, safe from attack, until the poison wore off.

When she was just a few hundred feet up, only scant seconds from safety, she lost all control of her muscles. Her head and tail slumped and the force of the wind pushed her limp wings uselessly behind her. Unimaginable sorrow filled her as she thought of her precious little one alone, slowly starving to death in their dark cave. The poison had set in so thoroughly that she did not even feel the impact of the sand when she struck. Darkness consumed her, and a final tear traced its way down the fine golden scales of her lifeless cheek.

Ulric marched his men toward the east wall of Groveswood to "liberate" the wealthy nobles from the clutches of the raiders who had been looting and terrorizing its prestigious citizens for the better part of the day. Groveswood had a large guard force who did an excellent job of keeping the thieves and commoners out of town, but they were poorly equipped to take on five hundred mounted mercenaries who lived for battle and mayhem.

Ulric sent a messenger into the city to inform Kayne that he would be driving him out that night and to have his men prepared to depart with their substantial plunder. Once the night fully arrived, Ulric led his men through the lightly guarded gates. Kayne's men held the gates not to keep Ulric out but to keep any citizen of Groveswood from fleeing the town and sending for help until they were ready for them to do so.

The battle at the gates was quick, and Ulric rode at the head as his army raged through the streets "battling" the invaders wherever they found them and routing them out of the town's west gate. Within an hour, not a single raider remained inside the town's walls. The "dead and wounded" were taken away in the duke's wagons where Ulric promised to dispose of the corpses and captives alike so that they would not sully the pristine air of Groveswood any longer.

The mayor lauded Duke Ulric, as well as bestowing the town's highest honor upon him for their deliverance from the hands of the invaders. Ulric nearly choked, stifling laughter at the irony of the award.

The pillaging had not been bloodless, but it had been acceptably controlled. As per Ulric's directive, Kayne and his men killed only a small number of the lesser citizens, those merchants with minimal political influence whom he had denoted as expendable. There was more than enough degradation, humiliation, brutalization, and assault to help properly enrage the citizens and bend their favor and gratitude toward the duke.

Duke Ulric found Kayne and his men at the agreed upon campsite, well off the traveled roads where anyone would chance upon them.

Once again, Ulric failed to spot the sentries that he knew Kayne had posted at several points leading up to the campsite. He found Kayne and his officers still tallying and recording the wealth of treasures they had carted off by the wagonload during the night. Once he had an accurate accounting, Kayne would then distribute the plunder amongst his men as their contract and pay dictated, with the bulk of it going to Kayne himself.

"It looks like you fared quite well, Kayne," Ulric called out as he approached with his men.

Kayne handed the ledger and quill to one of his trusted men and strode toward the duke, smiling brightly.

"Aye, we certainly did. May I presume that you fared equally well in your own way?"

"You may, Kayne, you most certainly may. I must congratulate you once again on you and your men's excellent performance. You are going to make me have to change my rather poor opinion of mercenaries."

Kayne chortled loudly. "Don't do that, Ulric. No other mercenaries are Hell's Legion. Stick with your first opinion; it will serve you better in the long run. Care to share the next step in your grand plan, Duke?"

"Now is the time to call up your infantry and support personnel. Coming from the south, they should have no problem marching as far north as Southport, even in the winter, unless you know a place farther south that will be warmer to sit out the remainder of the cold season. It would have to be out of the way enough to minimize accidental discovery but close enough to move north on short notice."

Kayne rubbed his chin thoughtfully. "There are canyons in the Bloodstone Mountains where I could hide them. They could reach Southport in two weeks at the latest. When do you plan to use them?"

"Jarvin has sent out three armies to secure the roads between the four major regions. I had hoped to trap at least one of them between our two forces and destroy them within the month, but I fear I risk tipping my hand too soon. I will have to march on North Haven afterward and put her to siege after we crush Jarvin's army, and I do not relish the thought of besieging that city in the winter. I expect to bring her down within a matter of weeks if not days, but it would be foolish to risk getting stuck outside the walls during their horrendous winters."

"So you plan to have us take North Haven first thing in the spring, before they can bring in their harvests just in case she proves to be a harder nut to crack," Kayne mused, stroking the small wedge of hair on his chin with a finger.

"Precisely. I would like you and your cavalry to winter in Southport as my guests. I can integrate you into my own forces, and no one will suspect your identities so long as your men do not bring undue attention to themselves. Then, under the cover of night, I will send you out on small raiding runs just to keep Jarvin on his toes and force him to maintain his patrols. When I decide to crush them, his army will be tired and their morale low. From there, we will ride to North Haven and bring that frigid bitch and her fiery daughter to heel!" Ulric crowed.

CHAPTER 5

B randon heard the unmistakable sound of splintering bone and drew his cutlass, turning slowly in circles. "Carter…Carter, are you okay? Damn it, man, answer me!"

Brandon saw the dark silhouette approaching through the fog. He knew right away that it was not Carter. The man was easily a head taller and a good deal wider than even the big oarsman was. It was not until the figure was within three or four feet that the guard could make out the man's features. He was tall, his long blond hair was braided into several unruly ropes down the back of his neck, and he wore nearly no clothing at all. How the man managed not to freeze to death was beyond him.

The big man reached out at Brandon as if to embrace him in a brotherly hug. Brandon swung his cutlass with all his might, discarding any attempt at skilled swordsmanship, and severed the giant's left arm at the elbow. The only thing more disconcerting than watching the pale limb drop nearly bloodlessly to the ground was that the northman still did not make a sound, did not cry out in pain, shock, or rage. The man did not even change the blank, seemingly unseeing stare on his ashen face.

"Alarm!" Brandon shouted as he tried to reverse his stroke, but he had swung with so much force that it had carried his blade too far to his left to bring it back around, and the mute creature clubbed him hard in the left side of his head with his remaining arm.

The blow sent Brandon crashing to the ground, his ears ringing like church bells, and his vision full of dizzying, flashing lights. He watched the big Eislander stalk silently toward his prone form and raise a big, fur-lined boot to crush his head like the shell of a snail. Brandon tried to grasp his cutlass in his nerveless hand through the haze of pain and his concussion, but his hand was so numb it may as well have belonged to someone else.

The long steel head of a pike burst through the shirtless chest of the man who had just killed Carter and nearly himself. The force of the thrust sent the big man toppling to the ground, yet he was impossibly trying to regain his feet as John stepped on his back, pulled the big pike out, and thrust it home a second, then a third time when the man refused to die.

Tent flaps were thrown wide as Toron and the rest of the southern men bounded out into the frosty night air, fully dressed with weapons in their hands. They barely had time to take in the scene when more large forms began scrabbling over the man-high wall of snow. Some, much like the one that had killed Carter, moved with a mindless slowness, but others moved swiftly, swinging weapons or just using their big fists.

The chaos was compounded as the sailors realized that their weapons were having little effect, and only after inflicting the most horrific of wounds would the attackers fall to the ground and lie still. Even worse were the monsters that leapt over the berm with the powerful legs and bodies of huge stags but the torsos of an Eislander or Akkadian jutting up where the thick neck and antlered head should have been.

One of the grotesque stag creatures trampled the tent, toppling the stove inside and setting the oiled canvas aflame. Despite the loss of the tent and bedrolls, the men were grateful for the extra light as they battled the inhuman monsters for their lives. Even the things they first thought had been humans were often parodies of human form. Some men had the arms of ice bears, which they wielded with like speed and power.

"Hack them to pieces with your blades!" Toron shouted as he decapitated a man with the head of a stag and an extra set of arms with which it wielded two swords, an axe, and a large femur, possibly from the same animal to which its head had once belonged. "Forget the spears! Chop them down like trees. Take their arms, legs, and heads if you can!"

Most of the men followed the experienced minotaur's words, but all were men accustomed to fighting and made improvisations of their own. Some simply did not have their cutlasses close to hand. A big man named Tom thrust the heavy spear into a man who looked normal with the exception of the impressive rack of antlers jutting from his head. The monstrosity paid the wound no attention and shoved itself down the length of the spear until the crosspiece stopped it. Tom was sure that the beast would have forced the spear all the way through its body until it could reach its wielder and rip him apart with its bare hands.

With a shout of defiance, Tom set his feet in the packed snow and shoved the creature back onto its heels, forcing it to backpedal until he reached the conflagration that was once the tent and shoved it into the blazing flames. It was the first time any of the monsters had made a sound. Green flames wreathed the beast as it struggled against the spear that kept it pinned within the dreaded fire. Tom bore his weight down onto the pike haft, pinning the flailing creature down into the flames, ignoring the heat that singed off his facial hair until the monster's screams died and it stopped moving.

Farley cracked his personal hunting spear across the back of the knees of another of the macabre creations, then pinned it to the ground when it fell, while Derran used an axe to sever the head from its shoulders. More and more of the creatures approached from out of the mists toward the horribly inadequate wall surrounding the camp. Zeb cursed when he saw the large number of abominations approaching the feeble barrier: far more than his men could shove back with the pikes no matter how furiously they tried. Zeb knew it was only a matter of moments until all was lost and they were overrun.

A hard blow from behind sent Zeb crashing onto the icy ground, and he felt as if he had been trampled by a horse. Ignoring the pain that lanced through his body, the aging captain rolled onto his back, bringing his cutlass across his chest, bracing the blade with his free hand in a guard position. Another of the four-legged stag men had leapt the wall and caught him in the back with its hoofed forelegs. It wielded a spear, and unlike most of the others, had a look of rage and hatred on its once human face.

The monstrosity raised the spear over Zeb's heart, preparing to launch a thrust that the captain had little hope of dodging or deflecting.

He was staring up at the hate-filled eyes when, over the beast's human shoulder, he saw the dark silhouette of another, more human form, leap high from atop the low wall with a huge battle-axe, similar in every way to the one Toron favored, raised above its helmed head. Zeb thought that the beast had come to steal the other's kill until the axe flashed down and split the torso of the stag creature nearly in half, the stroke of the blade not being arrested until it lodged deep into the intersection where the human pelvis joined its stag torso.

The big, blond-haired, shaggy-faced human wrenched his double-bladed axe out of the creature he had just slain, using his foot to apply leverage as if he were pulling the axe out of a stubborn log, except that no log ever made the sick squelching sound that followed the weapon's violent removal from the monstrosity's carcass.

The mighty Eislander raised his gore-covered axe high over his head and shouted, "Modi!" before racing off and burying his weapon into another creature's spine.

All around, Zeb began hearing the shouts of men, of real men, not those of these foul creations. Shouts of Gullantanni, Magni, Modi, Wuldor, and many others echoed through the fog and across the chaotic battlefield. Zeb was certain they were the names of the Eislanders who had appeared out of nowhere, seemingly to their rescue.

Zeb forced himself painfully to his feet. "'Ware the Eislanders, my lads! They be friends, at least for now! Check your swings, and be sure it's the monsters ya cut down!"

"Rick, follow me, I got an idea!" Matt shouted, pulling his friend along with him toward the two scorpios.

"What are you doing? These things aren't going to do much to these beasts!" Rick shouted.

"They will if we hit 'em with these!" Matt returned with a wicked grin, holding up one of the cloth-wrapped, oil-soaked flares.

Rick laughed, grabbed up one of the flares, and lit it with the flames from the burning tent before sticking the butt of the wooden stake into the snow atop the low mound where the scorpio was set up. Both men worked the windlass to draw the thick cord back and bend the powerful arm. Once cocked, Rick touched the oil-saturated canvas of another of the flares to the one stuck into the snow next to him before setting it on the track of the big crossbow.

Matt took aim at one of the creatures. It was huge, with the body of an ice bear and the head of a man and sent men tumbling with each swipe of its mighty paws. A dozen wounds marred the filthy coat of the creature, but it showed no sign that any of them bothered it. The scorpio bucked in the sailor's hands when he pulled the trigger and released all the pent-up energy held in check by the bow's thick cord.

The arm of the crossbow snapped forward with incredible force, launching the flaming brand at fantastic speed. The scorpio, a weapon designed to fire a small spear more than four hundred yards, struck the brute in the chest just a scant number of yards away. Matt half expected the brand to be extinguished by the monster's own innards and blood, but whatever foul magic or technique had been used to create it made it exceptionally vulnerable to fire. Instead of being drowned by the creature's blood, the oily flame caused whatever was inside the beast to flare violently into green flames. The monstrosity howled in anguish as its animated form was rapidly and painfully consumed from the inside out.

"Wahoo!" Rick and Matt shouted at their handiwork. "C'mon, crank it back again!"

The two men worked the windlass as fast as they could. Their former grimaces turned into evil grins as Rick set another brand onto the scorpio and sent it flying into another of the creatures trying to clamber over the wall, toppling it backward in a flash of green flame.

The battle was dying down, the numbers of the foul horrors finally dwindling until Zeb's men and the unexpected arrival of the Eislanders beat them back. The swifter creatures began fleeing southward, possibly toward the distant forests. When there was no longer a common foe, Valerian and Eislander eyed each other warily. The Eislanders had the southern men outnumbered by a good handful of men, and the smallest of them was equal to any of the burly oarsmen, most far larger, and many nearly matched Toron in height, discounting the horns.

Zeb broke the standoff by seeking out the man who had made the amazing leap from the top of the wall, cleaving the body of one of the creatures nearly in twain and saving his life. Zeb spotted him standing amidst the bodies of the dead creatures and one of his own fallen Eislanders near the dying flames of the tent remains where most had made their stand.

Zeb had nearly reached the big man when several of them spotted a flash of movement nearby. Hands gripped weapons tighter as men from both lands spun to face the mound where Rick and Matt had used the scorpio to good effect. One of the stag-men appeared through the fog, leapt over the wall, and bounded atop the mound. The foul beast knocked Rick down one side of the mound with its forelegs and clubbed Matt senseless with a blow to the head from one of its powerful fists before throwing the unconscious sailor over its broad shoulders and dashing off into the night.

Zeb and every one of his men still ambulatory made to run after the creature, but the big Eislander grabbed the captain's shoulder in a vice-like grip and shouted, "No, you will not catch the creature and would only die upon the frozen tundra if you tried!"

"Damn it, man, I can't just let that thing take one of my men away!"

"Then you must wait until morning and track it. It is tireless and can run for days. With luck, we can follow it to its lair and master and end his vile sorceries," the Eislander replied forcefully, then softened his tone. "They have taken many of my men as well, Utgardr. Trust that I will not rest until every one of these abominations are destroyed and the skull of the vile witch who has created them adorns my lodge."

Zeb was so furious he spat on the ground, not knowing what else to do. "Toron, Derran, get me a head count and tell me how many dead, wounded, and missing we got!"

The captain then turned back to the big Eislander who had spoken. "I'm Zeb, currently captain of the *Iron Shark*, and I lead these men. I thank you for your intervention." He extended his hand as he looked up into the vibrant blue eyes of the seven-foot-tall northman.

The Eislander paused before grasping the smaller man's hand in his own, fully engulfing it. "I am Magni, meaning courage, leader of this war band."

"Why don't ya have yer boys gather round our fire? It's big enough for all of us now," Zeb offered, glancing over his shoulder at the flaming remains of the tent and its contents.

Magni's face split into a grin before he barked a deep, heartfelt laugh. The big Eislander raised his hand into the air and made a circling gesture with it. His men began crowding around him and the fire, taking a seat on the frozen ground, some using their fallen, deformed foes as a bench.

"We have been watching you since you set anchor in the bay," Magni said.

Zeb nodded his head. "We figured as much. Toron smelled you close by a couple times, but we never saw you."

"Nor would you have until we opened you up with our axes had you shown yourselves to be aligned with the evil that has befallen this and other lands. It is fortunate that the ragmen attacked you, proving your innocence."

"You know what those things are? What are they? Where did they come from?"

Magni stared into the flames of the fire. "We call them ragmen because their bodies look like they were stitched together like rag dolls and brought back to life. Other than that, I don't know what they are. They are not alive anymore, not in any sense you or I would consider life. As far as where they came from—many were once my people, some from my very own clan. I have looked into the eyes of what was once my own brother before I laid him to rest."

"How did this happen?"

"Zeb," Derran interrupted, "we have one man dead, two wounded, and two missing. One, of course, was Matt. We all saw that. The other is Ruben. Probably pulled from his pallet during the fight."

"I doubt that," Zeb replied. "Knowing Ruben, he crawled out of that tent with a weapon in his hand before it collapsed around his ears, and then he got himself snatched up."

"He was wounded before?" Magni asked.

Zeb nodded. "Took a swipe to the chest from the ice bear that used to wear that big skin folded up on the sled outside the wall."

"Your men fought bravely, like real warriors. I would imagine he was taken fighting, no matter how dire his injuries."

"Aye, that'd be Ruben and most any man I brought with me. That's one of the reasons I chose this lot. They may not all be experienced sailors, and they sure wouldn't fit in at the king's ball, but by the gods they'll fight for ten minutes after they shoulda fallen just on pure orneriness."

Magni nodded his appreciation at the Utgardr's praise of his men. He knew the feeling of leading good warriors into battle as well as anyone, and better than most.

"I still don't understand what's going on," Zeb said. "What did you mean they were your people?"

"For many months, the northern forests, have been plagued with men and women crawling out of their graves and creatures like you saw tonight began stealing my people away. When we realized that someone was using the foulest of necromancies to create the beasts we slew or that ran off with our family, friends, and neighbors, I decided to take a band of my most trusted and steadfast warriors after them. We have been tracking the creatures and battling them for nearly two months now. The men you see before you are just over half the number we started out with and less than a quarter that demanded to accompany us."

Zeb cast his eyes about the fire, looking into the faces of every man present, those of his own men as well as the determined countenances of the Eislanders. "I don't quite rightly know what to do."

"It depends on what kind of man you are and the type of men you lead. If you are smart and wise, you will pack your things, return to your ship, and flee this cursed land. But if you are brave to the point of recklessness, honorable to the point of foolishness, and angry to the point of unyielding vengeance, then you and your men will take up your weapons and fight, and probably die, next to mine and purge this vile evil from the land for all time!" Magni declared, his moving speech reaching a defiant shout.

Every man in the camp was shouting oaths of vengeance by the time the northerner's proclamation reached its crescendo. Zeb saw before him a leader of unparalleled confidence, ability, and charisma and could not help but raise his cutlass and voice in defiance of whatever evil had defiled the bodies of decent men and women, and killed and kidnapped his own.

"I won't leave good men in the hands of that kind of filth. You can count on me, and every able-bodied man I have, to chase down whoever is responsible and destroy them."

Magni clapped Zeb on the shoulder with a huge open hand. "That's the spirit! I knew there were real men somewhere in the southern lands."

Few men slept that night; those who did were the envy of those who could not. The Eislanders had the least trouble catching a few hours' sleep, having been on the war trail and battling the ragmen for weeks.

Zeb gathered his men about him as they broke their fast next to their newfound friends and allies. "Brandon, I want you and William to take John back to the ship on one of the sleds. Take a tent, a stove, and as much food as you think you'll need. Do you think you can do that?"

"Aye, Cap'n, but my head's mostly better now. I can still fight," Brandon assured Zeb.

"I know ya can, lad, but William's got that arm in a sling, and John ain't able to walk on his own. You're the strongest of our walking wounded, and I need to know that you'll get William and John back to the ship and let Balor and the others know what we've come up against. You tell him to wait as long as he can, but get the *Shark* out of that bay before it freezes solid and crushes her."

"Aye, sir. That makes sense. Just get yourself and the others back, all right?"

"I'll certainly do my best. As much as I've always wished for a second pair of hands at times, I ain't ready to pay this kind of price for 'em," Zeb said in disgust, looking over at one of the dead ragmen.

"Captain Zeb," Magni rumbled a few paces away. "I would have a word with you if you've a moment to spare."

"Of course, Magni." Zeb stepped closer to the big battle jarl. "Is there a problem?"

"A concern. I have wounded who are not able to continue with us. I have seen far too many of my men die to leave any more behind now."

"Leave them behind? You have been fighting these things for weeks. Surely you have had wounded before now. What did you do with them?"

"Those with injuries that would heal in time we carried on litters or a travois. Those whose wounds would only slow or weaken the party were given a warrior's death," Magni answered, stifling the regret in his voice and covering it with pride for the bravery and sacrifice of his men.

Zeb's face paled at the thought. "What would you have of me, Battle Jarl?"

"First, I would have you call me Magni as is fit for one battle jarl to another. Then I would ask your leave to send my men with those returning to your ship, where they might be taken care of and recuperate, despite their protests to the contrary."

"Of course," Zeb replied, surprised that the jarl thought he even needed to plead for such an accommodation. "If you have at least two men who can walk and help pull the sled, they should be able to carry two more, but they'll be just about sitting on each other's laps."

"That's good to hear. I have one who simply cannot walk though he would hop on one leg all the way to wherever we go to do battle if I let him. The other should not walk, but I know he will get out of that sled the minute someone is not looking until he collapses. The other two should have little problem keeping pace. One's arm is near useless and he has a deep gash to his ribs. The other has a dent in his skull deep enough I could eat soup out of it. He walks like he's fine, but he can't remember what he's doing out in this gods-forsaken land and forgets half of what you tell him a minute later."

"Aye, I got a good bone cutter on my ship maybe can help him. I had a lad fall from the rigging halfway up the mizzenmast and cracked his skull when he hit the deck. Bones put him to sleep with some concoction he made, opened his scalp, and reset the pieces of his skull as if it was nothin' but a broken arm. The lad smiles a bit lopsided now, and I wouldn't hire him to balance my ledgers, but he does all right."

The big man allowed a small smile to crease his stern face. "Aye, that sounds like a good bet then, so long as there's no sorcery involved. Braken would probably tear that ship apart if he suspected anyone was trying to use witchcraft on him."

Zeb waved off Magni's fear. "It's no witchcraft, I swear. The stuff he uses is made from some kind of swamp weed he boils, then he runs the fumes through a tube and has the patient breathe it in."

"Dream weed! Our herbalists and healers use it for much the same thing, though they have never vaporized it like that. They always boiled it and distilled it into a liquid to drink."

"Consider it done, friend."

Zeb got his wounded prepared to travel, as did Magni after a great deal of coercion, debating, and threats. The two leaders introduced all the men who would be traveling together. Brandon insisted that Zeb take the second tent, arguing that the bearskin was big enough to cover all seven of them in a pinch and that the stove that survived the fire relatively intact would keep them warm until they reached the ship.

Zeb finally relented, bowing to the wounded men's argument that the ship was no more than three days out while the war party could be gone far longer, especially if they did not get back before the ice pack completely closed the bay, trapped the ship, and crushed it.

Zeb and Magni's band watched the seven wounded men head off toward the bay and the relative luxury of the ship. True to Magni's word, they saw one of the men stagger out of the sled and begin walking as soon as they were far enough away he could pretend not to hear his battle jarl's command to get back in.

"He got farther than I thought before jumping off," Magni commented. "I guess we better be on our way too."

CHAPTER 6

Azerick made a brief stop in Langdon's Crossing to rest and resupply before continuing his trek across the desolate and seemingly lifeless wastes of sand and hard-baked earth. Looking like an angry red welt across the horizon, the Bloodstone Mountains were visible to the north.

There were no roads leading to Rapture, the sardonically named town which the Black Tower wizards called home, nor would you find Rapture on any civilized maps since few if any civilized people had any business or desire to go there.

Rapture was a town built and inhabited by rogues, bandits, and criminals of every order. Only those of the lowest morals and most evil intent would call Rapture home: them and the unfortunates who were born there and lacked the money to leave. It was a truly lawless land with right and wrong often determined by the end of a sword.

The wind picked up and forced Azerick to wrap a strip of cloth around his face to filter out some of the dust and sand threatening to fill his lungs. He even had to do the same for Horse who complained bitterly for a while, shaking his head in an attempt to dislodge the foreign material covering his large nostrils, but he either got used to it, gave up, or realized that it made his breathing a little less unpleasant and eventually relaxed and ignored it.

The desert stretched endlessly and silently before him, the only sounds being the wind, Horse's plodding steps, and the occasional screech of a vulture or bird of prey. How anyone could live their entire lives in such a wasteland was beyond him. The monotony of the almost monochromatic landscape was enough to drive him mad after only these few days of travel.

A sound like the deep rumble of distant thunder made its way to his ears, but the rumbling did not end. It continued its low droning and got steadily louder. Azerick raised his head to peer into the distance. He was forced to squint in an effort to protect his eyes from the blowing grit. A massive wall of dust and sand bore down on him like a colossal avalanche intent on sweeping away everything in its path.

Azerick tugged on Horse's reins, guiding him toward the nearby mountains, and kicked him into a run. Horse must have sensed the looming danger and galloped without protest. The sorcerer spotted a dark void in the face of the red cliffs and pointed Horse directly at it. The wind became stronger as the massive dust storm drew near, and Azerick lost the entrance to the large cave in the reddish-brown haze. He kept Horse moving in a straight line until they reached the red rock of the steep-sided expanse of stone.

Azerick jumped off Horse and led him up the incline, his steel horseshoes ringing and scrabbling on the red, brittle rocks. The dust was so thick that he could hardly breathe, and he did not realize he was in the cave until the already dim light went almost black around him, the dust grew less substantial, and the wind died down to a bitter howl like the angry wailing of a giant predator whose prey has just escaped.

The cave was large and deep, the floor covered in a thick carpeting of sand. Azerick conjured a light and led Horse deeper into the cave's sheltering walls. He saw that the passageway opened into a larger cavern just ahead and could not help but see the similarity between this cave and the one that had belonged to the…

"Who dares enter the cave of the mighty and fearsome…" a deep voice echoed out of the chamber ahead, hissing and growling the last part of the question.

…dragon?

Azerick assumed that the hissing, spitting, and growling sound was the name of whoever had spoken. The voice was unusual, like someone was trying to make themselves sound deeper and more imposing than they were. Azerick dropped Horse's reins, gripped his staff, and cast his protective wards.

He walked slowly forward trying to see who the speaker was. "I am a traveler and only seek shelter from the sandstorm."

"Stop. Come no closer, puny human, or face my wrath!"

The voice was much different from the deep, menacing rumble of the large dragon he had been forced to slay, and any creature even close to its size should be visible by now. Azerick could almost make out the dark, shadowy wall at the rear of the chamber but could see nothing between him and the wall with the exception of a few scattered bones. He continued to creep slowly forward, wary of a sudden attack.

"I do not mean you any harm, whoever you are. I just wish to shelter within the cave until the storm passes."

A geyser of sand burst up just in front of him, and something large leapt out from its concealing surface. Azerick swiftly brought the hard head of his staff around and chopped down at the reptilian, tooth-filled jaws that snapped viciously at his face, striking the creature hard on its snout. The first thought that burst into Azerick's mind was of the dreaded sandworms, but there appeared to be only one, and the sandworms did not seem to be capable of speech.

"Mama!" the creature cried, then disappeared with another spray of sand.

It sounded nothing like the hiss or yelp of pain from an animal. It was more like the cry of a child, and Azerick could hear the muffled whimpering of the creature from the rear of the cave. Azerick slowly advanced, keeping his staff held in check in case of another attack. The whimpering and snuffling grew more distinct as Azerick neared the back of the cavern.

"Hello?" Azerick called out. "Are you all right?"

"No, you hit my nose!" a childlike voice accused.

"You can come out. I will not hurt you," Azerick assured the creature.

"Liar! You already did. Now go away, you're mean!"

"I'm sorry, but you startled me."

"I did?" the voice asked timidly.

"Yes, you did."

"Was I really scary?"

Azerick was beginning to understand the mentality of the creature in the cave. Whatever it was, it was very young for its kind and frightened.

"Yes, you were. I was very frightened. I thought you were going to hurt me."

"Were you so scared that you soiled yourself? Mama says that when something gets scared enough it soils itself."

"It was a very near thing. I'm sorry I hurt your nose. Would some food make it feel better?"

"Yeah." The creature whined and snuffled once more.

Azerick went back to where Horse was pawing at the sand, pulled the magic sack out of his saddlebag, and walked back into the cavern.

"Would you like some meat?" Azerick asked.

"Yeah," the creature whined again.

"Do you like it raw or smoked?"

"Can you breathe fire on it like Mama does and cook it?"

"No, I'm sorry, I cannot."

"Smoked, please," the creature answered softly.

Azerick reached into the bag and pulled out one of the large smoked hams. "Here it is. You can stop hiding now and come get it."

Azerick saw the wedge-shaped reptilian head pop out of the sand from the farthermost part of the cavern and look at him warily with large, green eyes. A willowy neck slowly extended, followed by a broad back and a long tail. As it drew cautiously closer, Azerick could see the short, leathery wings pressed firmly to its brassy scaled hide. It was a baby dragon.

The little dragon crept forward and gently took the ham from Azerick with its mouth then sat back on its haunches, gripped the ham in its taloned hands, or forefeet, and tore large mouthfuls of meat off with its sharp teeth.

Azerick did not speak to it until it had finished eating the entire ham. The baby dragon was obviously very hungry.

"Would you like some water?" Azerick asked when it finished devouring the ham.

"Yes, please," replied the dragon politely, nodding its head in a rather human gesture.

Azerick brought out a skin of water and held it above the little drake's head. The dragon tilted its head back while Azerick poured the water into its wide-open mouth.

"Thank you. The meat was very good. I never had any like that before," the little dragon said once the skin was empty.

"What is your name?"

The little dragon made hissing and growling sounds similar to the ones it had made with its initial warning.

"I am afraid that name is beyond my ability to reproduce. What does it mean?"

"It means Beautiful One Whose Scales Shine with the Glory of the Morning Sun," the dragon said, swelling with pride.

"That is a bit much to say all the time. How about if I just call you Sandy?"

The little dragon frowned, amazing Azerick with her ability to mimic such human-like facial expressions.

"It doesn't really sound as grand, does it? It really diminishes my defining characteristics," she replied.

The little dragon's use of words continued to surprise Azerick. He was unfamiliar with the growing cycle of dragons, but he was fairly certain she was quite young, even by human standards.

"It does," Azerick agreed, "but anyone who looks at you would see that your beautiful scales do shine quite brilliantly. Using it in your name would be needlessly redundant."

She looked thoughtful for a moment. "I guess you're right. It is obvious. I suppose you can call me Sandy. Oh! Is that because I can dig through the sand so fast?"

Azerick smiled. "I suppose so."

"Mama says I'm the best digger she has ever seen."

"Where is your mother, Sandy?" Azerick asked, knowing there could be a serious conflict if she returned to find a human in her cave with her young one.

Sandy's head drooped and she began crying once more. "I don't know. I can't feel her anymore."

"What do you mean you cannot feel her?"

"Baby dragons can feel their dams until they are old enough to leave the nest. She went to find food a few days ago. She was happy because she had found food, but then she was hurt and then very angry. Then she got scared and really sad, and then I could not feel her anymore!" Sandy wailed.

Azerick sat next to Sandy and stroked her shimmering scales in an attempt to comfort the distraught baby dragon. Sandy nuzzled her large head into Azerick's shoulder and wept loudly.

"I am so sorry, Sandy. I lost someone I loved very much too. I know how badly it hurts. Are you still hungry?"

Sandy snuffled and nodded her head. Azerick pulled a smoked sausage from his bag and gave it to her. She grabbed the sausage in her claws and ate, but at a much more sedate pace. She had stopped crying by the time she finished eating.

"So how old are you, Sandy?"

"I hatched two years, three months, and eleven days ago."

"You speak my language very well for being so young. You must be very smart."

Sandy nodded enthusiastically. "Oh yes, Mama says I am the smartest baby dragon she has ever seen. She said it was important to be able to speak well to the humans, because if I could talk to them they might not be so afraid of me and try to hurt me out of fear." She rubbed her snout with her paw. "Even though you did anyway."

"I'm sorry I hit your nose. If I had known you were a baby, I would not have hit you."

"That's okay. I scared you because I have sharp teeth and you thought I was going to bite you."

"So you learned to speak my language in just two years?"

Sandy shook her head. "Not really. I remembered a lot of it from my egg memories. Mama and I practiced a lot though."

"What are egg memories?"

"Baby dragons remember things from the egg that their dams learned and their dams before them all the way back a long, long time. Mama was very smart, and she gave me a lot of memories, and she told me all about them and practiced them with me."

"She sounds like she was a very good mother," Azerick said compassionately, fascinated at the thought of inherited memories.

"She is…was."

Horse nickered and clopped forward, not wanting to be left out of the conversation.

"Is that a horse?" Sandy asked.

Azerick nodded.

"I've never seen a horse before. They sure are big. Mama brought home a few camels before, but the big ones are hard to carry very far. What is his name?"

"Horse," Azerick replied.

"You named him Horse? I'm glad my mama had a better imagination than that. You're not very good at naming things, are you?"

Azerick laughed, thinking about his first conversation with Wolf. "No, I guess I'm not."

Sandy's full belly was making her eyelids heavy, and Azerick was ready for a nap himself. He took off Horse's saddle and used it for a pillow. Sandy buried herself up to the base of her wings in the sand with practiced ease, curling into a ball and tucking her snout under her tail like a dog.

"Too bad you can't breathe fire. Mama always heated up my sand for me and made it all nice and warm," she said with longing.

"I might be able to do something," Azerick said, standing up.

He shoved the arcanum-shrouded shaft into the sand near Sandy. A dwarven rune for fire flared on the haft, and the sand began getting steadily warmer as Azerick fed the magical energy into the ground.

"Let me know when it is warm enough."

The sand became hotter than what Azerick would have found tolerable before Sandy told him that it was warm enough and lay back down to rest. He watched the small dragon curled up into a scaly ball, for several minutes, before finding a suitable place to rest.

When Azerick awoke, the sun had already set and the temperature had dropped. He created a magical fire that would keep burning without any apparent fuel and seared a few of the fresh steaks over the flames. They were quite good with the salt, pepper, and herbs Azerick rubbed into them.

The smell of the cooking meat woke the little dragon. "Oh, that smells good!"

"Would you like some?"

"Oh yes, please."

Sandy's eating habits further reminded him of Wolf with the exception that she was fastidiously clean. She used the sand to scour away any remnants of grease and polished her brassy scales.

She liked the fire, so curled back up very close to it and fell asleep before Azerick leaned back against his saddle and fell back asleep himself. When he awoke, sunlight was just creeping into the cavern through the mouth of the cave. Sandy was still sleeping contentedly, so Azerick took care to move slowly and quietly as he saddled Horse. He recast the campfire spell so it would continue to burn for several more hours. He wished he could make it burn forever, but such a thing was beyond his skills.

Azerick laid the last smoked ham close to Sandy's sleeping form and led Horse out of the cave and down the rocky slope to the desert floor below. He needed to start moving south soon before he overshot Rapture. There were no real landmarks to orient himself, so he had to use his best guess. Rapture lay about three days south of the Bloodstone Mountains, but it should not be hard to find. The land flattened out the farther south one traveled, so it should be visible from quite a distance. As long as he could get within a few hours of it, he should be able to spot it even from far away.

About an hour out from the mountains, he glanced back over his shoulder and saw a form in the distance following his trail and slowly gaining on him. It was a low-slung figure and moved with an unusual waddling gait. He had a hunch as to what it was, and when the sun reflected brightly off her scales, it confirmed his suspicion. Azerick sat atop Horse and waited for Sandy to catch up.

"Sandy, what do you think you are doing?" Azerick asked as the little dragon trotted up to him.

"Ollowin oo," she said as she looked up at him, talking past the large ham clamped in her jaws.

"Why are you following me?"

"I ont oo oh it oo."

"You cannot go with me, Sandy. I am sorry, but where I am going is going to be very dangerous. I do not even know if I am going to make it back."

"Ah an't ay i a age. Ah il ar oo ech."

"Please take the ham out of your mouth so I can understand what you are saying."

Sandy sat back and held the ham in her paws. "I said, I can't stay in the cave. I will starve to death."

Azerick had to remind himself that no matter how smart she seemed or how articulate she was, she was only two years old, maybe five or six in human years. A very smart five or six.

"All right, Sandy, but when we get near the town, you will have to hide and avoid all humans. There are a lot of bad people where I am going, and they will not hesitate to hurt you, although they are more likely to capture and sell you."

"Anybody tries to touch me, I'll bite them and scratch them!" Sandy snarled, baring her small but sharp teeth.

"Promise me you will dig deep and hide, or you will have to wait for me at the cave and hope I make it back," Azerick said sternly.

"I promise," Sandy sulked.

"What is it with me and attracting orphans, half-elves, wolves, and now a dragon?" Azerick muttered to himself.

"Just lucky, I guess," Sandy replied, answering the rhetorical question.

Azerick narrowed his eyes at Sandy as she looked up at him innocently with her big green eyes.

"Mama always said I had the best hearing of any little dragon she had ever seen."

"Eat your ham so we can get going, and you better keep up," Azerick told her grumpily.

Sandy bolted down the ham and trotted along next to Horse, constantly chattering away about all the things her mama had told her and asking a seemingly unending stream of questions. After about an hour of constant chatter, Azerick looked down at her.

"You know, you remind me a lot of my apprentice."

"Oh, is she really pretty too?" Sandy asked.

Whatever annoyance Azerick had been building up was gone in an instant as he laughed long and hard at Sandy's honest reply. "I suppose she is."

It took Azerick's mind a full second to comprehend what was happening. Sharp stabbing pains erupted in both his shoulders, and the ground fell rapidly away from him. Horse's high-pitched shriek filled his ears as leathery wings flapped hard above him.

"Mama!" Sandy cried out and dove beneath the sand.

Azerick called his staff to his hand and thrust the spear tip deep into the wyvern's stomach. His wounded shoulders ached from the exertion that was demanded of them, but fear and adrenalin forced them to obey. A rune flared brightly at Azerick's mental command, and lightning seared the wyvern's vital organs.

The sudden pain and resulting death caused the wyvern to release its grip on what it had mistakenly thought was prey. The distant ground rushed toward Azerick, but only for a second. An air and spirit rune flashed on the staff, and his uncontrolled plummet became a slow drift like the seed from a dandelion. Azerick was able to twist his body in mid-flight so he could see the battle raging below.

Two wyverns were trying to make a meal out of Horse but were finding the terrified animal less than cooperative. Horse was bucking, spinning, and lashing out with his powerful rear hooves, screaming loudly in protest while the wyverns tried to attack him from opposite sides.

Azerick was just close enough to send a blast of lightning into the back of the nearest wyvern, knocking it off its feet while he continued his lazy descent. Horse saw the wyvern fall, reared up on his powerful rear legs, brought his front hooves down, and beat a rapid staccato on the injured wyvern's narrow head.

The second wyvern tried to bring its long, flexible tail over its back like a scorpion and drive its stinger into the equine, but the appendage refused to respond. With a loud hiss, the wyvern whipped its head around and found Sandy hanging from the end of its tail just above the stinger. It tried to snake its head back and snap at the feisty little dragon, but she skipped to the opposite side still worrying and shaking the wyvern's tail in her powerful jaws.

Horse lashed out with his hind legs and caught the wyvern square in its chest, shattering the light, hollow bones. He followed up his attack with a second powerful kick just under the wyvern's chin and upper chest when it snapped its head back around to face the more powerful opponent.

Azerick sent a stream of magic bolts slamming into the wyvern's side as Horse pummeled the creature with his forelegs, smashing it into the sand and seemingly dancing upon its head and neck long after it stopped moving.

Azerick's feet finally touched down, and he ran toward Horse and Sandy to see if either of them was hurt. Blood ran down his back and chest from where the wyvern's talons had pierced his flesh, but he was unconcerned with his injuries for the moment. Horse had calmed down enough that his eyes were no longer rolling in terror, and he pranced in an agitated circle around the two dead wyverns.

Sandy crouched a few feet from the head of one of the wyverns, her rump high in the air. She swished her tail like a cat just before she pounced upon the dead creature and sank her sharp teeth into the back of its neck, shaking it like a terrier on a rat.

Despite his pain, Azerick laughed when a nerve reflex made the wyvern's tail twitch, causing Sandy to call out for her mama in fright and disappear under the sand in a flash. Azerick slowed to a walk and retrieved one of his precious healing potions, then downed the bitter concoction. Fire spread through his body as the potion knitted his flesh closed and stopped the profuse bleeding.

Sandy's head popped above the sand several yards away from the twitching wyvern. Seeing that the creature was not coming back to life, she regained her courage, burst out of the sand like a large fish leaping out of the water, and pounced onto the wyvern's back.

She glanced up from gnawing on the wyvern's neck as Azerick sat down in the sand. The little dragon waddled over to where Azerick was sitting, and she saw his blood-soaked shirt.

"You're bleeding! You're not going to die, are you?" Sandy asked, almost on the verge of tears.

Azerick gave her a reassuring smile and stroked her broad head. "No, little one. I will be fine. I'm just a little tired and sore right now."

Horse ceased his prancing and nuzzled the back of Azerick's shoulder with his soft nose. Azerick stroked the velvety, rubbery proboscis and pulled out a couple of the sugar cubes he had bought at the bakery as a treat for him. Horse's silly, flappy lips clopped together as he gratefully took the treats from Azerick's palm. A thought crossed Azerick's mind, and he reached back into his pocket and brought one out for Sandy as well.

She sniffed it warily before her long, forked, purple tongue snaked out, wrapped around the morsel, and popped it into her mouth. Her sparkling green eyes widened in delight as the sweet brown sugar cube melted in her mouth.

"Is that horse food? It is soooo yummy!" Sandy exclaimed, darting her snout into the folds of Azerick's cloak looking for more.

Azerick laughingly pushed her head away and gave her another. When the second sugar cube dissolved, she ran her tongue all around the inside of her mouth to get every bit of lingering flavor.

"Did you see me bite that big ugly wyvern on his tail?" Sandy asked excitedly. "He was going to sting Horse and I was like, rawr! And I chomped on his tail, and he tried to bite me, but I was way too fast for his old, ugly head!"

Azerick nodded. "I did, and I also heard you cry for Mama and hide under the sand."

Sandy gasped in indignation. "That was a battle cry, and I was not hiding. It is a tactic we sand dragons use to surprise our foes," she haughtily informed the human, who obviously knew nothing about how sand dragons fought.

"Oh, my mistake, my mighty and fearsome little hunter!" Azerick said, holding his hands up in surrender and laughing.

Sandy cocked her head, narrowed her eyes at Azerick, and looked at him suspiciously. "Are you mocking me?"

Azerick had to hold his stomach as he rolled over onto the sand, laughing so hard it made his wounds hurt. "I would not dare to even dream of it."

Sandy was unconvinced of his sincerity, but the memory of the wonderful sugar cubes and the promise of more later kept her from begrudging the human for too long. She turned her back on him with a huff and resumed stalking her prey. She pounced back on the wyvern, but a large lizard poked its head out of its den to see if the danger had passed and distracted her.

Seeing live prey, Sandy bounded across the sand and snapped at the reptile, ending up with a mouthful of sand for her trouble. The lizard darted back down its hole, but Sandy followed it under the sand with a speed that amazed Azerick. She burst back up a few feet away from where she had gone under, hot on the heels of the fleeing lizard.

"Be careful, Sandy, it might be a cousin of yours!" Azerick called over to her.

She instantly forgot her prey and stalked deliberately over to where the human sat, grinning as if he had actually said something funny. She stuck her snout close to his face and fixed him with her gaze.

"Those cold-blooded, primitive creatures are no relation to us majestic dragons," Sandy informed him in slow, precisely clipped words.

"I'm sorry, Sandy. I did not mean to insult you."

"Humph!" Sandy retorted, then turned her back on him, pouting.

"Would you like another sugar cube?" Azerick asked, trying to placate the proud little dragon.

Sandy looked over her shoulder. "Yes, I would, but it does not excuse you from insulting me and my entire race. It would be like me calling you a, a, well I don't know what, but something crude and primitive."

"An ape?" Azerick said helpfully.

"What's an ape?"

"An ape is a hairy, long-armed creature that swings from trees in the jungles of Lazuul and has some human facial characteristics."

"Yes, you are an ape then. How do you like that—ape boy?"

Azerick pulled another sugar cube from his pocket, chuckling at the dragon's pique. "You really do remind me of my apprentice."

"Yes, yes, we have established that I am pretty, but you cannot fatter me into forgiving you."

"I think you mean flatter, unless you get into the habit of eating too many sugar cubes."

Azerick sidled over and held the sugar cube out for her as she tried to think of a comeback for his latest remark. He jerked his hand back when she darted her head at his hand and snapped up the treat.

"I bet you would not have been so afraid for your hand if I was just a lizard."

"All right, you win! You are nothing like a pathetic, cold-blooded lizard. You are a beautiful, powerful, fearsome, and majestic dragon whose history goes back to the dawn of time. Please forgive me, oh beautiful one whose scales shine with the glory of the morning sun."

"Well, I suppose, and you did feed me, so I will forgive you. We dragons are also very magnesium."

"I think you mean magnanimous."

"Can we go now? The wyverns are beginning to smell," Sandy complained.

CHAPTER 7

Zagrat shuffled about the large chamber of the cave he called his laboratory, examining the bubbling, brewing concoctions heating over oil burners and checking the sharpness of his tools, which looked more like torture devices than surgical equipment.

The floor was sticky and stank of rotted blood. No one ever cleaned up after the horrific experiments he conducted. A barrel of foul-smelling liquid contained the arms of various humans and creatures, which stuck up out of the top like the handles of shovels at a general store. Another held legs, others heads.

Torsos were too large to preserve at this facility, but when Varnath completed his goals, his master would reward him with his choice of any castle in the kingdom, except for Castle Stonemount of course. The capital was reserved for the lich lord's throne.

Perhaps Castle Brightridge. It was known to be the fairest of all the castles and sported a large population from which to collect his subjects. Southport had the luxury of being a port city with many transients from which to choose. People were less likely to foment a revolt or vociferous protests if you left their own alone.

"What do you think, Grogan?" the sadistic and completely insane hobgoblin shaman asked the huge golem.

The golem did not answer; he never did. Zagrat had not even bothered to equip him with a tongue when he had constructed him from the finest specimens he could acquire. It would not have mattered. Golems did not speak, did not even think, they simply obeyed, and that was what pleased Zagrat most.

The construct was a full eight feet tall, its limbs muscled to the point of obscenity. Not a single hair follicle marred its pink flesh. Hair did not survive well after all of the necessary preparations were done. The sustaining agents he had concocted preserved the flesh most excellently, but it was very harsh on the hair, and the fluids needed to construct the true golem were by far the most caustic.

Unfortunately, he needed minions that could think as well as obey so that they could bring him fresh specimens. That was one reason why he created the ragmen. He did not have a name for them until one of his pets brought back one of the big blond humans who had used the term while cursing the ambivalent shaman. Zagrat had liked the term and adopted it for his own.

The shaman crossed the room where a lovely, nude female lay strapped to the stone table, one of several occupying the center of the chamber. "And how are you today, my pet?"

The petite, raven-haired woman cursed unintelligibly through the rolled cloth that gagged her. Zagrat liked to hear the screams of his subjects, but this woman's ranting and caterwauling contained no fear or pleasant sobs for mercy, only an unending string of profanity and promises of the horrible things she would do to him if she ever got free. He eventually became tired of hearing it and gagged her.

"I have something very special in mind for you, my dear. Your light, sleek, muscular body simply cries out for one of my special modifications. You will be my finest creation yet, except for Grogan of course."

Hati tried to shriek another curse at the pointy-eared, pug-nosed, scrawny hobgoblin, but it came out as just another unintelligible gurgle. She satisfied herself with the rudest one-handed gestures she knew—and she knew several. Being half Eislander and half Thule and living amongst the rather intolerant, larger, and fairer people, she had learned how to defend herself verbally as well as physically. She was short, especially next to the gargantuan Eislanders, but she was quick and strong. Many of the big blond girls had learned the hard way that despite her small size, she fought like a demon and would win by any means possible. That also made her rather unpopular amongst the so-called honorable fighting people.

"Grogan, we need the young female chained to the ceiling and floor. Please make it so."

Hati renewed her ineffectual screaming. The stupid hobbi thought she was not afraid. She was in fact terrified, but her fiery spirit would never let the shaman know that. The moment the golem unpinned her shackles, she lashed out, scratching and gouging the animated blob of flesh and bone with her nails, going for the eyes and face. She may as well have been scratching at the cavern's walls. Her attacks did not even raise so much as a red welt on the creature's pink skin.

It handled her with the ease of an infant, picking her up and holding her upright with one huge and incredibly powerful hand while reattaching the iron shackles dangling from the ceiling. It then carefully attached her leg irons to rings secured in the stone floor.

The golem frightened her despite the fact that it was always gentle in handling her, but that was because the shaman never told it to harm her. It would rip her arms off with the same emotionless detachment with which it gently strung her up if its master commanded it to.

It was the fact that she knew she could never harm it that was the most infuriating. The hobbi was the master and a powerful user of magic despite his obvious insanity, but Hati knew if she could ever get her hands free and get close enough to use them, she would choke the life out of the ugly, sadistic freak.

Zagrat turned a wheel mounted to a pulley and pulled the chains taut. The increased tension forced Hati's arms over her head, but at least her feet remained mostly in contact with the ground. Then the hobgoblin turned the wheel further and lifted her off the ground, tightly stringing her up like a hide ready for scraping. Her arms felt as if they were being stretched from their sockets, and it was hard to breathe.

"Bring in the donor subject, Grogan," the hobgoblin commanded.

The golem walked silently from the room and returned a minute later with an enormous bird in his arms. Its wings and taloned feet were bound, and a cloth sack covered its head. Hati knew that it must be a dire hawk given its size and the russet body and wings trimmed in bright red flight feathers.

Hati felt sick to her stomach at the thought of what he was going to do to such a magnificent creature. Eagles, hawks, and falcons had long been her most favored of totems. She often prayed that she could transform into one of the powerful raptors so that she could fly away and leave everyone who had ever been cruel to her far below, maybe giving them a few deep scratches before she flew off.

It was then she realized the significance of the bird's presence. *Oh gods, be careful what you wish for. Not like this, not like this, I never wanted it like this!* she screamed in her mind as the golem bound the enormous hawk to one of the stone slabs.

She closed her eyes and tried to block out the ear-piercing shrieks of the doomed dire hawk as the room filled with the smell of fresh blood. The animal's agonized cries seemed to go on forever despite only a few minutes passing.

Hati opened her eyes when the hawk finally fell silent. She saw its motionless, blood-soaked, feathered body on the table, but she could no longer see Zagrat. Then she felt the knife cut deeply into her back. The giant raptor's shrieks seemed like an eye blink compared to how long hers went on for. She screamed until her throat was so raw she tasted blood. Once the carving of her flesh finally stopped, she felt tugging and pressure followed by a sharp instrument, like a needle the size of an awl, being jabbed through her skin over and over again.

The suturing finally stopped, and Hati hung from the chains sobbing in agony, fear, and disgust. She had never felt so violated. Not even when one of the young warriors of her village nearly succeeded in forcing himself on her had she felt this much shame and loathing. She felt the hobgoblin wrapping some sort of wet poultice around the incision sites on her back, then a tingling as he chanted strange guttural words of magic.

She thought she could never feel any more violated, but the foul taint of magic he used on her was more than she could bear. Her defiance failed and her spirit shattered as she hung there, sobbing and praying for death. Hati realized that the shaman was now standing before her. She looked up at the vile necromancer without raising her head. Blood covered his apron as well as the long, razor-sharp blade gripped in his right hand.

"You are so beautiful for a human. Now I shall make you magnificent!" Zagrat cried, then pressed the giant scalpel against her breast.

Hati thought she was beyond the ability to utter another scream, but her body managed to surprise her. This time, she passed out before the hobbi was even halfway finished.

Hati awoke in a cell covered with fresh straw. In the corner was what passed for a clean jug of water. Her throat was raw, and her craving for a drink was undeniable. She crawled across the floor, expecting the chains to draw her up short where she could only look at the water with longing, but then realized there were no chains attached to the manacles. Hati scrabbled forward even faster and grabbed at the jug as if she feared it would somehow run from her or simply disappear like a mirage.

She almost dropped the vessel. Her bandaged fingers felt strange and did not want to cooperate. Hati managed to gain control over the jug before more than half of the water sloshed out. She carefully lifted the container to her mouth and drank deeply, spilling a heavy rivulet of water down her neck and aching chest. Her chest. What had the monster done to her? She set the pitcher of water down, nearly empty, and began looking at herself.

Hati had always been slim and flat-chested, yet another source of torment from the buxom Eislander women, but now her chest was big, really big, but not like a woman's. It was more like a man's, a very muscular man's, except that the cleft between the pectoral muscles was not as pronounced. There was still a hint of femininity to her breasts, but no one would mistake them for being anything other than abnormal. A bulky shirt should suffice to conceal her disfigurement. It was not as if men had been knocking down doors to see her chest before.

Her fingers were all bandaged, but she saw that they were considerably longer than they had been. Hati knew it was probably a bad idea, but fear and rage shoved caution into the corner of her mind, and she began unwinding the rune-scribbled cloth. She wept when she looked at what were once her slender, dexterous fingers.

Every one of her digits had been snipped off as if they had been pruned like undesirable branches on a tree. They were half again as long as they once had been, and the last two-thirds of them were the toes and talons of the dire hawk. Hati buried her face in her hands, nearly gouging her eye out with a talon. She took a deep, shuddering breath and steadied herself.

Get a hold of yourself, girl!

She forced herself to be as calm as was possible under the circumstances. She felt a weight tugging on her back near her shoulder blades. She gently flexed the aching muscles of her back. The muscles felt larger and stronger than they had been despite the soreness, much like her chest. She gaped in wonder at the enormous wings that spread out to each side. They must have spanned well over twelve feet. They were so long she could not even fully extend them in the small cell.

Hati the bird woman wondered if she could really fly or if these things were simply decorative to satisfy the bizarre tastes of the shaman. They certainly looked big enough, and although her muscles were sore beyond description, she felt strong, really strong. So, she had been turned into some kind of bird. It was not the worst thing Zagrat could have done to her. She had seen the worst he could do, or so she hoped, and shuddered at the memories.

Why do I still have control of my mind?

The minds of all the ragmen she had seen before had been destroyed. Even the ones that were brought in alive and not turned into brainless zombies were stark raving mad. They hated all creatures that were not defiled as they were. Only Zagrat's power over them kept them from running rampant across the countryside, killing every living thing in their path.

As if summoned to answer her questions, the hobgoblin shaman walked through the door. Before he had taken a single step, Hati lunged at him, her new talons ready to rend the flesh from his bones.

Zagrat's eyes widened in surprise for a fraction of a second before he barked, "Stop!"

Every one of Hati's muscles seemed to lock at once. Only an amazing sense of balance saved her from toppling over onto her face from the sudden halt in her forward momentum.

"That's a good girl. As you can see, you cannot hurt me. You are forbidden to harm me or allow me to be harmed. Do you understand?"

Hati's mind raged in defiance but the only thing she could say was "Yes, master."

The idea that she had suffered the worst violation possible was proven to be a premature judgment. The vile shaman had stolen her mind, or at least her will, and that was by far the worst thing she had ever felt. She could think what she liked, but she knew in her heart she would follow Zagrat's instructions to the letter, and it made her sick.

"You have seen much of what I have gifted you with, but the most impressive is within you," the shaman continued. "Not only have I given you wings to let you fly and muscles strong enough to power them, I have also given you the great bird's heart."

Hati could not believe what she was hearing but instinctually knew it to be true. Her blood burned hotter and her heart was beating twice as fast as normal even without exertion. She had attributed those factors to the surgery and the stress that ran through her, but she knew that it was normal...*now* it was normal.

"Yes, you feel it, don't you? You needed that heart to fuel those powerful muscles. Even my magic was not enough to do everything, though it has helped greatly. I thought of adding the hawk's tail feathers; you would need them for proper control, but I decided to use my magic to aid you in that for modesty's sake. It would be quite hard to wear clothing with the feathers protruding like that. Besides, it did not match the symmetry of the artistic picture I envisioned in my mind."

"Why did you not make me insane or mindless like the other abominations?" asked Hati, her voice full of scorn.

"A very simple answer, Hati. I need officers, and officers must be able to think. A battle will be waged and very soon. You will be one of my generals, or a captain at the least. Your ability to spy upon our enemies from above will prove invaluable."

"I will tear your heart out and eat it one day, shaman!"

"No doubt you will try, little bird, but you will fail. You cannot harm me nor allow another to do so. What you cannot see is the mark I have burned into your forehead, though you have doubtlessly seen it on the others. It is linked to a similar mark, a master's mark, which is etched upon my body. Even if you managed to succeed, what would you do then? Your people would kill you without question. Humans will see you only as a monstrosity, an abomination to be destroyed. You need only look at your own feelings of revulsion toward my beautiful children. So why go? Why destroy the only one who loves you, the only one who can ever love you? Here you are beautiful, perfect in your creator's eyes."

"Because you are evil! You will make me do evil things. I could never live with that knowledge."

"Am I evil? Are my plans and those of my master truly evil? We accept you and the others without hesitation. Those we fight shun you; they shunned you even before your transformation, did they not? We fight against the intolerance of those in power. Even my own people drove me away many years ago because they did not understand me, said I was mad. Can a madman create such beauty, such perfection as I have created in you? No, he cannot. You are my vindication, Hati. Now rest, my little bird. It will take a few days before you are ready to test your new gifts."

Zagrat retired to his chambers in the underground caverns where he made his home, fortress, and laboratory. The human girl's transformation had exhausted him more than any other with the exception of Grogan's creation. He had instilled a great deal of his magic in making her into what he needed. Attaching the wings, muscles, even the heart was not overly difficult for him these days. He marveled at how far he had come over the years. Today was the first time he had successfully transferred the heart of an animal into a human.

But all those were just parts, simply connecting tubes and arteries and enspelling them to take root inside their new host. All those grafts were still insufficient to give Hati the power of true flight. He made her new muscles and made the existing muscles stronger, but he still had to cast several permanent spells into her to make her perfect.

He had studied the flight of birds for years, and his early experiments taught him that flight was a very difficult feat. The human body was simply not properly balanced for it. Even the largest wings would not lift the muscle and solid bones of a human, and the muscles required to work them would have to be massive to the point of uselessness.

Overcoming such obstacles had taxed him severely. He was not a strong hobgoblin, not like the warriors of his people, not even like their average citizen. He was thin and frail amongst a people known for their strength and bullishness. He preferred books to swords and brains over brawn. It was this that led him to study under the tribe's former shaman, the shaman he had slain when he felt he had learned what he could from his living mind and body. Zagrat had learned so much more from him after he had killed him.

A nagging thrumming sound seemed to echo through the chamber although there was no sound. He could feel the disturbing vibrations resonating through his pallid, ochre flesh and into his bones. The shaman crossed his room and stared into the large black pool of water that occupied the far side of the chamber. Ripples spread out from the center in ever-widening concentric circles as if something was disturbing its dark surface. Something was, and the source disturbed him as well.

"Yes, master," Zagrat whispered to the pool.

A shadowy, spectral image appeared in the pool's dark surface. Red pinpoints of light shone brightly under a deep burgundy hood where eyes should have been. Even through the reflection of the pool, the shaman could feel the terror, freezing cold, and pure evil emanating from the creature, yes creature, for although it was once a man, it had surrendered its humanity long ago.

"Have you been ignoring my summons, Zagrat?" Varnath asked.

"No, master. I have been very busy building warriors for your conquest."

"Excellent. How many have you constructed today?" the image asked hollowly.

Sweat beaded upon the shaman's brow. "Just one master, but—"

"One! You are supposed to be building me an army, Zagrat. One is not an army!"

"But, master, it is a most splendid specimen, the finest I have ever created! With what I learned, I can make you a unit of fighters that could not be matched, given time."

"I am not interested in your toys, shaman. You are spending too much time on your personal projects. I need an army, an army that cannot be simply turned away by Solarian's cursed Chosen or mindless minions that can be hacked apart by the greenest of conscripts. I have plenty of those at my disposal already. The ground is filled with them. I am sufficiently pleased with your ragmen, so get busy!"

The image faded away as the black water boiled and steamed: a clear indication of his master's displeasure. Zagrat paced his room. Varnath did not understand how important his work was, how important the things were that he learned today with the Hati construct. With time, he could make an entire company of flying warriors, wielding bows or dropping incendiary pots upon enemy ranks with impunity. Just the reconnaissance value alone would be invaluable. But the lich lord was not going to give him the time he needed. Oh well, he would have time after the slaughter and conquest of the southern lands and his very own castle to work in without interruption.

CHAPTER 8

Azerick and Sandy stood atop a low rise looking out across the sands to the distant town of Rapture, which sat growing like a malignant tumor a mile to the southeast.

"I want you to stay near this dune as much as possible," Azerick told Sandy. "I do not know how long I will be, but if—when—I return, I will look for you here."

"Okay, I'll wait here. Are those goats I see over there?" Sandy asked, looking at a large number of black specks milling around outside Rapture.

Azerick squinted into the distance, but his eyes were nowhere near as keen as the little predator's. "Probably, but you need to stay away from them. I will leave you with food, so there is no need for you to risk getting into trouble with the people here. Remember, these are mostly very bad people, some of the worst that humans have produced."

"Yeah, yeah, I know. I'll keep away from the humans and hide under the sand."

Azerick pulled most of the remaining smoked and salted meats from the magic bag, wrapped them in an ordinary linen sack, and left it for Sandy along with a couple of water skins. The herd of goats was near a large oasis with plenty of water if she ran out and got desperate.

With one last suspicious look at Sandy, Azerick rode Horse down the hill toward Rapture. The town was even more decayed and ramshackle than Azerick had imagined, and the smell rivaled that of the stockyards at Langdon's Crossing. Most of the buildings were crudely fashioned from whatever materials could be carted in from more civilized locations or salvaged. Barely clothed, filthy, swarthy-skinned children ran amok, looking wilder than the dog packs with which they shared the streets.

The great black tower loomed over the town. Fashioned from the blackest stone, it was several stories taller than Azerick's tower in North Haven and twice as big around. It was the only building he had yet seen that did not have hard-eyed men loitering around its walls and was not surrounded by trash.

Azerick chose a tavern near the tower and had a stable. A tough-looking youth with a split lip and a black eye shuffled lazily out to take Horse's reins. Before the lad took Horse away, Azerick pulled the magic bag out of his saddlebag and extracted a large bag of oats. He returned the sack to the saddlebag, strapped it down tight, and cast a simple locking spell onto the buckles that would keep anyone from being able to open it.

"Feed him a double handful of oats twice a day, brush him down, and make sure his water is fresh. Do not try to get into the bags. You cannot, and I will know if you try. He and all my gear had best be here when I return," Azerick told the youth firmly, handing him a gold coin.

Azerick held up a second coin. "You will get this when I return and find that you have followed my instructions to the letter. If I find you have not..." Azerick left the threat hanging and stalked off into the tavern.

He kept his staff close at hand, which brought some covetous looks his way from the rough-looking men and few women in the bar as he took a seat at one of the rickety tables facing the door. Dressed in his dark clothes and black cloak probably made him resemble one of the Black Tower wizards well enough that no one felt compelled to challenge him for the obviously valuable weapon.

He sat at his table sipping at the swill they served for ale and pondered how best to approach the tower and its occupants. He had not yet determined precisely what course of action he was going to take. Azerick knew that he was a formidable spellcaster given his level of experience, particularly in wielding the staff, but he was under few illusions that he could take on an entire enclave of wizards that likely boasted at least a few archmages, several adepts, and an untold number of lesser wizards.

He thought about lying in wait and ambushing one of them and extracting the information he wanted, but that plan was wrought with pitfalls. Assuming he could capture one of the leading wizards without getting himself killed or bringing on the wrath of the entire enclave, he could not be sure that the one he captured would have the information he sought.

Perhaps he could infiltrate the tower as a student or colleague. He could casually ask questions and search for answers once he was inside. Azerick drummed his fingers on the rough, cracked tabletop. Those thoughts had barely crossed his mind when two young men dressed in black robes strode into the bar with the self-assured arrogance that announced them as untouchable.

The pair brought a few hostile glares from some of the seedy patrons but most looked away when the two wizards glanced in their direction. It did not take long before the young man with the magnificent staff drew their attention. One leaned toward his companion, speaking to him in hushed tones while looking between Azerick and the staff he held in the crook of his arm, most of its length concealed under the table.

The two stood up as one, confidently strode toward Azerick's table, and sneered down at him. One looked about Azerick's age, the other a few years older, and apparently the senior of the two.

"That is an awfully nice staff you have there," the older of the two told Azerick, "much too nice for the likes of you. You steal it from your master?"

Azerick looked up at the speaker and replied flatly. "No, it was made for me by friends."

"You are not from the Black Tower. We would know. Trying to pass yourself off as a Black Tower wizard in this town is a crime punishable by death."

"I am not trying to do any such thing, though I do have business I would discuss with the Tower: one of the masters, not one of their lackeys."

Both of the young men's faces burned scarlet. "Are you looking to join the Tower? Give me the staff, and I will see that you get to meet one of my senior associates alive; otherwise, I will take them your dead corpse to do with as they please."

"Dead corpse? Your redundancy gives credence to your stupidity. I suggest you and your girlfriend leave me be while you still have lungs with which to draw breath," Azerick warned them in a hard-edged voice that matched his glare.

"You dare insult and threaten wizards from the Black Tower within the tower's very shadow?"

"No, I insult and threaten two foolish little apprentices who are too stupid to recognize one of their betters," Azerick growled.

Azerick heard the screech of chairs being pushed back by their occupants as they sought to remove themselves from the line of fire. The hands of both young wizards began to move, no doubt reaching for the Source to unleash their wrath upon the man who insulted them.

"I am an adept, you fool, and I will show you who is whose better!" the brash young wizard shouted, spittle flying from his lips as he and his companion completed the forms to the spells that would tear this upstart to shreds.

The moment the two wizards made their move, Azerick brought his legs up and shoved the table into the thighs of both wizards, causing them to stumble back and foul their castings. Free of the table, he leapt, spun his staff, and in one fluid movement, thrust the arcanum spear through the talkative wizard's chest. Azerick sent a burst of energy through the staff so powerful that it blew a hole clean through the wizard's torso large enough that Azerick could look through it and watch as the dead man's heart slapped against the wall behind the bar close enough to the shocked bartender that it spattered his face in gore.

With his left hand, he released an invisible blast of force that sent the other wizard sprawling several yards across the floor, fetching up against the bar and trying to draw breath. Before he was even able to take a full breath, fear helped propel the Black Tower wizard onto his feet and out of the door. He gave the lethal stranger a wide berth, bouncing off the doorframe as he made his escape. Azerick did not attempt to stop him. He was a small fish in a much bigger pond and posed no threat now.

Azerick looked around the room to ensure that nobody else was foolish or reckless enough to try and lash out at him. Nobody was. One who was not smart enough to know when they were clearly outmatched, did not survive long in Rapture

Well, I am certain that will get the attention of some of the Tower masters. Probably more than I need right now, Azerick thought to himself, then made his way slowly toward the door.

Krendall had just gathered up his traveling supplies and was crossing the spacious bottom floor of the black tower on his way out when a voice called out to him, a voice that made him hunch his shoulders in irritation and just a little dread.

Gods, it is like pulling the entrails from a living imp, the wizard thought as he turned to face the one who hailed him. "Yes, Shakrill?"

The mage strode down the wide winding stairs toward the other wizard. "Krendall, what is the status on Dundalor's armor? That general of yours has had plenty of time to recover it by now. You have practically delivered it into his hands. I fail to see why it is taking so long."

"I was just on my way to pay him a visit, Shakrill. My agent already reported to the general that he had recovered the helm and was on his way to deliver it. I have had a difficult time scrying or making contact since then, so I am going to see to it personally. The general is probably waiting for me to retrieve it at this very moment, unknowingly camped with his men in an area that interferes with such magic," Krendall replied, forcing his voice to remain neutral.

He had no love for the temperamental wizard, as few if any did, but he was not foolish enough to provoke her.

"You had best hope he has it, Krendall. You parted with a great deal of the Tower's treasures to pay for its acquisition, foolishly in advance, I might add."

"Do not worry yourself. General Baneford is too honorable a man to deceive us and intelligent enough that he sees the inherent risks of possessing such a highly desired object. I will return in less than a fortnight with it, I assure you."

A senior apprentice burst through the tower door, barely able to draw enough breath to explain his panicked state.

"M-master Krendall, there is a strange wizard at the tavern!" he rasped out. "He, he, killed Paul! He blew his chest clear out of his back and sent me halfway across the bar like I was nothing but a novice!"

"Anthony, Sasha! Come to the atrium, now!" Shakrill shouted, lacing the command with magic that would carry it to the other wizards no matter where they were in the tower.

"Slow down, Jarred; right now you sound like a novice," Magus Krendall told the youth. "What happened?"

"Paul and I went into the bar up the street and saw this guy about my age sitting at the table with a powerful-looking staff. Paul marked him as a wizard but not from the Tower, so we confronted him. He stabbed Paul through the chest and blew him to the abyss and sent me sprawling before we could even begin to cast a spell."

"What does this wizard look like?"

"He is my age, brownish-bronze hair, dressed in dark clothes with a black cloak, and he is carrying a silver and blood-red staff-spear thing."

Two more full wizards came rushing down the steps at Shakrill's command.

"Krendall, take Anthony and Sasha and bring me this wizard who darcs flout the Tower's authority and attacks its members. Preferably alive, if at all possible," Shakrill demanded.

"Of course, Shakrill. It is not as though I have anything else to do but jump at your commands."

Shakrill glared at the wizard. "You have taken your sweet time thus far, Krendall; a few more minutes will not matter." *When I command this tower, that will be another one I will enjoy licking at my feet,* the dangerous wizard thought as the three mages departed the tower.

Krendall spied the man that Jarred had described, hustling across the street within plain view of the tower, and pointed him out to the others who fanned out to the sides to avoid them all being caught with a single spell. He sent a lightning bolt arcing out at the young spellcaster without warning. Only fools and soon-to-be-dead fools openly challenged another before striking.

Azerick's skin prickled in warning. He turned just in time to see three black-robed wizards spreading out before him. The one in the center released a powerful blast of lightning just as he spun to face them. Azerick stuck out his staff and absorbed whatever energy his wards failed to deflect. It was a convenient if inefficient way to recharge his staff's power without casting any of his own spells into it.

Azerick created several illusionary duplicates of himself while he sprinted across the large open square. The wizard named Anthony foolishly sent a volley of magical bolts lancing out at him, which Azerick's wards easily blocked, although it did serve to destroy three of his duplicates.

Sasha sent a massive fireball streaking across the plaza where it detonated with a crackling whoosh and a concussive blast. Azerick smelled burning hair and cloth, and his exposed skin reddened and burned, but his wards and dodging protected him from incineration. The nearby building was not so fortunate. Its wooden walls burst into flames like the dry tinder it was.

Azerick tucked into a tumble as the fireball sped his way. He rolled into a crouch and let loose a powerful blue and white ray, crackling with energy, at whichever wizard was unfortunate enough to be in his sights. The beam struck one of the male wizards in the chest.

Anthony's wards flared brightly as the spell overcame the protection they provided. The beam burned deep into his chest and sent a jolt of electricity running through the wizard's body so powerful he broke his own spine when his muscles contracted, arching his back in agony.

Earthen hands erupted from the ground, grabbing at the sorcerer's ankles and wrists. The large sandstone hands wrapped around both his legs and his left wrist just as Azerick released his spell at the now-dead wizard. Runes flared on Azerick's staff as he brought it around with his free hand and struck the hands with its arcanum sphere. The moment the gleaming orb touched the grasping arms, they burst apart into useless sand.

Azerick cast another spell, and stone spikes erupted beneath Sasha. The wizard screamed in surprise and pain when one of the spikes penetrated her wards and slashed a deep wound in her thigh. The force of the stone thrusting up beneath her struck her magical shield hard enough to lift her up and throw her several feet.

He then brought his staff around to bear on the only wizard still standing—the one who had summoned the hands. Before Azerick could release another spell, a second pair of massive hands erupted out of the earth and tried to grab him. Azerick rolled aside and leapt to his feet, pointing his staff at Krendall, thinking he had avoided the grasping hands. He felt himself struck hard in the side and went tumbling, his staff knocked from his grip.

Azerick turned his head and saw that these hands were not anchored to the ground, that they were in fact floating a few feet above it and were rushing toward him. He tried to dodge them, but the huge hands slapped him down once more. Azerick sent a lightning bolt into one of the hands, tearing huge chunks from its form, but failed to destroy it. The hands spread apart then slammed into him from each side as if he were a bug to be squashed. His wards shattered with a flash, and he heard several ribs crack, and his left arm hung limply and painfully to his side, refusing to follow any of his mental commands.

Azerick called his fallen staff to his bruised, battered, but still functional right hand. He jabbed the bright sphere into one of the hands, instantly turning it to dust, but before he could face the wizard, the remaining hand wrapped itself around him and squeezed, pinning his arms to his sides and crushing the air from his lungs.

Azerick forced his brain to think past the panic of not being able to breathe and to find a way out of this predicament, but his vision was narrowing to a pinpoint as his oxygen-starved brain slowly suffocated. He watched as the male wizard walked toward him smiling in satisfaction.

"You are probably going to wish I had killed you long before Shakrill gets finished with you," were the last words Azerick heard before the roaring in his ears drowned out all other sound, and his vision faded to black.

CHAPTER 9

D ue to the sporadic appearance of new students over the last few weeks, no one took particular notice of the children Ellyssa had rescued from the former Lord Potsworth's estate, and they simply joined the classes to which Magus Allister assigned them.

The classes were run far differently than they were at the Academy in Southport. History of magic and magical theory were shelved for the time being. The students who could read well were put directly into an accelerated course of applied magic, and this was the source of Allister and Rusty's argument.

"I cannot believe you, of all people, are supporting this crazy plan of Azerick's," Rusty said to the old magus in frustration. "By skipping magical theory and history, we are failing to instill the basic wisdom every responsible wizard needs to safely and wisely wield magic. Without it, we are doing nothing but creating a bunch of hedge wizards and setting them loose on an unsuspecting populace!"

"Franklin, I am just as surprised at the stance I am taking as you are, and in any other situation I would fully agree with you," Allister replied calmly to Rusty's vehement objections. "However, these are not normal times. Azerick has already been attacked once in these very halls, and we could well come under attack again. Azerick has gone through a great deal, more than most, and certainly more than you can fully appreciate. He wants his students to be able to defend themselves."

"From whom?" Rusty shouted, waving his arms around over his head. "Don't you think it's possible that *because* of everything Azerick has gone through that *he* may be the one not looking at the situation objectively, that his own experiences have clouded his judgment?"

"Franklin, the reality is that there are reports of large roving bands of marauders harrying the countryside. They started in the south and have methodically worked their way north and west. There are disconcerting rumors out of Southport of strange doings and an increase in the size of Ulric's military."

"Rumors, Allister, and from what I have heard, Ulric is the only one who has even had the stones to confront these raiders! It only makes sense that he is building up his troop strength so that he is not plucked like a winterfest goose as these other towns have been."

Allister stroked his long white beard. "It does appear that way, at least on the surface of things, but I have lived in Southport and known Ulric far longer than you have, and I have never known that man to do anything out of the goodness of his heart. If there is an altruistic bone in his body, he stole it off the corpse of someone he killed."

Rusty sighed and tried to appeal to Allister's logical reasoning. "Look, even if the raiders came this far north, they would have to have a much bigger force than what has been reported to attack North Haven, and who would attack what is by most accounts an orphanage?"

"They may well find enough allies to attempt to invade North Haven. Southport is too large, and Ulric has too many forces for anything other than a true army to attack. However, North Haven has no army and less than two thousand men on the city watch. Even calling in the militia only adds another three thousand. Three thousand spears with less training than the Watch! It is not a secret that a certain 'wizard' has started an orphanage, pumped a considerable amount of gold into the city's economy, and started a very successful trading company. If these marauders are after plunder, then a rather wealthy orphanage is quite a tempting target."

Allister set a hand on Rusty's shoulder. "And what would happen if someone did lay siege to North Haven? It would take only a few heavily armed warships to seal her port and a few thousand determined, well-trained men to seal off the city and prevent any message from reaching King Jarvin to beg for aid. And speaking of the 'orphanage,' do you think an invading army's leaders are going to look at this fortified keep and simply ignore it? Not only could someone slip away and get word to Jarvin, it would make an excellent base of operations for the invading officers."

"Surely Ulric would send help if we were attacked. His army must be nearly as large as King Jarvin's."

"You are discounting the possibility that Ulric is in league with these bandits. Ulric despises the king; that is no secret. He has just as many aspirations as any man and far more gall than most. North Haven is largely loyal to His Highness, and if Ulric is considering a coup of some kind, he cannot afford to leave an enemy at his back."

"You don't think Ulric would attack his own countrymen?"

"I do not put anything past that man's greed and ambition. He tried to court Duchess Mellina and failed. He tried to court Lady Miranda and got himself humiliated. Twice he has tried to link their two cities and failed. Who is to say how far he will go to achieve what he wants."

"But even if he did conquer North Haven, Jarvin would never recognize his claim and would raise the other dukes and lords against him."

"Unless he had a plan to replace Jarvin. I told you, the man has ambitions, and only he and the gods know how high those aspirations go."

"Promise me that when the threat passes we will go back and teach them the way they do at the Academy. You and I both know that what we are doing right now was the reason the Academy was instituted, to prevent the kind of unchecked power that undisciplined wizards have at their command."

"Of course we will, Franklin, and it is not as though we are simply handing over vast amounts of power without taking a close look at who we are training. I know you watch the personalities of your students and drill into them the responsibility each of them must have for their conduct, and I hope that you respect me well enough to know that I am doing the same."

"Of course I do, Magus, and that is why I am so worried."

"Have you seen something that troubles you?"

"Have you watched the kids playing?"

Allister furrowed his brow, trying to think of what his former pupil was getting at. "Of course I have. I have watched them play in the snow and play other games out on the grounds."

"Have you seen the ones *not* playing?"

"What do you mean?"

"I have been watching them, Allister, and very closely. Anytime the kids let go and play, there are always a few who stay at the edges watching for danger or anyone who might pose a threat. When an adult comes near, most of them stop and go on alert until they pass. You never see them in groups of less than three and are usually in packs of five or more, especially the ones who have been on the streets the longest. Ellyssa comes from a loving home and is only here because of her family's abject poverty. Peck lost his family but was lucky enough to get a job and live at the stables of a nice inn shortly after. Even Roger and his siblings were only on the streets for a couple of years. Most of these kids have spent the bulk of their lives learning that everyone bigger than them is a source of danger. They learned that in order to survive, they had to do whatever was necessary to protect themselves."

"That is why Azerick started this school, so that these children did not have to keep going through what he did."

"That is exactly my point! I love Azerick like a brother, but he scares the hell out of me," Rusty finished quietly.

"Franklin, you know that boy would never hurt you or anyone here."

"I know that, but what about everyone else? His first line of defense is an overwhelming and often lethal response. A group of city guards came to do their duty, as they saw it, and he came within a hair's breadth from scattering them all over the courtyard."

"But he didn't," the archmage defended Azerick. "He warned them and they backed down."

"What if they hadn't? We have heard and seen what he is willing to do when he feels he or those he cares about are threatened. Now we have over two hundred young boys and girls being raised in a very similar environment, nearly seventy of whom we are teaching magic. We are training more than three score of Azericks who will one day go out on their own. How are they going to deal with challenges and threats?"

Allister was beginning to understand why Rusty was so adamant. "Have you seen something specific?"

Rusty let out a long breath. "I saw some kids playing, and one knocked over a bucket of mortar one of the masons was using. He shouted at them to be careful and to go play somewhere else. Allister, the instant he raised his voice and shook that trowel at them, I watched three young wizards reach for the Source. The mason turned away and went back to work, but I know that if those kids felt he was a threat, they would have incinerated him on the spot to defend themselves. We are putting all of our time and effort into teaching them how to use magic when it is even more important to teach them when not to. We have to change their survival instincts, or we are responsible for the disaster that *will* come."

The archmage's face blanched at Rusty's words. "I have been a fool. I am so used to my students coming from wealthy, stable homes that it did not occur to me to change my approach. Very well, I am not sure how we assure these children that they are safe now, but I will pass on to the other teachers that we need to focus more on their behavior and reactions. I do believe Azerick is also right. There is a real threat to this school, and these kids have accepted it as their territory, and like you said, they will defend it. We must continue to do what we can to give them the best chance to do so."

"All right, Magus. Thank you."

A bell began ringing out on the grounds. A young man by the name of Brother Thomas had arrived at the gates of the school shortly after Azerick departed. He had spoken to Allister, Rusty, and Simon about providing services for the large number of children and the faculty. He told them that he had recently graduated from the seminary in Brightridge and was looking for a congregation of his own when he heard about the orphans' academy, as people were calling it. He said that he received a vision from Solarian the next day to make the pilgrimage to North Haven to bring His beneficent light to the children.

Brother Thomas's request was met with such enthusiasm from both the children and faculty that Simon appropriated the funds and workers to build him a small church and made him a full-time faculty member. He was already teaching a class of twenty-five students in basic reading, writing, and numbers, and had eight children volunteering to become initiates of Solarian. Even more amazing was that over the past two weeks, three of them had shown signs of being a Chosen of Solarian, a blessing that shone down upon barely ten percent of all who entered the Church's service. To have three out of eight initiates receive such a blessing was unheard of.

The bell signified the first services being held in the recently completed church. Until now, they had held services in the main hall of the keep. The church was a log and timber structure like the more recent billets. It was the largest building with the exception of the keep itself. It had a high vaulted ceiling with an incredible stained glass window set high above the floor, which let in the morning sun just like all of Solarian's temples and churches.

The church was nearly filled to capacity as students, faculty, and workers filed in and took a seat on the long padded benches. Brother Thomas glowed every bit as much as the sun streaming through the stained glass, reflecting off his wavy chestnut locks. His youthful face mirrored the deep feeling of joy he felt as he stood upon the pulpit watching his flock file into the church and fulfill his holy mission from Solarian.

CHAPTER 10

M agni's scouts began reporting seeing tracks running across the ones they were following, indicating that they were probably getting close or were at least inside of their enemy's territory. They spotted a few ragmen roaming about, apparently on some kind of patrol, but they were far from alert or vigilant. Magni and Zeb's war party easily avoided them.

The number of tracks increased the farther they went, to the point of obscuring the trail they were following. It became increasingly difficult to separate the different signs, but the scouts were confident they were nearing their objective.

Along with the increase in tracks came the upsurge of the creatures that made them. They recognized the two primary categories of ragmen: the ones that were basically animated dead—zombies, and ragers—the ones that were full of rage, hate, and the desire to kill any living thing in their path. It was the latter that they had to be most wary of. The ragers studied their surroundings, scanning their territory for any signs of life. The zombies mostly just stood about or shuffled behind a rager. Zeb figured the zombies would not notice them unless they actually stepped on them.

The Eislander scouts avoided the paths now that they were in a heavily patrolled area and stuck to low-lying areas and dense clusters of trees to prevent being seen. They were currently hiding in a deep bowl on the leeward side of a clump of evergreen trees.

Zeb, Magni, Toron, and two of Magni's scouts lay prone just at the lip of the bowl, watching the movements of at least a dozen ragmen— and ragwomen. They gathered in front of a cave entrance in the side of a ragged dome of rock thrusting out of the ground like the single remaining tooth in an old man's mouth.

Given the relatively small prominence of rock, the cave floor had to angle down rather steeply. Seeing the number of ragmen and women that came and went, the inside of the cavern had to be quite substantial. For the past two hours, at least three score of the creatures had entered and left the cavern. Considering the number they had already seen on patrol, and assuming the other three directions were similarly guarded, that added up to a whole lot of trouble; far more than their small band could hope to deal with.

"As much as I hate to say it," Magni told Zeb, "us going into that cave would be like a few honeybees invading a hornet's nest."

"It looks like they may be forming up. Maybe they're fixin' to go somewhere," Zeb said hopefully.

A dour look crossed the big northman's bearded face. "The only reason they would go somewhere is to make some poor souls' lives a living hell."

"We can't do nothin' about that, Magni, but we can be sure there ain't much they can do to their captives when they bring them back."

"Aye, I get your meaning, Zeb. We'll kill whatever black devil is doing this. At least then whoever falls into these beasts' hands will get no worse than a swift death."

Zeb was correct in his assertions as a large bulk of the ragmen began moving out toward the southeast, leaving a much smaller force to guard the entrance of the cave and walk their patrols. Magni sent word back to his men to be prepared to move. Zeb's men imitated the Eislanders as they got up and began limbering up their arms and legs, restoring warmth and movement lost by sitting immobile for the past three hours.

A simple flick of the finger brought the Eislanders to the top of the bowl with Zeb's hunters in tow. The skilled movements and actions of the formidable warriors impressed the old captain. He could appreciate the difference between strong fighting men like his sailors and oarsmen and true soldiers, but these big combat veterans were in a class far beyond them.

The warriors' discipline made them keep their heads below the rim of the depression no matter how much their instincts and curiosity urged them to look at what lay beyond their hiding spot. It was yet another display of the Eislanders' discipline and professionalism, the warriors trusting in the guidance of their leader. They would take in and judge the particulars of the battlefield in the few seconds it took them to charge down the slight slope and cleave their heavy axes into their enemies.

"Magni," Zeb whispered to the battle jarl, "I know our crossbows aren't much good against these monstrosities, but a few head shots, particularly against them that look to have something akin to a functional brain, might give us an edge."

Magni nodded at the suggestion. He was in full battle mode and did not waste words when none were needed. He would rather his warriors led the charge anyway, not wanting the sailors to get in his men's way. He respected their courage and resolve, but they were not warriors, not Eislanders.

Zeb looked back at his men, pointed at the crossbows they carried, and tapped his head with his finger. Most of the men understood; the ones that did not had his intent whispered in their ear. He made eye contact with Magni, who gave him another nod, raised his arm, and then slashed downward.

Half a dozen heavy crossbows twanged almost in unison, launching their thick-shafted, broad-headed quarrels across the short score of yards separating them from their targets. Every missile struck flesh, living and otherwise, but only two managed to score a direct hit against two of the ragers' heads. Zeb yelped excitedly when the two that had been shot in the head dropped to the ground. One was a quadruped, the other a powerful looking beast with four muscular arms.

The Eislanders were up and charging before the crack of the crossbows ceased echoing off the trees. The air filled with the fearless and powerful warriors' battle cries as they kicked up snow in their headlong charge down the slight slope. Hand axes went flying through the air, slicing muscle, tendon, and bone. The northmen swung their huge battle-axes off their broad backs even as their hurled weapons struck home.

The battle was fierce but short, and was almost over by the time the slower southern men reached the fight. Toron, whose large feet and powerful legs allowed him to forgo the use of snowshoes, was only slightly behind the big northerners.

The element of surprise gave the human attackers the edge they needed to sway the battle steeply in their favor. They cut the ragmen down in minutes with only minimal casualties to the attackers. Two of Magni's men suffered some deep cuts, but they tied them off with bandages and assured their jarl they were still battle ready. Zeb lost an oarsman when a rager's stone-headed mallet caught him square in the face with an unexpected backhanded blow.

The battle jarl and his men swarmed into the cave without hesitation or coordination. They were in their battle frenzy now and would slow for nothing until they or their enemies were dead. The lead warriors ran straight into more ragmen, either alone or in small groups. The zombies, lacking specific instructions from their master, were slow to react and defend themselves and were cut down.

The ragers gave them far more trouble. They heard the sounds of battle and possibly smelled the scent of non-mutilated men in the caverns and reacted quickly. The Eislanders began taking more casualties as resistance began increasing. Who gained the advantage of the narrow passages was anyone's guess. Eislanders jockeyed for position, competing with Toron for the honor of being at the head of the battle group, sometimes going so far as to throw an elbow along with a grin and a wink as they charged past.

Zagrat awoke with a start when the wards he had placed at the entrance to the caves and along the halls warned him of intruders. Running across the small room, he gazed into the black water of the shallow pool and conjured forth an image of the passageway as seen through the eyes of one of his creations.

The shaman sprang backward and fell hard onto his bony rump when a huge axe seemed to erupt from the surface of the water to split him in half. He scrambled to his feet and looked warily back at the pool just in time to see a broad, grinning face staring up at him and spit in his eye before the image went black.

Zagrat waved his pus-colored hand over the water and watched as a new image appeared. He saw through the eyes of another of his minions that his cave was crawling with Eislanders, southerners, and what appeared to be a minotaur missing a good portion of one of his horns. He screamed in outrage as he watched these interlopers hew down his beloved creations, his objects of art and war.

How dare they! The shaman raged internally, nearly throwing himself into a tantrum. He turned his thoughts to his hunting party, which had departed only a couple of hours ago. *Return to me, my pets, quick as you can. Our home is besieged!*

"Grogan, we must prepare to defend our home. You are my greatest protector. See that no harm comes to me in this dark hour."

The golem showed no reaction, not even a blink of its pink eyelids. It preceded its master through the open doorway of his chamber and stomped off toward the main passage at the mental instructions of its master. The shaman walked behind his nearly invincible creation, listening to the sounds of battle rapidly approaching from the halls up ahead.

Zagrat and his golem rounded a short bend in the passageway and came upon the rear element of ragmen fighting a losing battle against the infuriated humans and the unwavering might of the minotaur.

"Fight, my pets, fight!" Zagrat commanded, knowing if his constructs did not hold, all was lost. Even if he was able to flee, he was likely doomed. Varnath did not take failure well. "Stand fast and guard me, Grogan. Do not allow my ragmen to be forced back any farther."

The flesh golem shoved at the backs of the ragmen, forcing them toward the machine-like swinging axes of their foes while the shaman chanted the words of a dark spell in his guttural tongue. A black fog billowed forth from his outstretched hands and rolled up the passage, washing over his constructs as well as the attackers. Where the fog touched his creations, minor wounds closed and bleeding slowed, renewing his pets with its black energies.

Seeing the effects of the black fog at first infuriated the northmen, but then they began losing hope, wondering how they could defeat an opponent that seemed to feel no pain and only ceased fighting after inflicting numerous crippling wounds. Their swings slowed as they lost their heart for battle. The invaders began losing ground and taking injuries.

"Do not give in!" Toron's deep bellow came as he strode forward and single-handedly held the line, his massive axe cleaving the air and cutting through any flesh it encountered. "It is the fog! Do not let the foul magic weaken your mind and resolve! Look at these creatures. Some of them are your people, your friends, neighbors, and family, and more will fall to this terrible fate if we fail here!"

"Listen to him, men!" Magni shouted, slapping his men on the shoulders or the backs of their heads to get their attention. "We are Eislanders, and we do not bend to the foul magic of cowardly tricksters!"

The roar of the warriors' defiant shouts echoed off the cavern walls as they heaved themselves back into the battle with renewed fury. First a few, then more and more returned to the fray as the others saw their brothers shaking off the magically induced gloom.

Zagrat hissed as the invaders overcame his spell and renewed the slaughter of his precious creations. The shaman waved his arms and spoke another line of incoherent words. Zagrat drew a long blade from the belt at his waist and casually tossed it in the direction of the battle. It flew as fast as an arrow, slashing deep cuts into any nearby flesh before clattering against the cavern wall several yards behind the attacking humans.

The shaman's use of magic just seemed to infuriate the rabid Eislanders even more. Their determination to reach the evil spellcaster quickened their blows as they shouted curses and promises of painful retribution. There were few ragmen left between Zagrat and the gore-covered axes that sought his lifeblood.

"Come out from behind your flesh wall and fight like a man, wizard!" one of the Eislanders called out.

"Wizard!" the shaman sputtered. "I am a shaman and necromancer!"

Zagrat pulled a sharp piece of bone from a pouch and enchanted it with his dark power. It grew and elongated until it was the size of a shortsword and flew from his hands. The shard of bone pierced the chest of the northman who had challenged and insulted him. Toragar felt a deep burning in his chest, and then an icy coldness spread through him just before he dropped to the ground dead.

"Ha! Why lower myself to fighting like a man when I can fight like a necromancer! Grogan, they are nearly past my pets; crush them for me."

The powerful mound of flesh strode forward and swung its massive fists. One of the Eislanders nearly lost his axe when he attempted to parry the blow with his weapon. The steel blade struck the fleshy arm with a wet smack and was turned away, making only a superficial cut on its forearm. The heavy steel head should have severed the appendage, but it felt like striking soggy wood with a dull axe.

The golem followed through with its strike and smashed the northman in the chest. The shattering of his bones made even the hardest of warriors give a sympathetic wince. The warrior flew back as if launched from a catapult, bowling over several men behind him. The men his body knocked down regained their feet, but the one Grogan struck never moved again.

The battle took on a new dimension. Instead of hacking wantonly at the construct, the powerful warriors were doing all they could to stay alive. The golem simply stepped into their weapons, heedless of the minor harm they inflicted, and ground them down with slow but tireless and unstoppable force.

Grogan reached forward with both hands, grasped an unfortunate Eislander by the front of his hauberk, and began using him like a huge club. The golem swung the hapless warrior from side to side like a scythe, smashing the man into his comrades as well as the narrow walls. The makeshift club ceased its struggles after several solid connections with flesh, stone, and armor.

The golem strode forward, obliviously treading on any fallen invaders in his path. With a mighty heave, Grogan hurled his human club into the press of warriors making a fighting retreat, knocking down nearly the entire front rank.

"Woo ha ha, yes my pet! Kill them, punish them!" Zagrat cackled, dancing in place.

"Fall back, men!" Magni shouted as he and Toron stepped to the fore. "Come on, beast-man, try and keep up, if ya can!"

"I would have to run backward and strike myself in both legs to hold pace with an Eislander," Toron retorted with a loud huff.

"Ha ha, that's the spirit! Now let's see if you can put it into practice, horn-head."

The two elite fighters stepped up, axes swinging. Toron swung high while Magni swung low. Grogan attempted to parry the minotaur's axe and ignore the human's strike. Both were mistakes. Magni's ancestral weapon cleaved deep into the golem's thigh, causing it to stumble. Toron's axe met flesh halfway through his swing and cut into the bone of the construct's forearm, cleaving clear through the smaller of the arm bones.

The creature was incapable of uttering a sound, but its facial expression registered the severe damage the two foes had caused it. Grogan did not feel pain like a living creature, but it knew it had suffered a serious injury and could not ignore the attacks of these two foes. When Magni swung low again, the golem brought its arm down to intercept the swing, catching the axe on the haft.

Grogan threw its other arm up over its head to block the powerful overhand strike the horned creature delivered. Toron pulled his swing in toward him at the last second so that the blade struck the upraised forearm instead of the haft. The weapon sheared through the upraised arm and sank deep into the golem's left shoulder.

Magni's reverse strike cut through the already damaged leg. Grogan started to topple, his ruined right leg no longer able to support his great weight. Toron brought his axe swinging down at an angle, burying the thick blade deep into the construct's neck. When the big minotaur wrenched his axe free, he could see a gaping cavity in the side of the creature's neck as it collapsed onto its side.

Magni extended his axe toward Zagrat with one hand, holding it perfectly level by the end of its haft without so much as a tremble in the heavy weapon. "Your turn, you sick hobbi bastard."

"Grogan! Oh my pet, my beautiful pet!" Zagrat wailed, then turned furious eyes onto the smirking creatures who had killed it. "You will pay for this!"

Zagrat raised his arms and spoke twisted words of magic. A swarm of blades spun around him like chaff in a whirlwind.

"Well that complicates things a little," Magni said.

The necromancer never paused in his casting, bringing forth a black shadowy blade. Zagrat tossed the black blade away from him, taking Magni and Toron by surprise when it darted forward and began swiping at them of its own volition. The shadow blade moved swiftly and was hard to see in the poorly lit cavern. The two warriors dodged and parried the animated ghostly weapon with all the skill they could muster.

"You will pay for your desecration with your lives! I will enjoy using your bodies to replace those you destroyed!" Zagrat spat.

The shaman thrust his hands forward, and a pair of snakes materialized and flew at the two warriors like hurled spears. One of the snakes struck Toron in the chest, sinking its fangs into his hide and injecting him with a powerful poison. He could feel the burning toxin enter his bloodstream and course through his body. His arms began to fatigue, and his legs became weak as the effects of the poison took hold.

Magni brought his axe around and cut the serpent missile in half, but his distraction left him unable to parry the black shadow blade. The ethereal sword cut through his side, causing frost to rime on his rent hauberk and blacken the puckered wound with frostbite. The Eislander grunted as it felt as though part of his life had just been brutally pulled from his body.

"Toron, that hurt. I think I may be getting a bit concerned now."

"Yeah, me too. Let's end this."

Toron lowered his head and charged, releasing a bellow of rage right along with Magni's battle cry. The two warriors barreled down on the shaman, completely disregarding the swirling blades wreathing his body. They felt the sharp steel slicing into them, opening numerous bloody wounds on their bodies as they slammed into the necromancer and bore him to the ground.

The remaining warriors and oarsmen let loose a ragged cheer and charged forward. The black blade and swirling cloud of knives disappeared as Magni and Toron shifted atop the hobgoblin. Both warriors went flying back as a hideous demon now stood where they had pulled the necromancer to the ground.

"Did you fools think it would be so easy to defeat me?" the huge winged creature demanded. "I am the most powerful shaman to ever come out of the tribes. My necromancy is second only to my master's! I will tear you all apart with my bare hands!"

"Boys," Zeb shouted, "cut that thing down to size."

Eislanders and oarsmen overcame their shock and fear and charged heedlessly at the demonic presence with their weapons held high, ready to strike. The shaman-turned-demon tore the axe from one of the warriors with one hand, then his head from his shoulders with the other. The brutal death only spurred his comrades on all the harder as they surrounded the transformed shaman and hacked at its red knobby hide. Toron and Magni slowly regained their feet, blood oozing seemingly from every inch of their bodies, and sank their axes deep into the demon's back.

Zagrat screamed in pain and outrage, as much from being struck as knowing he could not emerge from this battle victorious. Gathering up all of his concentration and ignoring the numerous attacks abusing his body, he cast a spell that would allow him to escape.

Magni swung his ancestral axe with all his might, hoping to decapitate the demon, and nearly struck Toron with it when the weapon met only smoke. The cloud bore a faint resemblance to the shaman as it sped up the cavern toward the entrance. A few men took swipes at it as it passed, but their weapons had no more effect on it than they would have on regular campfire smoke. The warriors could only watch helplessly as the shaman floated away.

"Get back here, you cowardly wizard—shaman—necro-whatever the hells you call yourself!" Magni shouted after the retreating mist. "Bah, damn spell hurlers are slipperier than slug eels."

"Let us be sure that we do what we can to prevent him from returning and wreaking more havoc once we leave," Toron suggested.

Magni nodded as he slapped away the hands of his warriors who were trying to tie bandages around some of his wounds, and led the men deeper into the cave. They came upon a narrow passage with sturdy wooden doors attached to iron hinges driven into the stone. The prison guard, if there was one, was nowhere to be found, but a closer inspection of the doors showed that they were all secured with a simple drop bar on the outside.

Out of the nearly dozen small chambers carved into the stone, only four of them were locked. Magni lifted the bar off the first one and threw the door open. Huddled in the corner, his knees pulled up to his chest, was young Matt. He looked up with red-rimmed eyes that had not yet lost all of their defiance, though they clearly showed the stress and fear he had been feeling for the past few days.

"Toron, is that you?" Matt asked, shielding his eyes from the light cast by the torch Toron had grabbed from the wall.

"It's me and Zeb and the others," Toron rumbled over the Eislander's shoulder.

"I knew you would all come! Gods, they have Ruben! They took him somewhere, wherever they make the monsters, I think!"

"Calm down, lad. We'll find him," Zeb called to him past the bulk of the large warriors.

"Let's see who else is in here," Magni said, then went to another door.

The next chamber had the corpse of a man in it, who had apparently died from wounds he had sustained during his capture before he could be turned into one of the ragmen. The foul necromancer probably would have still found a use for the body given time, Magni thought as they moved to the other secured door. The second room held another body, this one a woman who had used a length of cord to strangle herself before the shaman took her and desecrated her living body.

Magni lifted the bar from another door and peered into the dark cell. He took a tentative step inside and his flickering torch drove away the deep shadows enough for him to spy a form lying against the far wall. He took an involuntary step back when he saw the enormous wings but halted his retreat when he noticed the creature's human legs sticking out from beneath them. The jarl crept closer and circled the form until he could glimpse its face.

Magni dropped his torch and cradled what had once been a young woman in his arms. "Hati? Oh gods, girl, what have they done to ya?"

Zeb stepped close to Magni and winged woman. "Did ya know her?"

Magni looked up. "She was the daughter of a very good friend of mine. He returned from an exploration and trade trip to the far north. Not only did he return with furs and ivory, but a new wife as well. Hati's mother died of a fever when she was not even nine. I tried to help him look after her. I failed. I failed them both."

Zeb saw the gruesome wound in the girl's throat that had clearly ended her life and the blood coating one of her taloned hands. "She died on her own terms, as a proud woman and courageous warrior who chose death over servitude."

Magni scooped Hati up in his arms. "I'll not leave her in this cursed place."

Zeb nodded. "We'll do the best we can for her away from this place, but we must hurry. There might still be some we can save."

Several of the Eislanders made a hexing sign as the battle jarl carried Hati out of the cell.

The rescuers moved swiftly down the dimly lit passages. They encountered a few more ragmen, but they were alone or in small groups. The cavern system was not exceptionally large and had few branches leading off large enough to have been used by the occupants. It did not take long for them to find the shaman's laboratory. They found Ruben strapped to a stone slab inside the blood-spattered chamber. He turned his head to look at them when they entered.

"Toron, Zeb, is that you?" he croaked in a dry, raspy voice.

"It's us, Ruben," Zeb assured his brave hunstman. "We've come to get you out of here."

"Did ya kill that filthy bastard of a hobbi?"

"Not quite, lad, but we whipped him pretty good."

"Then the others will be returning," Ruben said. "That hobbi can talk to these monsters with his mind, and I doubt he's taken kindly to his defeat. He's also got a master who he seems to terrify him something fierce."

"We need to get out of here. We are too few and too wounded to try to take on the group that left out of here this morning." Magni replied somberly.

No one argued the battle jarl's point, and they hastily left the cavern behind. They made their way as swiftly across the snow-covered ground as they were able. Their travel was slowed by the number of warriors who needed help walking or were carried on improvised litters made of stripped saplings and wool blankets.

Many of the brave warriors begged to be left behind so they would not slow the others, but Zeb, Magni, and the other men refused their demands.

"We've lost too many men to these beasts and that depraved hobbi. I'll not lose any more without a fight. We all get out or none of us will. Either way, you'll die with an axe in your hand, so don't look so glum," Magni said, his way of cheering up his men.

The battered party force-marched the whole day before they spotted the first of their pursuers. It was the four-legged ragers they saw first, but they did not race ahead to engage the band, only getting close enough to keep an eye on their prey.

"I wonder what they're waitin' for, for us to drop dead of exhaustion?" Zeb asked.

"He does not want to lose more of his creatures," Magni replied. "He knows your ship is a few days' travel from here, and his creatures will be able to catch us before we reach it. We have to rest eventually; they don't."

"We'll need to keep moving," Zeb said. "I know your men are strong, Magni, and so are mine. We won't stop nor rest, and let's hope we can make it to my ship before they catch us."

The band of fighters forced themselves beyond the point of exhaustion, marching through the night without pause. Their bodies ceased aching hours ago, the pain replaced by a feeling of total numbness. The sun was well over the horizon by the time many of them realized it had risen. Even if they could continue at this rate and not stop to rest, they were still a full day from the bay and the waiting ship.

"We aren't gonna make it, Zeb," Magni said, his voice heavy with exhaustion.

"We gotta keep pushing on. It's our only chance no matter how slight it might be," Zeb replied, his head in a daze.

"No, look behind us. It's over. Get your men ready to defend themselves, and send some of these abominations to the abyss where they belong."

Zeb slowly turned around and saw that the host of ragmen were just a few hundred yards behind them and gaining. The ragers were stamping their feet in agitation as the zombies marched just behind them.

Zeb let out a deep breath. "Get ready to fight, men! This is our last battle, and it'll be our finest hour!"

The men with the litters set them down and slid out their weapons, facing the approaching army. There must have been nearly a hundred of them coming over a rise, ready to charge into the humans and the lone minotaur who waited for their deaths at the bottom of the slight depression. The wounded warriors who had been borne upon the litters rolled off and stood, several holding themselves up only by using their weapon or a litter pole as a crutch. They would get one good swing in before they toppled over and the ragmen cut them down.

The ragers began to speed up to a trot, unable to restrain their fury any longer, wanting desperately to kill the men who mocked their lives with their unaltered perfection. The men set themselves for the charge, lifting their weapons a little higher as the monstrosities bore down upon them. Thick quarrels sprouted from the charging ragers' bodies, dropping some of their targets into the snow with hits to the head by the steel broadheads.

Zeb and the others glanced over their shoulders at the sound of screaming men and pounding feet coming over the top of the rise behind them. Zeb's eyes widened and a grin split his face when he saw Balor leading the charge of what must have been nearly every man aboard the *Shark*.

The exhausted men fell in behind Balor's unexpected relief force as they charged past and crashed into the ranks of the leading ragmen. The initial clash stopped the ragmen's charge in its tracks, but the humans were horribly outnumbered, and many of the men were succumbing to their exhaustion. The ragmen began driving them back and exacting a heavy toll in blood.

Zeb's previous excitement turned dour as he realized that Balor's appearance only meant that they would not die quite as quickly, and he would lose nearly his entire crew. The screams of wounded and dying men filled the air as steel met flesh, and flesh and bone crushed the life out of the humans.

Another thrumming sound filled the air, deeper than that made by their heavy crossbows. Long black shafts began sprouting from the bodies of the ragmen. Green fire flared inside the wounds caused by the black shafts as the creatures underwent some kind of spontaneous combustion.

Zeb and some of the other warriors looked toward the source of the noise that was repeating so fast it almost sounded like a band of minstrels strumming a rapid staccato on huge lutes. A dozen cloaked and hooded figures stood atop the ridge of the shallow bowl where men battled unnatural beasts, wielding longbows nearly as tall as the archers and at a rate that defied possibility.

Every arrow found its mark, and where it struck, green fire jetted out from the wound as internal flames consumed the creature. Several constructs fell and died under the rain of arrows every second. In less than a minute, the archers cut their beastly numbers in half. The ragmen became disoriented and seemed to lack guidance, making it easier for the warriors to defend themselves and slay the abominable creations with their axes and swords.

The few remaining ragers tried to flee, but even as they sped away, arrows found their way into the creatures' backs, dropping them instantly. Some of the stag-based ragers made it nearly three hundred yards, certain of having reached safety, before a lethal shaft unerringly found its mark, slaying them just as quickly and easily as the others.

The humans bandaged their wounded as best they could as the strange figures walked lightly down to them across the surface of the snow. As they drew near, Zeb swore they were a bunch of youngsters: fair of skin, slight of build, none over five and a half feet tall. Their huge longbows topped some of their heads when unstrung. How the fragile-looking people managed to draw the powerful weapons at all, much less with the inhuman speed and accuracy that they did, was beyond him.

What he could make out under the heavy hoods were sharp, angular faces, bereft of any trace of facial hair, with bright, almond-shaped eyes that were just a little too large for their long, slender faces.

He was further surprised when the apparent speaker or leader of the small band approached Toron first. "Honorable minotaur," the figure said in a soft, lilting, and obviously feminine voice, "it has been a very long time since my people have met one of yours face to face. We are pleased with such a rare happenstance."

Toron simply ducked his big horned head in reply. The figure then turned and looked between Zeb and the big Eislander, Magni.

"It appears there are two disparate groups that have found themselves allied against a common foe, and now there are three."

It was the Eislander who spoke first. "I am Magni, Battle Jarl chosen to lead the fight against the monstrous creations that have been preying upon my people."

"Upon others as well, brave battle jarl. I am Coranalathana, Corana, for ease of use." She smiled, revealing a set of perfect white teeth.

"I'm Zeb, ship captain of the southern men you see here. We had come here to hunt and fish when these creatures attacked us. We would have been destroyed if it hadn't been for Magni and his warriors. We'd all have been destroyed again if it hadn't been for you and your friends, for which me and my men are most grateful."

Corana inclined her head at Zeb's words. "It is good to see that the humans have gained enough wisdom to set aside their differences when faced with a common enemy. Such has not always been the case. I would be most grateful if you are able to tell us more of what you know of these creatures, and most importantly, the one who creates and controls them so that we may complete our mission and return home."

"Their leader was a hobgoblin. A shaman or necromancer of some sort," Zeb said. "Toron and Magni took him down, but he used his magic and got away. He was set up in a cave a hard day's travel back the way we came. We tore up his laboratory as best we could before we left."

Corana looked grim and nodded. "We must continue our mission now. I pray we can find this necromancer before he reorganizes and renews his unnatural experiments. I will leave you all with some salves to treat the injuries of your wounded."

Corana and some of the other elves pulled several beautifully crafted glass jars out of their small packs and gave them to Magni and the others with instructions to rub the salve onto their cuts and worst bruises.

"Wait," Zeb called just before the elves departed. "My man said something about the shaman having a master. The hobgoblin may be the most pressing concern but not the greatest threat."

Corana's face looked pensive. "That is very distressing to hear. All the more reason for us to make haste. Fare thee well, humans and minotaur."

Zeb and the others watched in awe as the elves bounded across the snow without the use of snowshoes, yet barely left a mark of their passage. It took them only seconds to dart gracefully over the edge of the depression and out of sight. This trip was going to make some mighty good tavern stories when they got back. Few people had seen the reclusive elves for several generations. Such an event, especially in their natural surroundings, was unheard of.

The salves worked miraculously on their wounds, easing pain and closing cuts almost as quickly as one of Azerick's healing potions. Despite their extreme weariness, they rested only about two hours before marching on toward the waiting ship. Magni and Zeb's men finally reached the point of undeniable exhaustion barely an hour later and were forced to make camp.

Balor had brought only the bare essentials so as not to be slowed down more than necessary, but it was enough to get everyone fed, and provided blankets and bedrolls so they would not freeze. They were back into the strange nightly fog, but the skies remained clear and thankfully dry.

They took turns around the two small iron stoves that Balor's relief force had brought. Zeb had abandoned their sled and supplies back near the ragmen's cave.

A ragged cheer went up late the next day when the bay and the ship anchored within came into view just before the fog settled in. Zeb led the men out onto the ice, abandoning the sleds and excess gear. Those who were unable to climb the rope ladders and netting draped over the side were helped aboard using the cargo winch and the hoists used to pull up the longboats.

Bones went to work on the newly arrived wounded as Zeb ordered the icebreakers put into action. The crew aimed the heavy booms with their thick iron wedges over the sides and dropped them, punching through and shattering the ice around the ship. The least exhausted men repeatedly raised and released the icebreakers, and the ship began to move.

"You know, Zeb," the battle jarl remarked as he strode onto the wheel deck where the captain was expertly guiding the ship through the ice-choked channel, "I think my people made a mistake moving inland and abandoning the sea."

"Aye, it's in your blood, my friend, passed down from your father's father. It takes a lot to dilute all that salt once it gets in there. Probably three or four more generations until your kin are finally free of it," Zeb replied with a knowing smile. "If you ever decide you want to return to the sea, I might be able to arrange something," Zeb offered.

"As a crewman on your ship?" Magni asked with a raised eyebrow.

Zeb chuckled. "On one of them. I've got five, and at least until you get your sea legs back. I suspect it wouldn't take more than a couple seasons to remind that old sailor's blood what to do. I know you're a leader and a damn fine one, but it takes more than leadership to captain a ship."

"Aye, I see what you're saying. My old pride makes me say foolish things sometimes."

"It does it to the best of us. But I mean what I say. If you and any of your men ever want to take a hand at being a sailor, get me a message down in North Haven, and I'll get a ship under ya somehow."

"That's a fine offer, Zeb. I may take you up on it one of these days. For now, I need to get back to my people and tell them everything that has happened and see to laying Hati to rest. Thank you for your help not just with the fighting, but for getting Hati home where she belongs."

Zeb clapped the big man on the back. "That's what friends are for, and I got a feeling in my aching bones that we'll all need as many friends as we can get in days ahead."

CHAPTER II

Shakrill stared at the body Sasha and Krendall dropped onto the floor near the stairs. She walked languidly down the black marble stairs and stopped three steps from the bottom, preferring to look imperiously down upon the others.

"Where is Anthony?" Shakrill asked, wanting one of them to put words to what she already suspected.

"Outside drawing flies," Krendall replied simply and without emotion.

Shakrill was surprised only by the fact that this unimposing boy had managed to kill not only an adept who had been expected to go far in the Tower, but now a full wizard while being supported by another full wizard and an archmage. The wizard's death concerned her very little. No one considered Anthony an exceptionally talented spellcaster. Shakrill and the others figured he would likely never make archmage, and now there was certainly no doubt of it. She saw that Sasha sported a rather serious wound, which bled profusely even through the cloth bound around it.

"He certainly is not much to look at, is he?" Shakrill commented as she studied Azerick's unconscious form.

"One would think not, although you know as well as I that when it comes to wizards, or sorcerers I imagine in his case, looks can be deceiving," Krendall reminded the wizard.

"A sorcerer, is he? How very interesting. Is that the staff Jarred said he wielded?"

"Indeed, and an impressive weapon it is. The runes appear to be dwarven, which is an even greater surprise than seeing one so young wielding such an artifact."

"Dwarven? This young man just gets more interesting by the moment," Shakrill said, licking her brightly painted, red lips. "Do you think he stole it from his master? If so, I would love to hear how he or she got that magic-hating race to craft it."

Krendall shook his head. "From the astral readings I have gotten from it so far, this young sorcerer has been its owner nearly since its construction only a few years ago. He is certainly linked to it."

Shakrill descended the remaining steps, took Azerick's staff from her associate, and studied the arcanum and blood-red weapon.

"Most impressive. You say it qualifies as an artifact in its power?"

"Nearly, though its exact abilities and limitations would take years of study to identify and define. My short look into it gave me the impression of enormous depth."

"So the staff was the sorcerer's primary source of power?" Shakrill asked, slightly disappointed.

"I would be hesitant to make that claim. The staff certainly makes him a force to be reckoned with against most any wizard, but it would be foolish to underestimate the young man's own abilities. He showed a very good grasp of magic, his wards were exceptional, and the spell he slew Anthony with would give any archmage cause for concern. Now then, if show and tell is over, I have my own business to attend to, as I am sure you have a host of wonderful things with which to entertain our young guest," Krendall said lightly, then walked away.

Gods, that man is irritating! I would wish him an agonizing death in the desert, but that would rob me of the pleasure of using him as my footstool once I summon Klaraxis. "Joshua!" Shakrill shouted.

"Yes, mistress!" Joshua replied, hastening down the steps from where he had been anticipating his mistress's summons.

"Find another apprentice to help you take this man to the summoning chambers and chain him to the floor. And get a novice to clean up Magus Sasha's blood."

"Yes, mistress."

Joshua ran to the novice and apprentice chambers located on the first three floors and did as his mistress commanded. He sent one of the novices down with a scrub brush and a bucket of water and asked his friend Umair to help take the man lying on the floor downstairs to the summoning chamber.

Joshua grabbed Azerick under his armpits while Umair took his feet and tried to carry him down the steps. They found that this method was making them work far too hard since his middle tended to sag and the height difference when they got to the stairs made it even harder. They decided that it would be easier to throw his arms over each of their shoulders and carry him between them, like trying to get a drunken friend home.

"Did you hear what happened?" Umair asked, trying to suppress a smile and failing miserably.

"No, I was busy scrubbing Mistress Shakrill's floor," Joshua replied.

"Jarred came into the room sobbing that a wizard had killed Paul at that seedy little bar with the stable just down the street!"

"No!"

"He said he blew Paul's heart out through his back with so much force it hit the barkeeper in the face!"

Paul and Jarred had been the bane of all the apprentices and lower-ranking casters at the Tower who were not part of their little clique, which consisted of the strongest and most arrogant mages in the Tower. Anyone who showed even a hint of decency was automatically excluded. Joshua was fortunate that he was skilled enough that most of Paul's group left him alone.

"So what did Jarred do?"

Umair snorted. "What he always does when Paul isn't there to cover his ass, he ran like a little girl and cried to the wizards."

"And you think this is the guy?"

"Wait, it gets even better. Mistress Shakrill sends Archmage Krendall, Magus Sasha, and Magus Anthony out to get him. They catch him crossing the square, hotfooting it toward an alley, and unload on him. He takes Archmage Krendall's lightning bolt as if he blew him a kiss, casts a duplicity spell while running full tilt across the square, and gets little more than a sunburn from Magus Sasha's fireball. Then he jumps up and hits Magus Anthony with a ray that nearly folds him in half backward, snapping his spine loud enough for those of us watching from the windows to hear! Then he nearly impales Magus Sasha on these stone spikes that shot out from the ground."

"So how did they finally bring him down?" Joshua asked, amazed that he was carrying the unconscious form of a sorcerer who had killed an adept and a wizard and nearly fought off another archmage and wizard.

"Archmage Krendall smacked the crap out of him with that big stone hands spell of his," Umair replied.

"That is a really good spell. I hope to get him to teach it to me one day."

They finally reached the bottom of the stairs far below the tower and dragged Azerick into the large summoning chamber. A set of shackles was bolted to the floor in the center of a rune of summoning and containment. The rune ensured that anything summoned into the circle stayed in the circle. The dried blood on the walls was left there as a constant reminder of what happened when wizards summoned a creature beyond their power to control. They secured the manacles around the sorcerer's wrists and paused a moment, looking down at him.

"You say Archmage Krendall said he was a sorcerer?" Umair asked.

"Yeah, that's what he said."

"He looks too young to have that kind of power. He doesn't look much older than you," Umair said to Joshua.

"Archmage Krendall said it would be a bad idea to underestimate him."

"Krendall is a good deal wiser than many of the fools upstairs," an old, cracked voice cackled from behind them. "You'd be smart to heed his advice."

The two apprentices started and spun around to face the old woman standing in the doorway, leaning heavily on her staff.

"Hello, Agatha," Joshua greeted her. "You should not call the Tower magi fools; it will get you into trouble."

The old woman made a rude noise and an even ruder gesture at the ceiling. "I've been a mage from before this tower was raised. Hells, I helped raise the thing, before all the scum started moving in and building those dreadful shanties all around us."

Both apprentices had heard the old librarian's angry ramblings before. The wizards tolerated her because she could take you to any of the thousands of books in the library located at the end of the hall from the summoning chamber just by telling her what you needed. She had also been here as long as any mage could recall, all the way back to some of the masters' masters.

"Come along with me, boys, I have a little gift for you," Agatha ordered, crooking a long, bony finger.

The two apprentices followed the shuffling old woman down the dark corridor to the library. The brightly lit library stood in stark contrast to the gloomy halls and summoning room. Rich mahogany bookshelves and reading tables filled the chamber, and candelabras stood against every empty space along the walls.

Agatha shuffled behind a large desk covered in books and scrolls where she was nearly always to be found no matter the time of day or night. It was rumored that the old woman never slept, and that was one reason why she was completely batty. She pulled out two worn leather satchels like the type couriers were often seen using to deliver dispatches and mail.

"These are for you, but listen well, more than just your own lives may depend on it," the old crone warned them in her rasping voice. "Do not open them until darkness falls and lights your way, for only when darkness falls will you be able to see the path you must follow."

The two apprentices looked at each other and then at the old librarian.

"What is that supposed to mean, Aggie?" Joshua asked.

"Hmm? Oh, hello boys. Are you looking for a book?" she asked as if seeing them for the first time.

"No, Aggie, what do you mean by being able to see the path only after darkness falls?"

"Seeing the path after darkness falls? I guess you had best have a torch with you. Silly damn question, unless you're an elf, and you ain't got pointy ears to be one of them."

"Come on, Josh, let's get going before Mistress Shakrill screams for you to clip her toenails," Umair said, slinging the satchel over his shoulder.

Joshua followed suit, hefting the other bag. "Knowing her, she would make me chew them off."

The two friends laughed as they walked out of the library, neither one hearing the old woman muttering, "Gonna need more than a torch to light the path when darkness falls."

"So what do you think old Aggie meant by that?" Umair asked as they climbed the stairs after checking that the chains were still secure on the captive.

"You got me, but I think we had best do what she says for now and not look in the bags."

"You think she actually put something useful in here and isn't out of her mind?"

"I just have a feeling it's best to do as she says. It doesn't hurt us to not look in them, which is safer than the off chance that she knows what she's talking about."

"I guess so, but if it starts stinking like one of her salami and cheese sandwiches I'm going to open it."

Shakrill bent over her scrying bowl, gazing into its black depths. "Klaraxis."

"Why are you disturbing me again, little mage?" came the demon's irritated voice.

"Klaraxis, is that anyway to talk to the one who is going to bring you to the realm of mortals? And I have such a nice present for you," Shakrill crooned in a fake pout.

"Are you stepping up the summoning? Have you discovered a way to force the planets to speed along their alignment? With such power, you would have little use for me."

Shakrill smiled despite the demon's irksome personality. "Even better, I have found you a more worthy host."

"Why, have you discovered a fondness for your apprentice all of the sudden?"

Shakrill curled her lip into a sneer. "Hardly, but a young sorcerer dropped in and killed two of my wizards and battered two others. I thought he would make a far better host than that sniveling little apprentice of mine."

"Hmm, a killer—and one of power; I like it, Shakrill. You have done well, mage. I look forward to meeting this young sorcerer."

"I am glad you are pleased, my demon prince. I look forward to seeing you here next to me, as together we rule this realm."

Oh you foolish little mage. I cannot wait to see the look on your face when I devour you and your little wizard friends. I must save you for last so that I may savor your terror.

"Skunk, get your worthless hide in here!"

The little fire demog popped in with a puff of sulfurous smoke. "Yes, oh great and powerful prince of pits, lord of lost souls, demon of the damned, minister of misery—"

"Shut up, Skunk. I tire of your false flattery. I know you hate me," Klaraxis told the demon.

Skulk had the decency to look shocked. "Hate *you*, my prince? Never could I feel anything but the utmost joy and honor to serve the likes of your awesome presence."

"Skunk, if you did not hate me, then I would feel that I have not done my part to make your life properly miserable. Do I need to redouble my efforts to obtain a proper level of cruelty, Skunk?"

"I loathe you. I would rather rip off my own wings than spend one more minute with you. You are the vilest creature to have ever inhabited this or any other part of the abyss or any form of hell in existence in this universe or any other. I would sooner eat my own entrails than—"

"Shut up, Skunk. I need my horns polished. Make sure you use plenty of blood so they do not dry out and flake, and polish them well with the brains of...a fallen priest. That always gives them a nice shine."

Skulk turned around and began flapping out of the hall toward the prison chambers, muttering, "You want me to polish your horns? I'll polish your horns, all right, by ramming then into your guts you bloated piece of—"

"And, Skunk, do not pop into my chambers again. I have told you I do not like your stink."

"Yes, oh omnipotent one. Your miserable servant hears and obeys!" Skulk called back over his shoulder. "I'll leave you a stink, all right. I'll drop a big stink under that chair that's always propping up your big, fat, black butt. Maybe I'll use a little of that to polish your horns, eh? Leave you walking around sniffing, wondering where that smell's coming from." Skulk continued his bitter muttering as he fluttered down the gloomy passageways.

CHAPTER 12

Shakrill shouted through the open door. "Joshua!"

"Yes, mistress," Joshua said as he darted into the room.

"Thank me, Joshua."

"Thank you, mistress," the apprentice responded without hesitation.

Shakrill turned in her chair and sneered at her apprentice. "Do you even know why you are thanking me?"

"Because you told me to, mistress," Joshua responded automatically, knowing that was the wrong answer, but sometimes he could not contain his extreme dislike of his mistress and said foolish things.

Shakrill looked at her apprentice dangerously. "If I thought for a moment that you were clever enough to be mocking me, I would have you whipped. No, you little twit, I just saved your worthless life. You should be extraordinarily grateful."

"Then I thank you most gratefully, mistress," he responded, feigning as much sincerity as he could.

"That is better, Joshua. I had originally planned to use your body as the vessel to house the demon, Klaraxis, but that man you took down to the summoning room was kind enough to volunteer to take your place. Don't worry too much though, Joshua, I am sure you will find another way to make yourself useful. Take this potion down to him, make him take it if he is conscious, and clean him up. If he is hungry get him food, if he is thirsty bring whatever he wishes. I want him healthy and presentable when Klaraxis arrives."

"Yes, mistress."

Joshua walked back down the stairs to the summoning room in a daze. Shakrill's declaration of sacrificing his soul so his body could house a demon lord had stunned him like a kick to the head. He stopped off in the kitchens to grab a wineskin, bucket of water, and a clean rag. When he entered the summoning room, he saw that the sorcerer had indeed regained consciousness and was watching him.

"Are you thirsty?" Joshua asked as he knelt down beside the prone sorcerer. "I brought some watered wine."

Azerick turned his head away. "You must think I am a fool if you believe I would drink anything you have for me."

"It's just wine. I got it from the kitchen myself. I can take a drink first if you want, to show that it is not poisoned." Joshua downed a mouthful when the sorcerer looked his way.

Joshua held the skin to Azerick's mouth and let him drink as much as he wished until the sorcerer told him he had had enough.

"My mistress wishes for you to drink this also," Joshua said, bringing out the vial.

Azerick arched his eyebrows at the young man. "Wine is one thing, strange potions are quite another."

"She said it is to help heal your injuries."

"Do you believe everything your mistress tells you?"

Joshua shook his head. "I only trust her to do what is in her self-interest, and in this I believe her. She wants you healthy for her purposes."

"You do not sound as though you are fond of your mistress."

The young man looked askance. "It would not be proper, or healthy, for me to speak negatively about her."

"What is it she plans to do with me?"

Joshua shook his head. "I do not think it is my place to say. She gave me no instructions to tell you such things."

"Did she tell you not to tell me anything?"

"No, she did not."

"What is your name?"

"Joshua."

"I am Azerick. Tell me, Joshua, if you were in my position and I told you what was going to happen to you, would you be frightened, distraught?"

Joshua shuddered, knowing that he had very nearly been in this very position. "Yes, very much so."

"Knowing your mistress, does she take pleasure in other people's misery, enjoy causing them fear and pain?"

"Yes, she does. I have never met anyone who relishes the suffering of others the way she does."

"Then she would probably enjoy knowing that I know what is in store for me, since it could only cause me further anguish," Azerick reasoned.

Joshua could not fault the logic and failed to see that it made any difference whether the sorcerer knew or not the horror awaiting him.

"She plans to use your body as a vessel to bring a demon lord from the abyss to our realm." Joshua squeezed the washrag he held in his hands. "She was going to use me until you came along. For all of these years I have served her, taken her abuse and beatings, listened to all her insults, telling me I was useless, and still I served her, hoping that one day she would accept me as a wizard. Through all of that, she was going to kill me; worse, she was going to give my body to a demon and force my soul out into the abyss!" Joshua seethed.

"Give me the potion, Joshua. My arm and ribs are killing me," Azerick said.

Azerick took the potion from the apprentice and drank it down. The same familiar heat and tingling that he knew from his own potions suffused his body. It was a different color and had a different taste to it, but it was still bitter and unpleasant. His arm and ribs stopped hurting, and he found he could move his arm and take a full breath without serious pain.

"Joshua, none of us can ever know what is going to happen to us. Even when all appears hopeless and things are at their bleakest, chances arise to change our situation, our status. The hard part is recognizing when those opportunities present themselves and having the courage to strike when we do."

"Aren't you afraid of what they are going to do to you?"

"Not really. What good would it do me? I will remain focused, use my mind as best I can to resist whatever they throw at me, and be ready to take advantage of the slightest opportunity that may present itself.

It is all I have ever done, and it has gotten me through a few situations that most would have seen as inescapable."

"How old are you?" Joshua asked.

"How old do you think I am?"

The apprentice shook his head. "I don't know. When I first saw you, I thought you were not much older than me, but now, listening to you, seeing the strength in you, and knowing you killed two wizards even when you were outnumbered, I just don't know."

Azerick smiled wanly at the young man. "I am barely older than you are Joshua, although I have seen and been through much. You may think I am an extraordinary spellcaster, but I am not, not really. I am just a man who has found himself in extraordinary circumstances and done what I must to survive. That is all any of us can do."

"I am sorry about what they are going to do to you. I do not think you deserve it."

Azerick let out a small laugh. "There are those who would disagree with you, but I think most of them are as poor of character as your mistress, so I would not take any heed of their opinions."

"You do not seem like an evil man, Azerick. What were you doing in Rapture?"

"Are you familiar with a man called the Rook?" Azerick asked. He got his answer when he saw Joshua's eyes go round. "Someone sent him to kill me, and I found out he was connected to the Tower. Several years ago, seemingly a lifetime ago, someone murdered my father. That too was connected with the Tower, or so I believe. I do not know if the Rook was the same man who murdered my father, but given his association with the Tower and his methods, I suspect it is so. I came here for answers, and to ensure no one threatened my home or my family again."

"I wish I could get you out of here even though Mistress Shakrill would kill me. At least I would die knowing I did something right in my life," Joshua said forlornly.

"Now is not the time. We would both likely be killed. Remember what I said about doing what you must when the time comes. I cannot tell you when that is. Only you can be certain of that."

Joshua shook his head again. "I couldn't. I wish I had your courage, but I am a coward. I'm too afraid of Shakrill."

"Courage is not the absence of fear, Joshua. It is doing what you must in spite of those fears. It is about not allowing fear to prevent you from doing what you know you must do. A person who knows no fear is a fool and will likely die gloriously and uselessly before they get the chance to do the most good."

"I will try, I promise."

"That is all any of us can do."

"I had better go back before Mistress Shakrill calls for me. I don't know when the summoning will be, but I suspect it will be soon. This may sound stupid, but I wish you luck."

Azerick smiled at the young apprentice. "It has served me rather well so far."

Joshua departed, and Azerick stared up at the ceiling. "Sharrellan, if you truly do have greater plans for me, this would be a good time to step in and be more than just a voice in my head." He counted his breaths for a full five minutes. "That's what I thought. I'm just crazy."

Azerick and Joshua spoke several more times over the next two days when the apprentice brought him food, water, and wine. Time had lost all meaning very early on. Azerick often fell asleep, but he had no way of knowing for how long. Only his meals gave him any sense of time, but he had no idea if Joshua brought them with any regularity. When the door opened, he raised his head off the floor and looked up, expecting to see Joshua with his meal or at least a drink. When he saw that it was a woman, Azerick thought for a moment that his time had come to an end.

"Are you comfortable?" Shakrill asked.

"I've stayed in worse."

"Really? I would love to hear about that. It is a shame we won't have more time together. Seeing as how you have no more use for that lovely staff, would you tell me about it?"

"Tell me who sent the Rook to kill me, and maybe I will tell you something about my staff," Azerick told the cruel wizard.

"I would be far more concerned with what I am going to do with you now than some attempt on your life. He tried, failed, and now is gone. Why should you care when any chance of revenge is beyond your grasp?"

"I despise a mystery, particularly when it involves me directly. If I am going to die, I would like to know. Maybe I will get a chance to haunt them later."

Shakrill laughed with genuine pleasure. It was her kind of humor. "Some foolish nobleman," she said, waving her hand as if it were inconsequential. "Apparently he is still a bit miffed about you blowing his only son to bits some time back. I do not understand it myself. Why risk yourself antagonizing a dangerous opponent for something so trivial? I suppose that is why I have no sentimental attachment to anything other than my own life and ambitions."

Azerick could not believe that Travis's father would go to such measures to avenge a son who had brought about his own death. Then again, none of them seemed to be the type to accept responsibility for their actions. Few nobles were. Now, here he was, staked out for sacrifice because he had followed the wrong trail. Or perhaps not.

"Did he kill my father as well?"

Shakrill looked at him in a mixture of confusion and irritation. "How should I know? The Rook kills so many people. Even if I cared, I could not keep track of them all."

"He was a ship's captain in Duke Ulric's jail. He was murdered in his cell because someone had tricked him into smuggling an artifact into the kingdom."

The wizard shrugged ambivalently. "I am not privy to all of the Rook's dealings, so I would know no more than I really cared to, which is not at all. You should focus on what is going to happen to you now, not all of the little inconveniences that have already come and gone. I answered your questions as best I could, now answer mine."

"What do you want to know?"

"How did you come to possess it?"

"Some friends made it for me."

"Dwarven friends? You must be full of stories. It is bound to you in blood, is it not?"

Azerick's chains clinked as he shrugged. "Something like that."

"Has Joshua told you what I plan to do with you?"

"Host for a demon lord."

"Klaraxis will inhabit your body; therefore he should be able to wield your staff. I think that is a poor choice for succession. Help bind the weapon to me, and I will make your transition as painless as I can."

"No one can or ever will wield that staff other than me, but you will witness its full power when I destroy you and this entire tower."

"I am glad you plan to fight to the end. It will make your anguish all the more pleasing."

The dark archmage smiled as she left, finding pleasure in only two things in life: inflicting pain upon others and increasing her own formidable powers. As luck would have it, her current task was going to accomplish both, and that pleased her indeed.

CHAPTER 13

Sandy lay half-buried atop the dune and reading a book she had secretly borrowed from Azerick while he was resting just before he left for the town. It had taken her nearly an hour to understand how the magic bag worked, but her dragon knowledge allowed her to figure it out. With the sack bereft of sugar cubes, the book was the only thing she found that piqued her interest.

The wind shifted and carried the scent and bleating of the goats roaming the nearby oasis to her senses. Her hunter instincts caused her to pop her head up from the pages of the book and focus on the cloven-hooved little vermin. Her sharp eyes brought the herd into perfect focus even though they were nearly a mile away.

Her stomach rumbled despite the several smoked sausages she had just finished an hour ago. Sandy turned her gaze back toward the book and tried to renew her reading. She was not *really* hungry, and she promised Azerick she would stay here and not attract attention.

He made her promise. Him, a human, ordering her, a dragon, to make promises against her nature, a resentful little voice said inside her scaly head.

Who was he to tell her when and where to hunt? Besides, this had nothing to do with hunger; this was instinct—dragon instinct! She was a huntress: the most beautiful, powerful, and wise of predators. What gave an inferior species the audacity to dictate to her!

The little dragon turned her gaze back upon the unsuspecting goats and sank into the sand with a malicious chuckle. It took her only a short time to swim through the sand. She had no need to raise her head above the surface to see where the goats congregated. She could hear them milling about, bleating and munching the coarse grasses and shrubs that circled the oasis for a hundred yards in every direction.

Sandy sensed the change in the goats as she burrowed nearer. Their casual bleats were reduced to a few nervous noises as if the creatures could sense that a predator was near but were unable to see, smell, or hear it. Instinct made them group together, putting their young in the center while the rams stayed to the outside, waiting to butt heads with any interloper.

Six feet beneath the sand and directly below one of the goats, the little sand dragon launched herself upward with all her strength, breaching through the surface of the sand like a great-toothed devil shark breaching the surface of the ocean, taking one of the smaller sea mammals down into its cold depths to be devoured by the unstoppable predator.

At least that was what was supposed to happen. She flawlessly executed the breaching attack, but it started going wrong after contact with the enemy. Enemy, no longer prey, as the foul-smelling mammal kicked its hind legs like a mad drummer, striking Sandy in her sensitive snout and face. The counterattack was so sudden and effective that it caused her to lose her vice-like grip on the animal.

She spun about, hissing in pain, anger, and humiliation at the fleeing, wounded goat. A big ram took advantage of her distraction and butted her hard in the side. Sandy spun and snapped at the cantankerous beast and was hit from the other side by one of the younger males. Sandy realized that the goats were a bit larger than she had first thought, and they put up a much stronger fight than she had anticipated.

Hissing in frustration, the little dragon lashed out with her powerful tail and snapped at the foul beasts with lightning quick strikes, but the agile goats were adept at avoiding her attacks and lunged in for a bone-bruising headbutt whenever she was distracted. Learning from her mistakes, she feinted toward one of the younger males, then whipped her tail around at the senior ram when he tried another rush, sending the goat sprawling in the sand.

Her victory was short-lived as two more young males collided with her armored side, knocking her over, and eliciting a yelp of pain. Having had enough of this frontal battle, Sandy dove under the sand just as the young shepherd, who had been dozing in the shade of a large palm tree, came running at the sound of the commotion. He reached his herd at the same time Sandy burst out from under the sand, grabbed the goat she had initially wounded, and pulled it under the surface.

The young shepherd, no more than twelve years old, looked on in fear at the sight of the goat seeming to have disappeared in a burst of sand. Gripping his long crook, he stared helplessly at where the goat had just been standing, trying to make sense of the blood droplets he saw in the sand.

The ground burst skyward in another spray of sand, showering him with grit. He tried to leap away but fell onto his back as the reptilian demon glared down at him with fierce green eyes and a maw full of wickedly sharp teeth still showing traces of blood and fur.

"What are you? Please don't hurt me!" the boy wailed.

Sandy replied in perfect Sumaran. "I am the great and powerful," Sandy hissed her dragon name. "You will bring me treasure as a token of my greatness."

"What do you want? I am poor and have nothing," the shepherd said, quivering in fear.

"You will bring me sugar cubes, all you have, or I will eat your goats and then you. Go, bring me my tribute, or I will find you in your home near the edge of town and devour you while you sleep!"

Sandy snorted in laughter as she watched the boy flee back toward the city, his sandals flapping against his feet, throwing up small sprays of sand. The little dragon cast a glare of extreme hatred at the huddled mass of goats several yards away who watched her with wary, hostile eyes. She sank down into the sand with little effort of movement, never taking her eyes from the disgusting little beasts.

It took less than an hour for the shepherd to return, running back toward the herd with a small clay jar in his hands, his light muslin robes flapping behind him. Sandy watched the boy from where she lay in wait about halfway between him and the dune where Azerick had left her. The boy was breathing hard, partly from the exertion of running across the sands and partly out of fear. As Sandy came waddling up to him, his breath caught in his throat, and she thought he might actually make himself pass out despite the force of his previous respirations.

"You have brought my tribute?" she asked haughtily.

The shepherd dropped to his knees and pressed his face into the sand as he held out the clay pot shaking in his hands. "Great sand demon, I could find no sugar, but I brought you the honey we use to sweeten our tea. Please do not eat me; we are poor, and it is the best I could do."

Sandy glared at the boy. "I will spare you this one time, but should you ever fail to follow my demands in the future, I may not be so generous. You may depart—after you rub my scales down with sand."

The shepherd's normally tan skin blanched nearly white at the thought of touching the demon, but he dared not refuse. He set the pot of honey down before the dragon he thought was a demon and carefully rubbed handfuls of sand all around Sandy's sides and back while she clasped the pot in her paws and dipped her long, violet tongue into the honey.

"Harder, goat boy. Work the muscles while you are at it!"

She purred like a cat, fully contented by the relaxing buffing and massaging, and the exquisite taste of the honey. The dragon found the honey even more scrumptious than the sugar cubes. She would have to ask Azerick if he had any. If not, he would need to get some.

Sandy stared remorsefully at the empty pot of honey before casually tossing it away. She stood up, stretched, and yawned, shaking the loose sand from her scales.

"You have pleased me, goat boy. Your hands are most strong and dexterous, and the honey was delightful. I shall reward you by allowing you to repeat your ministrations tomorrow. Do not forget to bring more honey. You may go now."

The shepherd stood on quivering knees, his arms exhausted from rubbing the creature's scales, but he was slightly less terrified than he had been. He breathed a sigh of relief knowing that the demon was placated and was not going to dismember him on the spot. The thought of returning on the morrow filled him with dread, however.

The goats needed little prodding to herd them toward the grassy oasis the next morning. However, as Fazheel drew nearer, the memory of yesterday's events caused a few complaints and hesitation within the herd. Hunger won out over fear, and the contrary beasts started chomping on the tough grasses. Fazheel caught a movement out of the corner of his eye and turned just in time to see glittering gold scales dive below the sands between him and the large dune some way off.

Even knowing the demon was coming, he cried out in fear when it burst out of the sand a few feet from him. The shepherd dropped to his knees in supplication and offered the small pot of honey. The creature nearly pounced on the jar with barely contained desire. It flicked the lid off with one large claw and ran its long forked tongue into the amber delight. After a few licks, the demon looked up at him and purposefully cleared its throat.

Fazheel knelt next to the creature with a sigh and began dutifully rubbing its hard scales with handfuls of sand.

"Did you sigh?" Sandy demanded. "You should be grateful for the blessing I have bestowed upon you. It is a very rare few who are granted the honor of polishing a sand dra—demon's scales."

"Yes, great one," Fazheel replied subserviently.

Sandy let out a rumble of contentment. *This is how it is supposed to be: tasty treats and a dutiful creature to polish my scales and rub my sore muscles. Nasty little goats. I should eat another one on principle.*

It was a hollow threat and she knew it. The goat did not taste as good as smoked ham, and it kicked too hard. She only ate the thing out of spite for having been abused in the hunt, the greatest damage being to her enormous pride.

After she finished the jar of honey, she allowed Fazheel to continue his ministrations for another twenty minutes or so before she became bored and decided that she would be gracious and let the human go on with his duties.

"You may go now, goat boy. You have done well, and I am pleased. I shall retire to my den and see you tomorrow."

Sandy wondered if perhaps she was letting this newfound power go to her head but dismissed the idea. It was all in good fun. Besides, it was not *that* much more than her due.

Ancient memories flashed through her mind of enormous, ancient, and powerful dragons being worshipped almost as gods. She saw the ranks of humans, orcs, goblins, and even elves bringing gifts of gold, jewels, and magnificent feasts to please the mighty dragons that claimed dominion over all that lay within their vast territories.

Then newer memories came forward, memories of dragons mad with power and disdainful of the lesser races; horrible massacres committed by dragon-kind against those they had subjugated and the retaliation of the lesser races, particularly the cunning humans and the wise elves. She saw the eggs of dragons stolen and used in dark magic that formed a living link between the tiny embryo that grew inside the dragon egg and the implanted essence of an elven mother.

Then, an even darker memory took hold, something evil and beyond the power of even the mighty dragons: a faceless master they hated almost as much as they feared.

Yes, little dragon. We are vanquished, but do not despair. Soon we shall return, and once again, you shall take your rightful place at our feet.

Sandy shuddered. She knew that last thought was not an egg memory but something dreadful speaking to her. It took all of her stubbornness to shake off the ancient memory.

That was a long time ago, she told herself.

It was not as if she were enslaving the goat boy or was going to eat him. He probably tasted worse than the goat. She just wanted something sweet and something to do other than lie around in the sand and read all day. It was Azerick's fault for not taking her with him or at least leaving her with some sugar cubes.

Speaking of food, she still had a chunk of goat haunch that needed finishing. Mama always told her never to let food go to waste, especially if it had been live prey. With a wistful sigh, she plunged deep below the sand, brought up the haunch, and began eating, more out of a sense of duty than any pleasure.

Stupid, nasty old goat, she grumbled.

Fazheel herded the goats back home and pondered his untenable situation. There was no way his father and uncle would fail to notice the missing goat two days in a row. He knew better than to lie. Both he and his mother had an uncanny ability to suss out a lie, but what else could he do when the truth was so unbelievable as to be ridiculous? Of all the more deserving mortals in the world, why had the gods chosen to torment him?

A feeling of dread even greater than last night's quandary had instilled hung over the young shepherd as he drove the goats back to their grazing lands in the morning. His nerves thrummed inside him like the strings of a lute playing a lively traveler's tune.

It did not take long for the dragon to make its appearance, bursting out of the sand just as the goats were settling in to graze. At the creature's sudden appearance, they huddled together for safety and fled for the far side of the oasis when the predator's scent filled the air.

Fazheel was much closer to the edge of the oasis than he had been previously, but the dragon apparently felt confident enough in its command of the situation that it came near without hesitation. He set the pot of honey on the ground and stepped away. The dragon pounced on it like a cat on a mouse, greedily flipped the top off, and swirled its long, purple tongue around the inside.

Fazheel stepped to its side as if to give it a sand bath, but instead of scooping up a double handful of sand, he grabbed a thick rope his father and uncle had buried the night before. He had intentionally placed the pot where the dragon would step into the noose, and when he heaved up on the rope, it cinched tight around the creature's foreleg, trapping it.

His father, uncle, and three of their friends burst out of the trees and thick foliage surrounding the oasis with more ropes in their hands the moment Fazheel pulled the rope taut.

"Hey!" Sandy cried out in surprise, then saw the humans rushing toward her. "Uh oh."

Her first emotion was fear, but that turned to anger at the thought of being tricked by her human servant and trapped like some wild animal.

I will teach you humans what it means to have a dragon by the tail, she swore bitterly, biting at the rope with her powerful jaws and sharp teeth.

Several strands parted, but the rope was thick and well made. There were still several strands keeping the rope intact, and they were enough to continue restraining her.

Sandy knew she was out of time and decided to go on the offensive. She dove under the sand, narrowly dodging the lasso thrown by one of the humans, only to appear behind another and whack him in the back of his legs with her strong tail, sending the man tumbling to the ground. Before she could fully enjoy her momentary victory, another man threw his rope and lassoed her around her long neck.

A powerful tingling ran through her body as another ancient memory stirred inside her. She focused upon the sudden surge before the humans could get in place to get another rope around her. Sandy shaped and directed the energy into the ground around her, and the sand seemed to come alive, blowing around her and the humans in a small but fierce sandstorm. Were she an adult, she could bring forth a storm that could practically bury the entire town.

The dragon snapped its clear, diamond-hard inner eyelids closed to protect the delicate orbs as she dove beneath the sand once more. She burst up behind another of the humans while he was trying to affix a scarf around his head and face to block the blowing sand. A small growl was the only warning he got before she sank her needle-like teeth through the thin material of his robe and into the tender flesh beneath. The man howled as if he had been swatted with the goat switch, a sound and feeling Fazheel knew all too well.

Sandy was trying to spit the horrible taste out of her mouth when another rope found its way around her neck. She reared back in fear, hoping to pull the rope from the human's hands, but another caught her other foreleg. The men pulled the two ropes around her front legs in opposite directions, sending her sprawling face first in a most undignified fashion into the sand. Another rope caught one of her back legs, and before she could think of a plan, they wound all three ropes around her legs and hog-tied her.

Being pinned and rendered helpless brought upon a feeling of humiliation she had never experienced before. She hissed, snapped, and cursed the humans with every vile word she could think of, which were not many because her mother told her that ladies did not use foul language. Another rope wrapped around her snout and tied her jaws shut, cutting short her continued invectives.

Azerick was going to kill her unless these humans beat him to it. Why had she not listened to him? Why had she been so greedy and provoked the humans? Because she was a dragon, that's why. Full of pride and a sense of importance well beyond her young age, she thought herself superior with the right to do as she pleased. Mama would have been very disappointed in her, she realized.

A tall human approached, her former servant looking wide-eyed but slightly smug in tow. "So, little dragon, are you ready to talk more peaceably?"

"Yes," Sandy replied morosely, her words muted by the rope around her muzzle.

"What are you doing out here all by yourself? Where is your mother?"

"She's gone."

A look of empathetic understanding crossed the tall human's face. "I see, but I cannot have you eating all of my goats. It would make me and my family paupers."

"It was only one stupid goat, and it tasted terrible!"

"Ah, one so far, but how many would I lose if you stayed? You see, I cannot have you thinking my herd is your private hunting ground, not to mention you frightened my son half to death."

"Sorry," she said, looking at Fazheel standing behind his father as he crouched next to her. "I won't eat any more of your goats. I did not like it much, and we should be leaving soon anyway."

"So, you are not alone? Is there another dragon nearby?" Fazheel's father asked, eliciting nervous looks from the men with him.

"No, he is a human but very powerful. I would not want to make him mad if I were you," Sandy responded with a hint of warning.

Actually, Azerick was much more likely to be mad at her than these humans were, but she was not about to reveal that fact.

"Ah, I think I see now."

They had all heard about the battle that had taken place between the wizards in the tower square, but Fazheel's father decided it was not his place to tell the little dragon that the stranger had been taken since he did not know what had happened to him.

"We will let you go, but you must promise not to eat any more of my goats, and stop terrorizing my son."

"Fine, I promise. Can I have the rest of the honey?"

Fazheel's father laughed, a rare break in his normally strict nature, and placed the clay pot next to the dragon while the others untied her.

Sandy picked up the pot in her mouth and bounded toward the dune where she made her lair below the sand.

"You should remember this day, Fazheel. It is a rare thing for a man to see a live dragon these days, much less to speak to and touch one. She owes you a debt for your services and gifts. Perhaps one day, should your paths cross again, you may be able to call in that favor if your need is truly great."

"Do you think the dragon would see it that way, Father?" Fazheel asked. "It seemed rather selfish and arrogant to admit to such a thing."

"You are lucky it was a sand dragon, one of the more beneficent of the dragon kinds. She is just young, and the young lack wisdom and make many mistakes. I think she saw her errors and will gain wisdom in the years to come the more she learns from them. A goat and a few pots of honey is a small price to pay for such an experience. Now, go tend to your duties."

"Yes, Father."

CHAPTER 14

It was late the second night of his capture when Azerick was awakened by several people entering the summoning chamber. Five forms in black robes stood in a circle around him. Azerick identified two of the wizards. Shakrill and the woman he had injured during the fight stood with three other men he had not seen before.

No one bothered to speak to him. Instead, they all seemed to have their own duties to attend to and went about them without preamble. Shakrill pulled a knife from beneath her robes and slashed Azerick across his chest. He hissed more in surprise than pain when the sharp blade opened a three-inch gash in his flesh. Shakrill showed no emotion, only focused determination, as she dipped a small fox-hair brush into the bright blood flowing from the fresh wound and painted several unfamiliar runes around his prone form.

Sasha used a minor spell to light five of the six braziers that stood near the circular wall of the summoning room, surrounding both captive and captors while the others cast several spells of protection. Shakrill began chanting in a low, droning voice that the others took up.

Azerick tried once more to call his staff to his hand, but it failed to materialize just as it had every time he had tried to summon it since his capture. Something in the room, or possibly the chains that bound him, blocked his ability to reach out for it.

Azerick felt nothing at first and had a momentary glimmer of hope that the spell was not working, but then the room began to spin. It was nothing like the spinning feeling one got from drinking too much, where one felt as if they were spiraling with the room. It felt to Azerick as if the room was spinning yet he remained stationary, each of the wizards' faces flashing past his open eyes. Every few seconds, the door came into view then disappeared as the room spun faster and faster.

He could not contain the scream that tore from his chest when the floor dropped out from under him. He saw the five wizards' faces as if peering down at him through the opening of a well, and they drew farther and farther away as he fell down a deep, dark hole. The faces vanished as he plummeted too far away for him to see, and the orange glow of the braziers became nothing more than a pinpoint of light, like a single star in an endless black sky before it too winked out of existence.

Azerick had no idea how long he fell or if he even kept falling. Once there was nothing to fix his eyes on, it felt as if he simply floated in the ether of nothingness. It reminded him a great deal of when the psyling had invaded his mind, but this time, there was no flaw or fissure through which to escape.

After an indeterminate amount of time, he began noticing that the darkness was changing color. The black began to fade and take on a reddish, rusty hue. Azerick soon stared up into a grey, lifeless sky and discovered solidity under his back. He had never thought he would ever welcome the feeling of a stone jabbing uncomfortably into his flesh, but at this moment, it was the most wonderful sensation he could imagine.

He got to his feet and stared at the bleak landscape. There was no sun, but there was light, a reddish diffused sort of glow that came from no obvious source and cast no shadows. The ground and land all around him were reddish stone and sand. Far in the distance, he spied the black walls of a sinister-looking fortress built in an architectural design he would not have thought possible. With no other real options, he began walking toward the strange fortress.

Without knowing how big the castle was, it was impossible to tell how far away it lay. He felt as if he had been walking for at least an hour, but it did not seem as if he were getting any closer. Azerick could not shake the feeling that someone, or something, was watching him. He scoured the rocks that projected out of the ground in clumps and piles but saw nothing. He cast a look over his shoulder several times but could not see the source of his discomfiture.

The sorcerer continued his trek toward the black fortress. He tried to call his staff to him, but wherever he was must have been beyond its ability to reach him. He did not even have his rings or bracers to help him touch the Source or provide additional protection. He had become so accustomed to wearing them that it felt as if he were missing a part of his body.

Azerick spun toward a flicker of movement out of the corner of his right eye. He stopped and looked at the jumbled pile of stones for several minutes, but nothing moved. Azerick began walking faster. He thought that the castle looked a little closer now.

The clatter of small stones falling down a slope was the only warning Azerick got when the creatures finally got up the nerve or numbers to attack him. Hideous, long-limbed monsters with knotty hides the same color as the landscape leapt from behind piles of rocks and out of narrow crevasses in the ground. They looked almost like smaller versions of trolls, perhaps a foot shorter than he was. It was hard to tell because they bounded across the rocky landscape on all fours.

Long, sharp claws tipped each of their twelve fingers and toes, pointed teeth filled their overly large mouths, and solid, glossy black eyes glared hatefully from their hairless heads. Azerick ringed himself in stone spikes he conjured from the ground. Several creatures ran heedlessly onto the protrusions, shrieking in pain when the stone tips pierced their pinkish flesh.

The ravagers behind the first ranks leapt high into the air, effortlessly clearing the ten-foot-deep field of spikes. Azerick barely had time to cast a protective ward and roll out of the path of the bounding ravagers. He sprang to his feet and cast a flesh-freezing wave of cold air and frost, catching nearly every one of the creatures that landed inside the small area surrounded by the stone spikes.

The ravagers caught in the icy blast shrieked in agony as their skin froze to the point of splitting when they tried to move, and many died a painfully horrific death. Two of the creatures crouching to each side of the sorcerer sprang at him in tandem. Azerick ran forward, spun, and released a blast of lightning, striking the two creatures that collided in their haste to draw the sorcerer's blood. The ravagers became even more entangled as they flailed under the painful lightning strike.

Azerick sent a swarm of magical bolts pounding into their reddish, pebbled flesh until they ceased their struggles.

Azerick waited several minutes, crouching and scanning the land all around him for any further signs of attack. When no other creatures presented themselves, he picked his way through the spikes and continued to march toward the castle, much more wary of his surroundings. It would appear that this land was not so lifeless after all.

The fortress was definitely drawing closer now. It was a massive structure, easily twice the size of the castle in Southport or even the Academy. Whoever, or whatever, lived in the massive ziggurat must be a giant. The colossal black structure could easily house most of the population of North Haven without being horrendously overcrowded.

The wayward sorcerer did not even question his reasons for approaching the castle. Wherever he was, whatever the intentions of the master of the ebony fortress, that was where he would find answers—even if the answer was simply his own death.

He wondered if he was actually alive or if he was even physically in this place. Azerick was confident he was in the abyss. What little he had read of the hellish dimension seemed to fit this desolate world. Whether he had been sent here bodily or just spiritually, he could not tell.

Azerick's spine tingled, and he dove to the ground without conscious thought. A large body swooped past the space he had just occupied, shrieking its rage at having missed its prey.

The sorcerer scrambled back to his feet and was forced to jump and roll away once more when a second creature strafed him. He did not even try to stand a second time as a third creature circled, waiting for an opening to attack. Azerick stayed on his back, not taking his eyes off the sneering cambions, and cast his duplicity spell before rolling to his feet.

Azerick tried to retaliate with an offensive spell, but the winged demons forced him to dodge as they hurled fiery orbs at his moving form. Two of the orbs struck the ground behind him, but one tore through one of his illusions and destroyed it. He sent a spread of magical darts into the nearest cambion. The creature shrieked and flew up higher. Azerick avoided another pair of fireballs, losing another image while he avoided the attack.

He scooped up a handful of stones, each one the size of a man's eye, and infused them with his magic. He hurled the stones at one of the female demons. The stones sped to the velocity of a heavy crossbow bolt and tore into the cambion's flesh and wings. The demon screeched and tumbled from the sky, one of its bat-like wings ruined by the speeding bullets, and struck the hard ground.

He released a lightning bolt at another demon just as she hurled a fiery sphere. This orb, instead of simply tearing through one of his images, arced between them, destroying his remaining duplicates, scorching his clothes, and blistering his flesh. The lightning bolt caused the cambion to stagger in mid-flight. Eager to finish the demon off, he sent another half-dozen luminous darts slamming into her chest.

Azerick smiled in satisfaction as he watched the demon fold up and fall. So intent was he on the demon he had just killed, he made the grievous error of forgetting about the first cambion that had flown off. A heavy object struck him in the back, pitching him headlong onto the rocky ground. Pain erupted across his back from the talons the demon raked across his flesh.

Azerick rolled in an attempt to pitch the weight off his back, but the cambion moved with him and straddled his prostrate body. The sorcerer looked up into the malevolent, red, glaring eyes of the demon as she swiped at his face with her clawed fingers. He brought his arms up to fend off the creature's blows. Azerick managed to get a grip on the demon's wrists and tried to throw her off him.

The demon was surprisingly light but immensely strong. It was all Azerick could do to maintain his grip on her wrists as she flailed about. He managed to roll the both of them onto their sides but dared not let go. He kept his body pressed against the cambion's very feminine, albeit alien, form in an effort to keep her taloned toes from tearing into his abdomen. Even taking this precaution, he still received several long gashes carved into his thighs and shins.

Azerick knew he had to end this quickly. Having her hands and feet all but neutralized, the cambion snapped at the sorcerer's face with her needle-like teeth. Without the use of his hands, Azerick had to shape his spell without them, which required a great deal more effort and concentration.

He managed to pull the energy from the Source and articulate the spell well enough to bring the desired effect, but on a smaller scale. Several stone spears erupted from the ground, impaling the cambion through one side of her chest and out the other. A second stone spike pierced her right thigh, spitting the demon through her left side and lifting her off the ground.

Azerick rolled away while the cambion shrieked in rage and anguish and cast him hateful glares before finally dying upon the stone skewer. He examined the wounds on his legs, one of them caused by one of the spikes he had conjured a little too closely, but it was not terribly deep. His legs were a bloody mess, more from the number of scratches he had received than the severity. He felt blood trickling down his back, but the wounds did not feel severe enough to be lethal or overly incapacitating.

He wished he had his healing potions, but they were gone as well. Tearing his cloak to shreds, he was able to bandage most of his wounds. With a resigned sigh, Azerick resumed his trek toward the dark, enigmatic bastion.

As he finally drew near, seemingly hours or even days later, Azerick spied two large, grotesque demons standing to each side of a huge closed door. The door, as everything else concerning the fortress, was built at twice the scale of anything Azerick had seen of the castles back home. Thick, pointed spikes erupted from every corner and angle. Dozens of minarets sprouted from the tower like giant black horns.

Azerick watched the two immobile figures as he drew warily closer. They were huge and powerful, standing at least eight feet tall and four feet wide. They had a vaguely insectoid appearance with their bodies covered in hard chitin. Each possessed a pair of large arms with powerful pincers and a pair of thin spear-like limbs that grew from their backs and articulated over the tops of their wide shoulders. The creatures stood rigid until Azerick closed to within a score of yards of them and the door they apparently guarded.

"We have been waiting for you, human," one of the bug demons called out, the voice coming out almost like a hiss between the large mandibles that clacked together as it spoke. "The massster hasss been mossst anxiousss for your arrival."

"Good, does that mean you will let me pass?" Azerick asked without a trace of the fear buried beneath the thick layer of righteous anger he felt.

Both demons laughed a hissing reply. "You have not yet been found worthy, sssoft little human. You mussst prove yoursssself to our princcce before you will be granted an audienccce."

Azerick gave the two big bugs an annoyed look. "You know, being sent to the abyss is bad enough, but your complete lack of hospitality is really beginning to aggravate me."

The two demons hissed another laugh before they rushed toward the sorcerer in a loping, skipping gait on powerful, grasshopper-like legs. Azerick swept his arm upwards and summoned a line of stone spikes, but the attack did not catch the creatures by surprise. They both leapt up and back, easily avoiding the deadly protrusions.

"We have been watching you, flessshy human," one of the demons hissed. "We know your little tricksss."

"Is that right? I bet you do not know this one," Azerick smiled wickedly, then thrust both his hands forward as if he were trying to push them away.

A dozen of the stone spikes snapped off two and three-feet down their length and flew at the demons like javelins from a ballista. The stone spears slammed into the demons, pierced their hard carapaces with loud cracks, and hurled them back with great force. Azerick approached the large door that now had one of the insectoid demons hanging from it like a winterfest wreath.

He stepped up to the demon that lay on the ground next to the wall and examined its corpse. He had never tried using his sunder spell on a living, or once living, creature before, but he severed the five-foot chitinous spear at the joint where it extended over its shoulder.

With his short spear in his hand, he walked up to the door, grabbed the pincer of the hanging demon, and used it like a door knocker to rap loudly against the portal. Azerick heard a distinct click, and the huge door swung silently open, seemingly of its own accord.

Flickering torches, which surely would have blackened the walls were they not constructed of black stone, lit the halls. Enormous double-sized doors stood closed in random places down each side of the passage. Wall hangings, tapestries, and paintings depicting grotesque and highly imaginative macabre scenes adorned much of the onyx walls.

Azerick had no real idea which direction to go in this bizarre place, but he figured the lord of the castle would reside in a large hall near the center or rear, so he followed the long passage, not deviating through any of the closed doors. After what he assumed to be several minutes of travel in this timeless world, he spied a small winged demon on its hands and knees muttering to itself and scrubbing at what looked to be dark blood spatters with an ordinary brush and pail of water.

"Stupid cow-headed prince thinks Skulk has nothing better to do than clean up his messes. Skulk is a demon, not a scullery maid to scrub floors and polish his stupid skulls. One of these days, Skulk is going to make that bloated windbag respect—ouch!" Skulk cried out, then leapt up, rubbing his posterior where Azerick had jabbed him with his spear.

"What da hell ya poke Skulk in his rump for?" the little fire demog demanded, giving Azerick an indignant glare.

Azerick thrust the point of his makeshift spear under the hovering demog's chin. "Take me to whoever is in charge of this place—now."

Skulk flew up out of the spear's reach, spun away, and began flapping his way down the hall. "You comin' or what?" Skulk turned and asked irritably when Azerick made no move to follow.

Azerick walked below and just behind the little demon as he fluttered slowly down the hall, muttering once more. "Stupid human poke Skulk in the rump like a piece of roasting meat and demand he take him to see big cow-headed prince then stand there like a wart on a blattazuu's butt. First Skulk is Prince Hornhead's maid scrubbing floors, then he is stupid pasty-faced human's escort. One of these days Skulk will show all of them, then get some respect."

Skulk eventually stopped in front of an enormous set of double doors carved with detailed scenes of slaughter and mayhem. "Lord Klaraxis in there," Skulk informed the human with a jerk of his thumb.

"How do I gain entry?"

Skulk looked incredulously at Azerick. "You knock, stupid, what else?" Skulk fluttered off back toward his scrub brush, muttering.

"Squishy human is too stupid to know how to knock on a door. Maybe he thinks Skulk got a promotion from escort to doorman. Like Skulk has nothing better to do than open doors for stupid, lazy human who is probably just gonna get eaten as soon as he walks in the room anyway."

Skulk turned back toward Azerick who had just raised his fist to pound on the massive door. "Hey, try not to bleed so much! Skulk gots better things to do than clean up stupid human blood because he gotta bleed so much!"

Azerick watched the strange, bitter little demon fly away, bobbing down the hall, continually muttering his complaints about his lot in life. He took a deep breath and pounded on one of the doors, making little more than soft, dull thuds against the impossibly thick wood.

To Azerick's surprise, it swung inward to allow him admittance to the huge throne room. Azerick strode purposefully down the wide red carpet that ran from the doors to the foot of a tall dais. Twenty feet up sat a throne made from the bones of various creatures. Upon the throne was an enormous black demon with blood-red eyes, horns, and claws.

It had to be at least ten feet tall not counting its long red horns that thrust up and forward from its huge head. Its facial features were largely human, notwithstanding the horns, though the nose looked more ape-like than human. Huge bat-like wings were folded tightly against its body and draped over a backless throne of skulls and bones.

"Ah, my honored guest has finally arrived. I am Klaraxis, demon prince of the fifth circle of the abyss. I am master of all you see around you," the demon told Azerick imperially, making a sweeping gesture with one of his powerful ebony arms.

Azerick looked around the enormous but largely empty chamber then back at the demon sitting on his gruesome throne. "You mean the carpet?"

"No, not the carpet, you simpleton!"

"You don't own the carpet? How can you claim to be the master of anything if you do not even own the carpet?"

"I am master of *everything* within the fifth circle! Every demon, every stone, the air you think you are breathing all belongs to me! The lesser masters of the lower circles show me deference as their better! I am…ah, you are being clever," Klaraxis said with a smile. "I despise cleverness in my subordinates. You have proven yourself to be a worthy vessel to house my spirit and transport me back to the material world. I was especially impressed with how you dealt with the mantar'ri demons: quite entertaining."

"I hate to disappoint you, demon, but I am not here to be anyone's *vessel*. Tell me how to return to my home, and I will leave you in peace."

"There is no way home for you, little human. This is your home now, and you had best get accustomed to it."

"You will find me a rather bitter and troublesome houseguest and highly resistant to any plans you may have for me. You had best get accustomed to that," Azerick returned.

Azerick sent a concentrated electrical beam at the seated demon prince without warning, but Klaraxis simply deflected the spell with a flick of his wrist, sending it to strike the distant wall where it burned a deep hole into the black stone. Obsidian ooze slithered down the black surface, and a faint screeching reached Azerick's ears as if the stone were crying out in pain.

"Not only are such attacks rude, they are quite futile. Come, allow me to show you something that may interest you," the demon lord invited him. He stood to his full, imposing height and descended the steps of the dais to tower over the much smaller sorcerer.

With little other choice, Azerick followed Klaraxis through a doorway that was more than large enough to allow the enormous demon to pass through without fear of even coming close to scraping the wing joints that peeked over his shoulders and head.

They traversed a long, descending hall and stopped before an ornate door that appeared to be made of solid bronze. The door swung open at the demon's touch, and Azerick followed him into a room that looked much like Azerick's own vault chamber, only much larger.

"Here is where I keep all of my most precious artifacts. Since you will be residing as a shade here for, oh, about an eternity, I thought you might like to amuse yourself by looking at them and studying them. Of course, as a shade, you will not be able to interact with anything, but I think it is a fair trade in exchange for what you are giving me. Would you not agree? No? Well I suppose I might feel I was getting the short end of the deal if I was in your place, but since I am not, I feel quite good about it," Klaraxis chuckled.

The demon began pointing out some of the more significant artifacts in the room, describing where he had gotten them, and whom he had to kill to get them. He directed Azerick's attention to a black-bladed shortsword hanging on the wall.

"This is by far my most prized possession," Klaraxis told Azerick. "With that sword, I can trap the soul of any creature, even a god. I hope to put it to use one day, preferably against that damnable Solarian."

He retrieved a clear glass or crystal sphere from a velvet-padded box sitting on a shelf. "I suppose it is time for the show to come to an end." Heavy black chains erupted from the wall and wrapped themselves around Azerick's wrists and ankles.

As the demon stalked toward him, Azerick retreated until his back struck the wall. He knew he was only going to have one chance at what he planned, so he waited until Klaraxis stood just before him and pressed the crystal orb lightly against his forehead.

Azerick reached out with his power, using a spell similar to the one he had used to hurl the stones at the cambion, but this time, he pulled rather than pushed. Since the distance between him and the object was greater, it took more effort to achieve the effect, but the sinister black shortsword flew from the wall and into his outstretched palm. Azerick thrust the blade forward without hesitating. The demon's eyes widened as the blade sank deep into his bare flesh just above where a human, or almost any other creature born of a mother, would have had a navel.

Azerick felt a burning in his hand and tried to drop the sword, but his fingers would not release their grip, either that or the sword would not release his hand. The sorcerer felt an evil intelligence emanating from the blade, and it held his body immobile.

Klaraxis's knees finally bent, and he fell kneeling onto the floor in front of Azerick, yet was still looming over the human when the room filled with a deep, gratified laugh. The demon prince toppled to the side, but the laughter continued, and it took several moments before Azerick realized it was coming from his own mouth.

He tried to scream, but he could only continue laughing as he felt himself being forced from his own body. Blackness overcame him, and he could no longer see out of his own eyes.

Klaraxis looked at his body through his new eyes as the chains uncoiled from around his wrists and ankles. Far above, on another plane, five wizards watched as the five braziers flared black flames for several seconds before returning to their normal orange glow.

CHAPTER 15

Joshua paced the gloomy hall outside the summoning room just in case his mistress needed him to perform some task. His conscience warred with his inability to do anything regardless of how he felt about the situation. He heard the sorcerer shriek a long and frightful scream, but no further sounds had issued from the room for many minutes now. Not even the droning chant of the archmages slipped under the crack beneath the thick door.

Unable to stand it any longer, he stalked down the hall and into the library where he saw Aggie behind her desk, as usual, though looking a bit fretful.

"Ah, Jonathan, I'm glad you stopped by," the senile old librarian said as he walked into the room.

"It's Joshua, Aggie."

It was funny how she would always get his name wrong but could tell you where every book was within the library and what it contained.

"Joshua Aggie! Why you have the same last name as my first name," she cackled.

"No, Aggie, it's just Joshua."

"Well, whatever you want to call yourself, I am glad you're here. I seem to have lost the key to my desk drawer, and I could use a good spellcaster to get it open for me. I used to know a nice little spell that would do the trick, but I've forgotten it over the years."

"I'm sorry, Agatha, but I haven't studied that one."

Aggie waved a gnarled old hand dismissively. "No need to fret. This is a library, for Solarian's sake." She began sifting through sheets of vellum and paper scattered across her desktop. "I have a scroll around here that should do the trick."

She picked up one of the scrolls and pressed it to her nose before shoving it in Joshua's face. "What does this one say at the top?"

Joshua told her and she waved her hand once more as if she were shooing away a fly. "No, no, that one would unlock everything from shackles to a dimensional portal. This is just a desk, not a wizard's ward." She began picking through the scrolls once more. "Ah, I think this is the one! Tell me what this one says."

Joshua took the scroll from her and read its title.

"That's the one! Be a dear and use it to unlock my desk for me."

Joshua read the scroll, its scribbled runes flaring away to nothingness as he recited the magical words. He heard the click of the locking mechanism release the instant he read the last word on the scroll.

The old librarian opened her desk drawer with a little shout of triumph. "Well, there's my key, right in the drawer. Now how did I manage to lock that in there without having the key? Oh well, such mysteries can wait until after my lunch to be solved," she said, pulling out a salami and cheese sandwich and taking a full bite.

"You want a taste?" she offered Joshua, pointing the end of her sandwich at him.

"No thanks, Aggie," he replied, then walked out of the door.

Joshua resumed his pacing and every few steps glanced down at the scroll he still held in his hand.

"Skunk!" Klaraxis shouted. "Skunk, get your worthless hide down here, do you hear me?"

"Of course I hear you. Everybody between here and the third circle of the abyss can hear you," Skulk muttered as he flew down the stairs and through the hall. "Skulk would have to be deaf not to hear you. Hmm, not a bad idea. Maybe Skulk can jab his eardrums out so he does not have to listen to big-mouthed, cow-headed demon lord."

Skulk flew through the huge bronze door that still stood open. "Yes, oh magnificent lord of the under…balls of fire, he's dead! Puny human done killed da big horn-headed blattazuu's rump! Oh, joyous days! Skulk's dreams have come true!" Skulk cried, then began dancing a jig on the demon lord's chest.

"Skunk, get off my chest," Klaraxis told the demog who was busy shaking his posterior in the face of the demon prince's body, making flatulent noises with his tongue.

Skulk bit off his raspberries with a squeak and looked at the sorcerer, his black tongue sticking out between his puckered lips. Skulk looked between the human and the seemingly dead Klaraxis, which he was still squatting over, in confusion. The demog flapped up and peered intently into each of Azerick's eyes then rapped on his forehead with his knuckles.

"You in there, oh prince of darkness whom Skulk serves with utmost loya—ack!" Klaraxis's new hand wrapped around his scrawny throat and cut off Skulk's words.

"I should tear your wings off, followed by your arms, legs, and finally your brainless little head for that display," Klaraxis threatened with a low growl. "But I have a more important use for you. First, you will go and summon two of my tar'raun'atu to heft my body onto that stone slab. Then you will be responsible for ensuring that no one disturbs me or my possessions for the next one hundred years while I bring about a reign of torture and misery for the feeble inhabitants of the mortal world."

"Yes, great demon lord. Prince Klaraxis is wise to know that Skulk is his most loyal and adoring subject with whom to trust such an important honor," Skulk croaked past the demon prince's crushing grasp.

"Trust?" Klaraxis laughed. "Hardly, you little dungpile with wings. I know that you are too much a coward and too feeble to attempt to destroy my body and usurp my throne while I am away."

"Dat too, your benevolent wickedness."

"Now go get my porters to lift me off this floor." Klaraxis slung Skulk through the doorway where he smacked into the wall before he could arrest his uncontrolled flight.

"Stupid, pasty-faced, human skin-wearing demon squatter. Bad enough he thinks Skulk is scouring maid, stupid human think Skulk is doorman, now he supposed to be some kinda mortician to take care of his stinkin' body. He thinks he can just throw Skulk against da wall like he is stupid little puppy, and den I'm supposed ta just sit around and watch his stinkin' corpse collect dust? Skulk gonna get his revenge, make him regret ever throwing Skulk around."

Skulk returned with the two hulking tar'raun'atu. The tar'raun'atu were massively muscled, wingless demons who were nearly as wide as their eight-foot frames were tall. They had long ringed horns like a gazelle, jutting slightly back from their bristly, black-haired heads. Their ridiculously muscled arms were so long that their knuckles dragged on the ground. Their enormous strength was only equaled by their stupidity.

"Pick up my body and lay it *gently* upon the slab," Klaraxis instructed the two brutes.

If the demonic duo was surprised to find the body of their prince lying seemingly dead upon the floor with his voice coming out of the mouth of a human, they gave no sign of it. They simply bent down, lifted the thousand pound plus demon prince up as if he were a sleeping child, and placed him on the black stone table as they were instructed.

"Face up, you imbeciles!" Klaraxis growled irritably.

The two tar'raun'atu righted the lifeless body of their liege then stared at him expectantly.

"You may go now," he told them with forced patience then turned to Skulk. "You will guard my body with your life, Skunk."

"Oh joy of joys! Skulk is most happy to sit on the cold corpse of the Lord of Lies, the Duke of Degeneracy, the Emir of Immorality, the—"

"Shut up, Skunk, and if you so much as touch my body, I will tear one of your wings off and laugh as I watch you fly in circles."

Klaraxis turned to leave but spun back around as soon as he stepped through the door and narrowly missed catching Skulk shoving one of his fingers up his body's nose and sticking his tongue out at him as he walked away. The prince of demons glared at the innocently hovering demog and returned to his throne.

Klaraxis sat back on his throne of bones, waved a hand over an upturned skull in the arm of the throne, and saw Shakrill's expectant face in its reflection.

"It is complete, and I am ready."

"Excellent, my demonic prince. We are prepared to bring you to your new home. He is ready," Shakrill informed the other wizards, then led the chanting of the complex spell that would bring the soul back from the abyss and return it to the vessel.

Klaraxis felt a moment of disorientation before his new body seemed to leap from the throne and fly upward at an incredible rate. He looked down and saw his mighty fortress dwindle to a black speck amidst a rosy field until it disappeared. Before he was able to comprehend the sensation fully, he found himself staring up at a black ceiling just above the heads of the five humans looking down at him.

"Welcome, Klaraxis, we have all been eagerly awaiting your arrival so that you may lead us to our rightful place of domination," Shakrill crooned.

Klaraxis looked at his wrists and down at his ankles, giving the chains a test tug. Had he been in his demon body, he could have snapped the feeble restraints with ease, but stuck in this form, some of his powers, most notably his physical prowess, were greatly diminished, but not his innate magical power, as these foolish wizards were about to learn.

Klaraxis called upon his demonic source of power only to find it beyond his grasp. His mouth opened in mute surprise at the sudden understanding that he was helpless and realization that these were no ordinary chains. Somehow, they managed to block his ability to reach back to the abyss, the source of his infernal magic. He tried to access the sorcerer's Source and found that it too was beyond his grasp.

"What have you done, Shakrill? How am I to aid you in your ascension when you have bound me and my power?" the demon asked, trying to control the rage he desperately wanted to unleash on these fools.

"Calm yourself, my prince. It is but a temporary measure until we come to a full understanding of one another," the wizard said, then bent down next to his ear and whispered, "or should I say *Dur'ar'ang'sen*."

Every muscle in the demon's new body spasmed at the sound of his soul name.

"How do you know that, you traitorous bitch?" Klaraxis grunted through the pain.

"How is not important. It is only important that you know that I am the only one who knows it, for now."

Well, she was the only one until she just told me, Azerick's voice sounded through the demon's mind.

What, how? I destroyed you! I replaced your soul! How are you still here? Klaraxis demanded.

I made a vow that no one would ever control my mind and body ever again, demon! Now, take a seat while I get us out of here.

Like hell I will! I am in control of this body. It is mine, and I will never give it up!

You were never in control, you disgusting boisterous braggart, now shut up while I think! Azerick commanded the demon.

Klaraxis shrieked in impotent rage as Azerick forced his essence to the far reaches of his mind. Azerick found that his connection to the Source was indeed severed as long as these shackles remained. He decided he would simply have to wait until an opportunity presented itself, which it did when Joshua came bursting through the door, reading from a scroll he held in his shaking hands.

"Joshua, what do you think you are doing? I did not summon you!" Shakrill screamed at her apprentice.

The magical bonds chaining Azerick to the floor and blocking his access to the Source released their hold as the metal shackles fell to the floor with a clank.

"What have you done, you stupid little fool?" Shakrill asked, her voice hoarse, fury lacing every syllable.

With a great smile of triumph, Azerick leapt impossibly fast to his feet from his fully reclined position and brought Klaraxis out of the darkness to which he had banished him.

All right, demon, do you want to make these people pay? Then let's do it, and do not try to fight me.

The smile on the sorcerer's face took on an even more menacing cast as Azerick's hazel green eyes glared with an evil red glint.

Azerick called his staff to his hand and felt its reassuring power slap into his palm. He raised the weapon high and struck its gleaming shaft onto the floor. A burst of power exploded out from all around him with such force that it sent the wizards sprawling and extinguished the braziers in a cloud of sparks. Even Joshua, who was farther from the heart of the blast, was sent flying back through the open door to land heavily against the wall.

Azerick shouted a word of command and called forth every ward he knew, shielding his body with a series of spells strung together to be brought up all at once. Several illusory duplicates sprang up around him, and his body was invigorated with a sudden burst of energy, which increased his reflexes even beyond the unnatural speeds that Klaraxis's possession instilled in him. Such a casting would normally be exhausting, but the demonic possession seemed to give Azerick an immense well of power from which to draw upon.

The sorcerer stretched out a hand and sent an electrical ray into the chest of the master of the Black Tower, instantly searing a massive hole through him before he even got halfway through the spell he was trying to cast. An intensely hot jet of flame splashed harmlessly against Azerick's demonically-reinforced wards. The demon Klaraxis stretched out a hand, and a black ray lanced through the wizard's body, turning it into a desiccated husk.

One wizard tried to cast a binding, but his efforts were futile against the dual spirits that now resided within one body. Azerick imitated the previous wizard's attack and sent a hellish stream of liquid fire into the archmage's torso, incinerating his body and melting the black stone behind him.

Another archmage tried to grab the sorcerer with hands wreathed in black flames. Klaraxis dodged the grapple, grabbed the foolish wizard by the wrist, and slammed him repeatedly against the wall until he slumped down, leaving behind a bloody streak.

Azerick stood over the cowering form of Shakrill, holding up her arm, which appeared to have grown a second elbow. "Klaraxis, please," the wizard pleaded. "I never meant to betray you, I swear! Together we can conquer the world; no one can stand against us! I only learned and used your soul name so that you would not betray me."

"And for that I am truly grateful, Shakrill. It makes controlling the demon much easier," Azerick replied with a grim smile.

"You…you could not possibly still be alive."

"Oh, but I am. Sorry, Shakrill, but you do not fit within my plans, nor do any of your other Black Tower ilk," he informed the wizard, then thrust his arcanum spear through her heart.

Azerick strode through the door and looked down at Joshua who was still huddled against the wall, staring at the destruction the creature before him had wrought.

"Please, I set you free. Please don't kill me," Joshua begged.

Azerick's spear quivered under the force of his grip as the demon battered at his host's mental defenses, longing to crush the cowering human. With another mental surge and the use of the demon's soul name, he forced the demon further back into his psychic cage.

"Are there any others who share your decent nature in this nest of vermin?" Azerick asked.

The apprentice nodded vigorously. "My friend Umair, a few other apprentices and younger students, maybe an adept or two have not been terribly corrupted."

"You are not as incapable as your mistress liked to tell you. I see within you great potential and even now you possess a respectable amount of skill. Would you like to continue your studies, free of threats and insults, perhaps even teach those younger and less accomplished than yourself?"

"You would take me as your apprentice? Are you Azerick, or are you the demon?" Joshua asked tentatively.

Azerick grinned down at the frightened young man, which did nothing to ease his distress. "A little of both at the moment, and no, I would not have you as an apprentice. I would have you as a colleague at my school."

"I could learn and even teach?"

"Get yourself and any who are decent, trustworthy, and willing to follow you to North Haven. Anyone there should be able to direct you to the orphans' academy. Take whatever you wish from this tower. Those who remain will have bigger worries than some pilfering. Now, go get those who will follow you, but be swift about it. You do not have much time."

Joshua nodded, jumped to his feet, and sprinted up the stairs to get the satchel Aggie had given him and to gather Umair and the others he thought deserved to be spared from whatever fate the sorcerer had in mind for the tower.

Azerick looked up and down the hall with his red-tinted eyes, about to follow Joshua up the stairs when he noticed light streaming through an open doorway farther down the hall in the other direction. Azerick turned to his right, stepped into the library, and saw a stooped old woman puttering about behind a large desk.

Agatha looked up and squinted at the newcomer. "Well, hello there, young man, come to check out a book? I don't seem to recall seeing you here before, and I never forget a face; a name on occasion, but never a face!"

"No, revered grandmother, I am afraid I do not have the time to enjoy the treasures you have here. Though I wish I had a few years to peruse your grand library. I am afraid I must ask you to leave the tower and with some haste."

"My, my, honored grandmother, am I? Such a polite young man, unlike those stupid wizards who mock old Aggie and call her a useless has-been. Well, I suppose it's finally time for me to move on, though I don't know about the swiftly part," she cackled as she shuffled out from behind her desk.

"Please move as fast as you are able, Grand Magus."

"Oh, don't worry about me. You go on and do what you have to do while I collect up a few things. I'll be gone before you're finished, don't you worry about old Agatha," she ordered, shooing Azerick away with a bony old hand.

Azerick nodded once and left her to her own devices.

Agatha looked around at her precious library with longing. "I guess I had better figure out what books to take with me." She looked at the rows upon rows of books. "Oh hells, I can't decide. I guess I had best take them all. It's not like you didn't see this coming, you daffy old broad."

Aggie raised her old, unadorned staff and spoke words of magic that she had not used in decades, but still they came clearly to her mind. Runes, cleverly carved into the wooden bookshelves that appeared as nothing more than part of the larger, more elaborate artwork, flared. The bookshelves became two-dimensional like an extremely well-crafted painting, before they folded themselves into sections and disappeared, leaving behind bare walls that had not seen light in decades.

"Well, that's done," she said looking about the library with satisfaction. "Now, if my memory serves me correctly, I should have another sandwich around here somewhere."

Azerick stepped back into the summoning room where the wizards still lay as dead as they had been a few minutes ago. Sometimes you could never be too sure when it came to wizards—or sorcerers. He found and retrieved his bracers and rings from Shakrill's dead body, glad that he was not going to have to search the entire tower for them. He looked over the other bodies and stripped off the rings, necklaces, pendants, and wands the wizards carried on them as well. It looked like they had come prepared for a battle, just not the kind he had given them.

He sighed when he slipped on his ring and felt his connection with the Source grow stronger. It was like having a missing limb reattached. He left the dead where they lay and turned toward the stairs. A young wizard leapt out from around the corner of a stairwell and raised a wand at the sorcerer.

Most people were familiar with the phrase "if looks could kill," but in Azerick's case it was true. With little more than a glare, Azerick allowed Klaraxis to summon his demonic power. Azerick's eyes flared crimson, and the wizard's robes simply burst into flames. The hapless wizard flailed and screamed as his flesh burned away under the intense heat of the demon fire before the flames reached his lungs and he collapsed in a heap at the bottom of the stairs.

The smell of burnt clothing, flesh, and hair filled the corridor with an acrid scent that made Azerick queasy at how much he enjoyed it. He stooped over and casually retrieved the wand the wizard had dropped. Seeing that it was a little charred but undamaged, he slipped it into the pocket of his cloak and continued up the stairs. When he reached the top, a fusillade of lightning bolts, power strikes, and bursts of fire flared across the room.

The nervous wizards had mistakenly let loose the moment the top of Azerick's head cleared the stairs. He calmly ducked and let the spells strike the wall above his head as he fed more power into his wards.

Without bothering to climb the stairs any higher, he swept his staff in an arc, collapsing a large portion of the ceiling onto the wizards who had been foolish enough not to flee when they had the chance.

A great cloud of dust wafted through the room as Azerick climbed to the ground floor of the tower and began picking his way toward the stairs to search the upper levels. A wizard stumbled out of the dust and raised his wand at the sorcerer. Azerick saw that he was little more than a journeyman, probably not even old enough to shave yet. He lunged forward impossibly fast, snatched the wand from the youth's outstretched hand, and delivered a stinging, openhanded slap to his face.

"Get out of here, boy. If you are smart, you will catch up with Joshua and get your life straight!" Azerick snarled at the terrified youngster, then shoved him toward the door.

Azerick continued toward the stairs. Another wizard, a real one this time, stepped out from behind a large stone column and tried to cast a spell. With a word and a gesture, Azerick sent him hurling into the wall some fifteen feet behind him and ten feet up. The wizard fell in a crumpled heap and did not stir.

On the stairs, the possessed sorcerer ran into a few of the younger novices and apprentices who had been slow to leave the tower or chose not to heed Joshua's warning, but he let them pass. The young students gave the sorcerer a wide berth as they tracked him with terrified eyes. Some even ran back up the stairs and waited for the deadly stranger to pass before bolting down the steps as fast as they could and fleeing through the front door.

Azerick saw that the first few floors were dedicated to the novices, journeymen, and apprentices, so he skipped these rooms as well as those rooms set aside for the adepts, only pausing to shout at anyone he saw to flee the tower and his wrath. His interests lay in the rooms of the archmages near the top of the tower.

He did not want to spend a great deal of time looting the tower of its precious items. He was more interested in making good use of his time to give Joshua and the old librarian a chance to get away. His treasure hunting was secondary, or so he told himself. Allowing the demon a measure of active consciousness altered his own perceptions and attitude to some degree depending upon how much he let the demon come forward, and right now, he was allowing Klaraxis a considerable amount of consciousness.

Why are you letting these mewling children get away? Exterminate the lot of them! You know that these wizards have corrupted them all and cannot be trusted. Besides, children have the most flavorful souls.

"Shut up, demon, or I will stuff you back in your little, dark box in the furthest recesses of my mind," Azerick told him, choosing to speak aloud.

The demon grumbled but remained silent, savoring the memory of the wizards he, and the sorcerer, had killed. As much as he hated sharing the human's body, he had a suspicion that his existence was going to be far from boring. The fates had their hooks deeply into this one. Nothing could satiate the demon's desire for death and destruction, but he could be pleased, and so far, the first several minutes of his new existence were quite pleasing.

Azerick found a rucksack in one of the archmage's rooms and was delighted to discover that it contained an enchantment similar to the magic bag that was still in Horse's saddlebags. He had hoped to liberate a few spell books, scrolls, and magical items, but the rucksack made his choosing what to take and carry much simpler.

Azerick looted anything that looked interesting. Klaraxis was able to tell at a glance if an item possessed any sort of enchantment, which also helped him in selecting which items to grab. Azerick was already in the master of the tower's suite near the top, and anyone who wanted to get out had had enough time to do so.

Azerick casually descended the stairs and made for the entrance where he paused amidst the rubble near the collapsed ceiling. He shaped the familiar spear point onto his staff, jammed it between the closely set stones of the floor, and walked away. He was nearly halfway to the tavern where he had left Horse when he turned around and concentrated on his staff.

Inside the tower, every rune on the staff flared until the entire chamber was awash with a blinding light. Azerick and Klaraxis poured energy into the weapon until motes of light began dancing in front of Azerick's eyes from the exertion. The staff released all of the pent-up energy it contained in a single, massive pulse of energy. The walls blew apart, sending stones flying across the open square and into nearby buildings. The floors within the tower crumbled and the excess energy sent the roof and several tons of stone blocks flying hundreds of feet into the air just before the entire structure began to topple.

Had Azerick been untainted by the demon's presence he may have considered the innocent lives that may have been lost when the tower blew apart, fell, and crushed several buildings, but such was not the case, and coupled with the general morals of the populace, he was not about to let it concern him now. His staff popped back into his hand with a thought, if a bit sluggishly, and he went to retrieve Horse and leave this disgusting warren of thieves and murderers.

He walked past the crowds that were beginning to throng the streets to see what had happened. A huge cloud of dust floated over the center of the town where the tower had stood uncontested in its private plaza. Azerick snaked out a hand and snatched a familiar boy by the collar, who was running past him to get a closer look at the ruined tower.

The boy's eyes went wide and his face turned pale when he looked up at the grim face of the wizard who had killed the other wizards a couple of days ago in the tavern and in the square before he had been captured.

"I have come for my horse, boy," Azerick told the terrified and stammering stableboy. "Don't just stand there gaping. Spit it out."

"Y-you were captured and taken inside the t-tower. Nobody returns from the t-tower."

"Well, I have, and I have come for my horse. I told you that I would be back for him. Now, where is he?"

"S-sold, sir. He was sold!" The boy was almost crying.

Azerick lifted the youth a foot off the ground with one hand and stared him hard in the eyes. "I can easily find my property, but I am weary," Azerick snarled. "You had best go and get my horse and have him and my stuff, all of my stuff, in the next half hour."

"Y-yes, sir!" the boy said, nodding his head so hard Azerick thought he would snap his own neck.

The sorcerer set the boy back down on his feet but did not let him go. "He is that way about seven blocks in case you forgot to whom you sold him."

The stableboy took off in the direction Azerick pointed, his sandals kicking up clouds of dust as he ran faster than he ever had in his life. Azerick went into the bar to wait. Even the swill they served here sounded good right now. The few patrons and the bartender all stopped their excited conversations about the recent happenings and stared in abject terror at the red-eyed stranger who walked into the tavern.

Word had already gotten back to the tavern about the young man who had walked away from the tower just before it was destroyed. They also knew that he was the one the wizards had taken two days before. The fact that the tavern keeper had been the one to sell Horse and his possessions nearly made the man lose his water when Azerick approached the bar.

"Give me a beer, the best you have," Azerick said, his voice rough from inhaling dust and the stress of recent events.

The bartender dropped three glasses by the time he was able to pour one from his personal stock. Azerick did not try to pay, and the barkeeper did not ask him to. Azerick drained the glass in a few quick gulps, slammed it down, and demanded another. He drank this one more slowly and waited for the stableboy to return with Horse. He had no doubt in his mind that he would, and whatever the barkeeper had to do to make restitution to whomever he sold him to was none of his concern.

Azerick did not have long to wait. He had just finished the second beer when the lad burst in through the door. "Sir, he's out front, saddled and everything, with his bags and all. They weren't never opened, couldn't, so I'm certain everything's in there!"

Azerick nodded and left. What gold he had on him prior to his capture was gone, and he was not in the mood to take the time to go into his bags to get more. The boy had failed to fulfill the contract as far as he was concerned. He could get it from the tavern owner if he wanted it badly enough. Azerick frowned at his thoughts and bad attitude. He banished the demon to the back of his mind where he would not influence him, at least not significantly, despite Klaraxis's vociferous protests.

Azerick's eyes took on a more natural hue with only tiny specks of red interspersed with the hazel and green, and he felt much better. He almost felt like he had recovered from a bad hangover. He had not noticed how heavily the feelings of anger and hatred had been weighing him down and pressing on his soul until they were gone. This was something he was going to have to be very wary of in the future.

Azerick pointed Horse to the north where he had left Sandy atop the small knoll. He nudged Horse into a canter, wanting to leave the town behind him as quickly as he could. He was also concerned about Sandy. Who knew how she had reacted when he destroyed the tower.

"Sandy!" Azerick shouted as he neared the rise.

Sandy's brightly scaled head popped out of the sand near the top of the mound where he had left her. "Azerick, you're back!"

Azerick rode nearer, and it seemed to him that Sandy was avoiding looking directly at him. He looked at her as she turned her head away, and noticed a small, shiny, black hoof sticking out of the sand.

"Sandy, what did you do?"

"Nothing. What do you mean?"

"Why won't you look at me?" Azerick asked.

Sandy turned her head and looked at him but only far enough so that she trained her right eye on him. "There, I'm looking at you. Happy?"

"Look straight at me."

"There's no need. We dragons have very keen eyesight. I think I have some sand in it too."

"Sandy, look at me."

Sandy huffed and faced her surrogate parent. If dragons could get a black eye, Azerick figured this was what it would look like. Several scales were missing or cracked around her left eye and snout and did not gleam nearly as brightly as the rest.

"You went and attacked those goats, didn't you?"

"No!"

"Then what is that sticking out of the sand next to you?"

Sandy looked down and saw the small cloven hoof. "I think it's an old skeleton. The desert is full of them," she replied.

"Sandy, it still has hair on it!"

Sandy looked like she was battling with the truth and finally gave up. "Who would have thought that those hairy little demons would kick and head-butt like that or actually form a concerted attack? I knew they were herd animals, but Mama never said anything about them forming a cohesive defense bolstered by a mass of solidarity before!"

"Where did you learn to use those terms?" Azerick asked.

"I read it in one of the books I borrowed from your magic bag. I learned how to use it by watching you when you took the food out of it. Speaking of which, do you have any more sugar cubes or, better yet, honey?" Sandy asked, wagging her thick tail.

"You did not do as you were told and got hurt in the process, so I think not."

"Ugh, that's not fair! I'm not hurt, and the goat was the one that got eaten! You just don't understand the mind of a superior predator!" Sandy shouted. She turned away with a huff then spun back around. "I have instincts, you know! A million years of instincts can't just be turned off like a, a, any woman you smile at with your ugly little flat teeth!" she shouted, then began stalking off again.

"Sandy?"

"What?"

"Where is my book?"

Sandy dug furiously in the sand, sending the spray unnecessarily far and high, then popped up a moment later with the book in her mouth.

"There's your stupid old human book!"

"Sandy?"

"What? I told you about the stupid goat, I gave you your stupid old book, and you won't give me a sugar cube, you don't have any honey and probably wouldn't give me any anyway because you are mean and stingy, so what do you want now?"

"We're going that way." Azerick pointed about ninety degrees north of the way Sandy had been heading.

"Fine!" the little dragon shouted, then began clomping off in the new direction.

Azerick could no longer contain his laughter as he watched the dragon stomping away, her hind end swaying furiously in aggravation.

CHAPTER 16

Joshua and just over a dozen former Black Tower students, including his friend Umair and an adept named Maira, made haste down the dirt streets of Rapture and heard the horrific crash. The young apprentices and novices turned around just in time to see the tower crumble and fall.

"Only when darkness falls will you be able to see the path you must follow," Joshua whispered, but Umair was close enough that he heard what his friend said.

Umair and Joshua had both grabbed the satchels Agatha had given them along with a spare set of clothes, quills, and an inkpot: the only things they really owned. The other students who decided to go with them had brought their own few necessities and followed. Both apprentices undid the buckles holding the satchels closed and looked at the contents.

Inside was not a half-eaten salami sandwich as they had half-feared, but a couple of traveling spell books, a small pouch of coins, and several magical scrolls: everything they needed to make a long journey.

"You don't think that loony old librarian knew what was going to happen?" Umair asked.

Joshua shook his head. "I don't know. She is definitely an odd bird, but look at what she gave us."

It was a mystery, one they were unlikely to get a clear answer to, so they just accepted it as a good omen and focused on getting out of Rapture. They made it to the west end of town where a large caravan was lining up to take a load of ill-gotten goods to Langdon's Crossing.

Using some of the gold Aggie had given them, Joshua was able to convince the caravan master to provide them with passage.

The wagon train arrived in Langdon's Crossing well after nightfall a few days later. Langdon's Crossing was technically not on the sea, so the former Black Tower students walked the three miles to the port of Langdon's Crossing where a second town had sprung up to accommodate ship traffic.

Joshua, Umair, and Maira began asking around the taverns of the small shipping town about passage north. They had no idea how much a captain would charge for fifteen passengers to North Haven and prayed that they had enough. There was also the real fear of being offered passage and then taken south and sold into slavery. Any captain who tried that was going to regret it, Joshua vowed.

The caravan trip had not been one without peril. A day out from Rapture, Sumaran raiders had attacked them, and the student wizards had acquitted themselves well. The weak did not fare well within the black tower's walls, and their magic, minimal as it was, had been a deciding factor in their victory.

In answer to their queries regarding passage to North Haven, the tavern owner pointed to a small group of sailors sitting at a table in the corner. All three looked nervously at the huge graying minotaur that sat at the table with two men, but necessity reinforced their courage.

"Excuse me, gentlemen, might I have a moment of your time?" Joshua asked, keeping a wary eye on the formidable minotaur.

Joshua knew from his readings that minotaurs were prone to sudden outbursts of anger and were easily provoked.

The older man at the table turned and faced them with a friendly smile. "Name's Zeb, what can I do for you young 'uns?"

"Mr. Zeb, my friends and I are looking to book passage to North Haven. The man at the bar said that you and your ship are out of that city and would be returning soon. Would you be able to take on a few passengers? It is very important we get to North Haven."

Zeb rubbed his chin. "Depends, is it just you three?"

"No, sir, there are fifteen of us in all," Joshua replied.

"Fifteen! Hmm, that's gonna take up a lot of space, and we would have to purchase more provisions. I suppose we could make room, but it ain't gonna be comfortable, and it ain't gonna be cheap."

Joshua took out the small pouch of coins Aggie had put in the satchel, added it to the few that the caravan master had paid them for saving his cargo, and handed it to the old sailor.

"That is every coin we have, sir."

Zeb poured the coins out in his hand and frowned. "It ain't much. Barely gonna cover your food."

"Please, sir, we must get to North Haven," Maira begged. "We are all young and can work hard, scrubbing the decks or mending sails, whatever you need us to do."

Zeb thought a moment and groaned. "I've always been a sucker for a pretty young lass, and it ain't like I haven't hauled a bunch of kids north before. Becoming a regular habit these days. All right, but you'll all work."

"We will, sir. You have our word," Joshua swore.

"Pfft, don't need a boy's word when I can just have Toron here pitch any slackers overboard." All three students paled, and Toron's toothy grin did nothing to assuage their fears. "Why are you all so hot to get to North Haven anyway?"

"A sorcerer named Azerick told us to find our way to North Haven and to ask there about a place called the orphans' academy. Do you know of it?"

Zeb, Balor, and Toron all leaned forward with eager excitement.

"You've seen Azerick? Where, when?" Zeb asked.

"A few days ago in Rapture. Do you know him?"

"Know him? He owns this ship!" Zeb laughed. "He'd have my hide if I didn't get you kids to North Haven even if I had to toss half my cargo overboard to make room." Zeb pitched the pouch with its meager coins back to Joshua.

"What was he doing in that horrid place? Was he all right?" Balor asked.

Joshua and the others took a seat and explained everything they knew about what had happened to Azerick, from his capture to the destruction of the tower. In the morning, they were all aboard Zeb's ship and sailing north to their new home and future.

Aggie strode up the newly cobbled road toward the tower nestled against the dark grey backdrop of the Northern Range. She whistled a jaunty tune that would have made a sailor blush if she had sung the words. She abruptly cut the tune off and called into the woods.

"It's not polite to spy on folks, ya know. Come on out and greet me properly."

Wolf and Ghost slipped noiselessly through the brush and stepped out onto the road. "I can't believe you saw me. Nobody ever sees me!" Wolf complained with his wide smile plastered across his face.

"I didn't have to see you; I could smell you a mile away."

Wolf sniffed under an armpit and shrugged. "I'm Wolf and this is Ghost."

"I'm Agatha but my friends call me Aggie. Nice to meet you both. Do you live in the keep up there?"

Wolf gave her a scathing look. "Pfft, no way. I live in the woods and do what I want; at least until it gets really cold, then Ghost and I gift them with our company."

"I see, but you know what goes on up there, you know some of the people who live there?"

"Oh yeah, mostly a bunch of kids reading books or whacking each other with sticks. I know Azerick, who thinks he's in charge, and a few of the other old people. They're all right for the most part, even if they are boring. So where did you come from, North Haven? You look too old to have walked very far."

Aggie laughed at Wolf's refreshingly direct manner. "Oh, I get around rather well, even for an old broad. I suppose I will have to bestow my presence upon those in the tower for a spell as well. Maybe I can help loosen them up a bit."

Wolf slapped his knee and laughed. "I like you; you're funny for an old person. Maybe you can teach Azerick to have a sense of humor. He needs it. Have fun. It's about lunchtime, and I saw some rabbits yesterday that looked tasty!"

Aggie laughed along with Wolf and waved as the boy and his wolf disappeared back into the forest. The first thing she noticed as she neared the keep was that it looked more like an armed camp preparing for a siege than the school she had heard about. Men and boys manned the walls, wearing armor, and carrying swords and crossbows. The gates were firmly shut and looked less than inviting.

"Halt. Who are you and what is your purpose!" a large boy of perhaps fifteen called down from his place just above the gate.

Aggie looked up at the beardless youth with a scowl. "I'm an ogre and I have come to eat the children, you big lout! What do you think I want?"

The serious-looking young man turned red. "I don't know, looking at you I would say someone to pre-chew your food for you!"

He's big, but he is sharp, Aggie thought to herself. "I heard you were looking for teachers. I thought I would come and apply for a job."

"Gods, not arms trainer, I hope. Master Ewen is mean enough," the youth mumbled none too quietly, which got a grin out of Aggie.

The boy motioned to someone on the inside, and the postern gate opened to allow her entrance. She walked into the compound and looked around in wonder. The only building visible above the walls other than the keep was the church. She gawked at the blacksmiths, fletchers, carpenter shops, and what looked to be billets and other living quarters. Over half the structures were made of solid logs and timber, although all had slate or clay roofs.

The other thing that amazed her was the number of children she saw, which she was certain did not nearly represent the whole. She turned toward the sound of battle and saw at least sixty youths in three different groups going through battle drills and arms training. A bell rang and dozens of book-toting children came running out of several of the log buildings, which must have been classrooms, and ran into another.

The Black Tower had had at most twenty students from novice to adept, and only two or three of them were likely to graduate to full wizard. Aggie focused upon the children with her wizard sight as they scampered about the grounds. She identified at least three dozen children with respectable magical potential.

Aggie strode down the wide avenue leading to the keep. The cobbled street did not lead directly there; it doglegged twice to curve around a few stout stone buildings, and given the look of their recent construction, she seriously doubted that their placement had been accidental. She noticed that most of the stone buildings inside the expansive walls were built along this one wide avenue. Each had a flat roof and sported low crenellations from where archers could set up and wreak havoc on any enemy that got through the gates.

The obvious militancy of this *orphans' academy* gave her serious pause and concern for her children who were likely to arrive soon on the ship they had managed to get a berth on in Lesser Langdon's Crossing. She hoped she had not made the mistake of trading one subservient school for another.

She stepped into the portico of the keep and knocked loudly on the sturdy wood and iron door. After waiting perhaps a minute, the door swung in and a beautiful young woman holding an equally beautiful baby girl greeted her.

"Good day, madam, I am Colleen. How can I help you?" Colleen asked warmly.

"I heard you were looking for some teachers and hoped I might convince you to take me on. I know I'm not much to look at, but my mind is still sharp, and I'm sure I have a few good years left in me."

Colleen gave a kind, soft laugh and made room for the older woman to pass. "You will have to speak with my husband, Franklin, about that, but I am sure we would be glad to have you. We are so busy, especially since the twins came and I had to set aside my own teachings for a time."

Colleen led Aggie into the main hall and bade her sit on one of the padded sofa's that adorned the room. "So, what do you teach...? I'm sorry, I did not catch your name."

"Agatha, but most folks call me Aggie."

"What do you teach, Aggie?"

"Oh, I have become a good hand in just about everything over the years. I even have a little skill in the dabbling of magic."

"That would be wonderful! We are so short on magus instructors. Rusty will be thrilled to have you. I think I hear them coming down the stairs now. We are just breaking for lunch. You must join us," Colleen insisted.

Rusty and Allister came down the stairs and into the hall where Colleen and her guest were waiting for them. Colleen and Aggie stood up, the former about to introduce the latter, when Aggie spoke out.

"Hey there, sailor, care to buy a lady a drink?" Aggie called up to them.

Magus Allister's eyes went wide and he nearly fell down the stairs when he saw the woman standing below him, but he recovered his composure.

"Sorry, Colleen does not drink since she is still nursing, and I don't see anyone else around here that would qualify as a lady," Allister growled.

Aggie smiled at the insult. "I wasn't talking to you, you old windbag. I was talking to the handsome young hunk next to you that actually looks healthy enough to handle me."

Rusty's face burned as red as his hair at being dragged into the two older people's verbal sparring.

"By the gods, Aggie, it is you! I thought you were dead by now!" Allister exclaimed as he hurried down the stairs.

Aggie raised her hands above her head and shook her hips. "Far from it: tall, grey, and handsome."

"Uh, you two know each other?" Rusty asked as the old mage embraced the woman.

Allister turned toward Rusty and Colleen, keeping one arm wrapped around Aggie's trim waist.

"Aggie and I go way back," Allister replied with a broad smile.

"Don't tell them how far, Al, a girl has her pride," Aggie warned him with a soft elbow in his side.

"So, is she a wizard as well?" Colleen asked.

"One of the best; I taught her everything I know," Allister answered with a wink.

"And then we made out for the rest of the afternoon. He certainly had nothing to teach me there."

"Despite her low morals and crass personality, she is nearly equal to me when it comes to mage craft."

It was Aggie's turn to look at Allister with a scowl. "I seem to remember being the one that put you out after you set your robes on fire in class! I would have to have a stroke to be almost your equal, you old windbag."

"Were you two students at the Academy together?" Rusty asked.

"Hardly, I was his applied magic teacher when he almost burnt down the school trying to impress me," Aggie told them, this time setting Allister's ears glowing.

"So, other than humiliating me, what brings you here?" Allister asked.

Aggie became serious as she explained. "I have a number of my more decent children, the ones who were not hopelessly corrupted by those Black Tower fools, coming in on a ship, and I wanted to make sure they would be treated right this time. I couldn't do much for them at the tower, but I'll be damned if I'll watch it happen again! Finding this old windbag here makes me feel a little better about my decision. Seeing the place geared for war had me concerned."

"I will explain all that later," Allister said. "So, what happened? I take it you broke away from the Black Tower."

"More like the tower broke away from me—and everybody else for that matter." Allister gave her a quizzical look. "A polite young man came in and cleaned house before demolishing the entire thing. He told most of the students to get to North Haven and check in here. I suspect they will be here in a day or two on a ship I think I heard belonged to the young man who started this place."

"You saw Azerick? Was he all right? What happened?" everyone exclaimed at once.

"He created quite a stir, and some of the archmages got a hold of him, but he got free and let them know in no uncertain terms how he felt about that. He sent the whole tower crashing to the ground last I saw of him. I am sure he is alive, but is he all right is the real question, and that will only be answered in time."

"Why, what happened to him?" Rusty asked.

"I think that is best left to him to talk about in his own time, young man. I imagine he will be back here soon enough and will need your love and support to keep his spirit bright."

"He has had a difficult past. We understand he falls into episodes of gloom and bitterness at times if that is what you are speaking of," Allister told the wizard.

"I am sure he will be fine with friends like this. Someone said something about lunch. Do you have any salami and onions?"

"We need to find you a place to stay," Colleen said abruptly, not sure where to house the esteemed wizard.

Aggie waved the thought away. "Don't trouble yourself, sweetheart. I figured I would just shack up with this old goat again, if he thinks he can handle it."

Allister turned beet red and tried to sputter a reply but failed to form a coherent sentence. Everyone laughed at the archmage as they all made their way to the kitchens.

CHAPTER 17

A zerick watched the still pouting sand dragon sitting across from him on the other side of the small fire he had made from the dry, scrubby plants that often blew across the desert, driven along by the winds like a herd of antelope.

Sandy had not spoken to him since their disagreement earlier that day, preferring to trot alongside or just ahead of Azerick and Horse. The sorcerer was astounded at the little dragon's stamina. Despite her awkward gait, she never asked to stop and rest and never lagged behind Horse, even at a trot.

"Sandy, I have been thinking about what you said, about your instincts, and I think you may be right. It was unfair of me to judge you so harshly knowing that you are descended of the mightiest predators in the land," Azerick conceded. "However, you must overcome those instincts at times for the sake of safety and discretion."

Sandy looked at Azerick through the bright orange flames. "Does that mean you apologize?"

"Yes," Azerick replied after a short pause.

"Does that mean I can have a sugar cube?"

"I suppose."

Sandy drew herself up haughtily. "Very well, even though we sand dragons are the fiercest of our kind and implacable enemies, Momma always said that we must be forgiving when someone realizes the errors of his ways and confesses his fault. You may give me a sugar cube now as a token of reparation."

Azerick was unable to contain his mirth at the little dragon's hauteur. Great bellows of laughter escaped unimpeded from deep within his belly as he rolled over onto his side holding his stomach.

"Why are you laughing? I am quite serious!" Sandy insisted indignantly. "This is a standard gift for admission of guilt amongst my kind, and you are mocking it! If you do not stop laughing at me, it is going to cost you two sugar cubes, and the price of forgiveness goes up from there!"

Sandy's outrage only caused Azerick to laugh even harder. Sandy stood up and swung her heavy tail into the sand in pique, sending a large spray of sand to wash over the prone sorcerer, nearly extinguishing their fire.

Azerick finally got his laughter somewhat under control and pulled out a pair of sugar cubes. He sidled around the dying fire, still chuckling, and gave them to the irritated dragon. Azerick fell asleep sniggering to himself under Sandy's green-eyed glare.

It took several days of travel before they left the dry desert behind and began approaching Southport from the southeast. The pair avoided roads and traffic as much as possible, but the farther north they traveled, the more difficult it became for them to avoid the more heavily traveled roads.

By the time they were within two days' ride of Southport, traveling by anything other than the roads was nearly impossible. The land and hills were too thickly wooded and overgrown to try to ride through without tripling their travel time on their way to North Haven.

Fortunately, Sandy found that she was able to burrow into the denser dirt of the northern terrain much as she did the sands she was more accustomed to, albeit with more difficulty. Instead of being able to dive below the earth almost as if it were water as she could do in sand, it took several seconds for her to submerge herself beneath the damp soil.

"Ugh, what is this horrible substance?" Sandy complained bitterly the first time she had to hide from an approaching traveler.

"It is called dirt, Sandy."

"Dirt. The name is as disgusting as its substance."

Azerick found that Sandy's amazing burrowing ability lay far beyond just her sharp claws and muscular body. When asked, Sandy replied that she simply made the dirt or sand move out of the way as she propelled herself along with her powerful legs and hard talons. She complained that the dirt was more stubborn and refused to move as quickly as the sand did, and she was sure it was simply being rude to her.

The pair met a large contingent of the king's soldiers a little over a day from Southport. The military force was not moving swiftly, and Sandy had plenty of time to hide herself.

Azerick and Horse stood patiently off the road as the approaching force drew near. He hoped that they would continue past without bothering him, but three men brought their warhorses to a trot and rode up next to him, dashing such hopes.

"Good day to you, traveler," one of the men greeted him when they drew near.

Azerick marked him as an officer by his red cape and plumed helmet.

"I am Captain Cooper, an officer under King Jarvin's standard."

Azerick inclined his head in greeting. "Good day to you, Captain. You and your men are a little far from home, are you not?"

The captain furrowed his brow, obviously unhappy with their assignment. "Aye, we have been patrolling the roads around Argoth, but Duchess Paullina has enough men-at-arms to deal with most any incursion, being so close to the border of Sumara. Word reached me that there were still sporadic raids happening along this route, so I took my men this way to secure the roads. Apparently, something has happened to cause Duke Ulric's vigilance to lapse," Captain Cooper intoned almost under his breath. "Have you perchance seen or heard anything during your travels? Seen any large groups of men or raided towns or farms?"

"Sorry, Captain, I rode from out of the desert and avoided the roads much for that very reason. The only people I have seen are a few travelers and merchant trains. A few of them spoke of depredations but nowhere near the scale of earlier this year."

Strike him down and destroy his men. He suspects you of something, the demon urged from deep within his mind. *They want to chain you, make you a prisoner once more. They are weak. Destroy them!*

Shut up, demon, and get back in your cage, Azerick replied, his voice thick with scorn. He mentally shoved the demon lord further into the recesses of his mind.

Captain Cooper sighed. "If I could just find where they are hiding and get within striking range! I haven't enough cavalry for a decisive victory, and I cannot catch them dragging along my infantry. Well, I'll catch them eventually. Good travels to you, sir."

"Good hunting to you, Captain."

Azerick stood by the side of the road until the army was well past before calling for Sandy to come out of hiding. Twenty feet from the roadside, a mound of earth rose up like a giant, breaching molehill. Sandy pulled herself out of the ground and shook vigorously, sending a spray of dirt and globs of mud in every direction.

"This stupid dirt is ruining my scales. Sand has the decency to stay on the ground where it belongs and even helps shine my scales. This stuff is like a parasite!"

"You will clean up soon enough. It looks like rain before the day is out," Azerick told her as she rolled in the tall grass in an effort to remove the contaminant.

The sorcerer was correct; it started raining less than two hours later, and even though it did wash away the dirt, Sandy simply found another thing to complain about. It was late winter bordering on spring, and the rain was still cold and bitter.

Azerick had hoped to enter Southport for at least a few hours to see if he could learn anything about what was transpiring in the land, but he found the gates of the great city locked to nearly all non-residents. A long line of angry merchants, caravans, and travelers shouted at the guards and demanded entrance so they could sell and trade their wares and return home before the summer runs, but their shouts and pleadings were met with stony stares and threats by the city guard.

Many of the merchants swore to take their goods to North Haven even though it meant risking late snows and being stranded in the northern city instead of returning whence they came. Better to sell their goods in North Haven and spend an extra couple of weeks there than return home with wagonloads of useless goods and no coin.

Azerick and Sandy kept a brisk pace as they rode toward home. Although she never complained of fatigue, her nonstop griping about the cold and dampness of the north was beginning to grate on the sorcerer's nerves.

A few days out of North Haven, Azerick finally relented to renting a room at the same small town that he had stayed in with Lady Miranda and her remaining entourage after the bandit attack. It had an outside stairway, so Azerick was able to sneak Sandy into the room after dark where they enjoyed a fresh meal and a blazing fire.

Sandy lay so close to the fireplace that Azerick was afraid it might burn her, but it apparently had no ill effect on her as she rested contentedly on a pile of blankets.

They had to leave early the next morning before the townsfolk began stirring so no one would see the small dragon and make a fuss, but Azerick was becoming less concerned with discovery the closer they got to home.

An unusually late snow began falling later that afternoon. Sandy was initially curious and stared at the gently descending flakes in wonder, licking them off her snout as they settled onto her scales. She was not unfamiliar with the cold. Deserts got extremely frigid in the winter months, but the air was so dry that it almost never snowed. The snow soon lost its initial appeal and simply gave her another reason to complain.

Sandy's griping paled in comparison to the demon's near-constant whisperings, urgings, and nagging. Every traveler they passed, the demon urged Azerick to kill. Klaraxis would say that he was a spy or another assassin sent to kill him. He told Azerick that he could see into the stranger's heart and knew the evil within, and that the man or woman would kill others if Azerick did not stop him.

Once, the demon caught Azerick inattentive, and projected an image of the Rook's face onto a passing traveler. He then gently prodded Azerick into action. The sorcerer bit his spell off mid casting, realizing what was happening just a split second before he incinerated an innocent man.

Azerick mentally lashed the demon, used his soul name to inflict pain, and banished him to the point of almost nonexistence. Even then, Klaraxis's laughter echoed in his mind. Azerick knew he could not rid himself of the demon and had serious doubts whether anyone else could either. The demon was part of him now, their souls deeply intertwined.

Azerick and Sandy crested the hill and gazed down upon the spectacular view of North Haven, the valley, and the sea far in the distance. Sandy gasped at the sight that spread out before them for miles in every direction. Even Azerick could not help but smile in appreciation of the view.

As the late morning ground inexorably into early afternoon, Azerick and Sandy walked at a leisurely pace along the newly cobbled road that led to the keep despite Azerick's anxiousness to be home again. Home; even now it felt so strange to feel so comfortable here.

Wolf's shrill call broke the tranquility of the moment. "Azerick, you're back! What is that?" Wolf asked as he and Ghost broke out of the nearby wood line.

"This is Sandy. She is a sand dragon."

"Wow, a dragon! Does it talk?"

Sandy took an exaggerated sniff at Wolf. "Does it bathe?"

Wolf held his belly and doubled over in laughter. "I like her. She reminds me of Ellyssa."

"I really must meet this human girl that everyone finds so beautiful," Sandy responded.

As they drew nearer the keep, Azerick was astounded at the changes wrought upon his school while he had been gone. The towering church with its magnificent stained glass drew his eye. The peaks of other wooden buildings poked up over the surrounding walls as well. What their purpose was, Azerick could only assume. More living quarters, if he were to guess.

The gates were open to allow the season's workers to come and go unimpeded, but they were under the watchful eye of several young men and a few older ones manning the walls. To the east, Azerick spied worked parcels of land just waiting for the snows to stop so they could be planted, and a couple of small log homes, their chimneys sending white plumes of wood smoke into the crisp air.

Several calls of greeting rang out as Azerick, Sandy, Wolf, and Ghost entered the gates. The students who were not in school rushed to see him, especially when word got around about what appeared to be a small dragon accompanying him.

Sensing Sandy's unease, Azerick slid off Horse's saddle and laid a reassuring hand on her back as they walked amongst the astonished crowd. Ellyssa, Roger, and a few of their closest friends broke through the throng of people. Ellyssa surprised Azerick by rushing forward and wrapping her arms tightly around his waist.

"Azerick, is that a dragon?" his apprentice asked excitedly.

He guessed Ellyssa was technically his former apprentice since her magical talent likely exceeded his ability to teach her much within the bounds of her own type of spellcasting.

"Her name is Sandy, and she is a sand dragon. She will be staying with us for a while."

Ellyssa smiled and moved closer to the young dragon. "Hi, Sandy, I'm Ellyssa."

"Hello, Ellyssa, nice to meet you," Sandy responded politely, then looked over at Azerick. "I suppose she is cute for a human, but she lacks the brilliancy of my scales to adequately describe the two of us as being anything alike. It is like comparing a lovely candle to the glory of the sun."

Azerick only smiled and shook his head at Ellyssa's questioning look. Rusty, Allister, and Colleen came out of their classrooms to greet him, releasing their students for the rest of the day. Azerick avoided their many questions until he could get safely inside his tower.

"Everybody, this is Sandy. She is a young sand dragon who recently lost her mother and will be staying with us."

As Azerick introduced everyone, Sandy committed all of their names to her formidable memory. Each person welcomed her warmly to her new home. Aggie strode through the crowd and stroked the dragon's neck.

"You poor dear. What is your name?" she asked.

"Sandy," she replied, wondering if the older woman was forgetful or something.

Aggie smiled and her eyes twinkled with mirth. "Sandy is hardly a proper name for such a beautiful creature as you, dear. What is your real name?"

Sandy hissed out the name her mother had bestowed upon her at her hatching.

"Now that is a lovely name, and quite apt, I would say. You do have the most brilliant scales."

"You speak dragon?" Azerick asked.

"Oh, I have picked up quite a few odd bits of knowledge in my wanderings."

"The woman is so old she's probably half dragon herself," Allister teased with a mirthful snort.

Aggie turned toward the old mage and feigned crossness. "I would rather be half a dragon than a complete ass like you, you old goat!" Aggie hiked up her skirts to her thigh. "Look at those gams. I have the legs of a woman half my apparent age."

"Half her age but twice as hairy!" Allister guffawed.

His beard coiled around his throat like a python and choked off his laughter. Allister clawed at his animated whiskers, trying to break their vice-like grip.

"Blast you, woman. Can't you take a little joke?" the magus shouted as he untangled his beard.

"Of course I can. I've been putting up with one since I got here, and quite frankly that joke was old when the elves were young."

"It is nice to see that you made it, revered grandmother, though you look considerably different than when we first met," Azerick said with a small bow.

"Oh, still the polite one, aren't you? It's just Aggie to my friends and that old, used-up scarecrow who calls himself a wizard."

Azerick looked between the two senior wizards. "I take it you two know each other."

Aggie slipped an arm through Allister's. He tried to glare at her but could not keep the smile from creeping onto his wizened face. "Oh yes, we go way back."

"Did Joshua and the others make it all right?"

Rusty answered Azerick's question. "Yes, he and several others arrived just yesterday. Three of them are quite talented and are willing to teach a class for the younger or less skilled students. Allister and Aggie will work with them to improve their skills."

"That is very good to hear." Azerick turned to Ellyssa. "Why don't you and your friends take Sandy to get something to eat and then maybe get to know each other better up in your room?"

"Okay, come on, Sandy, let's go raid the kitchen."

"I heard that!" Wolf crowed, then urged everyone through the doors of the dining hall.

When all of the youngsters were gone, Azerick turned back toward Aggie. "I wish I had a library worthy to replace the one you had at the Black Tower."

"Oh, that reminds me! In all the hubbub I completely forgot about my library. Let me see what I can set up."

Everyone hurried after the wizard as she bounded youthfully up the stairs to the landing where the library was located. She stepped into the room and stopped.

"You call this a library? I have more books stacked next to my privy than this."

"Yes, we have been meaning to expand it, but with the construction and getting the classes together, none of us found the time to seek out more and make it a proper library," Azerick explained as they all looked at the single bookcase that was only about three-quarters full.

"Of course, each of the students has their own textbooks and materials," Rusty added.

"Well this just won't do at all," Aggie muttered, then began an incantation.

Several square objects appeared, hovering a few feet over the floor of the library, and began unfolding themselves. When the two-dimensional items finished unfolding, they looked like masterfully created paintings of bookshelves full of thick tomes and books. Another gesture placed them where Aggie wanted them, where they took on depth and settled onto the floor. Fully stocked bookshelves now lined every inch of available wall space with several others standing in the open areas of the library.

"Wow," was all Azerick was able to utter at the impressive display.

"Wow is right," Rusty concurred.

Allister hugged Aggie with one arm around her shoulder. "You are an amazing woman."

"Of course I am. I've been telling you that for…quite a while. It's about time you realized it."

"Oh, I have known since I first saw you," Allister told her. "I just did not voice it for fear of feeding your already overgrown ego."

"Pfft, such a pittance could hardly make an impression on that beast."

"Cripes, Azerick," Rusty exclaimed, "every time you leave, you bring back something crazy. First, it was a minotaur, then hundreds of orphans, now a dragon, and a magus with an entire library in her pocket. What else have you dragged back with you?"

"You do not want to know," Azerick responded with all seriousness.

Aw, come on. What's the matter, you don't want to introduce me to your friends?

Shut up, demon. I can smell your breath even in my head.

Laughter filled Azerick's thoughts until he pushed them deeper down.

After stripping Rusty and Allister of every bit of information about what had happened while he had been away, Azerick spent the next several days simply resting, relaxing, and readjusting to the semi-chaotic life of being back at his school.

Sandy soon made friends with everyone in the keep. Even the territorial cooks enjoyed it when she popped her head into the kitchen looking for a snack to feed her rapidly growing body.

It was late in the evening a few days after he had returned when strange sounds coming from the floor above his own caught his attention. Closing the book he was studying, Azerick crept up the stairs to investigate.

The noises were coming from Ellyssa's room, and were accompanied by the sounds of children's laughter. Azerick knew that anytime that many kids were laughing, there was almost certainly some sort of mischief in the making. He cracked open the door and poked his head into the room.

"What is going on in here? What were those noises?"

Ellyssa, Roger, Sandy, and a few other children were sitting in a large circle on the floor, dressed in their nightclothes and gave him guilty stares until Ellyssa finally confessed.

"We were having a burping contest," Ellyssa answered with an impish grin.

"A burping contest," Azerick repeated flatly.

"Not me, Azerick," Sandy interjected. "I'm a lady, and Momma said that ladies don't—oh, hold on."

Sandy stretched out her neck and tail until they were parallel with the floor and let out a ten-second belch that rattled the shutters and made the door handle in Azerick's hand vibrate.

"Whoa! Did you hear that?" Sandy asked with a look of pride. "What?" she demanded as she glared at Azerick, daring him to reproach her.

Azerick shook his head and returned to his room, gales of laughter following him all the way back down the stairs.

As the evening grew late, Azerick set aside his book and dimmed the luminous glass globe that provided the light for his room. The howling winds of an approaching storm soon lulled him into sleep.

"Azerick? Psst, Azerick?"

The sorcerer's eyelids fluttered open and he looked into the large green eyes set in Sandy's wedge-shaped head.

"Are you awake?" she whispered.

"What is it, Sandy?"

"There is a loud storm outside."

Azerick turned his attention to the shuttered window, and heard the high winds and the loud peal of thunder.

"I thought you might be scared, so I came down here to see if you needed my company."

"No, I'm fine, Sandy."

"Oh, okay then."

Azerick saw the crestfallen look in the dragon's eyes and understood what she was really asking. Sandy was frightened, but her draconic pride would never allow her to voice it. Another peal of thunder rattled the shutters.

"On second thought, this is a bad one. Would you mind staying here with me tonight?"

Sandy's head perked up but she resumed a nonchalant pose. "I suppose I could. Ellyssa is sound asleep and snoring, so she should be fine on her own."

Azerick's bed groaned in protest as the not-so-little dragon climbed up and lay at the foot. Fortunately, Azerick's bed was a large affair, constructed for him by a team of carpenters last year, and sported a huge, overstuffed mattress. He could tell that Sandy had already grown some since he had first found her. She was at least a foot longer and several inches taller: the size of a very large dog but significantly heavier.

Sandy curled up at the end of the bed and tucked her snout under her tail. Azerick saw that she was shivering, but whether from cold or fright he did not know, so he took an extra quilt and threw it over the top of her body. Times like these reminded him that she really was just a small child of her species, despite her advanced learning and impressive mind. It seemed the world around him was full of orphans, but at least they all had family.

Zeb, Toron, and Balor returned from Sumara with more than just several young mages. They brought with them numerous soft, warm white furs, one big enough to cover even the largest of beds. Zeb presented Colleen with a long coat made of smaller, suppler white furs that she absolutely loved.

"I am surprised to see that you brought so many of the furs back for us this time. Not that I am complaining, but I thought they were your big moneymakers," Azerick said to Zeb as they all sat around the dining table drinking tea and coffee.

"I wouldn'ta had nearly so many, but Southport had her port closed to all incoming ships, and I wasn't about to try and make my own overland caravan to get them to Brelland or Brightridge, what with all the stories of bandits prowling the roads."

"I saw that Southport had its gates closed to land traffic, but the port as well? That seems odd to me," Azerick replied.

"Aye, what's even stranger was we got close enough to see several large ships at anchor in the port before we were chased off by threat of attack. They were big affairs and heavily armed as if they were expecting an attack."

"Or preparing to launch an attack of their own," Toron put in.

Rusty asked, "Who would Southport want to attack?"

The minotaur shook his huge horned head. "I would not know, but if a nation or group is going to launch an assault, the last thing you want is for anyone to get away and warn the target."

"That would explain the restricted gates and closed port," Azerick replied.

"I know my dad said that Ulric has had his sights on the crown for a long time," Rusty said.

Allister scoffed. "You can't reach Brelland by ship."

Azerick made up his mind. "We can conjecture all day long about Ulric's intentions, but none of us knows what he is planning. Regardless, my instincts are telling me he is up to something. I want the guard doubled after dark and manned by grown men and older students. You can use no more than two of the younger ones to act as runners. They are not to engage in combat. I know it is cold and miserable, so let us put out plenty of braziers and fuel and erect some overhead covers."

"Did you make any connection between Ulric, the assassin, and Dundalor's armor during your recent escapades?" Allister asked.

Azerick shook his head. "No, Baneford said that a wizard from the Black Tower had him searching for the armor. The assassin who I believe murdered my father, and tried to kill me as well, was also connected to that same scorpion's nest, but I could find nothing to indicate Ulric had any dealings with them. Travis's father was the one who hired the Rook to kill me because of his son's death; it had nothing to do with the armor. It was purely personal."

Azerick looked pointedly at Aggie. "Speaking of the Black Tower, how is it that you came to be part of that less than pleasant bunch?"

Allister's face darkened at Azerick's question, and he too looked hard at Aggie. "Indeed, in my excitement of seeing you again, I completely forgot about that bit and how you just up and disappeared from the Academy one day."

The old magess let out a long sigh before answering. "It came to the senior council that several wizards were building a new tower and re-establishing their black order. The council thought it would be best if they had someone on the inside to keep an eye on them. We decided that I would be their mole. I reported directly to the headmaster, Arkam back in those days, and then to Dondrian when he ascended the position. For a long time, there was little to report as they seemed to keep mostly to themselves and did not appear to be trying to regain power in the kingdom. That started to change about ten years ago. I told Dondrian that it looked like the Tower was giving aid to a usurper, but it was seemingly indirect. Then I got wind of them actively aiding in the recovery of Dundalor's armor. I continued to inform Dondrian of this, but he never acted on it as far as I could tell."

"Dondrian was working with the Tower and betraying the king," Azerick informed the senior mage.

Aggie sighed and her face fell. "I suspected as much, but I had little to go on. I figured the best thing I could do was stay put and act when I thought I could make a difference. I began studying the fate lines and got a hint of your coming, Azerick, though I could not divine what exactly it meant."

Azerick looked at the old woman. "What do you mean you saw my coming?"

Allister interrupted and explained. "You remember what I told you about the few wizards who are foolish or crazy enough to delve into temporal space manipulation? Aggie is one of those, as well as transdimensional scrying and traveling. Some wizards can catch a glimpse of the future that way."

"You can see the future?" Azerick exclaimed as the possibilities of such an ability raced through his head.

"Don't be silly, boy. Not even the gods can see what has not yet happened. What I saw was, for lack of a better term, your fate strand."

"Fate strand?"

Aggie shrugged. "Some people might call it destiny, but that's a little too strong a word. You see, when certain events of significant importance collide, those people who will play a major part in it are said to get special attention from the fates or the gods. Their thread of life, spirit, or whatever you want to call it, is more pronounced— profound even. It allows someone with the right skill and a lot of luck to catch a glimpse of it. During one of my studies, I caught a glimpse of yours."

"Hey, Rusty, you hear that? I'm profound," Azerick said with a grin.

"I know you're a profound pain in the arse of most everyone you meet."

Azerick smiled and turned back to Aggie. "So, you can see what will happen to me and what I will do? You can tell my future?"

"No. I was able to glimpse the direction it was going, but like anything with free will, you can turn and change direction at any time, so seeing your fate strand cannot be used to see yours or anyone else's future."

She lies! the demon raged. *She came here to kill you. She is a Black Tower wizard, and you killed her friends and destroyed her home and she wants revenge. Strike her down before she does the same to you! She is too powerful to let live.*

You know nothing, demon, so shut up.

I smell blood in the air, lots of it, and it smells so sweet! You know Ulric is a threat. Let us go end it before it comes to you and yours.

Azerick ignored the demon while the others talked about preparing for any surprises and the general running of the school. Rusty repeated his misgivings about ignoring magical theory and history in favor of applied magic, and Azerick repeated his earlier arguments and supported them further with the strange goings on in Southport.

If there was a threat coming, Azerick vowed to be ready for it. No one would threaten his home or his friends again. Deep in the recesses of the sorcerer's mind, Klaraxis chuckled.

CHAPTER 18

Wolf stared deep into the forest. "You feel it too, don't you, boy? Someone is in our woods that don't belong. I thought it was just my nerves from being cooped up too long, but it's not, is it?"

Ghost glanced up at his half-elf friend with his golden eyes, then stared south once more.

"I didn't think so. Let's go see what it is."

The snow was still deep even beneath the thick boughs of the evergreen trees as they walked south in search of whatever it was that disturbed the spirit of his forest. Wolf wore a pair of snowshoes he had made from deer sinew and soft pine branches earlier in the season. He did manage to take down a winter hare and a pair of grouse with his bow, for which he was grateful. He knew he would not find whomever or whatever he was looking for before nightfall.

Wolf found a hollow under a young evergreen and shoveled out the remaining snow until he managed to reach dirt and old pine needles, and cleared a large enough space for the two of them. He then kindled a small fire inside the hollow and roasted the two birds and the rabbit. Wolf dropped a fist-sized chunk of coal from his fire kit onto the fire, which would stay smoldering and giving off heat for hours, and soon fell asleep.

He found himself loping through the snow-covered woods. Because the pristine white snow covered nearly everything, it took several minutes before he realized that he was colorblind. Wolf saw that where the snow had fallen from some of the tree branches, the needle-covered limbs were a dark grey, not green.

His lack of color vision was far from a handicap. Whatever happened to him, he could see more shades of grey than he thought were possible. He could also hear with amazing acuity, and the scents that came to his nose were so strong and clearly definable that it was almost like a second type of vision.

His view was also oriented lower to the ground than he was accustomed to. He looked down and saw his broad black chest and forefeet. He was not Wolf but Ghost. The feeling was strange but exhilarating. Wolf-Ghost caught the scent of a deer and raced off in the direction from which it came. He could tell just by the smell that there was a buck and at least two doe not far from where he was standing.

His delicate nose picked up the scent of fear that roiled off the prey animals as their own acute hearing detected the sound of his careless charge. Wolf-Ghost caught a flash of movement ahead and saw the broad white rumps of the deer spring away into the woods. Wolf-Ghost laughed aloud, but it sounded more like a yip, and was about to give chase when another scent intruded onto his senses — smoke, men, and horses, and not far away.

He resisted his chase instinct and moved toward the source of the smell, but with much more caution than he had the deer. The scent of a lone human separated itself from the others. It was stronger, closer. Wolf-Ghost crept nearer, skirting around the base of the trees so his black coat would not stand out so much and would appear as just another shadow.

He heard the human's breathing before he saw him. He was dressed in white and grey clothing and furs, blending in with the surroundings quite well. Wolf-Ghost knew that he would have to get past this human if he were going to be able to see who else was in his woods without his permission. Though technically outside the area he frequently marked as his own, in both his forms, he still considered these woods his, and he did not tolerate interlopers — especially ones that stank of foul intent as these did.

The human was vigilant, but he did not belong here as Wolf-Ghost did. He was out of his element, and it was going to cost him dearly. Wolf-Ghost was able to creep to within a few paces of the man before the human turned and saw the crouched black form against the base of a nearby tree.

The human tried to pull one of the long steel claw-fangs hanging from his side, but Wolf-Ghost was too fast. Before the human could shout a warning to the rest of his pack, Wolf-Ghost's powerful jaws pierced the soft flesh of the man's throat and crushed his windpipe, riding the falling body to the ground.

The human was dead before his head hit the snow. Bright red blood, dark grey to his wolf eyes, ruined the pristine snow all around the body. Wolf-Ghost's black coat did not show the blood that covered his jaws and chest, but he could taste it. It was not the pleasant taste of his usual prey food, but it was not altogether vile.

He followed the human's tracks back toward the rest of his pack, more by smell than by the sight of the prints, but he could use those too. Even when he was just Ghost, he knew what tracks looked like and could decipher their meaning. Within minutes, he saw the dying fires of the humans and the dens the humans made of hides that came from plants. *Canvas*, the Wolf part of Wolf-Ghost said in his bilateral mind.

The pack was huge, bigger than any he had seen outside of a human city. The count was beyond his ability to reason, but he knew that this was the source of his troubles. He had to warn the rest of his pack. Wolf-Ghost decided it was best to get back to his den, but he picked up the scent of another lone human not far from the first one he killed.

Well, I have time for one more, he thought, then set out to leave another example of how he dealt with intruders in *his* forest.

Wolf awoke from the strange but wonderful dream with a yawn and a stretch. He smacked his lips at the coppery taste filling his mouth like the shadow of a memory. He plucked a pinch of young pine needles from the tree and chewed them, taking care of the strange morning taste. He squinted at the darkness and felt around for Ghost, but the wolf was not there.

Probably went out to expand his territory again. Not a bad idea, come to think of it.

He laid his hand onto the silver wolf's head pommel of his shortsword and was surprised to find that it was warm to the touch.

It was probably under Ghost and he just left.

Wolf gave his chest and arms a quick scratch then crawled out from under the thick boughs of the young tree. Rough hands grabbed him and lifted him to his feet. Wolf cast a startled glance behind him and looked into the fur-hooded face of the man holding his arms tightly to his sides.

"What do we have here?" a second man with a drawn sword asked. "You ain't no wolf!"

"I am so!"

"Ya look more like a wood rat than the wolf we tracked back here. What do ya know about that, boy?"

Wolf dropped to his knees without warning, slipping from the man's grip, rolled to the side, and drew his small sword.

"I know you orc lovers better leave me alone," Wolf warned, brandishing the masterfully crafted shortsword with much more bravado than skill.

Both men grinned disdainfully at the half-elf's bluster. "Now ain't that a pretty little thing. Am I supposed to be scared of a little boy with a pretty little knife?"

"I would be more afraid of Ghost if I were you."

"I'm a grown man, boy. Ghosts don't scare me none no more."

"Well, I guess that will be the last mistake you ever make then."

Before the man could reply, a black blur leapt out of the trees, pinning his sword arm uselessly against his chest as he fell with Ghost at his throat. Wolf lunged forward and slashed at the other man before he could even get his blade halfway clear of its sheath. The wolf-headed sword sliced through the thick fur coat and steel-linked armor as if it were made of paper. Blood blossomed in a thick line across the man's midsection as he dropped to his knees then fell face down into the snow.

"I think it's time to go, Ghost."

Wolf gathered his bow and quiver, and strapped on his snowshoes, never noticing the dark, dried blood covering Ghost's chest. He looked at the bodies of the two men, unaffected by the sight of their blood.

Definitely not from around here; too tan and they stink.

Wolf and Ghost began the long trek through the snow back the way they came. He knew all he needed to know and was in a hurry to get back and tell Azerick. Whatever these men were doing, it was not going to be good for the school or North Haven.

It took most of the day for him to reach the keep late that afternoon, and he sought out Azerick and the others. He was doubly lucky in that it was almost time for the evening meal. That way they would all be together, and he could fill his hungry belly.

Wolf and Ghost strode into the dining hall and took a seat without preamble. Wolf began helping himself to everything within reach, fixing a second plate for Ghost and setting it on the floor. He did not like that Ghost was required to eat on the floor like an animal, but Allister had got mad last time he set him a place at the table with the rest of them.

Humans. Go figure, he thought.

"It is nice to see you actually sitting at the table and not darting out from under it to steal a ham or swinging down from the rafters," Azerick said from the head of the table.

Wolf just shrugged and shoveled food into his mouth with inexpert use of the metal utensils, yet another reason he rarely ate at the table with the others.

"There are people in my woods—men," Wolf finally said once he slowed down enough to draw breath.

"I imagine there are from time to time. Does this surprise you for some reason?" Azerick asked.

Wolf shook his head as he bolted down a large piece of roast. "There are a lot of men. I killed some, one, and Ghost killed three—although I may have killed three and him one, not sure. Maybe we should split the first two."

All conversation stopped and every eye turned to look at the young man still eating, seemingly unperturbed by what he had just said.

"You don't know if you killed one or three?"

"I don't know, maybe it was a dream. I'm not sure."

Azerick spoke with measured slowness. "Who did you kill, Wolf?"

"Some men, soldiers from the looks of them. Guards, maybe scouts. Definitely scouts, I think. They had a really big camp with lots of tents and horses." Wolf glanced out of the corner of his eye toward the ceiling. "I think there were anyway, but that may have been a dream too, but I don't think so; not *just* a dream anyway."

Aggie asked, "Wolf, what do you mean by you think it was a dream, and what did you see?"

Wolf shook his head as he swallowed nearly half a potato, barely chewing it. "I went to sleep, I think, and then I was Ghost. I chased some deer then I smelled humans. I killed a guard and saw a huge camp with lots of tents and horses. When I woke up, two men grabbed me. Ghost killed one and I killed the other with my sword. By the way, have you found my present yet for those feathers?"

"No, Wolf, I have yet to find something appropriate," Azerick replied in exasperation.

Aggie looked at Ghost who was peering over the top of the table as if he were following the conversation. He gave a deep yawn, his tongue jutting out and curling, and punctuated it with a squeak.

"What do you make of that, Aggie?" Allister asked his lady friend.

"I think we had best heed the young man's warning. I won't pretend to fully understand what he is talking about in regards to the dreams, but I think he has seen enough that we would be foolish not to be ready and quickly."

Azerick nodded at her suggestion. "I agree. Coupled with the news Zeb brought, and what I saw with my own eyes, I think we need to be extra vigilant and warn North Haven as well. Wolf, how far away were they, and how many do you think there were?"

"It took me the entire day to get back, so figure two, maybe three days for them. I'm not sure how many men. There were tents for as far as I could see, and I could see pretty far with Ghost's eyes. At least as many humans as I have ever seen in one place before and several hundred horses."

"Bags, hundreds of horses and likely not even their entire force," Allister muttered.

Jansen spoke up, breaking his usual silence. "A heavy cavalry-equipped army you can figure perhaps five footmen and one archer per cavalryman, a standard army—perhaps two to three times the ratio of men afoot to horses."

Alex concurred with the bodyguard's estimate with what he had learned in his years at the Martial Academy.

Rusty released a distressed sigh. "Let's hope it's a cavalry-oriented army then."

Aggie spoke up. "I'll see if I can get a better look at what Wolf saw.

The senior wizard grabbed a shallow silver dish from beneath the bowl of potatoes, filled the bottom inch of it with water, and recited a spell. She gazed into the reflected image for several long minutes before finding what she was looking for.

"Oh dear," she mumbled. "It would appear our wild young friend is quite correct. There are several thousand men in a large encampment just days to the south."

"I think I had best go see the duchess and warn her," Azerick said as he stood up.

"And maybe Lady Miranda?" Colleen asked, then sipped at her goblet of red wine.

"I had best go with you, lad, just so you don't ruffle any feathers while you deliver your warning," Allister said, then rose with him.

Azerick had Peck bring Horse and a well-tempered mare around, and they went on their way. Azerick summoned his staff to his hand even though he could have left it at the keep and called it in an instant. He liked the feel of it in his grip and the impression the powerful weapon made.

Was it always that way, or was this a new feeling? He usually just left it behind, not bothering to encumber his hands needlessly. The sorcerer ran his hand over the smooth burgundy wood, tracing the patterns of the many runes carved in its surface and felt the thrumming power just waiting to be unleashed upon a deserving foe.

Stop it, you demonic cesspool. I know what you are doing, Azerick ordered his unwelcome parasite.

And I know what you will be doing, and I like it! I can smell the blood in the air. Death is already being carried on the winds of fate, and it brings the sweet smell of wanton destruction and brutality! Finally, after weeks of this pointless existence, we can get back to doing what we do best—killing those who stand against us!

I thought maybe I would just sit this one out, stay in the rear and provide defensive support and let Allister, Aggie, and Rusty handle all the unpleasant stuff.

No, you cannot deny me this, nor can you deny yourself! I know you; you could not just stand by idly while others threaten those you love.

It was amazing how the demon could make the word love sound so disgusting. He was right though, he could never just stand aside even if he knew that his friends could handle it themselves. Azerick could hear the demon's gleeful laughter in his head and could almost picture him rubbing his palms together like a child waiting to open his winterfest gift.

The sun was down and the gates were closed by the time they reached North Haven proper. A guardsman called down a challenge from atop the gates.

"Ho, who goes there?"

"Magus Azerick and Archmage Allister. We have urgent news for the duchess."

"Oh, good evening to you, Magus, Archmage. Come 'round to the sally port and we'll let you in."

Azerick could already hear the large crossbar being raised from the smaller gate a few yards ahead. The two mages walked their mounts through the single gate into the open area beyond. Another guard rode up on a horse as two men lowered the stout crossbar back into its support brackets.

"Good evening, gentlemen. I will escort you to the castle. I am — holy halberds in heaven, it's you!" the guardsman shouted.

"Captain Cruthers?" Azerick asked, recognizing the former Watch captain of Sandusk. "What are you doing here?"

The man ran a hand over his face and groaned. "It's Lieutenant Cruthers now. I took your advice and moved north with my wife where it is nice and quiet and safe like you suggested. It's not going to be quiet for long, is it?"

"I don't think so," Azerick admitted.

"I should have known better, I really should have. I should have stayed in Sandusk where I only had to worry about killer dust storms, nomadic raiders, murderers, and thieves. It was so much safer. Follow me, please. Try not to kill anyone on the way to the castle," John said in resignation.

"You sure have a way of making friends wherever you go," Allister whispered with a grin.

Guards took hold of their mounts at the castle gates as they dismounted. Lieutenant Cruthers handed them off to the castle guards and returned to his duty at the gates. The duchess's seneschal met them just inside the castle entrance in the lavish reception hall.

"Good evening, gentlemen, to what do I owe the pleasure of your distinguished presence?"

Before either Azerick or Allister could answer, the hall echoed with hurried footsteps and the chiming of small bells.

"Good evening, Captain Brague," Azerick said without turning his head to see whom it was that approached.

"What are you doing here?" Captain Brague snapped.

"I have urgent news for the duchess, news that is best not delayed by petty rivalries," Azerick intoned as he turned to face the obstinate captain.

"Then you can tell me and I will decide if it is worthy enough to excuse interrupting the duchess."

Allister stepped forward to prevent unnecessary delays. "Captain, I assure you our message is urgent, and we should be taken to the duchess with great haste."

Captain Brague knew Magus Allister by reputation well enough to know that only a fool would disregard anything he had to say. "Very well, Magus, follow me."

The captain led them through the ornate marble halls at a fast, bell-jingling pace to the dining hall where the duchess was entertaining several nobles of the city. All eyes turned to watch the trio enter.

"Magus Allister, Magus Azerick, what an unexpected surprise," Duchess Mellina said without emotion at their unexpected entrance. "I must apologize for not inviting you to dinner. I did not think you would care to attend such a social function."

Captain Brague took a single step forward. "Forgive me, Your Grace, but Magus Allister said that he had an urgent message to deliver, and I felt compelled to bring him at once along with…him."

"Good evening, Azerick," Lady Miranda said with a warm smile.

"Good evening to you, Miranda," Azerick returned, matching her smile.

Captain Brague glared daggers at Azerick's failure to address Miranda by her title but said nothing.

Oh you have got to be joking! Please tell me we are having relations with that! Klaraxis said.

We *are* not *having relations or anything else with that. You will have no part of anything with Miranda. I will push you so far back in my mind that a speck on a grain of sand could encompass your entire world!*

My, what a complete overreaction for someone who is not having relations. Oh, this is fantastic! Hey, stop it, nooo! The demon's voice trailed away and disappeared behind an iron wall of absolute nothingness.

"Perhaps you would like to discuss this privately," Azerick said.

"Is it a personal matter, or does it involve the city?" the duchess asked.

"I believe there is a great threat to the city and possibly the entire kingdom."

Worried mutterings erupted around the table, but a frigid look from Mellina silenced them. "Then please proceed. Everyone at this table has a large stake in the safety and success of the city and has a right to know about anything that threatens it."

"Very well, Your Grace," Azerick replied with a nod. "We believe a large group of soldiers are no more than three days' march from here, possibly only two. Several hundred cavalry could reach the city in less than a day."

Miranda threw a delicate hand to her full lips and gasped. Duchess Mellina reacted with the same cold, calm demeanor she granted any other sort of news.

"Do you have an approximation of their total numbers, Magus?" Mellina asked after again silencing the worried mutterings of the nobles with a steely glance.

"At least three thousand, perhaps as many as twice that."

The mutterings took on an air of panic. All the nobles voicing their fear and shock sounded like a gaggle of frightened geese, honking wildly without coherent purpose or direction.

"Silence!" the duchess shouted in a rare show of emotion. "I thank you for this information, Magus. Once again, you have proved yourself a valuable friend to the city. Captain Brogue, head the readiness of the city's defenses. Double the watch and rouse the militia. Unlock every weapons store we have and arm every able-bodied man and woman in the city. If these men do indeed plan hostilities toward North Haven, we will repel them just as my grandfather and his father before him repelled the pirates and barbarians.

"Chamberlain, have my armor readied. If North Haven falls, it will be atop my cold, dead body. I want buckets and cisterns filled to fight fires and barricades erected along the streets to channel anyone who breaches our defenses into killing zones. It looks as though this year's winter festival will be celebrated in a display of blood, valor, and heroism."

An older, heavy-jowled noble cleared his throat. "Your Grace, perhaps it would be prudent to evacuate Lady Miranda and as many noncombatants by ship as we can. Most every merchant ship that calls North Haven home is docked for the winter. We could move several thousand if necessary."

Azerick answered the nobleman's suggestion for the duchess. "I would strongly advise against taking to the sea. One of my ship's captains reported that Southport had numerous warships standing ready, and closed its harbor as well as its gates. It is quite possible that those ships are to be used to invade North Haven by sea, or at the very least, provide a blockade against anyone escaping to seek aid, and could at this moment be waiting to capture or sink any vessel heading south."

"That vile, traitorous snake!" Miranda shouted. "I never thought that even he would sink so low as to take North Haven by force despite all his treacherous ambitions!"

"Chamberlain, send a runner to the harbor master and have him raise the chains to seal off the port. Have the harbor fortifications put on alert and see that the weapon emplacements are ready to engage any ships attempting to invade us by sea," Duchess Mellina ordered. "We do not know if that is Ulric's plan, but we will be prepared, and I would not put such treachery as being beneath him. If he is behind this, I will do everything in my power to see that he pays a reckoning for it. Magus, can we expect any magical aid from you and your people in our time of need?"

Azerick looked into Miranda's beautiful, liquid emerald eyes. "Your Grace, I am afraid my people and I will all be fully engaged defending the keep. If North Haven comes under attack, particularly if Ulric is behind it, they are not likely to leave us alone and risk us going to Brelland or Brightridge for help."

"You selfish, cowardly bastard!" Captain Brague raged. "You would allow the city that is your host and home to crumble about you just to save your own worthless hide! If you are truly worried about them and not just yourself, why not move the lot of them inside the city walls?"

Azerick did not return the captain's vitriolic accusation but calmly replied, "The citadel is home to over three hundred of this city's displaced youth and dozens of men and women. It is *my* home, they are *my* family, and I will defend it and them with my very life. I will abandon neither for anything or anyone."

The duchess held up a hand. "That is enough, Captain. Magus, I thank you for your warning, and I wish you well in your defense. If there is nothing else, I will bid you good evening while I and my counselors further discuss the defense of the city."

Azerick and Allister gave the duchess a small bow and departed the dining hall. Miranda excused herself from dinner, darted from the dining hall, and caught sight of the two men in the hallway a moment later.

"Azerick, wait!" Miranda called out as she went running after them

"I will wait for you outside, son," Allister said as she approached.

"Azerick, I heard only recently that you had returned. I am sorry that I have not found time to see you myself. This winter was every bit as difficult for us as the last one was. I had hoped you would come to see me when you returned."

"I am sorry, Miranda. I have been…preoccupied. I did want to see you, but things have been out of sorts for me since I got back. I wish I had come under more pleasant circumstances."

"Is there nothing you can do for the city against these invaders?"

"I wish I could, but I must defend the citadel. It is possible that whoever it is does not fully understand the nature of the school and will greatly underestimate our resources. If we break free of any siege, I promise you, I will come to the aid of the city—and you."

Miranda smiled at the sorcerer. "I know you would never abandon us, Azerick, and I know you are the least cowardly man I have ever known, despite Captain Brague's rather harsh opinions."

"I am glad you feel that way. I would not like you to think poorly of me. I will do what I can."

"I know you will. Good luck. I will see you after the battle," Miranda said, then looked at Azerick expectantly.

Azerick stared into her jade-flecked eyes, longing to feel her sensuous, full lips against his, but Klaraxis's mocking words haunted him and made him pull back.

"I need to attend to other matters in the city, Lady Miranda. Forgive me, I must go." Azerick spun on his heel and departed with haste.

Damn that man and his aloofness! What do I have to do to get his attention, club him in the head? Miranda wondered in frustration. Miranda heard the telltale jingling of Captain Brague's approach and stopped him in the hall. "Captain, when you have a moment, I need you to find me a mace."

Captain Brague looked at the lady, baffled. "Whatever for, My Lady?"

"So I can beat some sense into that frustratingly obstinate and oblivious sorcerer!"

The captain's face split into a wide grin. "Of course, My Lady! I have a very nice one of my own in my quarters you are more than welcome to. It has a fine balance that could powder stone! I'll go get it immediately!"

Allister followed Azerick to the docks where they found Zeb and his senior officers eating supper at Barnacles.

"Azerick, you're just in time for dinner, but the look on your face says you're not here to eat," Zeb observed as he spied the two magi approaching his table.

Since Toron was rarely far from Zeb's side, they were easy to find no matter how crowded the area they were in. Azerick and Allister grabbed empty chairs from another table and sat down near the group of sailors.

"Zeb, Balor, Toron, gentlemen," Azerick greeted them all. "Zeb, how many ships do we have in port?"

"All of them, lad. *Majestic* was going to ship out next week for a run to Lazuul, and the *Iron Shark* was being tightened up and calked after our last push north, but she's done now. Why?"

"I think the port may come under attack. I want every ship we have mounted with as many weapons and men as you can find and get into place. The duchess is already ordering the harbor closed off, but I want to be ready to engage any warships if we are forced to flee the city. There is a large group of soldiers that I believe are going to put North Haven to siege. Should the city's defenses fail, you are to get as many people out as you can. If we break the siege, I plan to join you and as many men as you can crew to engage the fools who dared to threaten the port and the city."

"Aye, lad, it sounds like a fine plan to me. We'll be ready for whatever you have in mind. You can count on it." The sentiment was loudly confirmed by the other men at the table.

"I know I can, Zeb. I have no worries about that."

By the time Azerick and Allister left the sailors, Zeb had already sent several of his men to relay orders to prepare the ships for battle.

When Azerick and his former teacher returned to the keep, preparations were already underway to fortify the school. Alex and Jansen were busy directing groups of men, women, and children in the defense of the keep. The younger children carried bundles of arrows and quarrels to the tops of the wall and the flat-roofed, crenellated buildings. Women set up buckets of water and sand to defend against fire, and men built barricades out of timbers and overturned wagons to cordon off the passageways between buildings.

Everyone worked through the night to ensure they were as ready as they could be to defend their home. They divided the work shifts the next morning to allow everyone a chance to get some much-needed rest while the others continued to shore up, recheck, and add to the defenses. Even Wolf and Ghost were out adding defenses of their own to the woods they called home.

Whatever came, the school would be ready to defend itself.

As Kayne's men marched toward North Haven, nearly a dozen white-sailed ships flying no colors of allegiance bobbed on the open seas just outside the city's harbor. They did not attempt to breach the defenses and invade the harbor, nor did they come within range of the shore defenses, but it was apparent that they were not going to allow anyone to leave North Haven by sea.

Zeb examined each of the ships through a spyglass from aboard *Dolphin's Grace*, something he was certain every one of his ships' captains were also doing. The ships were large war galleons, each one of them bristling with weapons, but as far as he could tell, were not crewed by boarding parties. Each of those monsters could hold nearly five hundred men, but he counted perhaps a fifth of that number actually aboard. It was possible that there were large numbers in the hull, but if there were, none had made an appearance on deck, which was highly unlikely. You could not keep that many men penned up below decks for very long.

Balor was captaining *Majestic* while Toron held a tight command of the heavy icebreaker, *Iron Shark*.

Three of Zeb's most trusted men captained the other ships he commanded, including the flat-bottomed *Freedom Winds*, but she was to be used as an evacuation vessel only, being ill-suited for sailing the open seas.

Zeb studied those ships with a professional eye. Outnumbered and far outgunned, he knew that even with the young sorcerer's help, it was going to be a dangerous, almost insanely difficult battle if it came to that, and he was not looking forward to such a prospect with nearly as much enthusiasm as Toron was.

Kayne had not even reached the city but was already suffering battle losses, and it annoyed him no end. First, he lost three men to some savage animal attack and another to the cleanest sword cut he had ever seen. Four men were killed outright by various booby traps employing swinging logs and sprung tree limbs with sharpened stakes lashed to them. Seven more had stepped into shallow pits with sharp wood and steel spikes in them. Those men would either lose their foot or die within days from infection caused by the filth spread on the spikes.

Word came back this morning that two of the night sentries were dead with arrows in their throats, and no one heard or saw a thing. He would have to double up the sentries from now on. He had not expected these kind of guerilla tactics from the peaceful northern people.

Still, the numbers were small considering the nearly five thousand men under his command. Ulric had done well recruiting and shoring up his forces. Kayne had had some reservations about attacking a city like North Haven with only the thirty-five hundred men he had expected to lead, but the bolstered numbers made him confident that he could take the city within weeks, if not days. He paid his engineers and sappers well, and soon they would earn their gold.

His engineers would be at the edge of the forest just a short distance from the gates of the city where they would lead men in the construction of siege engines. Rams and huge trebuchets should make short work of the walls and gates, but he would have men working on scaling towers as well should the barriers prove overly resilient. They should not be necessary, but he would be ready in any case.

North Haven was built to defend against pirates and other seaborne threats, not powerful sieges by land. The builders had always thought themselves too far north and far enough from any source of hostile forces to require the extra expense of the tall, reinforced walls of the southern cities like Southport, Brightridge, and Argoth. That assumption was now going to cost them dearly.

The sound of axes, saws, and mallets echoed throughout the once peaceful forest. The cracking and crashing of the majestic trees sounded like a death rattle to Wolf's pointed ears as he watched the invaders desecrate his home. He would make them pay for this he swore as he crept wraith-like from shadow to shadow.

He occasionally found a lone man or a pair of men chopping and sawing on his trees at the far edge of the ring of guards who were supposed to protect them. However, their great numbers left them feeling overly safe and not expecting any danger despite Wolf's previous ambushes. This allowed him to pick off a few more men from the fringes of the main body from time to time. Wolf knew he was a flea biting a bear, but he would not allow these men to foul his home unanswered, so he would keep biting them every chance he got.

CHAPTER 19

Kayne tasked a hundred cavalry and five hundred footmen to take what he had heard described as some sort of orphanage. He knew it was overkill, but his men mentioned it having a respectable wall and several people guarding it as if it were a military outpost. Even so, he wanted it taken quickly. A single ram should have little trouble breaching the gates, and then his men would easily take the tower.

All things considered, everything was going exactly as planned. This endeavor, although long and complex in the making, would prove quite profitable for him in the end. While his successful assault against the city of Lyonsgate had been a strategic success, crippling King Jarvin's ability to send reinforcement to North Haven was his only reward. While losing two hundred men with nothing to show for it was a bitter pill to swallow, it made sacking North Haven not only possible, it helped to all but ensure his, and Ulric's, victory.

Kayne relaxed inside his command tent, sipping tea from a fine set of porcelain he liberated from a nobleman's home in Groveswood. It was one of those rare pieces of plunder that he enjoyed, not for the monetary value, but for its fine artisanship and uniqueness. It was as thin as an eggshell and felt so fragile that it almost made him nervous to pick it up. It was pure white with a gold rim encircling the top and featured a very lifelike depiction of a stag hunt in fine azure lines beneath the flawless glaze.

"Commander Kayne," one of his guards addressed him just outside the tent, "there are three individuals who request to see you. They say they have been sent by Duke Ulric."

"Let them in," Kayne replied over the top of his delicate teacup.

He smiled in appreciation as he felt the cup vibrate under the sound of his voice.

The guard entered and held open the tent flap for the guests. Two of them appeared to be tall and lean, the other much shorter and possibly on the fat side. It was hard to tell. Heavy hooded robes of a dark material obscured their forms considerably. The robes of one of the tall ones and those of the short one were of the deepest black. The other tall one, the one standing in the center, wore robes of such a deep red that they were nearly black as well.

"You are Commander Kayne," the one in the middle said with a soft but commanding voice.

It was not a question but Kayne answered anyway. "I am. What can I do for you?"

The one who spoke lowered his—her—he now saw—hood. "I am Magus Lillis Bauer of the Magus Academy. These two gentlemen are both wizards of the Black Tower. Duke Ulric has enlisted our services and requested that we provide you with whatever assistance we can. I assure you, our aid can be quite substantial."

"Of that I have no doubt," Kayne said with a broad smile, flashing his perfect white teeth. "Please, have a seat. Would you care for tea? It is quite good."

"Tea would be excellent, Commander, thank you," Magus Bauer replied, then took a seat on an available campstool.

Kayne opened the ornate silk and cotton-padded case that held the entire service set and removed three more of the delicate porcelain cups. He then crossed the tent and retrieved the silver teapot that steamed over a lit brazier.

Ulric had told him that he had recruited some special talent, but he had no idea that it would be in the form of three wizards. As a fighting man, he was not overly fond of spellcasters, but he did not fear them either, like most people did. They were a tool, a weapon, and he would employ them to the fullest of their abilities and be grateful for it.

His intelligence had heard rumors that the man who ran the orphanage on the hill was some sort of magician, but he had paid little heed to it. However, if it were true, then these three should be more than capable of countering whatever resistance he threw at them, unless they were somehow inept or lacking in skill.

He could tell right off that that was not the case. Malicious power lay very close to the surface of Magus Bauer. He could feel it raise the hairs on his arms and could see it in her eyes. She was not one to cross. The other two had lowered their hoods as well and both had the look of men who were quite confident in their power but were smart enough to defer to the woman.

"Exactly what kind of assistance will you be able to provide me with, so that I may better plan my stratagems?" Kayne asked as he returned the teapot to the brazier and sat down.

"We can provide wards to protect your rams against fire, stones, and magical attack, and we can greatly reduce the effectiveness and accuracy of arrow volleys, as well as striking the enemy with powerful magical attacks if necessary. You know, fire, lightning, those sorts of things that impress and terrify the common rabble so much. But mostly, our role should be defensive in nature, particularly against the citadel atop the keep," magus Bauer said.

Kayne nodded his understanding. Perhaps there was more to the rumors than he suspected. "I had heard there was a wizard of some sort within the keep. Is he likely to be a problem?"

Kayne was surprised to see that the woman was capable of looking even more serious and dour than before. "The one who owns the tower was once a student of the Academy, a sorcerer. He left well before his training was complete, but he managed to pick up a measure of power on his own or with the help of someone unknown to the Academy. Although exceedingly young, he does not lack talent or audacity. Not long ago, he strolled into the Academy headmaster's office and killed him, doing a great deal of damage in the process."

"The headmaster? Then he is formidable."

"He is more crafty than powerful, I believe, but not to be underestimated. He is no archmage, and my associates and I can handle him with little trouble." Her face grew more shadowed. "A greater concern is that one of my former colleagues may be there as well. He had some kind of special attachment to the boy. If he is here, then that will certainly add a measurable challenge but not an insurmountable one. That is why our power is best left to providing defensive measures, to counteract those that would use magic against your men so that we might keep them alive long enough to kill them with steel."

Kayne nodded. "Very wise, Magus. I will defer to you and your associates in all matters magical. I just ask that you keep me informed so that I can direct my men most effectively."

Magus Bauer cracked a humorless smile, breaking her rigid countenance. "Ulric told me you were a smart man for a mercenary. I am glad to see he was correct. We have already had our apprentices erect our quarters. As soon as you are prepared to take the citadel, we will be ready."

The three magi stood as one and departed Kayne's tent. They crossed the muddy ground, churned up by countless boots and mixed with slushy snow. A simple cantrip kept the wizards from soiling their robes or soaking their soft leather and fur-lined boots.

They approached a small circular tent no more than fifteen feet in diameter, recently erected only a short way from the command tent, and strode through its open flap. They were not concerned with anyone entering unannounced. Such an attempt would be impossible. The magic of the tent allowed only those who were granted permission to enter its true confines. Anyone else entering would only find an empty tent.

However, those that belonged would find themselves inside a palace made of rich, colorful canvas and silks. The interior was enormous with half a dozen large, opulent bedrooms, a dining section, a library, and a reception room. It was neither hot nor cold no matter the weather outside.

Two apprentice wizards were busy setting up a tray of finger foods and wine. "Masters, mistress, everything is ready," the young woman told the three senior wizards.

"Very good, Cecilia," Magus Bauer replied. "Bring the tray to the library, Vincent. We will have dinner at six. I am in the mood for mutton and wild rice."

"Yes, mistress."

The siege of North Haven began two days later. Six massive trebuchets hurled stones weighing hundreds of pounds each. Some of the stones fell short and littered the ground between the attacking army and the city walls. Others sailed over the walls and occasionally crushed homes, shops, and anyone unfortunate enough to be in their path. Nearly half impacted the wall after a short bounce or roll across the frozen ground or struck it squarely, doing a great deal of damage to the barrier with every strike.

Onagers hurled dozens of fist-sized stones to help clear the walls of archers and to intimidate any forces that may be rallied against the ram crews. Magus Bauer and her two companions cast multiple wards upon the large wood and hide-covered rams that would be used against the gates.

For now, Kayne kept his men out of bow range and let the onagers and catapults soften up their targets before sending in the ram and the men to keep the siege piece safe. More aggressive tactics were put into place at the citadel. The three wizards stood several hundred yards from the school's walls with five hundred footmen and a hundred cavalry waiting for the order to charge.

"We are ready to begin our initial sortie. Are you ready, Magus?" the officer in charge of taking the citadel asked Magus Bauer.

"We are prepared, Captain."

With a nod to the wizard, the captain gave the order. "Cavalry, charge!"

A battle horn repeated his command, and the sound of thundering hooves filled the air.

Azerick stood upon the wall next to Alex and watched the soldiers arrayed in the field just outside the tree line. He looked at the young men and few women standing atop the wall with him, ready to defend their home with their lives if necessary. Azerick had offered to let anyone who wanted to wait out the battle inside the much stronger walls of North Haven, but not one person wanted to leave. From the youngest student to Agnes the cook, none would abandon the citadel.

The youngest students, Simon, Teresa, Brother Thomas, and Aggie stayed inside the tower along with Sandy. The little sand dragon had suggested that she might be more useful atop the wall where the enemy could see her, insisting that the mere sight of such a fearsome creature may frighten the humans enough to leave them alone. Azerick swore that these men were all insane and would not be scared enough to run, and that her awesome might was best used to protect the younger children in case they gained entrance to the tower itself.

Azerick could hear some of the students fearfully muttering at the sight of the army arrayed against them. No matter how much Alex and Jansen had tried to explain that there was nothing glorious about battle, he knew that most of them had not fully accepted that fact until now. The sorcerer could almost hear the doubts in the minds of what were mostly children: children in armor, wielding crossbows and bows, ready to take the lives of the men who threatened them.

The thought made Azerick queasy. It was how he was forced to grow up, and he was fully aware of what it had done to him, how it had changed him. It was not what he wished for his students, but there had been little choice. The greed of other men had stolen their choice just as the choice had been taken from him. Very well then, at least they would not stand alone in this battle.

Azerick looked to his left and saw Rusty with his characteristic flaming red hair and orange and red robes, standing next to Jansen halfway to the corner of the wall. To his right, Allister looked as if he were a statue, his steely gaze unwavering, all trace of his kindly, grandfatherly face gone, replaced with a look of grim determination and pent-up anger. Ken, the thin but incredibly strong blacksmith, stood near the old wizard, wearing a shirt of mail and gripping a heavy forging hammer in each of his calloused hands.

A horn sounded in the distance, and the ground vibrated under the brutal pounding of a hundred charging horses. The swift-running horses ate up the ground between the walls and the tree line with frightening speed. Wide, nervous eyes watched the invaders racing toward them, sweat dripping from the hands gripping weapons.

Alex was given the responsibility of issuing the battle commands, which is why he held the center of the wall. Jansen was undoubtedly the most skilled fighter any of them had ever met, but he was not trained to lead an army. Alex had been groomed for commanding troops for the past twelve years at the Martial Academy, the finest battle college known in the kingdom.

"Archers, ready!" Alex called in a high command voice that carried over the sound of the thundering horses and the shouting of men. "Loose!"

Every defender who held a crossbow or bow stepped between the stone crenellations and released their shafts. Panic and inexperience caused many of them to overshoot the fast-approaching enemy, and they forgot to adjust their aim for the speed at which they were approaching.

Rusty sent a massive fireball into the charging army, which burst directly in the midst of the lead horses. The resulting explosion of super-heated air was massive and shook the stones under Azerick's feet. The flash was so bright that spots floated in his vision; however, as soon as he blinked them away, he was shocked to see that the huge conflagration had done only minor damage. A few men and horses tumbled to the ground with severe burns while several horses panicked at the blast and threw their riders or bolted in another direction, but most emerged unscathed.

Azerick heard Allister curse and turned just in time to see the old mage raise his arm up over his head then whip it down as if he were throwing something onto the ground. Hailstones the size of his fist streaked down upon the charging cavalry by the hundreds. The thunder of their impact matched the pounding hooves of the horses in volume and rhythm. Again, the spell seemed to do far less damage than it ought to have. Azerick saw that many of the stones shattered before they struck the ground or the enemy. A few more men were knocked from their saddles but not nearly enough.

Azerick was desperate to stop or at least slow the charging invaders and slashed the air with his staff in a long, horizontal arc. A towering wall of flame erupted from the ground just yards in front of the oncoming cavalry. The blaze stretched higher than the walls of the citadel and was too close for them to avoid. As quickly as the flame wall sprang from the ground, it disappeared.

Azerick realized what was happening. They had wizards of their own, and they were countering the spells that he, Rusty, and Allister were casting! This added a completely new set of problems for the defenders. Magic was the only thing that was going to give them a chance of successfully defending the citadel.

Azerick cast one of his most reliable spells. With luck, it was unique enough and quick enough to prove effective before the enemy wizards could negate its effect. The sorcerer turned his hand up like an inverted claw and watched with pleasure as a long double row of stone spikes thrust through the earth, impaling the broadly muscled chests of the unfortunate horses.

Over a dozen of the animals tumbled to the earth at tremendous speed, throwing and rolling over many of their riders, crushing and pinning them beneath their enormous weight. Several more mounts directly behind those now impaled, tumbled to the ground as they tried to vault over or dodge around the twisted chaos of riders and horses.

Azerick felt sick over the senseless slaughter of the innocent animals, but he could not afford to let his sentiments stop him from using whatever force was necessary to protect his home, friends, and family. Arrows whizzed past his head as the remaining riders loosed their arrows as they passed in front of the wall, trying to sweep away the defenders. So wrapped up in his casting, he failed to hear Alex order the archers back down behind the crenellations. Azerick was unconcerned; his wards would protect him from the arrows, just as Rusty's and Allister's protected them.

Azerick saw that his stone spikes had crumbled to dust, obviously another casualty of the enemy wizards' counter-magic. It was unimportant, they had done what they were supposed to do, but he doubted that it would work a second time. Whoever these wizards were, they were very good.

Azerick cast his eyes along the wall and felt his stomach drop when he spotted two of his students being carried away with arrows sticking out of them. Brother Thomas and his Chosen would administer to their wounds in the tower. Azerick prayed that their injuries were not too severe for their ministrations.

"We have a problem, son," Allister rumbled next to Azerick.

"The other wizards," Azerick replied without looking away from the battlefield.

"Aye, so you figured it out already; good. We need to find a way to take them out, or we cannot hope to defend the school. I have some pretty good tricks up my sleeve, but I will have to gate over there and get close. It is unlikely I will be able to return before those soldiers cut me to ribbons," the old mage said dourly.

Azerick racked his mind for a solution. "Gating over there amidst five hundred killers is suicide. We need a better plan."

"Aye, you're right about that. You got one in mind?"

"I think so." Azerick called Alex over to them and explained his idea.

Alex was wary of such a plan. "Why don't we just seal the gates?"

"Because even if we were able to keep them from scaling the walls, which we could not, they would just get more men and swarm us. We have to crush them completely before they send for reinforcements," Azerick explained.

"Azerick, if you are wrong, if your plan fails, the keep will be lost and likely everyone in it," Alex said after hearing what his friend had in mind. "Even if you succeed with your part, there is a great risk of being overrun."

"The school is lost if we don't try. A slim chance is better than none at all. I believe in my people, Alex. They can do it."

Allister said, "Best let Aggie know. We're going to need her help with this one, maybe even some of the younger apprentices."

Azerick blanched at the thought of putting his younger students in harm's way, but Allister was right. The citadel would need to tap every resource it had to make this work.

"All right, but keep them atop the tower with Aggie. They can defend the inner courtyard from there. Alex, pass our plan on to Rusty."

Alex nodded. "Right after their next charge. It looks like they are forming up for another pass. Archers, ready!" Alex shouted as he ran back to his position.

The endless rolling thunder resumed when the cavalry charged the walls once more, their bows held ready to rake the defenders with arrows. The school's volley was much more effective this time. The defenders adjusted their point of aim with far greater accuracy, sending several riders tumbling to the ground or hanging loosely from their saddles.

Azerick unleashed lightning across the front ranks of the enemy, but much of its energy deflected harmlessly into the ground. He still managed to send three men and two horses crashing to the earth. Rusty let loose with a series of fiery bolts one after another in a seemingly unending barrage of flaming lances. His merciless assault sent several riders' scorched remains tumbling to the earth despite the fact that four out of five of his bolts splashed harmlessly against the approaching enemy or flared out before they even reached their targets.

Allister decided that simplicity may be the best course and sent half a dozen bolts of pure magical energy streaking out across the battlefield. Either the opposing wizards felt that the spell did not deserve their attention, or it was simply too quick to counter, but all six missiles struck home, knocking two riders from their saddles and leaving another slumped over either dead or too injured to carry out the charge.

Once again, the riders wheeled their mounts parallel to the wall and strafed the crenellations with arrows, keeping the defenders crouched low to avoid the missiles. The three wizards and the archers launched another attack at the backs of the retreating cavalry, sending a dozen more riders to Sharrellan's dark embrace.

Once the riders were out of range, Allister hurried to the tower to inform Aggie and the others of their plan while Azerick and Alex relayed their intent to Rusty and the rest of the defenders.

Captain Crayhill looked on as his cavalry made a second futile pass at the walls. "I believe it is time to send in the ram and attack the fortress with significant force. I am losing men with no gain," he informed the wizards next to him.

"Very well, Captain, but be aware that we cannot defeat the other wizards' magic entirely," Magus Bauer replied. "More men will mean more casualties, but we can keep those numbers low enough for your men to achieve victory."

"Very well, Magus. Prepare to advance. Man the ram!"

The ram consisted of a stout log suspended by ropes like a massive pendulum from a wheeled, shielded frame. The roof was made of heavy timbers covered in animal hides soaked with water to prevent the defenders from setting it aflame. Dozens of men hid inside the contraption, pushing its bulk forward until they nestled it against the gates. They would then grab a shortened limb or affixed handle like an oarsman on a ship, swinging the massive log back and forth until it battered the gates into submission.

The ponderous siege engine creaked forward on its eight large wooden wheels. Archers and footmen marched beside and behind it, shooting arrows at any defenders that appeared atop the walls. Lightning and fireballs rained down, but the wards the dark wizards cast upon it shielded it from much of the damage.

It was slow going, but the ram was finally into position and beat a steady, pounding rhythm against the stout wood and iron gate. Footmen threw grapnels over the walls and attempted to scale them by rope, but quick-acting defenders hacked the ropes off with axes as quickly as they appeared.

The defenders' vigilance often put them in danger of the attackers' arrows, and they began suffering casualties. The noncombatants pulled the wounded from the walls and hurried them to the keep upon litters. The thick wood of the gate cracked like a toppling tree under the ram's relentless pounding. The horde of mercenaries roared in triumph as they saw the gate giving way.

Azerick and Alex saw that the gates would not hold much longer. They had already suffered over a dozen casualties, and Azerick knew that at least a few of them were beyond any help the Chosen could give them, even with the healing potions the wizards had crafted, though their quick use upon the wall had undoubtedly saved several lives already.

"Move everyone off the wall, and have them prepare to defend the courtyard. Allister and I are going to do our part now," Azerick told Alex.

Alex nodded. "Fall back to the courtyard, fall back!"

Azerick met Allister below the northeastern corner of the wall.

"Are you ready, lad?" Allister asked as he hurried to the wall.

"Ready."

The archmage opened a shimmering portal through which they could see the trees as if they were just ahead of them instead of the several hundred feet they actually were. Azerick walked through with Allister right on his heels. The gate snapped shut the moment the magus stepped through into the tree line three hundred yards north of the citadel.

The two spellcasters shook off the disorienting effects of gate travel, though it barely seemed to affect Azerick at all. He was pondering the meaning of this when Klaraxis invaded his thoughts.

See, there is some benefit to having me around. Maybe now you will appreciate me and not keep me locked up so much.

Do not count on it, demon. You are foul, vile, and evil. I will never appreciate *anything about you, though I will use you as a means to an end.*

As long as I get to enjoy the slaughter of these lesser creatures, you may justify it all you like.

Azerick ignored the rest of Klaraxis's repugnant thoughts as Allister prepared to open another gate that would bring them within striking distance of the opposing wizards.

This was likely to be the most hazardous part of his plan, at least as far as the two magi were concerned. There were still about fifty soldiers guarding the wizards and what they assumed was the command element.

Azerick and Allister appeared less than a hundred feet behind the group of enemy that were watching the battle unfold before them. Sensing that the gates were only moments from giving way, they had begun moving closer to the forward line of battle to better support and command the bulk of the invaders attacking the tower. Magus Bauer and the other two wizards must have sensed the flare of magic behind them and spun about, spells of death already forming on their lips.

Azerick knew that it was going to take Allister a crucial moment to clear the fogginess from his head, so he sprinted forward in hopes of buying the archmage the time he needed to compose himself. Azerick could afford to take no chances. Each of these three wizards was likely an archmage and far more experienced than he was. The sorcerer's eyes glowed a fearsome red as he allowed Klaraxis to come to the fore of his psyche.

Azerick heard the demon's gleeful laughter echoing through his mind as he reached into the abyss for his infernal power, reveling in the chaos he was about to unleash.

Klaraxis opened his human mouth wide, and a massive cone of scarabs spewed forth into the ranks of men and wizards, their powerful, needle-like mandibles scouring the soft flesh from the humans' bodies. Many of those who lacked the magical protection of the wizards were nearly stripped of flesh to their very bones, their agonizing screams cutting the air for far too long in Azerick's ears. Their armor was useless as the beetles found every opening, scurried inside, and devoured them.

Magus Bauer managed to shield herself from the horrifying and unexpected attack. The other two wizards were not quite as swift. A large part of a wizard's ability to counter the spell of another was by either seeing the somatic gestures or hearing the verbal components of a spell being cast or by sensing the way that the Source was being tapped and shaped by the opposing wizard. However, Klaraxis did not use the Source as other spellcasters did. He had some access to it, but his greatest power came from the dark energies of the abyss.

Several of the plum-sized beetles pierced the wizards' wards and sank their mandibles into their pasty flesh, interrupting the lethal spells they were casting. Only their training and concentration saved them from even more grievous damage. The two archmages put the painful bites to the back of their minds long enough to cast another spell. The black scarabs that sought to burrow their way through the wizards' flesh burst apart with small flashes of flame before the mages bent their minds back toward blasting the upstart sorcerer to bits.

Magus Bauer completed her spell with a sneer of contempt for the former academy student. A dozen luminous orbs flared into existence around her and streaked out at the sorcerer. Missile after missile slammed into Azerick. He lost count of how many had gotten through his wards, but it felt like the punishing barrage was never going to end as the bolts of energy pounded into his body, driving him to his knees.

Azerick was barely able to keep himself from falling face first into the cold, sodden ground. His entire body ached as if a herd of horses had trampled him after he had fallen down several flights of stairs. His eyes could not even focus on the ground just an arm's length from his face. His lungs battled to pull in some air before he lost consciousness, but they seemed determined to disobey his mental commands.

Klaraxis, if you want to live long enough to kill these people, you had best do something quickly.

You will have to give me more control, human. Let me off my leash, and I will show these mortals the true meaning of pain!

Azerick had already given the demon all the freedom he was comfortable with, far more actually, but he was going to die here if he did not let Klaraxis have his way. Azerick knew he was too beaten to defend himself on his own.

He felt his senses sharpen, and his body gained unimaginable strength as he slipped off the demon's mental leash. Klaraxis rose to his feet with a laugh so loud, evil, and full of such dark hatred that the soldiers who were beginning to advance balked under his malevolent glare. Death radiated from his body like an icy cold wind.

The soldiers recovered their courage and charged at him once more, but a dark red pulse of pure hate surrounded him and beat with the rhythm of his own heart. Several of the soldiers who stepped within its pulse dropped dead with a rictus of horror and pain frozen onto their faces. Those of stronger heart and constitution died upon the tip of Azerick's staff or had their skulls pulped by a powerful blow from his bare hand.

Allister appeared at his side with a look of concern and fear for his young friend and former pupil, but he could not afford to spare him much thought as the wizards prepared to unleash more powerful and lethal spells.

The two Tower wizards relied upon their Academy associate to deal with the young sorcerer and focused their attention on the old archmage. Twin beams of brilliant death lanced out and struck the wizard's wards with incredible force. The flash from his own wards almost blinded him as they struggled to stave off the death-dealing arcane power.

Showing remarkable agility for a man his age, Allister dove and rolled to his left away from the rays. He did not bother to attempt to stand, instead unleashing a powerful blast of lightning that forked to strike both opposing wizards, causing their wards to flare brilliantly under the assault.

The demon stretched his fist out and pointed it at Captain Crayhill. With a splaying of the demon's fingers, the enemy commander's body burst apart. The bone fragments and concussive explosion struck a dozen men and sent them sprawling to the ground all around the floating red mist that was all that was left of the captain's body.

Klaraxis's glare blazed red behind Azerick's once hazel eyes, fixing Magus Bauer in place with his malevolent stare; the words of her incantation freezing in her throat, which went dry. The wizard's chin quivered in terror as she felt the demonic presence destroy her will. In the very last agonizing moments of her life, she realized what she stood against and knew they had never had a chance.

Klaraxis raked his fingers through the air before him. Though he was still several yards from the magess, her flesh was shredded with every swipe of his hand as if an invisible lion were raking her with its claws. Her throat loosened enough that her piercing shriek of unimaginable pain cut through the din of battle even as far away as the keep itself.

The demon lord tore strip after strip of flesh from the wizard as if he were peeling an orange, slowly and methodically, savoring the pain and terror he could feel deep within his black soul. Soldiers began to turn and flee, but the two dark wizards made one more attempt to destroy the two men against them.

The tall, black-robed wizard stretched his hand out toward Allister to release arcane destruction upon the archmage, but just as he was about to utter the final word of command, an arrow sprouted from his thin neck. The wizard looked about dumbly, not quite comprehending what had just happened for several seconds before folding to the ground.

The shorter, heavier archmage released his spell just before his companion toppled, but a streak of blackness struck him in the chest and clamped its jaws around his throat. Ghost tore the man's throat out with a quick jerk of his head before sprinting after a fleeing soldier and taking him down from behind.

Wolf gave chase along with Ghost, sending arrow after arrow streaking into the backs of the fleeing men faster than he drew breath. He nearly drained his packed quiver in less than a minute, every one of the steel-headed shafts finding the flesh of the fleeing men.

Allister sent fire and lightning after the soldiers who fled, leaving none of them alive to ever do harm or threaten another again. He turned to Azerick, his eardrums ringing with the shrieking of Magus Bauer's agony. Her robes had been stripped from her body along with nearly every square inch of pale, white flesh. Her blood melted the crushed snow beneath her body and soaked the earth until it was as black as the demon's heart, yet still she lived and still she screamed in an agony so great that the gods themselves must have been cringing in their celestial palaces.

"Azerick," Allister cautiously addressed his young friend. "Azerick, listen to me. That is enough. Let her go, let her die. Azerick, I said that is enough!" The old archmage strode forward and grabbed the sorcerer's arm.

The pulsing ring of evil and hate still surrounding Azerick caused the old mage to gasp and clutch his chest, but he did not let go of Azerick's arm. The screaming stopped and the magus' body collapsed to the ground in a rendered pile of flesh and bones when the demon spun on Allister and struck him in the chest with the palm of his hand, sending the archmage sprawling in a heap several feet away. Klaraxis took two long strides forward and raised the spearheaded staff, poised to pin the foolish old man to the ground.

"Azerick, get control of yourself," Allister told him calmly, looking up into the demon's burning red eyes. "Do not let him control you, you are stronger than him. It is your body and your mind, not his. Do not let him take that from you."

Allister could sense the battle taking place behind the eyes of the young sorcerer. He knew that as long as Azerick could fight, there was no force that could subjugate him for long. He breathed a sigh of relief even before the internal battle ended.

All right demon, get back in your cage. You have done quite enough.

That is where you are wrong, little sorcerer. It will never be enough. There is not enough blood in the world to slake my thirst, but it will suffice for now. It was a good fight.

Azerick looked around and saw Wolf, Ghost, and Allister staring at him. He reached a hand down to help Allister to his feet, which the old wizard gratefully accepted.

"I am sorry, Allister," Azerick said, abashed and frightened by his actions. "There are things I have neglected to tell you."

Allister embraced his friend and clapped him on the back. "We will speak of it later, son. Let's go help our friends first."

CHAPTER 20

The gates split asunder under the ram's relentless pounding at almost the same moment Allister and Azerick gated behind the wizards and their guard element. One half of the gate tumbled to the flagstones with a heavy thump. The other managed to cling tentatively by one hinge near the top. The ram crew pushed the ponderous siege engine back away from the breach to allow the waiting soldiers access into the fortified compound.

The waiting cavalry pushed past their foot-bound brethren in hopes of gaining the honor of spilling the first blood. All of the side streets had barriers of wood and stone erected to prevent the enemy from running freely throughout the compound. The soldiers were unconcerned, trusting that their numbers were far too superior to allow any kind of successful ambush. The footmen chased after the swifter horses with battle cries of incoherent sounds and promises of death.

Wagons turned onto their sides littered the main boulevard, requiring the riders to steer around the obstacles. They slowed the horses down, but only slightly, as they raced to the large open courtyard in front of the tower.

The mercenaries had expected rows of pikemen or archers to try to break their charge, but the grounds seemed deserted. Many began to realize that they were prepared for the actions experienced soldiers would take and recalled that this was some sort of school or orphanage despite its apparent militancy.

It was likely that everyone was hiding inside the tower, as if they could find safety there. They would probably entreat for surrender and mercy but they would get none. The mercenaries had no time for such niceties.

The ram crew cleared away the shattered gates and forced the siege engine through the breach toward the sealed tower doors. The commander of the ram crew shouted for some of the infantrymen to clear a route through the wagons so the nearly non-maneuverable ram could get at the tower unimpeded.

Men pushed and pulled at the wagons, righting them so they could wheel out of the way, as the ram rolled inexorably forward while the commander shouted for the footmen and horses to clear a path.

The street was not much wider than the gates, which allowed little more than enough clearance for the ram to squeeze through. The mass of soldiers wanting blood actually hindered the progress of their own ram. Several men standing below the tower became impatient and began hacking at the doors with heavy axes.

Inside the tower, the children and adults listened to the pounding of the axes on the door, and many of the younger ones wailed in fright.

Sandy looked at the mass of children she was with and tried to reassure them. "Don't worry, little humans, any bad men that get through those doors I'm going to bite and scratch them real good! They will learn what it means to anger a sand dragon."

The ram had made it less than halfway to the tower when there was a screech of metal, a short rumbling, and a heavy thump behind them where the gates once stood. A few men in the open rear of the ram looked behind them at the sound and saw two massive stone blocks, with what appeared to be a dozen steel wheels beneath them, roll together from the sides of the avenue, slamming together and completely sealing the opening.

None of the enemy had paid any heed to the steel rails that were set flush with the flagstones running parallel to the gate or that the street here had been built with a slight decline toward the center. The two enormous stone blocks looked like nothing more than part of the wall until the retaining pins were knocked loose from a hidden corridor behind them. A chain with links the size of a ship's anchor chain was attached to the ends of each block. The chains ran through the sections of wall that were now revealed. It would take a team of draft horses to reset each block to reveal the blocked egress.

The moment the blocks slid into place, defenders sprang up from the rooftops and began pelting the trapped army below them with arrows and large stones. From the crenellated rooftops and tower, a rain of arrows showered down upon the mercenaries who had shouldered their own bows and drawn their swords in anticipation of melee combat.

Atop the tower, Aggie sent a bolt of lightning into a mass of riders. It arced between the invaders, slaying half a score of them at once. Rusty sent bolts of fire into the ranks of men in a continuous barrage, this time with full effect, raking them across one enemy after another. Joshua and Umair unleashed their own formidable magic against the press of mercenaries who were beginning to panic amidst the magical killing storm that came crashing down upon them.

Maira, the former Black Tower adept, had a vengeful gleam in her eye while she directed more killing magic from another rooftop as she stood beside a half-dozen younger boys wielding crossbows. The students knew that they could expect no mercy, and none knew that better than the former Black Tower apprentices did, so they had no qualms in not showing their enemies any in return.

Despite the sheer volume of killing fire, electricity, and magical energy, there was still an enormous number of enemies below them, and they could not hope to kill them all in a single stroke. Some of the cavalrymen used their horses to kick and tear down some of the flimsier wooden barricades blocking the alleyways between the buildings and fled down them in search of a way to reach the defenders.

The men on the ground found shelter where they could, darting behind the erected barricades, buildings, and sometimes kicking in a door or climbing through a window to escape the death being dealt from above.

Some of the boys next to Maira spun about in time to see a couple of mercenaries clambering onto the rooftop behind them. They turned and fired their crossbows into the faces of the first two who breached the top, then threw them down and drew their swords as more of the enemy tried to gain the roofs. The same scene was unfolding across the roofs of several other buildings where more of the young men and women fought to defend their school and their home.

A huge mercenary wielding a massive double-headed axe finally chopped through the stout door leading into the tower. A few more swings and he had a hole large enough to stick through his large, helmed head.

"I'm coming, little kiddies! I'm gonna eat the flesh from your bones!" he shouted through the breach, then resumed hacking at the portal.

Another minute, and the ruined doors swung wide, allowing the tide of mercenaries another route to escape the slaughter happening in the courtyard. The big mercenary with the axe took his weapon to the inner doors that lay at the end of the foyer. These were an ornate set of carved doors and were not built to withstand any sort of attack. A few swings cleaved the bolt securing them, and scores of frightened and furious killers swarmed into the reception hall.

"I found ya, ya little vermin!" the burly mercenary shouted gleefully as he looked at the top of the stairs where Ellyssa, Sandy, and a few other of the younger magus students were waiting.

"You have found only your death here, scum," Ellyssa called down with barely a trace of fear in her young voice.

The apprentice raised a slim wand and spoke a word of command. A small ball of fire streaked from the end of the wooden rod then detonated between the leering man and the first group of his murderous band, which came through the door behind him. The fireball sent men flying in all directions, filling the reception hall with the sickly scent of burnt flesh and hair, but scores more began pouring in like water from a breached dam.

Roger and Missy raised their wands and sent lightning bolts and darts of arcane energy tearing into the rushing tide of bodies, but there were too many to be stopped. They were so close now that Ellyssa had to aim behind the men in the front-most ranks so as not to scorch her or her friends with the next fireball she unleashed.

The children were forced to scramble back up the stairs to avoid the swing of a mercenary who managed to clamber up the steps just below them. Ellyssa jumped back but tripped and fell over the step behind her and watched in terror as the man loomed over her, ready to plunge his sword into her young body.

A flash of glittering scales flew over her and struck the mercenary in the chest. Wings extended, Sandy sailed over the prone girl in a semi-controlled glide and sank her four-inch-long talons, the hardest and sharpest of almost any dragon species, deep into his chest. Her snake-like neck whipped down, and her sharp teeth took the mercenary in the throat, instantly ending his struggles.

The furious little dragon felt a flash of pain when another mercenary stabbed at her with his sword. The blade skipped off her hard, shiny scales but still managed to bite through enough to raise a line of blood. Sandy hissed in anger and darted forward with the reflexes of a pouncing cat before the man could recover. The sand dragon reared on her hind legs and raked her razor-sharp fore-claws through the attacker's chain throat guard. Blood sprayed into the eyes of the nearest invaders charging up the stairs behind him when he spun away and tumbled down the steps.

"Sandy, get back here!" Ellyssa shouted from higher up the stairs, ready to retreat to the roof where Aggie and the others were still pouring death down onto the forces below the tower.

Sandy took advantage of the mercenaries' troubles as they slipped in the blood-coated stairs, and bounded up to where her friends were waiting for her. Ellyssa looked down into the crowded reception hall and at the men swarming up the stairs and knew that they could never make it to safety. There were too many stairs to climb between them and the roof and only one flimsy door to slow them down. The men were simply too strong, too fast, and too many.

Just as a wall of mercenaries closed within a few steps of where Ellyssa was holding the door for Sandy, a translucent form floated up through the stairs, her shimmering robes and long spectral hair flowing about in a breeze that no one living could feel.

"Not my children!" the ghostly image of the woman shouted in rage.

The sudden appearance of the furious apparition stopped the attackers in their tracks, some of them jumping back so suddenly they tumbled backwards, knocking down several of the men behind them.

"Get out!" the banshee shrieked, the sound of her voice empowered with rage and the pain of her ancient loss.

The shout washed over the men on the stairs like a tidal wave, tearing weapons from hands as they were blasted off the stairs and over the heads of those down below.

"Get out! You will not hurt my children!" she shrieked as ghostly tears streaked down her anguished face.

Hearts froze with fear and the hair turned pure white on the men farther away or partially shielded by those in the front. The banshee repeatedly turned her killing voice against the men who dared threaten her home and children once more. She had failed to protect her family in life, and she refused to fail them in death.

The ethereal lady shrieked her rage until nothing living moved within the reception hall. Outside, the dying sounds of battle made their way through the sundered doors and up the stairs of the eerily silent hall. The lady floated up before Ellyssa and reached out a tentative hand toward the young girl. Ellyssa's breath began to fog as the air around her froze.

"Thank you," Ellyssa said quietly.

The Lady of the Tower touched a single lock of Ellyssa's hair. Her already blond hair took on a pure silver streak, mirroring the one on the other side of her head where the spirit had touched her the first time they had met. With a smile mixed with joy and sorrow, the lady sank back into the stairs and disappeared once more.

Azerick, Allister, Wolf, and Ghost ran toward the citadel. Azerick conjured a gate that opened atop the wall next to the colossal stone blocks sealing the entrance. The sorcerer let the other three pass through before he joined them on the wall to see how the battle was progressing.

It did not look good. There were scores of mercenaries lying dead in the streets and courtyard. Dozens of panicked, riderless horses trod on the wounded as well as the corpses, seeking a way out of the killing zone. A huge number of men were swarming into the near-defenseless keep in a tide of murderous frenzy. Still more were gaining a foothold onto the rooftops where they shot their arrows at the defenders on the other roofs or engaged them in hand-to-hand combat.

Rusty and the senior apprentices were killing men like a farmer scything down wheat stalks, but it was not enough to keep the roofs free of the enemy. A powerful explosion rocked the tower from within.

"That would be your apprentice if I were to hazard a guess," Allister said as he studied the chaos.

A crack of lightning followed the explosion. "Roger and Missy as well," Azerick returned. "We need to defend the roofs and stem the flow going into the keep. The gods only know how many are already inside, but there are too many outside in mortal danger."

"Don't worry, lad. Aggie can defend that roof for some time yet," Allister assured him.

Azerick was still concerned for his apprentice. Knowing her as he did, he doubted that she would be out of harm's way on the roof with the formidable wizard. The sorcerer raised a thick mass of stone spikes just outside the foyer, damming up the flow of human bodies trying to press into the tower and brutally impaling those in the lead.

Allister sent a massive fireball into the crowd of mercenaries who now found their passage into the tower blocked. The archmage then sent single target spells against the men who were too close to friends or too loosely packed together for larger assaults to be safe or economical.

Wolf snatched a handful of arrows from a small barrel set at the top of the wall, dropped them in his quiver, and used the remaining ones from the barrel to shoot at those below and on the roofs. Shot after shot found the vulnerable flesh of a mercenary. Ghost bounded down the stairs and disappeared into the shadows of the buildings. A loud snarl, a scream of terror and pain, and an occasional flash of black fur were the only signs of Ghost's predations.

Azerick was amazed at the young half-elf's uncanny skill with his hunting bow, but had no time to waste in appreciation. He too was busy picking off attackers with lightning and magical bolts of energy as they gained the rooftops.

The throng of mercenaries was greatly beginning to thin out under the defenders' relentlessness when an inhuman, ear-piercing shriek cut through the courtyard. Everyone, attacker and defender alike, dropped their weapons and clapped their hands over their assaulted ears. All sounds of battle abruptly ceased. Only the frightened whinnies of the horses and Ghost's piercing howl could be heard over the deafeningly shrill cry. Several more times the crippling shout rang out over the courtyard, dropping the people nearest to the tower to their knees.

Then there was silence. Only the sounds of the horses' nervous whickering and the crying out of wounded humans was heard above the ringing in everyone's ears. The defenders stooped to recover their weapons as did a few of the mercenaries, but the invaders dropped them to the ground, no longer in the mood to continue the fight. No man wanted to face more of the punishing magical assaults again. After that awful keening, none had the heart to do battle in this accursed place any longer.

After dropping their weapons, the surviving mercenaries went to their knees in supplication as the young men and women bound their hands behind them with whatever length of thong or cord they could find, including their own bootlaces and the laces of their captives. Jansen, bloodied and exhausted from engaging numerous opponents, ordered every captive relieved of weapons and boots before they secured them in one of the thick timbered classrooms. Azerick and the others would deal with them later.

Azerick and Allister ran down the steps to the ground while Wolf went in search of Ghost. "Allister, go get Aggie and the apprentices and have them meet me in front of the stables."

The old wizard did not bother to reply, but simply nodded, and headed into the charnel house that was once a rather grand reception hall, and bounded up the stairs. He told the older children atop the stairs in passing to go meet Azerick at the stables.

Sandy followed the apprentices out of the tower, hissing at a few of the corpses littering the floor. They found Azerick striding toward the stables and ran to meet him, glad to see that he was all right.

"Peck!" Azerick called out as he approached the stables.

The short stableboy came out of the stables at a run, a spear gripped in his hands, and a leather hauberk slung over his narrow shoulders. Peck had refused to leave the horses for the safety of the tower even when it became obvious that the mercenaries were going to breach the gates.

"Yes, Master Azerick?" Peck shouted before he came to a halt just before the sorcerer.

"I need every horse in the stable saddled and ready to go," Azerick instructed the boy.

Peck's freckled face broke into a wide grin. "Already done, milord. I figured once you was done tossing this bit of scum out you'd be wantin' ta go and drive off the rest of them what's beatin' on the city walls."

Peck's exuberance pierced Azerick's fatigue and foul mood. "Excellent work, Peck. In that case, grab some help, round up the rest of these horses, and secure them in the paddock before hitching up a team to reopen the gates," Azerick directed with a small grin of his own.

"Aye, milord, straight away." Peck saluted and ran off after the mercenaries' forfeited mounts.

"What are we going to do now, Azerick?" Ellyssa asked as they came up behind him.

Azerick turned and faced the small group. "I'll explain everything when everyone else gets here. Is everyone all right?"

They all said they were fine. Ellyssa told him about how the spirit had killed all of the mercenaries that made it into the keep.

Alex, Jansen, and Rusty approached from the direction of the classrooms while Allister was just now exiting the keep with Aggie and the rest of the children. Many of the children were crying and being comforted by several women.

Corpses littered the reception hall, and the courtyard was not much better. These were not clean kills like those made by arrows or simple stab wounds. Magic had been used: powerful magic that had torn men asunder and charred their flesh, and the smell was every bit as awful as the visual. This was something that was going to affect them for a long time. Azerick only prayed that the resiliency of childhood would be strong enough to see them through it.

"All right, lad, I think this is most of us. What do you have in mind?" Allister asked gruffly.

"I want you, Rusty, the senior apprentices, Ellyssa, and Roger to ride with me to North Haven where we will strike the enemy in their rear or flank. I also want Alex, Jansen, and any other fighting men we have to ride with us in case we run into a situation that requires some sword work."

"Leaving me to babysit again, are you?" Aggie complained. "What's the matter, afraid the old broad can't still hurl a fireball or two?"

"No, Aggie, quite the opposite. I am strongly debating whether to take you with us or not. I would greatly appreciate the formidable magic you wield, but I have to consider those I leave behind. If we fail to break the siege, then you all will have to flee, possibly all the way to Brelland. I would feel much better knowing that they will have at least one powerful spellcaster to protect them along the way if the rest of us do not make it back."

"Roger and Ellyssa are just children. You should leave them with the others to stay here," Aggie insised.

Azerick shook his head. "They are also the two most talented students we have, and I need every mage who can cast a spell, use a wand, or read a scroll if I hope to break this siege."

Aggie looked at the two young students and saw that the look on their faces reflected their willingness to fight, and chose not to argue.

"Wolf, I want you to lead them east through the woods, then south to Brelland if you do not get a signal from us by nightfall. In fact, I want you all to load up with food, clothes, and blankets and go hide in the east woods. If you do not hear from one of us before sundown, make for Brelland. We fought only a handful of their total force here. We will be facing several times as many at North Haven with even fewer people and no walls to hide behind nor rooftops to shield us."

"That's all right, lad. I have been saving my best for last," Allister replied with a wink.

"Aggie, if you want to come with us, you are more than welcome. I will leave Ellyssa and Roger to go with the others. I have enough wands and scrolls that they should be able to deter most anyone or anything that may threaten them."

Aggie thought about it for a moment. "I don't like the idea of those two children riding into that mess, but a journey like this is going to take more than just magic and wands. They're going to need someone who's been around a while. You can't get wisdom and experience out of a wand or from a scroll. Besides, it's been a long while since I've ridden a horse, and I'm not sure my old bones are up to it."

Allister opened his mouth to reply to her last comment, but Aggie saw the twinkle in his eye and shut him down before he could say a word.

"Shut your mouth, you old goat, before I stuff your beard in it!"

"All right then. Rusty, make sure everyone going with us has at least one wand with several charges in it. Aggie, have Agnes start packing food and water and equip the rest of the students who are capable of wielding them with whatever wands and scrolls remain."

Azerick grabbed Rusty by the arm before he ran off. "You may want to take a minute to say goodbye to Colleen and the babes before we go, just in case."

Rusty swallowed hard and mutely nodded his head.

"Azerick, there is something else you should know," Jansen said as everyone went about their business. "I took a minute to question a few of the soldiers we captured. Not all of them are mercenaries. A few are soldiers under Duke Ulric's command. They said he sent them to augment the mercenary forces. Then, when they took North Haven, they were to sneak away to rejoin Ulric when he leads another force north to 'drive out' the invaders."

"That traitorous bastard," Azerick snarled. "Once North Haven is safe, I am going to deal with Ulric once and for all. Do you know how many soldiers he has left?"

"It does not sound like a lot, mainly conscripts and men he hired, but he has over a thousand men of his own here who will be joining back up with him once the city falls. He has a similar plan in mind with the ships that are blockading the harbor. Several of those will sail out to be joined by a few more sailing north and make it look as if he defeated the sea forces as well."

Azerick shook his head trying to decipher the meaning of such an audacious plan but came up blank. "Why would he go through all this?"

Alex spoke up. "It's obvious when you think about it. By rescuing North Haven, he can insinuate himself on the populace. North Haven is the last major city that supports the king and is hostile to Ulric. He is already being hailed a hero in the southern lands and Brightridge. He could not only demand Miranda's hand in marriage as the cost of her rescue, thus increasing his influence and power, but also label Jarvin as weak and ineffective at protecting his people. He could demand the crown and take it by force if necessary. All he would have to do is march these mercenaries under his banner and no one would know the difference."

Azerick suspected that Duke Ulric's complicity went deeper than that. He could have started this campaign years ago, but this plan of creating and solving a national crisis to take the crown by point of virtue and heroism was wrought with pitfalls. So many things could have gone wrong and had him branded as a traitor instead of a hero.

He was probably the one who wanted Dundalor's armor all along. Ulric had probably spent the last several years trying to get it. The mercenary option would cost him a fortune, so using the armor to secure the throne was the better strategy. It only cost him time.

But something went wrong. Someone double-crossed him. Was it the Black Tower or was it Baneford? Azerick's father had been murdered in Ulric's prison. Ulric was the one who sought the armor, but the king's men found out about the piece his father had. Ulric then hired the Rook to kill his father.

Ulric was responsible for his parents' death, for Azerick's homelessness, Delinda's death, and every tragedy in his life. Duke Ulric and his schemes had put in motion the events that caused every heartache and loss Azerick had ever suffered.

Alex saw the raw emotions play across Azerick's face. "Azerick, are you all right?"

"No, but I will be better soon. Right now the city needs us."

Kayne sat atop his mount with a company of his cavalry watching as his trebuchets pounded the walls and flattened buildings just inside the city. Huge rents were already evident, and a group of his men fought furiously to penetrate one of the breaches. It would not be much longer until his trebuchets battered more holes in the wall, then nothing would stop his men from getting into the city. His ram crew had destroyed the portcullis, and the thick gates sported several deep cracks.

A thousand men were packed beneath the wall guarding the ram from counterattack. The defenders had tried to use oil and fire to burn the ram and dropped large stones to stave in its roof, but the wards the wizards had put in place were holding up well against the abuse.

Scores of men lay dead beneath the wall and around the breach: victims of boiling oil, arrows, and dropped stones, but Kayne's archers had advanced and were doing a good job of keeping the defenders' heads down and all but neutralized the threat they posed to the exposed soldiers beneath the wall.

Kayne had been involved in a few sieges in the past, and he knew they could last weeks or even months, but he doubted that North Haven would be able to keep his forces out for more than a few days, and that was granting them a great deal. They simply were not prepared for this sort of warfare. Their soldiers were unprepared, and their walls were weak to the point of being pathetic.

He turned at the sight of horses approaching from the northeast. *Ah, this must be my men coming to inform me they have taken the tower,* he thought as they thundered toward him.

He hoped the three wizards were with them. He thought he could see the flapping of robes amongst the riders. *Perhaps they can use their magic to hasten the breaching of the walls and gate.*

Kayne watched the approaching riders with mounting confusion. *Why are they riding toward the archers and cavalry instead of my command element?*

Kayne realized what was happening when the first fireball shattered a huge section of his massed archers, slaying scores of them with a single stroke. Within the inferno, Kayne saw his and Ulric's plans unraveling. Magical destruction began raining down upon his men. Each blast of lightning and every burst of fire was like a death stroke cutting into his flesh.

Captain Brague paced the battlements shouting orders to his men and cursing those below the wall. The jingling of bells chiming with every stomp of his boot and shake of his fist punctuated each outburst.

Between his shouting and cursing, he cast nervous glances at the assembled riders a short distance down the street.

Despite his vehement protests, Duchess Mellina sat atop her snow-white charger resplendent in her pale blue and white enameled plate armor. The duchess looked every bit the ice queen the people of North Haven affectionately called her. Surrounded by her personal guard, she sat impassively, studying the situation at the wall. Only her deep blue eyes betrayed the fury that lay just below the frigid surface.

Captain Brague also looked for Lady Miranda, knowing that the fiery opposite of her mother would disobey the duchess's command to stay within the castle, but he could find no sign of her. An arrow glanced off his breastplate, bringing his attention back to the attackers. After throwing a rude hand gesture in the direction of the lucky archer, he ducked down behind a crenellation, fully aware of the difference between bravery and foolishness.

An explosion brought his head prairie dogging back over the top of the battlements to see what sort of evil was transpiring now. Lightning, fire, and orbs of magical energy streaked out across the battlefield, shattering rank upon rank of archers and cavalry.

Captain Brague jumped to his feet, his face contorted with fury. The captain sprinted down the stairs to his cavalry and footmen waiting to engage any enemy that breached the gates or to plug any gap in the walls.

"Captain Brague," Duchess Mellina called to him, "what is happening out there?"

"It's that damn wizard and his ilk coming to make me look like an inept fool! I'll be damned if I let that little upstart make me look ridiculous again!"

Captain Brague began shouting orders to his waiting army. "Cavalry, follow me out of the southern gate, footmen through the eastern sally gates, and clear that breach! This is *our* city, and we will be the ones to crush this scum!"

The captain wheeled his mount to the south and charged toward the lightly guarded southern gates. Steel-shod hooves rang against the cobblestones as three hundred fifty men on horseback charged after the enraged commander.

"Open the gates!" the captain shouted as he and his men approached.

The huge wooden gates swung open and the portcullis was raised as the horses thundered past. Several hundred men afoot, many of them sailors, craftsmen, and laborers wielding whatever weapons they could get their hands on, followed the cavalry out the gates for the counterassault that would either break the siege or doom them all.

CHAPTER 21

The surprise magical assault virtually destroyed the ranks of archers. The small groups of survivors scattered, running in all directions to escape certain death. Kayne's cavalry was also brutalized, but was still largely intact as they charged at the group of spellcasters, intent on cutting them down.

Azerick swung his staff in a wide arc, raising a huge wall of fire in front of the charging cavalry. Rusty brought up a wall of flame nearly as large as the sorcerer's, further slowing the riders and forcing them to lose valuable time by circumventing the scorching flames.

Allister waved his arms and chanted. The old wizard blew on a small sphere of ice that formed in his hand, sending a cloud of icy fog roiling across a huge section of the battlefield. The fog bank rolled inexorably toward the enemy, obscuring the small group of defenders from the citadel. The enemy cavalry charged into the swirling mists, thinking it no more than a veil to screen the wizards from view. The men and horses felt the freezing, numbing effects of the fog the moment they plunged into its ethereal embrace.

Frost rimed the horses' large nostrils, and their breath came out in thick puffs of white nearly indistinguishable from the mists that surrounded them. The freezing vapors entered the lungs of man and horse, freezing and frost burning the delicate tissue so that they could no longer use the air they took in. Men tumbled from their saddles as their mounts collapsed or sought a way out of the killing miasma.

Ellyssa, Roger, Maira, Joshua, and Umair used their wands and scrolls to devastating effect, launching balls of fire that consumed dozens of men as they burst throughout the enemy's ranks. Walls of spinning blades and clouds of choking gas created impassable barriers and slew men and mounts without mercy.

Allister pulled a fistful of bean-sized pebbles from a pouch and began chanting a long and complex spell. At the climax of his mantra, he hurled the stones high into the air where they continued to streak skyward, enlarging and burning with a halo of bright flames until they disappeared into the dense clouds hundreds of feet over their heads. A moment later, the stones, each the size of a man's head, wrapped in fire, and trailing a tail like that of a comet, came streaking back down toward the earth.

The meteors struck across a wide stretch of the battlefield, each stone bursting with enough force to send scores of men hurtling through the air. It was the most awesome display of power Azerick, and probably anyone witnessing, had ever seen. The sheer scale of destruction was unimaginable as hundreds of men died in an instant, and still the spellweavers did not relent, would not relent, until they had no more power to use or they vanquished their enemy.

Captain Brague and his cavalry burst out onto the battlefield without slowing or even pulling their swords from their scabbards to engage the invaders just outside the gates. Instead, they simply ran over the surprised infantry with their armored warhorses, bent on engaging the main body of marauders to the east. He and his riders would let the infantry take care of this rabble.

North Haven's cavalry charged toward the eastern section of wall just in time to see the meteor shower blow apart a massive section of enemy ranks to the north. Captain Brague pulled his longsword from his scabbard with a roar of challenge and charged into the rear of the distracted enemy.

His arm pumped up and down like a relentless machine, cutting down any enemy within reach. He slapped away spears probing for vulnerable spots in his armor with his shield and trampled men beneath his destrier's powerful hooves. The captain fought like a madman, as if his soul had been possessed by the most fearsome abyssal spawn to ever inhabit the five circles of Hell.

Captain Brague would give birth to a legend that day. People throughout the kingdom would speak of him as the *chimes of death*, for every time he swung his sword, they heard the jingling of bells, and a man would die beneath his blade.

Deeper and deeper, he cut his way into the ranks of his foes as his men tried in vain to keep up but were forced to engage the enemy he left in his wake. His footmen routed the enemy at the southern gates and followed the path he and the cavalry blazed through the mercenary forces.

Captain Brague was the first to reach the outside of the breach in the city's wall and continued hewing life and limbs from the attackers pressing themselves into the fissure in an attempt to gain entrance to the city while the defenders pushed back from the inside. His men fought valiantly to reach their commander's side and aid him in clearing the breach, but the press of enemy soldiers slowed them as if they were trying to swim against a river's swift current.

So ferocious was Captain Brague's assault that for every man he slew another fled in fear of the ringing chimes that heralded another man's death. Within minutes, North Haven's defenders were able to push through the breach and engage the enemy on the outside of the walls thanks to the captain's relentless assault.

Kayne watched with growing fury as the defenders arrested his cavalry charge and decimated his soldiers without being able to return a single blow against the damnable wizards. As he wheeled his mount away from the killing fog, he saw that the soldiers of North Haven had come swarming out of the breach to join a contingent of cavalry and footmen pressing back his southern flank until they were almost at the gate.

Kayne realized that his soldiers and Ulric's wizards must have been defeated trying to take the citadel, and his assault against North Haven was in danger of meeting a similar fate. However, if he could stop their cavalry from routing his infantry, he might yet still win the day. Those wizards could not cast spells forever. If he had to win this battle by attrition, so be it. He had the numbers.

He ordered his remaining cavalry to charge into the enemy cavalry's flank. He still had more horses, and his men were better armed and better trained than those of the city. He would scatter their cavalry, rip apart the pathetic infantry, and send his forces through the nominally contested breach and gate that was ready to fall at any moment.

Kayne's charge drove his cavalry deep into Captain Brague's flank. Cavalry battled cavalry, but Kayne's charge gave his men the decided advantage of momentum. Captain Brague turned away from the foot soldiers he was battling and saw the vicious mercenary charge tearing his cavalry apart.

He cleaved in twain the skull of the man who had foolishly engaged him before wheeling his mount to the right and pushing toward the front of his beleaguered flank. His footmen surged forward to fill the gap their commander left and continued to press the enemy infantry.

Kayne thought he could hear the faint ringing of tiny bells as he cut another man from his saddle. Looking about for the source, he spied a large man in full plate armor wearing the cape and blue-plumed helmet of a senior officer. The man was fighting with a berserker's fury and doing a great deal of damage against his men, not just in terms of killing and wounding, but in providing a powerful symbol of resistance that bolstered the morale of his men and degraded that of Kayne's own.

Kayne struck several more North Haven horsemen down as he carved his way toward Captain Brague. When he slew this jingling leader, it would have a great demoralizing effect on his enemy. Kayne had been a soldier for a long time, and he knew how much difference one brave and determined man could make in the hearts of those who followed him.

One man, no matter the strength of his arm or the skill of his blade, could not turn the outcome of a battle. However, if that symbol of bravery could inspire the men around him and demoralize his enemies, then even the most assured victor could find himself on the losing end of the battle.

Captain Brague turned just in time to see the sword come slashing at his head in a vicious overhand chop. He pulled his sword from the crook of a man's shoulder and neck and parried the powerful blow. The stroke sent an arm-numbing vibration through his blade, but the captain ignored it as he looked into the furious, dark eyes of the man who nearly succeeded in ending his career and life.

Captain Brague took in the man with a glance. His gleaming, black scale armor rippled like the skin of a dragon, his cloak looked to have been dipped in the blood of his enemies, and the long scar that bisected his left eye socket, leaving a milky white orb in its place, gave him the look of something that had crawled out of the pits of hell.

The man put Captain Brague on the defensive with a series of swift, skillful strikes from his cruel sword. Wide and serrated along its spine, the blade slashed and thrust at him with speed, skill, and power that belied the man's small stature. Captain Brague knew that his success thus far was based heavily upon his rage, but this scarred man was a natural killer; skill and instinct came as naturally to him as breathing came to other men, and he knew he was in trouble.

Kayne slashed at the enemy commander and was certain the man would fall beneath his blade within moments. He could always tell the likely outcome of a fight within the first few exchanges by appraising his opponent's skill, strength, and technique.

Oftentimes, a man would try to fool his opponent by pretending to stumble or show less skill than he truly possessed to lure his foe into making a mistake, but it never worked on Kayne. He had an innate ability to see through such simple tricks.

Kayne attacked Captain Brague's right side, rendering his shield nearly useless. This also put him on the same side as his good eye, eliminating the minor inconvenience of his blind spot. The enemy commander fought well, and for a time managed to parry and dodge Kayne's assault, but the man's strength was flagging, his swings coming just a little bit slower, and his reactions just a bit delayed.

Kayne smiled in triumph as he swung a hard cut toward the captain's midriff. Captain Brague swept his sword across to parry the blow, but at the last moment, Kayne twisted his wrist and brought his blade over the top of his opponent's. The captain's eyes went wide as he recognized the feint, and the wicked blade came slicing unopposed for his head.

Men nearest the battle between the two leaders seemed to pause as the sharp ring of steel echoed loudly across the battlefield. With interspersed looks of triumph and horror, the soldiers watched the blue-plumed helm sail through the air. It was as if time had slowed to a crawl. It seemed to take several long seconds for the helm to hit the ground, staring face up from the muddy, hoof-churned battlefield.

"We need to move closer to the battle!" Azerick shouted. "Ellyssa, Roger, stay close to me. Do not let anyone get behind us."

The walls of fire, icy mists, and other magical death-dealing barriers were falling as the limits of their existence expired. Azerick led his group to the northern edge of the battle, figuring that if the enemy broke they would retreat south toward friendly lines, and he did not want his friends to be in the path of the retreating men desperately fleeing for their lives.

They were all beginning to fatigue from the near constant summoning and releasing of magical power. Even Ellyssa and Roger were beginning to feel the mental stress of focusing on their wands and scrolls to ensure that they were used effectively and accurately. They pushed closer to the battle, trying to get within range to aid North Haven's army.

They watched helplessly as Kayne's cavalry brutally slammed into the defenders' flank, effectively dividing North Haven's cavalry into several smaller groups where their greater numbers could more easily finish them off. Knowing the battle was far from won, the spellcasters pushed aside their fatigue and launched a devastating salvo of fireballs and ice storms against the tight groups of infantry fighting their way south against North Haven's desperate soldiers.

One piece of good fortune for the outnumbered and outclassed defenders was that with Kayne's archers scattered and all but destroyed, their own archers atop the high walls were now able to add their supporting volleys with near impunity. Despite the renewed support, the ram managed to batter the gates open with its rhythmic pounding, and North Haven's reserve elements were now fighting desperately to keep the mass of mercenaries from flooding through and wreaking havoc inside the city walls.

It seemed that no matter how hard they fought, the enemy continued to press slowly but inexorably through the gates. Only the hastily erected barricades kept the enemy forces from spreading out once they were through the sundered gates and running amok through the city streets. Civilians ran out of homes and inns wielding a variety of weapons from old swords and spears to pitchforks, broom handles, and butcher knives. Men, women, and children broke their nails tearing up the cobblestones and hurling them at the slowly advancing enemy.

Seeing her lines faltering, Duchess Mellina ordered her personal guard forward to bolster the brave men and women desperately fighting a losing battle to hold the gates. The duchess led her soldiers herself despite their protests, stilling their entreaties for her to stay back with an icy glare.

Their foes were beyond the barricades now and beginning to spread out. The trained mercenaries made short work of the civilians trying to defend their homes and families, but for every man and woman they cut down, two more jumped in, fearlessly taking their place.

Duchess Mellina's long, slender blade darted in and out of the vulnerable joints and visor slits of the enemy like a snake's tongue flicking in and out of its mouth. The duchess was a true lady in every sense, setting the standards of propriety and decorum that every woman in the kingdom could only try to emulate; however, beneath that veneer of civility lay the ruthless heart of a woman of profound strength and ability. Her father and then her late husband had taught her how to fight. Both great men often said that a leader must be capable of defending their people against any who sought to do them harm.

Seeing a leader standing proudly beside them in the heat of battle gave soldiers the strength and courage to fight against twice the number of men whose leader cowered in his castle or far behind the lines of battle and sent runners to issue orders to those fighting and dying in his or her name.

No cries of fury ever escaped the ice queen's perfect lips. Only the cold look of purpose and determination showed on the duchess's face as she bloodied one enemy after another. From the corner of her eye, she saw a spear questing for her side deflected by a slight man in the armor of her personal guard. His armor bore the dents and scratches of numerous turned blows. A slight kick to his mount's flanks brought the young man close enough to allow him to thrust his sword beneath the spearman's helm and through his neck.

Duchess Mellina nodded her appreciation to her guard then glared suspiciously when she saw the emerald eyes looking out from behind the enclosed helm and the long lock of auburn hair that fluttered in the late winter breeze.

Before she could say anything, the soldier kicked his mount ahead to engage another foe. Mellina could not afford to pay the matter further heed as she blocked the swing of a gap-toothed, unshaven man's sword. Bending low over her saddle, she thrust her blade right between his teeth, which looked so much like the hole left in the wall by her sundered gates.

Sound flowed back into Captain Brague's ears and light returned to his eyes just in time to see Kayne hauling his sword back to finish the lethal blow his helm had turned. The captain was not about to give him the chance. Kayne's follow-up stroke turned into a parry as Captain Brague's fury renewed itself with a vengeance. He hacked at the mercenary leader like a man chopping wood.

With absolutely no attempt at skill or finesse, Captain Brague screamed in rage, swung his longsword over his head, and battered against Kayne's raised blade repeatedly, giving the lethal man no chance to do anything but absorb the punishment his sword and arm were receiving under the captain's relentless assault.

Kayne saw in the enemy commander's eyes and the berserker fury in his blows that he knew he was outmatched as a warrior, and that the only hope he had of winning was through sheer brutality. Kayne knew the strategy, had even had it used against him on multiple occasions, but in the end, they all simply wore themselves out until Kayne was able to slip his sword into their bodies and kill them. Such a tactic would often work against lesser men, but not against him.

Kayne accepted the punishing blows upon the serrated back of his blade, figuring to let the Valerian notch and dull his sword until either it or his arm wore itself out. His hand and arm thrummed under the constant battering vibrations, but it was nothing he could not handle.

The mercenary leader saw that the captain was getting desperate as he threw his shield to the ground and gripped his sword with both hands, bringing it crashing down with all of his might, and releasing a savage roar of anger and frustration. For a second time, the battle around the two leaders paused as the peal of overstressed steel rang out in protest.

Kayne stared at his shattered blade in uncomprehending confusion. His eyes crossed in an attempt to look at the berserker captain's longsword, which was now firmly buried in his skull to a point just above the bridge of his nose.

Captain Brague wrenched his longsword free with a spray of bone fragments and brain matter and let the mercenary leader's corpse topple from his saddle, landing with a dull thud and the squelch of hoof-churned mud, blood, and slush.

As word spread of the undefeatable Kayne's death and the continued onslaught of magic killing scores of men at a time, the remaining mercenaries and Ulric's soldiers began a retreat to the south that became an undisciplined rout.

The mages gave chase to discourage any who might change their mind, hurling balls of fire and another terrifying meteor storm from Allister into the retreating ranks.

Azerick pulled up short after chasing the fleeing men to the edge of the forest. "We need to get to the docks! Ellyssa and Roger, go find Wolf and the others and let them know they are safe now. You can put shackles or hobbles onto the men we captured and use them to help clear the keep of corpses. Everyone else, follow me. We are not finished yet."

With an exhausted sigh, the others followed after Azerick as he raced toward the east city gates while Captain Brague and his men chased after the retreating mercenaries, ensuring that they did not get the chance to regroup and pillage the countryside.

Without the hundreds upon hundreds of men shoving forward through the shattered gates, the mercenaries that had won their way into the city were now being pushed back at a faster pace than that which they had gained the ground to begin with.

Duchess Mellina, her guards, and the defenders upon the walls were about the only true soldiers left to drive the invaders back out of the city. The rest were stalwart citizens, sailors, innkeepers, blacksmiths, and just about anyone who had the courage to pick up a weapon, stick, or rock and use it to defend their city.

Azerick and his friends raced for the gates. A few of the men guarding the eastern gate recognized Azerick as he approached and shouted to open the gates. Soldiers on the inside opened a smaller sally gate and let them into the city without question. The party galloped through the streets of North Haven toward the docks.

Azerick sent Horse sliding on his hooves to a stop just before one of the wooden piers. All five of Zeb's ships occupied the space at the end of the docks just as Azerick had instructed.

The sorcerer jumped from his saddle and began giving instructions. "Rusty, I want you on the *Iron Shark* while I take *Dolphin's Grace*. Umair, Maira, and Joshua, I want you three to split up between *Majestic* and the other two ships. Allister, you can lend your support to any of the other four vessels of your choice. We are going to help Zeb and his men take out those ships outside the harbor, intact if possible. I think Ulric put most every man he had on the ground, so I don't think they will have large crews. At least I hope not. As long as we can take out their sails and weapons, we should be able to capture them. I do not want to sacrifice lives to try and take them intact. If they prove too difficult or costly, sink them."

"For Solarian's sake, Azerick," Rusty complained, "we are all exhausted, and I know you are too. We cannot take on the whole bloody world in one day."

Azerick laid a hand on Rusty's shoulder. "I know you are tired, Rusty, we all are, just like you said; but we need to finish this, and the only way we can guarantee that it gets finished is to crush Ulric's ability to wage war. We have helped rout their soldiers, and now we need to take apart his navy. If we can capture some of these ships, then we can help North Haven build its own navy to repel any future threat. Besides, it is a good chance to increase the number of our own ships, and that is just good business," Azerick said with a smile.

"When did you get so wrapped up in the sailing business?"

"It's in my blood, Rusty, it's in my blood. Now, everyone make sure you have what you need and let's get going."

Azerick ran down the dock toward *Dolphin's Grace* while the others hustled toward the other ships. Zeb sent his cabin boy to look after the horses they left behind, not needing him for what they were about to do.

"All right, lad, you got us all here, so what are we doing?" Zeb asked.

The deck and rigging were swarming with men, and dozens more were in the hold, every one of them armed and ready to do battle.

"We are going to capture those ships. Barring that, we will sink them."

"Jumpin' seahorses, boy, those are warships! War galleons with thick hulls and twice as many cats and ballistas mounted on her than we have, not to mention the five hundred men each one of them can pack aboard."

"I can neutralize the ship's weapons, and I think we have already routed most of that five hundred on the battlefield."

"That sounds like a whole lotta thinkin' and not a whole lotta knowin'," Zeb countered.

"Look, Zeb, those men had to get here somehow, and I bet they didn't walk, or someone would have seen them and warned us. I am betting that nearly all those troops were loaded aboard those ships and dropped off a little ways south of here, and they did not have time to return to Southport to load up another full complement and return. That means they are probably carrying a standard complement of men at best, more likely a skeleton crew."

Zeb ground his teeth as he chewed over the idea. "You willin' ta bet your life on it, lad?"

"Since I will be on board, the answer to that seems rather obvious."

Zeb turned his head to shout toward the ship. "Cast off, ya louts, hoist the sails, and put your backs to the oars. We're goin' shoppin' for some new boats!" He turned back to face Azerick. "I hope ya haven't forgotten about the little detail of the chain stretched across the harbor, or this is gonna be a short trip."

He had forgotten. "I'll take care of it."

Azerick turned and saw the other ships casting off as well once Zeb ran up the signaling flags ordering them to get underway. Azerick took up a position at the bow of the ship and watched as they neared the harbor mouth and the massive chain stretched across it. The harbor was divided into two by a small rock formation jutting above the surface some ten feet at low tide with a chain running to it from a gatehouse on each shore.

As *Dolphin's Grace* approached the massive chain barricade, Azerick once more allowed Klaraxis to come to the fore enough that he could use his abyssal power of decay and corruption against the massive steel links. Several links near the southern gatehouse turned black and corroded with unnatural speed. The steel flaked and crumbled until it could no longer support its own incredible weight and shattered under the pressure, sending the chain to sink into the sand and silt on the ocean floor.

The moment the task was accomplished, Azerick pushed the demon to the back of his mind with a shudder of revulsion, still remembering and feeling the effects of losing control earlier that day.

The *Majestic* sailed out of the harbor mouth and into the open sea next to Azerick aboard *Dolphin's Grace*. The three other ships followed behind as they approached the enemy warships not far beyond North Haven's port. The ships were already close enough that Azerick could see men scrambling about the decks trimming sails, manning weapons, and preparing the big warships for battle.

It was soon apparent that the enemy crews had not expected North Haven's merchant navy to attack. The men on board likely thought them foolish, for even a poorly crewed warship could sink merchant ships with relative ease before they could hope to land a boarding party.

Zeb's ships spread out the moment they were beyond the harbor mouth and began tacking in a zigzag pattern. The key was to make their ships as difficult to hit as possible while bringing them within range of Azerick's and the other wizards' spells.

It was a plan fraught with danger. The spellcasters needed to get within a few hundred yards for most of their longer-ranged spells to be effective, while the big frigates mounted huge ballistas that could launch heavy stones nearly five hundred yards. Fortunately, each ship only mounted two of the massive weapons, one at the bow and one at the stern, and they were slow to reload.

The loud crack of the heavy ballista carried over the water as huge stones began arcing out toward them. Zeb and the other ships tacked diagonally toward the lethal war vessels trying to make themselves harder to hit.

Dolphin's Grace passed through the spray left by one near miss as another stone tore a large hole through one of the sails. The big cargo ship, *Majestic*, was struck by a stone just above the waterline, staving in several planks but failing to breach the thick wood and cause a hole. Men below decks busily braced the cracked wood with timbers and slapped thick tar mixed with chunks of hemp rope into the cracks to seal them against the inflow of water.

A second loud crash carried across the waves as a pair of stones weighing more than a hundred pounds apiece struck the slower and less maneuverable *Iron Shark* in rapid succession, but her double-thick hull and iron-shrouded bow shrugged off the assault with little real damage.

Azerick raked a bolt of lightning across the deck when his swift schooner came within range of one of the war frigates. His spell struck the forward heavy ballista, rendering the weapon inoperable and striking down its four-man crew. A second bolt split one of the main masts of the four-masted war galleon, sending the huge timber crashing into the forward mast, tearing sails and fouling ropes as it fell.

Azerick saw the flash of fire out of the corner of his eye when Rusty's fireball took out another ship's heavy ballista and set fire to the oiled ropes, rigging, and sails near the stern of a second enemy warship. Soon lightning, fire, arrows, and stones were streaking between Ulric's galleons and Zeb's merchant ships, killing men, shattering masts, and burning sails.

The damage to the sails and rigging of the warships was so great that even the slow and cumbersome *Iron Shark* was able to get within boarding range, nearly ramming the larger ship in the process. Grapnels attached to heavy ropes arced out over the gunwales of the merchant navy onto the rails of the frigates. Sailors threw boarding planks across the narrow expanse as they drew the ships together while others swung through the rigging to gain the decks of the enemy vessels.

Melee combat was brief. Azerick's assumption of there being only a light crew aboard the warships proved to be correct. Once they boarded the warships, the heavily packed crews aboard Zeb's ships were able to take the galleons with almost contemptuous ease. They locked the surrendered enemy crews into the holds while Zeb's men took over control of the ships they seized as lawful plunder.

They lost the ship Umair was aboard, but it sank slowly enough that most of the crew was able to make it to the longboats before it went down. The others were plucked out of the rolling seas by another merchant ship that lent its support to the war effort. *Balor's Beauty* was taking on water, but not to such an extent that the bilge pumps and men with buckets could not keep her bailed out enough to limp back to the harbor. They had to chase down three more ships, but only one managed to make it through the battle without getting her sails and rigging destroyed and was able to flee to the high seas and escape. There was too much at stake to spend hours or even days chasing after it.

With the help of other merchant ships that had been at anchor in North Haven's harbor, Zeb's men managed to tow seven of the ten ships back to port as spoils of war. One managed to flee and two had burned to the waterline before they sank to the sea floor. The crew continued working on the big merchant ship until she was safe from sinking and could be dry-docked and repaired later.

Allister and Rusty stood back on the docks and scanned the harbor for the sleek schooner, but it was nowhere to be seen.

"Where are Azerick and Zeb?" Rusty asked with a tinge of concern in his voice.

Allister shook his head. "I'm not sure, son."

Allister grabbed Toron by his powerful, shaggy arm as he went past. "Toron, have you seen Azerick's or Zeb's ship?"

The big minotaur looked down at Rusty and the old wizard. "They were sailing south as I was returning to port and signaled by flag not to follow."

Rusty let out a long breath. "He's going to get Ulric."

"Then may the gods have mercy on his black soul, because that boy sure won't," Allister intoned.

CHAPTER 22

At the same time Rusty, Allister, and their prisoners were digging mass graves and cleaning up the school, Azerick, Zeb, and a complement of sailors sailed to Southport.

Azerick spent the majority of the next two days resting and replenishing his energy as well as renewing the power of his staff. He finally made an appearance on deck late in the afternoon of the second day at sea.

"You're lookin' better, lad," Zeb appraised him as he walked up to the young man.

Azerick just nodded, his mind already in Southport, two days ahead of his body.

"You got a plan for once we get there?"

Azerick's mind returned to the ship. "Strike our colors and sail into the port as a neutral vessel. Signal the harbormaster that we have urgent news for the duke regarding the battle at North Haven. He will be expecting someone to return to tell him that Kayne has taken the city and for his men to move north.

"We will sail in at night and take any ship that is flying Ulric's banner. There should be fewer than we fought at North Haven, and they will likely not be fully crewed unless they are ready to set sail. With luck, the crew will be billeted on the mainland close by and only a guard force set to watch the ships. If they are loaded and ready to set sail, I will destroy them when we sail out; if not, your men will take them and return to North Haven. You wait here, if possible, while I take care of business within the city."

Zeb looked at Azerick and scratched his short beard. "What kind of business would that be?"

"Personal business," Azerick replied darkly, then returned to his cabin without another word.

Two days later, they lay at anchor outside Southport's harbor, waiting for the sun to set. When the hour finally arrived, Azerick's ship sailed into the harbor. An armed customs ship sailed out to meet them before they could approach any of the docks. Large bullseye lanterns bathed *Dolphin's Grace* in beams of bright light.

"This port is closed by the order of Duke Ulric, Lord of Southport," a voice boomed across the dark expanse of water.

"I have an urgent message for the duke regarding the battle at North Haven. Let us pass," Azerick shouted back.

"You can pass your message to me, and I will ensure that the duke gets it," the man returned adamantly.

Azerick was in no mood for the man's foolishness. He opened a gate, stepped from the deck of *Dolphin's Grace*, and stood directly behind the man on the customs ship.

A bright light flared at the end of Azerick's staff, casting his hooded head in deep shadows. "I was sent with two of my colleagues by Duke Ulric's order. He further commanded me to return with all haste once I had something to report. Are you now going to delay my report, or even more foolishly, countermand my orders?"

Hands flew to sword hilts as the startled customs agent spun around to face the angry man who appeared behind him.

"Well, you see…sir, it's just that I…"

"Quickly, man, your answer may well determine how much longer you get to enjoy breathing!" Azerick snarled.

"No, sir, of course, sir. Proceed with your duties."

Azerick returned to the deck of the schooner while the customs ship shuttered the lanterns and sailed back into the harbor. *Dolphin's Grace* grabbed the wind and sailed smoothly into the port behind the customs ship. Seeing that the schooner carrying the wizard was behind them, the nervous customs man ordered his ship to take up a position on the far side of the harbor, not wanting to be anywhere near them.

Against the darkness, Zeb's crew spotted the tall masts of three more ships similar to the big war galleons they had battled anchored just off the docks. Guards patrolling the decks gathered near the rail and manned the heavy deck weapons as the schooner sailed slowly by.

Their vigilance proved to be for naught. Azerick cast another gate spell, stepped onto the deck of the warship, and captured most of the crew with incapacitating spells before they could even respond. Zeb's men were able to take the ship nearly without a sound. Only the occasional ring of steel on steel or the heavy thump of a body hitting the deck broke the stillness of the night.

The same tactic proved equally successful on two other ships floating at anchor. After having seized the ships, Zeb pulled the schooner up next to the dock to allow Azerick to disembark.

"Remember, Zeb, get out of here before the sun breaks with or without me. The last thing you want to do is have a relief force arrive and sound the alarm."

"I got it, lad. You just be careful and get yourself back here before we go."

"I will do my best, Zeb, and thank you. You have been a reliable friend. I could not have done all this without you and your men."

"Yeah ya could have, but thanks. Me and more than a few of us owe you our lives. It's the least we can do. Besides, you own a majority stake in these tubs!"

Azerick shook his head. "Whatever you think you owe me has been paid in full, Zeb. That goes for all of the men. I would certainly count this as above and beyond the call of duty."

"That's what friends are for, lad. Now get going before ya make yourself late for your meeting."

Azerick and Zeb clapped each other on the back before the sorcerer stepped onto the dock and disappeared into the night.

So, we're going to go kill this duke worm then? Klaraxis asked in anticipation.

Actually, we are not. I intend to leave him alive. I just wish to have a talk with him.

Talk with him? I saw your thoughts, your memories! I know what he has done, and you are going to let him live? I understand that you are a weak-

willed human without a proper thirst for blood and vengeance, but I expected better from you.

I have something else in mind. Azerick let the demon in on his thoughts.

Oh, that is beautiful! You are more insidious than I thought. I truly underestimated the spine of your vengeance. Bravo, you have the makings of a demon in you yet!

Azerick ignored the rest of the demon's words as he made his way toward Ulric's castle. Perhaps it was the self-assured way he carried himself, or perhaps the men hiding in the shadows looking for easy prey felt the shroud of death wrapping the young man walking boldly down the poorly lit streets. Whatever the reason, no one dared accost him as he strode fearlessly down the cobbled streets toward the castle.

Duke Ulric awoke with a start, his body breaking out in a cold sweat with the feeling that someone was in the room watching him. The duke turned up the wick on the oil lamp next to his bed and furtively cast his eyes about the room. His heart caught in his throat when he spied the dark-cloaked figure sitting in his plush chair watching him. For a brief moment, Ulric thought it was the Rook, but as his eyes adjusted to the light, he was able to see the prematurely aged young face behind the hood of the cloak.

"Who are you? How did you get in here?" Ulric demanded as he gained his composure.

Azerick dropped the hood of his cloak and revealed his face. "I suppose I should not be surprised that you do not recognize me even though I have been told that I resemble my father a great deal. I doubt such a man as you remembers the faces of a fraction of the men you have had murdered."

Ulric narrowed his eyes at the intruder. "What are you talking about? I am certain I have never seen you before in my life."

"You met my father once though. Perhaps if you look closely, you will recognize him in me. No? Let me refresh your memory. Several years ago, you had men in Lazuul recover an artifact, part of

Dundalor's armor. You had them convince or trick a ship's captain by the name of Darius Giles into bringing it to Southport. When the king's men discovered it and arrested the captain, you had him murdered by an unsavory character who goes by the name of the Rook."

"How do you know of him?" Ulric demanded.

He was getting nervous as this young man began talking of things that he should not know, things that could get him in a great deal of trouble if they were proven. No, he was safe from the king's justice. North Haven would soon fall, and Jarvin did not have the men to bring him to justice even if enough evidence of his treachery was brought forward. However, it would not be good to have this young man spreading these tales to the peasants and nobles. He would listen for a moment then call his guards and have him killed on the spot.

"I know the Rook because your stupid cousin sent him to kill me after I inadvertently killed his son, Travis. He failed, as you can see by the fact that I am here now to seek my retribution."

Gods, he killed the Rook? Can that be possible?

If so, this man was far more dangerous than Ulric cared to contemplate. Sweat began beading on his brow as he slowly slipped a leg from under the thick blankets to touch the cool floor with his foot, ready to move at a second's notice.

"Guards, assassin in my chambers! Guards!" Ulric shouted as he sprang from the bed, a dagger clutched in his hand.

Ulric backed away from the man who was still sitting comfortably in his chair, watching him as he crept slowly toward his chamber door.

"Guards!" the duke shouted once more. "What have you done to my guards? Where are they?"

"I have done nothing to them. They stand just outside the door, as vigilant as ever," Azerick coolly responded.

Ulric reached behind him with his free hand, not taking his eyes off the intruder, and tugged on the door, but it would not budge. He turned toward it and used both hands without releasing the dagger and pulled harder. He began pounding on the sealed portal and shouting for his guards when still it would not open.

"You may as well save your voice; they cannot hear you, and you will need it soon. It would be a shame for you to strain yourself when you have such an important speech to make tomorrow."

Ulric spun back toward the man in his chair. "What are you talking about? What speech?"

Azerick stood and stepped slowly toward the duke, his eyes burning red as Ulric tried to push himself backward through the door.

"Relax, Ulric. Drop the knife. I am not going to harm you," Azerick said smoothly.

The dagger clattered to the floor at the duke's feet, his utter obedience compelled by the young man's hypnotic, dual-toned voice. One voice, smooth and higher in pitch than the other, seemed to mix with another much deeper and foreboding voice as if two people were talking at precisely the same time, speaking the exact same words.

"That's better. Are you relaxed now?"

Ulric nodded his head with a sheepish smile. "Yes, I'm fine now. Sorry, I do not know what came over me. Just nervous I suppose. It has been a very stressful time for me, you know."

Azerick returned his smile. "I know, Ulric, but that is all over now. Your forces have failed at North Haven. The city still belongs to the duchess, and your men have been routed, but that is not important now."

The duke frowned. "That is disappointing, but you are right, it is not important. What do I do now? Jarvin will have me banished, possibly executed for what I have done. I have done some very bad things, and a lot of people are going to be angry with me."

"I am going to tell you what you are going to do, and it will make it all better. You will not have to fear the king or anyone else," Azerick and Klaraxis intoned.

Ulric nodded as Azerick told him what he needed to do. "That sounds reasonable, thank you," Ulric said after Azerick finished speaking.

"Good, ensure that you have your criers sent throughout the city so everyone will come to see you and hear what you have to say. We want a nice big crowd. That is important."

"Of course. I will have my seneschal send them out first thing in the morning and announce it every hour on the hour. In fact, I will have the Watch send people to the square. I will make it mandatory to attend!" Ulric said earnestly.

"Good, that should work very well. Make sure you get a good night's rest. You want to look your best for tomorrow's event," Azerick said, then entered the portal he summoned and disappeared.

Yes, I must look my best. It is important, Ulric said to himself as he opened the door to his chambers.

"Is everything all right, Your Grace?" the guard asked as the duke stepped into the hall.

"Oh yes, very well. Please send for Lord Alton at once and have him attend me here."

"Yes, Your Grace," the guard replied, then flagged down a servant, and relayed the duke's command.

A few minutes later, a light rapping sounded outside Ulric's door. "Alton? Come in, quickly now. We must attend to some very important things right away. I am going to address my people. First, I need you to lay out my finest garments of state. Nothing too thick and cumbersome. White silk would be best. Then you must send out criers to every corner and announce to all that I will be commencing a speech of profound importance at exactly noon tomorrow in Rose Plaza. Instruct the guard to urge everyone they see on the streets to attend or face a fine."

The old chamberlain shook his head at Ulric's rather impulsive command, but Alton had been chamberlain for the previous two dukes of Southport, and he was ingrained to follow orders promptly and without hesitation.

"Yes, Your Grace. I will see to it at once."

"Excellent, Alton. I shall leave the details in your capable hands. I must get some rest now. I need to look my best for tomorrow's address."

Alton selected the garments that would satisfy the duke's wishes as Ulric slipped back into his bed and fell asleep. Once Alton was satisfied that the clothing was suitable, he shuffled out of the rooms to carry out the rest of his orders.

Azerick found himself in a richly appointed study standing just behind a man sitting in front of a warm fire in a high-backed, thickly padded chair sipping a glass of brandy despite the late hour. When the cool metal of the extended blade of Azerick's staff touched him lightly on the neck, the man nearly spilled the entire contents of his glass upon the red silk and velvet robe he was wearing

Azerick walked slowly around to the front of the man who now sat frozen in his seat with only the trembling of his glass to show that he was alive at all.

"Lord Beaumonte, we have some things to discuss, you and I," Azerick told the man as he removed the gleaming arcanum blade from his neck and leaned upon the burgundy staff.

"Wh—who are you?" Lord Beaumonte asked.

Azerick shook his head and flashed a humorless smile. "It must be something that runs in the family. You and your cousin, the duke, seem to have a talent for ordering the murders of others without even knowing or remembering their faces."

A look of comprehension came over Lord Beaumonte's face. "You are the one who murdered my son!"

"No! I did not kill Travis," Azerick said more softly. "Travis was killed by his own petty selfishness and the belief that his social status allowed him to act as he pleased. He thought he had the right to extort younger students, rape a young woman, and kill me because of the values *you* instilled. You are as guilty of his death as I am."

"That is nonsense! I raised him to be a man of breeding and power, all those things necessary for a leader of men, but you killed him with your cowardly sabotage!"

"You taught him how to be nothing but a two-bit tyrant with the wealth to hire enough muscle to intimidate people into doing whatever he wanted. That is not a leader, that is a bully. A leader is able to get men to follow him through the strength of his convictions, character, and purpose! But you would not know about that sort of thing."

"So what will you do now, kill me? Go ahead, you will be dead soon enough. I hired the best assassin in the known world to pay you back for your treachery, though why the Rook has not finished you off yet is beyond me. I paid him quite enough to ensure that it was carried out in a timely manner," Lord Beaumonte snapped back.

"Ah yes, the Rook. He was a very frightening fellow, wasn't he? Let me tell you something. If you thought he was scary, then I ought to terrify you. He died trying to fulfill your contract."

"He is dead? You killed him?"

"I have killed many men, more than I care to count or think about, enough that I am willing to offer you just one chance to go on and live your life, for whatever it is worth. Your cousin is going to give a speech tomorrow that people will be talking about for a very long time. I strongly suggest you attend so that you might learn what becomes of men who give in to their selfish desires, who attain their lofty positions of power by climbing the bodies and swimming through the blood of those they killed to attain it. Listen well, and learn from his example if you wish to continue to live."

With that dire warning, the sorcerer stepped through a tear in the very air behind him and disappeared, leaving the lord to ponder his words and decide for himself what to do, and to put the fate of his life into his own hands.

Azerick returned to the docks two hours before the sun rose and boarded *Dolphin's Grace* for the return home. Four ships sailed quietly off into the night, their captives pitched overboard, and a single longboat dropped as an act of mercy just after they passed beyond the mouth of the bay.

Azerick shuddered and felt physically ill when he thought about the use of such compulsion magic on another person, even one as vile as Ulric. It reminded him far too much of what Xornan did to him, and that brought back memories of Delinda. He tried to reconcile the need for what he had done with the awfulness of the act, but nothing made him feel any better about it. It was done now, and he would not change it even if he could.

Throughout the morning, pages and runners ran from inn to inn to announce the mandatory attendance of Duke Ulric's speech. Criers stood at every major intersection in the city repeating the same announcement several times every hour on the hour. As noon approached, the city watch was out in force clearing out taverns, inns, places of business, and herding everyone they found on the streets toward Rose Plaza, which was located within the castle grounds.

The tumultuous cacophony of thousands of voices drifted up through the open doors that led to the grand balcony where Ulric would soon give his citywide address. Alton was by his side trying to calm his lord, wishing that the duke would tell him something of what this was all about, but Ulric insisted that it must be him alone to reveal his message, and he would do so only to the people as a whole.

"It is nearly time, Your Grace," his chamberlain informed him, his voice barely above a whisper.

"Very good, Alton. Please leave me and join the crowd down below. Of course, you will stand at the head of the other nobles of the city," Ulric instructed.

Alton's aged hand trembled slightly as he raised it toward the duke. "I thought I might listen from here in case you needed me, Your Grace."

"No, my loyal chamberlain, you must join the others in the courtyard. I will be all right, I promise you."

Duke Ulric gathered his thoughts as he paced nervously within his rooms as the time grew near, and then boldly stepped out onto the balcony. The chaotic noise of the populace turned into subdued murmuring then ceased altogether when Duke Ulric raised his hands for silence. He looked down at Alton and the assembled nobles then spread his gaze out over the sea of bodies tightly pressed together, all eagerly awaiting his proclamation.

"People of Southport and guests from throughout the land," Duke Ulric called out in a loud but clear voice, his words carrying with perfect resonance thanks to the skillful engineering of those who had built the courtyard. "I come to you today to confess my sins and divulge the wrongs I have committed against my citizens, my neighbors, and the kingdom."

The frenzied questioning and murmurings of several thousand people broke the stillness in the courtyard. It took several minutes for the duke and the guards below to restore the peace enough for him to continue.

"I have committed numerous and grievous crimes, far too many for me to list them all. It was I who ordered the poisoning of the late Duke of North Haven over ten years ago and arranged the assassination of Duke William of Brightridge as well as our former king."

It took a full ten minutes to restore order after Duke Ulric's confession. When the crowd was once again quiet and able to contain themselves, Ulric continued.

"I tricked a local merchant named Darius Giles into smuggling an illegal artifact into the city with a set of forged documents supposedly from the king, then I had him murdered when he was discovered to ensure that no suspicion was cast my way. I sent my soldiers to acquire the pieces of Dundalor's armor so that I could challenge Jarvin for the throne, going so far as to slaughter his special guard and recover any pieces they had in their possession. I also paid men to try to kidnap Lady Miranda of North Haven so that I might force her into a marriage and one day eliminate the duchess and gain power over the northern city.

"When that failed and the men I had sent after the armor turned against me, I hired mercenaries to pillage several smaller towns in the kingdom so that I could ride in and appear to drive them away in order to gain the favor of the populace. The battles were staged, and nearly every casualty the invaders suffered was faked. I even sent them against Groveswood and allowed them to plunder the wealthy town full of some of our most esteemed nobles as payment for the services of the mercenaries as well as to add those noblemen's influential voices to my group of supporters when I made my bid for the crown.

"I then sent an even larger force of mercenaries, augmented by my own men, to sack the city of North Haven where I would supposedly liberate it in the same manner that had been so successful on a smaller scale for the past year. However, those forces have failed, and my complicity and duplicity has been revealed, so I stand here before you, confessing my crimes as part of my punishment and to serve as a warning to any who would think to try to gain power by spilling the blood of others."

Duke Ulric stood upon a chair and pulled out a dagger from the sheath belted around his waist. "As a further example of what happens to men who abuse the trust and power of their position, I offer you this last warning."

Without warning or hesitation, Duke Ulric plunged the blade deep into the side of his stomach, and a red rose of blood bloomed across the white expanse of silk and velvet. The rose turned into a river as he pulled the blade sharply across his abdomen before stepping up onto and over the balcony rail.

No one noticed the rope the duke had secured around his neck and trailed down his back until it snapped taut, sending a spray of blood and offal down upon the front ranks of nobles gathered some twenty feet below him. When the grisly scene unfolded, Lord Beaumonte understood the warning Azerick had given him, as well as the second chance he offered.

He continued to stare up at the swinging, dangling corpse of his cousin as people screamed, women fainted, and guards ran amok, unsure of what to do. After a brief moment of shock, Alton gained control of several guards and ordered them to clear the courtyard and recover the duke's body. This was indeed a speech that many people would be talking about for a very long time.

EPILOGUE

Azerick and Miranda rode down a deer path and entered a small grassy glade hidden within the woods not far from the keep. The bodies were gone and classes had resumed. North Haven was still busy repairing and fortifying the walls and gates around the city, but Miranda had urged Azerick to take her on a picnic until he relented.

The couple let the horses wander about the glade, munching green spring grass and drinking from the small brook that gurgled peacefully nearby. Azerick spread a plaid cover over the ground where he and Miranda took a seat and shared a bottle of wine.

"I hear that the repairs are going well in the city," Azerick said.

"Yes, you know Captain Brague chased the fleeing soldiers south until they ran into the support and baggage train that followed the mercenaries north. There were quite a lot of valuables on it. My mother insisted that much of it be returned, the more conspicuous pieces anyway that could be readily identified by the owners, but the rest has gone a long way to covering the cost of rebuilding. We have sent envoys to Southport to discuss the political ramifications and reparations due, but Ulric drained the city's coffers to the point that we can expect little if anything from them for some time."

"It is my hope that the extra ships under Zeb and my company's control will bring in quite a bit of extra tax revenue with the increased trade," Azerick replied.

Miranda flashed one of her perfect smiles that made Azerick's heart beat faster than when he was forced to fight in the arena. "It has, and the ships you donated to the city will also generate much-needed income when the ones we converted to haulers return with their goods, something for which Mother would have thanked you personally had you bothered to show up at the ceremony to receive your reward."

Azerick blushed under Miranda's teasing. "Please tell the duchess that I am glad I was able to help and for the award she bestowed upon me."

"So how does it feel being a noble, Lord Azerick Giles?"

"Like I just got dipped in oil and rolled in the dirt," Azerick replied, then wiped at his arms as if he were trying to rid himself of something foul.

Miranda laughed deeply then without warning leaned in and kissed him on the lips. Azerick returned the kiss, tentatively at first, and then with a passion he thought he had lost forever. The couple held each other tightly and looked deep into each other's eyes.

"Hooray, Azerick, you finally got the princess, you sly dog!" a voice shouted shrilly across the glade, spoiling the romantic scene.

Azerick turned and shouted. "Wolf!"

High-pitched laughter and the sound of several pairs of feet running away deeper into the woods filled the glade. Miranda's melodious laughter echoed through the trees, suffusing his heart with the warmth and joy that had been missing for so long. Perhaps now he would be able to live in peace for once and enjoy a measure of the happiness he had forever been denied.

The dark-robed figures gathered around a stone table under the flickering light of large tapers and torches once again. The secret cabal was meeting in what looked to be a dusty tomb or crypt with only the bones of the dead to hear their dark machinations.

"Ulric has failed miserably," one of the figures intoned unnecessarily. They all knew of the disaster at North Haven.

"It was not totally unexpected. His plan was overly complicated and rested upon the shoulders of too many unpredictable elements," another said. "It is why we backed him but did not openly support him. Our contingency plan is still in place and completely unsuspected."

"But the king is aware that a major plot to overthrow him only narrowly failed. He is certain to be more alert for treachery now."

"Not necessarily. Ulric may have done us a favor by failing in his grandiose conspiracy. Even if he had taken North Haven and managed to unseat Jarvin, well, men talk. It would have been only a matter of time before his duplicity was uncovered, and then the people and the nobles would both be howling for his blood. With such a dramatic failure and expenditure of resources, few would believe that another such attempt at a coup would be coming anytime soon. If exploited properly, it may actually work in our favor."

"Ah yes, I see what you are saying. Excellent, then we proceed as planned?"

"Absolutely. By this time next year, the bastard king's head will adorn a pike right next to his wife and misbegotten offspring. It is the will of Solarian."

"Blessed is the light of Solarian," everyone around the table chanted in unison.

To be continued in:
THE SORCERER'S SCOURGE
Book Five of The Sorcerer's Path

FROM THE AUTHOR

I hope you enjoyed this tale and will try my other works. Feel free to look me up on Facebook! You can also check me out on my website http://brockdeskins.com/ where I write serial fiction, free for your enjoyment, and answer questions!

Author page:
https://www.amazon.com/Brock-Deskins/e/B005M6VQ1O

Facebook:
https://www.facebook.com/brocksbooks/

Twitter:
@brockdeskins

PLEASE <u>**REVIEW**</u> **MY BOOKS** (Especially if you liked it). Customer reviews are the primary means of enticing others to purchase them. I am dependent upon the sales of my books to earn a living that will allow me to continue writing stories that I hope bring you some measure of entertainment. Thank you for your support.

OTHER BOOKS BY BROCK E. DESKINS

The Sorcerer's Path is an epic fantasy series.

The Sorcerer's Ascension: Torn from a life of comfort and luxury, his family destroyed by political intrigues and aspirations, a young boy must quickly grow into a man before the deadly streets of Southport devour him. Follow Azerick through a page-turning adventure that pits him against thieves, thugs, murderers, and men of power that will stop at nothing to achieve their goals.

Azerick must fight just to survive, but for him survival is not enough. A hunger to avenge the wrongs committed against him burns deep within. But that is not all that lies within the young man. There is a power waiting to be unleashed that may be the key to achieving the justice and security he seeks--if it does not destroy him first.

The Sorcerer's Torment: Azerick flees The Academy but quickly falls prey to powerful beings that use his skills and power for their own amusement. What these creatures do not understand is the power of the young sorcerer's will and the lengths he will go to for vengeance. Despite becoming a prisoner, Azerick finds his first true love, but can he keep it?

The Sorcerer's Legacy: Azerick has found himself a home and tries to settle down. He takes on an apprentice and tries to put all the death and desire for vengeance behind him. But when the Rook finds him, Azerick is once again pulled back into Ulric's schemes. Knowing that all he has worked toward and everyone close to him is in danger as long as these schemes are ongoing; Azerick decides to put an end to it, once and for all.

The Sorcerer's Vengeance: After narrowly avoiding being killed in his own bed by the land's most feared assassin, Azerick leaves his school behind to find out who sent him and to put an end to the threat once and for all. Azerick's search will take him to the very pits of the abyss and back to unleash hellish fury upon those that threaten him.

The Sorcerer's Scourge: With the siege broken and Ulric dead, Azerick can finally relax, study his magic, and run his school in peace. Unfortunately, Jarvin's reign is far from uncontested and the true usurper decides to make his move. Jarvin escapes with help from an unlikely source—a vampire named Landrin who still clings tenaciously to his own humanity. While Azerick and a large force from North Haven race to save the king in exile, evil forces are preparing to unleash a nightmare upon the kingdom that may well destroy them all.

The Sorcerer's Abyss: Now the master of the Fifth Circle of the abyss, Azerick is challenged by another demon lord for supremacy. Azerick must face this threat as well as his innermost demons, all the while searching for a way to escape his hellish prison.

Ellyssa fears she is going insane as she plagued by nightmares of her capture and enslavement. Deciding the key to saving herself lies in the total destruction of the object of her fears, she embarks on a crusade to find and kill the slaver, Captain Jake, and eradicate the slave trade.

Ellyssa's nightmares and battles spill out onto the streets of North Haven and gains the attention of The Academy. Fearing Azerick's school is turning out rogue wizards, The Academy decides to hunt down and destroy the rogue and place the school within their control.

The Sorcerer's Return: Azerick has come back from the abyss in order to try to unite all the races against the return of the old gods who seek to destroy them and subjugate the few they allow to survive a brutal purging. However, fighting ancient gods may be the least of his troubles as he battles to save a fractured kingdom, a brilliant son traveling a dark path, and the splintered soul of his own humanity.

The Sorcerer's Destiny: Brutally purged of his demonic influence, Azerick continues the struggle of uniting the kingdom to face the coming of the Scions, ancient gods banished by the mortal races during the Great Revolution two thousand years ago. The fallen gods' prison is crumbling, and Azerick is powerless to stop them from breaking free and enacting their cataclysmic vengeance upon the world.

The humans must ally with the other races in a final battle against impossible odds while their entire world crumbles to the ground and is trod beneath the feet of an unstoppable foe. How can they set aside their distrust of each other when they fear the very person trying to save them?

Rise of the Order: Banished to the abyss after helping defeat the Scions and saving the world from eternal darkness, Azerick languishes in perpetual misery as Lord of the Fifth Circle. The denizens of his hellish realm view him as a usurper and outsider. The chaotic creatures form an alliance with one goal in mind: destroy Azerick Giles, but Sharrellan stands in their way.

A powerful spell tears through the demonic planes, and when the dust settles, the dark goddess is nowhere to be found. It is up to Azerick to return her to her seat of power, but he has a price: return him to his mortal form and send him home.

Back home, a vast empire is on a crusade to conquer the world, and it has set its sights on Valeria. Their goal is to unite the world under a single banner, eradicate the spawn infestation unleashed by the Scions, and replace the gods who they feel have forsaken them with their mystical rulers.

Can Azerick save the dark goddess from the clutches of her demonic subjects and become mortal once again? Will he have the power to protect his people from The Order if he does?

Descent Into Chaos: The Order has arrived in force, and the fate of Valeria, and perhaps all the world, is poised to come under their iron-fisted control. Azerick and Daebian are forced to flee Southport and make a contentious alliance when King Miles capitulates to the invaders. Reduced to insurgent warfare, Azerick and his allies attempt to battle The Order's vastly superior forces in a series of hit and run strikes, but the enemy legions may not be his biggest threat.

Princess Sylvian Attar, daughter to The Order's godlike emperor and empress, has taken a personal interest in Azerick. Herself a powerful sorceress, Sylvian hunts Azerick in hopes of removing Valeria's legendary hero from the battlefield thus sapping her enemies' will to fight. Azerick decides there is but one course of action he can take against this unstoppable foe. It was time to inject a little chaos into The Order.

Brooklyn Shadows is a modern-day vampire tale. Full of action and snarky dialogue, Brooklyn Shadows is an enjoyable read for anyone who enjoys the supernatural underworld and butt-kicking vampires.

<u>Shrouds of Darkness</u> (Brooklyn Shadows Book 1) Leo Malone has been a vampire for the better part of the twentieth century. Once a prominent Sherriff (vampire cop), he now earns his living as a private eye and occasional bodyguard for anyone that requires some serious protection. Leo is hired by the daughter of a mob accountant who has gone missing.

The fact that her father is also a werewolf has Leo following a trail of grisly murders that will lead him through a web of intrigue and conspiracy involving his fellow vampires and the local werewolves that make New York their home, all the while trying to keep one particularly determined cop off his back and himself out of jail. Leo is not some pretty-boy vampire that all the girls ogle over, but a hard-eyed, remorseless killing machine who does not take crap from anyone.

<u>Blood Conspiracy</u> (Brooklyn Shadows Book 2): While dealing with the aftermath of the failed vampire council coup, Leo discovers that the modified Cure has fallen into the hands of a black ops government project designed to create vampiric super soldiers. When the inevitable happens, the off-book Homeland Security operation forcefully enlists Leo to help them resolve the situation. Worse yet, he has to work not only with an antagonistic werewolf named Meat, he is reunited with his hated creator, Lesile.

<u>Primacy of Darkness</u> (Brooklyn Shadows Book 3): Jack the Ripper, sadistic madman of old London, once thought long dead, has returned

to New York in an effort to quench his thirst for blood and mayhem. When the city's vampire enclave finds itself insufficient to deal with a madman of Jack's caliber, Vincent, the enclave head, enlists Leo Malone to put the maniac down before he reveals the existence of vampires as he throws the city into the throes of chaos and terror. Leo soon finds that Jack is not the only monster with which he must contend. A ghost from his past has also seemingly crawled from its grave and seeks to put an end to him and the rest of his kind.

The Transcended Chronicles is the story of an outlandish young man as he goes from being a troublesome youth to one of the kingdom's greatest secret agents. Blessed (or cursed) with an amazing ability to both fight and abuse his body with every conceivable vice known to man, Garran Holt is either the kingdom's greatest hero or its biggest embarrassment.

The Miscreant (The Transcended Chronicles Book 1): Garran Holt is a troubled young man. Unable to tolerate his self-destructive ways, his mother sells him into indentured servitude as part of a work crew building King Remiel's new trade road. When mercenaries sent to disrupt the road's construction attack his work camp, Garran discovers an inner power capable of turning him into a warrior of unparalleled ability. When the leader of his work crew recognizes Garran as being one of the transcended (a fighter able to slip into the swifter currents of time), he is trained as an agent, one of the kingdom's elite spies. Crude, abrasive, and deeply committed to destroying himself with drugs, alcohol, and debauchery, Garran might be the kingdom's only hope against falling to The Guild, the powerful trade cartel bent on becoming the true and undisputed power in the land.

The Agent (The Transcended Chronicles Book 2): The Guild rules the kingdom through their puppet monarch, and Garran must race to save the last living heir to the throne before the powerful syndicate's assassins complete their extermination of anyone who could oppose them. Garran and Prince Adam Altena struggle to find allies in hopes of rescuing Adam's sister, who was forced to marry the usurper in order to prevent even the thought of rebellion, and raise an army capable of defeating The Guild. With The Guild now in control of Anatolia's powerful army as well as their legion of mercenaries, their future is grim. How can a disreputable agent and a deposed prince convince their neighboring rulers to oppose The Guild, an organization that has had them cowed for decades?

Empire of Masks is an exciting and explosive new series that takes place in the world of Hedon and takes you across the land of Eidolan where ships sail through the skies and men and women wage war with magic, swords, muskets, and cannons.

<u>Highlords of Phaer</u> **(Book one of Empire of Masks):** Born a slave, descended of kings, Jareen Velarius just wants to provide the best life he can for his family, but Eidolan is a realm that challenges even the most stalwart of souls. Caught between his masters and those brave or foolish enough to strike against them, Jareen struggles to reconcile his role as a dutiful slave with that of a man who desires to be free. His goal: to return his people to a life stolen by the highlords more than a millennium ago.

Auberon Victore, sorcerer, alchemist, son of a powerful overlord, and Jareen's master, creates an alchemic compound he is certain will change the world; he just does not know how. Jareen sees it for the weapon that could break the sorcerers' iron grasp wrapped around the necks of every lowborn in the empire. It will change the world, but not in the way his master desires.

Across the Tempest Sea, a mighty storm has raged for a thousand years, keeping a terrible, long-forgotten enemy at bay, an enemy whose cruelty knows no bounds. Only the perpetual storm and their fear of the sorcerer highlords keep the Necrophages from returning to Eidolan and cloaking the empire in death and darkness. But the tempest is waning, and the dissidents' freedom may well come at the cost of their total destruction.

<u>Nightbird</u>: The Great Revolution ended the highlords' tyranny two hundred years ago, but the legacy of that epic war, and that of the principal architects' descendants, lives on. With the highlords' death and their taking magic, as it was once known, to their graves, Eidolan

fell into a time of darkness and its cities lived in isolation. However, some people, dubbed arcanists, discovered a new form of magic and the airships returned to the skies, rejoining the cities in trade as well as conspiracy, but a new darkness, more dreadful and deadly than any they faced before, is coming.

Kiera is a fifteen-year-old nightbird, one of many who flit about after dark, stealing whatever they can find in order to survive. She lives on a derelict airship in the poorest part of the city with Wesley, a young man who plies his trade as an escort to wealthy older women, and his little brother Russel, an autistic savant who communicates only through sign but who could secretly be the most powerful techno-arcanist the empire has ever known. Deep in debt to the underlord Nimat, Kiera dives into evermore dangerous schemes that put her at the heart of a secret war that could spell the destruction of not just the city, but the very empire.

Kiera is caught in the center of several factions on the brink of war. When she can no longer tell friend from enemy, there is only one side she can trust—her own.

Mourningbird: A creature of darkness lurks in the shadows of Velaroth, wearing the skin of its victims, and grips the city in terror. Dorian, a Necrophage bent on sowing chaos and paving the way for his people's invasion, has declared war on the humans of Eidolan, and there appears to be no one capable of stopping him.

Kiera's world is shattered by those who hold power, and she is forced to seek an ally. The nightbird is coming into power of her own, but can she stay alive long enough to seize it? Russel's behavior has taken a turn for the worse, and his actions have drawn the attention of those who would use his amazing talents for their own gain...and everyone else's loss.

The battle for Velaroth, and perhaps the world, has begun. Who will win? Who will live to mourn the dead? Will there be anything left for the victor to claim as their prize?

Standalone books

The Portal is a fun and exciting story of some less than popular teenagers that accidentally open a portal to a mystical land during one of their role-playing games. Drew, a dour and anti-establishment teenager, is pulled through and captured by evil creatures lying in wait on the other side. Now it is up to his friends and older brother to rescue him, but who will rescue Drew's captors from him?

Amelia (Battle for Ardentia): Amelia is a precocious, ten-year-old girl with a powerful imagination. In her alter-ego guise of a demi-goddess warrior princess, Amelia fights against a powerful demonic sorcerer named Romut and his horde of monsters in a never ending series of battles to protect the people of her imaginary world. However, the true battle strikes home when Amelia is diagnosed with a brain tumor. Now Amelia must fight not just the evil living in her imagination, but for her very life.

ABOUT THE AUTHOR

Brock Deskins was born in a small town located in rural Oregon. At age twenty, he joined the army and served as an M1A1 tank crewman, dental specialist, and computer analyst. While in the military, he became an accomplished traveler, husband, and father of three wonderful children. His military career completed, attended college to brush up on his skills as a computer analyst and gain new skills as a writer. Brock received his degree in computer networking and is now devoting his full time and limited attention span to writing.

BIBLIOGRAPHY

THE SORCERER'S PATH
The Sorcerer's Ascension
The Sorcerer's Torment
The Sorcerer's Legacy
The Sorcerer's Vengeance
The Sorcerer's Scourge
The Sorcerer's Abyss
The Sorcerer's Return

The Sorcerer's Destiny
Rise of the Order
Descent Into Chaos

BROOKLYN SHADOWS
Shrouds of Darkness
Blood Conspiracy

THE TRANSCENDED CHRONICLES
The Miscreant
The Agent

EMPIRE OF MASKS
Highlords of Phaer
Nightbird
Mourningbird

OTHER BOOKS BY BROCK E. DESKINS
The Portal
Amelia: Battle for Ardentia

Curious about other Crossroad Press books? Stop by our website:
http://crossroadpress.com
We offer quality writing
in digital, audio, and print formats.

Subscribe to our newsletter on the website homepage and receive a
free eBook.

www.ingramcontent.com/pod-product-compliance
Lightning Source LLC
Chambersburg PA
CBHW070308260626
47160CB00003B/764